Praise for *Girl with a Pearl Earring*:

'Beautifully written, mysterious and almost unbearably
poignant – a magical experience.'   DEBORAH MOGGACH

'It has a slow, magical current of its own that picks you
up and carries you stealthily along . . . a beautiful story,
lovingly told by a very talented writer.'   *Daily Mail*

'A wonderful novel, mysterious, steeped in atmosphere,
deeply revealing about the process of painting . . . truly
magical'   *Guardian*

'Ultimately absorbing . . . suspended in a particular
moment, it tr̲̲̲̲̲̲̲̲ ̲̲̲̲̲ ̲̲̲̲ ̲̲̲̲̲̲̲̲ *New Yorker*

GIRL WITH A PEARL EARRING

FALLING ANGELS

Tracy Chevalier

HARPER

Harper

An imprint of HarperCollins*Publishers*
77–85 Fulham Palace Road,
Hammersmith, London W6 8JB

www.harpercollins.co.uk

This omnibus edition 2009

1

Girl with a Pearl Earring
Copyright © Tracy Chevalier 1999

Falling Angels
Copyright © Tracy Chevalier 2001

Tracy Chevalier asserts the moral right to
be identified as the author of this work

A catalogue record for this book is available from the British Library

ISBN 978-0-00-785091-4

Printed and bound in Great Britain by Clays Ltd, St Ives plc

Mixed Sources
Product group from well-managed
forests and other controlled sources
www.fsc.org Cert no. SW-COC-1806
© 1996 Forest Stewardship Council

FSC is a non-profit international organisation established to promote the
responsible management of the world's forests. Products carrying the FSC
label are independently certified to assure consumers that they come
from forests that are managed to meet the social, economic and
ecological needs of present and future generations.

Find out more about HarperCollins and the environment at
www.harpercollins.co.uk/green

GIRL WITH
A PEARL EARRING

For my father

1664

My mother did not tell me they were coming. Afterwards she said she did not want me to appear nervous. I was surprised, for I thought she knew me well. Strangers would think I was calm. I did not cry as a baby. Only my mother would note the tightness along my jaw, the widening of my already wide eyes.

I was chopping vegetables in the kitchen when I heard voices outside our front door — a woman's, bright as polished brass, and a man's, low and dark like the wood of the table I was working on. They were the kind of voices we heard rarely in our house. I could hear rich carpets in their voices, books and pearls and fur.

I was glad that earlier I had scrubbed the front step so hard.

My mother's voice — a cooking pot, a flagon — approached from the front room. They were coming to the kitchen. I pushed the leeks I had been chopping into place, then set the knife on the table, wiped my hands on my apron, and pressed my lips together to smooth them.

My mother appeared in the doorway, her eyes two warnings. Behind her the woman had to duck her head because she was so tall, taller than the man following her.

All of our family, even my father and brother, were small.

The woman looked as if she had been blown about by

3

the wind, although it was a calm day. Her cap was askew so that tiny blonde curls escaped and hung about her forehead like bees which she swatted at impatiently several times. Her collar needed straightening and was not as crisp as it could be. She pushed her grey mantle back from her shoulders, and I saw then that under her dark blue dress a baby was growing. It would arrive by the year's end, or before.

The woman's face was like an oval serving plate, flashing at times, dull at others. Her eyes were two light brown buttons, a colour I had rarely seen coupled with blond hair. She made a show of watching me hard, but could not fix her attention on me, her eyes darting about the room.

'This is the girl, then,' she said abruptly.

'This is my daughter, Griet,' my mother replied. I nodded respectfully to the man and woman.

'Well. She's not very big. Is she strong enough?' As the woman turned to look at the man, a fold of her mantle caught the handle of the knife I had been using, knocking it off the table so that it spun across the floor.

The woman cried out.

'Catharina,' the man said calmly. He spoke her name as if he held cinnamon in his mouth. The woman stopped, making an effort to quiet herself.

I stepped over and picked up the knife, polishing the blade on my apron before placing it back on the table. The knife had brushed against the vegetables. I set a piece of carrot back in its place.

The man was watching me, his eyes grey like the sea. He had a long, angular face, and his expression was steady, in contrast to his wife's, which flickered like a candle. He had no beard or moustache, and I was glad, for it gave him a

4

clean appearance. He wore a black cloak over his shoulders, a white shirt, and a fine lace collar. His hat pressed into hair the red of brick washed by rain.

'What have you been doing here, Griet?' he asked.

I was surprised by the question but knew enough to hide it. 'Chopping vegetables, sir. For the soup.'

I always laid vegetables out in a circle, each with its own section like a slice of pie. There were five slices: red cabbage, onions, leeks, carrots and turnips. I had used a knife edge to shape each slice, and placed a carrot disc in the centre.

The man tapped his finger on the table. 'Are they laid out in the order in which they will go into the soup?' he suggested, studying the circle.

'No, sir.' I hesitated. I could not say why I had laid out the vegetables as I did. I simply set them as I felt they should be, but I was too frightened to say so to a gentleman.

'I see you have separated the whites,' he said, indicating the turnips and onions. 'And then the orange and the purple, they do not sit together. Why is that?' He picked up a shred of cabbage and a piece of carrot and shook them like dice in his hand.

I looked at my mother, who nodded slightly.

'The colours fight when they are side by side, sir.'

He arched his eyebrows, as if he had not expected such a response. 'And do you spend much time setting out the vegetables before you make the soup?'

'Oh no, sir,' I replied, confused. I did not want him to think I was idle.

From the corner of my eye I saw a movement. My sister, Agnes, was peering round the doorpost and had shaken her head at my response. I did not often lie. I looked down.

The man turned his head slightly and Agnes disappeared. He dropped the pieces of carrot and cabbage into their slices. The cabbage shred fell partly into the onions. I wanted to reach over and tease it into place. I did not, but he knew that I wanted to. He was testing me.

'That's enough prattle,' the woman declared. Though she was annoyed by his attention to me, it was me she frowned at. 'Tomorrow, then?' She looked at the man before sweeping out of the room, my mother behind her. The man glanced once more at what was to be the soup, then nodded at me and followed the women.

When my mother returned I was sitting by the vegetable wheel. I waited for her to speak. She was hunching her shoulders as if against a winter chill, though it was summer and the kitchen was hot.

'You are to start tomorrow as their maid. If you do well, you will be paid eight stuivers a day. You will live with them.'

I pressed my lips together.

'Don't look at me like that, Griet,' my mother said. 'We have to, now your father has lost his trade.'

'Where do they live?'

'On the Oude Langendijck, where it intersects with the Molenpoort.'

'Papists' Corner? They're Catholic?'

'You can come home Sundays. They have agreed to that.' My mother cupped her hands around the turnips, scooped them up along with some of the cabbage and onions and dropped them into the pot of water waiting on the fire. The pie slices I had made so carefully were ruined.

*　　*　　*

I climbed the stairs to see my father. He was sitting at the front of the attic by the window, where the light touched his face. It was the closest he came now to seeing.

Father had been a tile painter, his fingers still stained blue from painting cupids, maids, soldiers, ships, children, fish, flowers, animals on to white tiles, glazing them, firing them, selling them. One day the kiln exploded, taking his eyes and his trade. He was the lucky one — two other men died.

I sat next to him and held his hand.

'I heard,' he said before I could speak. 'I heard everything.' His hearing had taken the strength from his missing eyes.

I could not think of anything to say that would not sound reproachful.

'I'm sorry, Griet. I would like to have done better for you.' The place where his eyes had been, where the doctor had sewn shut the skin, looked sorrowful. 'But he is a good gentleman, and fair. He will treat you well.' He said nothing about the woman.

'How can you be sure of this, Father? Do you know him?'

'Don't you know who he is?'

'No.'

'Do you remember the painting we saw in the Town Hall a few years ago, which van Ruijven was displaying after he bought it? It was a view of Delft, from the Rotterdam and Schiedam Gates. With the sky that took up so much of the painting, and the sunlight on some of the buildings.'

'And the paint had sand in it to make the brickwork and the roofs look rough,' I added. 'And there were long shadows in the water, and tiny people on the shore nearest us.'

'That's the one.' Father's sockets widened as if he still had eyes and was looking at the painting again.

I remembered it well, remembered thinking that I had stood at that very spot many times and never seen Delft the way the painter had.

'That man was van Ruijven?'

'The patron?' Father chuckled. 'No, no, child, not him. That was the painter. Vermeer. That was Johannes Vermeer and his wife. You're to clean his studio.'

To the few things I was taking with me my mother added another cap, collar and apron so that each day I could wash one and wear the other, and would always look clean. She also gave me an ornamental tortoiseshell comb, shaped like a shell, that had been my grandmother's and was too fine for a maid to wear, and a prayer book I could read when I needed to escape the Catholicism around me.

As we gathered my things she explained why I was to work for the Vermeers. 'You know that your new master is headman of the Guild of St Luke, and was when your father had his accident last year?'

I nodded, still shocked that I was to work for such an artist.

'The Guild looks after its own, as best it can. Remember the box your father gave money to every week for years? That money goes to masters in need, as we are now. But it goes only so far, you see, especially now with Frans in his apprenticeship and no money coming in. We have no choice. We won't take public charity, not if we can manage without. Then your father heard that your new master was looking for a maid who could clean his studio without moving anything, and he put forward your name, thinking that as headman, and knowing our circumstances, Vermeer would be likely to try to help.'

I sifted through what she had said. 'How do you clean a room without moving anything?'

'Of course you must move things, but you must find a way to put them back exactly so it looks as if nothing has been disturbed. As you do for your father now that he cannot see.'

After my father's accident we had learned to place things where he always knew to find them. It was one thing to do this for a blind man, though. Quite another for a man with a painter's eyes.

Agnes said nothing to me after the visit. When I got into bed next to her that night she remained silent, though she did not turn her back to me. She lay gazing at the ceiling. Once I had blown out the candle it was so dark I could see nothing. I turned towards her.

'You know I don't want to leave. I have to.'

Silence.

'We need the money. We have nothing now that Father can't work.'

'Eight stuivers a day isn't such a lot of money.' Agnes had a hoarse voice, as if her throat were covered with cobwebs.

'It will keep the family in bread. And a bit of cheese. That's not so little.'

'I'll be all alone. You're leaving me all alone. First Frans, then you.'

Of all of us Agnes had been the most upset when Frans left the previous year. He and she had always fought like cats but she sulked for days once he was gone. At ten she was the youngest of us three children, and had never before known a time when Frans and I were not there.

'Mother and Father will still be here. And I'll visit on Sundays. Besides, it was no surprise when Frans went.' We had known for years that our brother would start his apprenticeship when he turned thirteen. Our father had saved hard to pay the apprentice fee, and talked endlessly of how Frans would learn another aspect of the trade, then come back and they would set up a tile factory together.

Now our father sat by the window and never spoke of the future.

After the accident Frans had come home for two days. He had not visited since. The last time I saw him I had gone to the factory across town where he was apprenticed. He looked exhausted and had burns up and down his arms from pulling tiles from the kiln. He told me he worked from dawn until so late that at times he was too tired even to eat. 'Father never told me it would be this bad,' he muttered resentfully. 'He always said his apprenticeship was the making of him.'

'Perhaps it was,' I replied. 'It made him what he is now.'

When I was ready to leave the next morning my father shuffled out to the front step, feeling his way along the wall. I hugged my mother and Agnes. 'Sunday will come in no time,' my mother said.

My father handed me something wrapped in a handkerchief. 'To remind you of home,' he said. 'Of us.'

It was my favourite tile of his. Most of his tiles we had

at home were faulty in some way – chipped or cut crookedly, or the picture was blurred because the kiln had been too hot. This one, though, my father kept specially for us. It was a simple picture of two small figures, a boy and an older girl. They were not playing as children usually did in tiles. They were simply walking along, and were like Frans and me whenever we walked together – clearly our father had thought of us as he painted it. The boy was a little ahead of the girl but had turned back to say something. His face was mischievous, his hair messy. The girl wore her cap as I wore mine, not as most other girls did, with the ends tied under their chins or behind their necks. I favoured a white cap that folded in a wide brim around my face, covering my hair completely and hanging down in points on each side of my face so that from the side my expression was hidden. I kept the cap stiff by boiling it with potato peelings.

I walked away from our house, carrying my things tied up in an apron. It was still early – our neighbours were throwing buckets of water on to their steps and the street in front of their houses, and scrubbing them clean. Agnes would do that now, as well as many of my other tasks. She would have less time to play in the street and along the canals. Her life was changing too.

People nodded at me and watched curiously as I passed. No one asked where I was going or called out kind words. They did not need to – they knew what happened to families when a man lost his trade. It would be something to discuss later – young Griet become a maid, her father brought the family low. They would not gloat, however. The same thing could easily happen to them.

I had walked along that street all my life, but had never

been so aware that my back was to my home. When I reached the end and turned out of sight of my family, though, it became a little easier to walk steadily and look around me. The morning was still cool, the sky a flat grey-white pulled close over Delft like a sheet, the summer sun not yet high enough to burn it away. The canal I walked along was a mirror of white light tinged with green. As the sun grew brighter the canal would darken to the colour of moss.

Frans, Agnes and I used to sit beside that canal and throw things in — pebbles, sticks, once a broken tile — and imagine what they might touch on the bottom — not fish, but creatures from our imagination, with many eyes, scales, hands and fins. Frans thought up the most interesting monsters. Agnes was the most frightened. I always stopped the game, too inclined to see things as they were to be able to think up things that were not.

There were a few boats on the canal, moving towards Market Square. It was not market day, however, when the canal was so full you couldn't see the water. One boat was carrying river fish for the stalls at Jeronymous Bridge. Another sat low on the water, loaded with bricks. The man poling the boat called out a greeting to me. I merely nodded and lowered my head so that the edge of my cap hid my face.

I crossed a bridge over the canal and turned into the open space of Market Square, even then busy with people crisscrossing it on their way to some task — buying meat at the Meat Hall, or bread at the baker's, taking wood to be weighed at the Weigh House. Children ran errands for their parents, apprentices for their masters, maids for their households. Horses and carts clattered across the stones. To my right was the Town Hall, with its gilded front and white marble faces gazing down from the keystones above the windows. To my left was the New Church, where I had been baptised sixteen years before. Its tall, narrow tower made me think of a stone birdcage. Father had taken us up it once. I would never forget the sight of Delft spread below us, each narrow brick house and steep red roof and green waterway and city gate marked for ever in my mind, tiny and yet distinct. I asked my father then if every Dutch city looked like that, but he did not know. He had never visited any other city, not even The Hague, two hours away on foot.

I walked to the centre of the square. There the stones had been laid to form an eight-pointed star set inside a circle. Each point aimed towards a different part of Delft. I thought of it as the very centre of the town, and as the centre of my life. Frans and Agnes and I had played in that star since we were old enough to run to the market. In our favourite game, one of us chose a point and one of us named a thing – a stork, a church, a wheelbarrow, a flower – and we ran in that direction looking for that thing. We had explored most of Delft that way.

One point, however, we had never followed. I had never gone to Papists' Corner, where the Catholics lived. The house where I was to work was just ten minutes from home, the time it took a pot of water to boil, but I had never passed by it.

I knew no Catholics. There were not so many in Delft, and none in our street or in the shops we used. It was not that we avoided them, but they kept to themselves. They were tolerated in Delft, but were expected not to parade their faith openly. They held their services privately, in modest places that did not look like churches from the outside.

My father had worked with Catholics and told me they were no different from us. If anything they were less solemn. They liked to eat and drink and sing and game. He said this almost as if he envied them.

I followed the point of the star now, walking across the square more slowly than everyone else, for I was reluctant to leave its familiarity. I crossed the bridge over the canal and turned left up the Oude Langendijck. On my left the canal ran parallel to the street, separating it from Market Square.

At the intersection with the Molenpoort, four girls were sitting on a bench beside the open door of a house. They were arranged in order of size, from the oldest, who looked to be about Agnes' age, to the youngest, who was probably about four. One of the middle girls held a baby in her lap – a large baby, who was probably already crawling and would soon be ready to walk.

Five children, I thought. And another expected.

The oldest was blowing bubbles through a scallop shell fixed to the end of a hollowed stick, very like one my father had made for us. The others were jumping up and popping the bubbles as they appeared. The girl with the baby in her lap could not move much, catching few bubbles although she was seated next to the bubble blower. The youngest at the end was the furthest away and the smallest, and had no chance to reach the bubbles. The second youngest was the quickest, darting after the bubbles and clapping her hands around them. She had the brightest hair of the four, red like the dry brick wall behind her. The youngest and the girl with the baby both had curly blonde hair like their mother's, while the eldest's was the same dark red as her father's.

I watched the girl with the bright hair swat at the bubbles, popping them just before they broke on the damp grey and white tiles set diagonally in rows before the house. She will be a handful, I thought. 'You'd best pop them before they reach the ground,' I said. 'Else those tiles will have to be scrubbed again.'

The eldest girl lowered the pipe. Four sets of eyes stared at me with the same gaze that left no doubt they were sisters. I could see various features of their parents in them — grey eyes here, light brown eyes there, angular faces, impatient movements.

'Are you the new maid?' the eldest asked.

'We were told to watch out for you,' the bright redhead interrupted before I could reply.

'Cornelia, go and get Tanneke,' the eldest said to her.

'You go, Aleydis,' Cornelia in turn ordered the youngest, who gazed at me with wide grey eyes but did not move.

'*I'll* go.' The eldest must have decided my arrival was important after all.

'No, *I'll* go.' Cornelia jumped up and ran ahead of her older sister, leaving me alone with the two quieter girls.

I looked at the squirming baby in the girl's lap. 'Is that your brother or your sister?'

'Brother,' the girl replied in a soft voice like a feather pillow. 'His name is Johannes. Never call him Jan.' She said the last words as if they were a familiar refrain.

'I see. And your name?'

15

'Lisbeth. And this is Aleydis.' The youngest smiled at me. They were both dressed neatly in brown dresses with white aprons and caps.

'And your older sister?'

'Maertge. Never call her Maria. Our grandmother's name is Maria. Maria Thins. This is her house.'

The baby began to whimper. Lisbeth joggled him up and down on her knee.

I looked up at the house. It was certainly grander than ours, but not as grand as I had feared. It had two storeys, plus an attic, whereas ours had only the one, with a tiny attic. It was an end house, with the Molenpoort running down one side, so that it was a little wider than the other houses in the street. It felt less pressed in than many of the houses in Delft, which were packed together in narrow rows of brick along the canals, their chimneys and stepped roofs reflected in the green canal water. The ground-floor windows of this house were very high, and on the first floor there were three windows set close together rather than the two of other houses along the street.

From the front of the house the New Church tower was visible just across the canal. A strange view for a Catholic family, I thought. A church they will never even go inside.

'So you're the maid, are you?' I heard behind me.

The woman standing in the doorway had a broad face, pockmarked from an earlier illness. Her nose was bulbous and irregular, and her thick lips were pushed together to form a small mouth. Her eyes were light blue, as if she had caught the sky in them. She wore a grey-brown dress with a white chemise, a cap tied tight around her head, and an apron that was not as clean as mine. She stood blocking the doorway, so that Maertge and Cornelia had to push their way out round her, and looked at me with crossed arms as if waiting for a challenge.

Already she feels threatened by me, I thought. She will bully me if I let her.

'My name is Griet,' I said, gazing at her levelly. 'I am the new maid.'

The woman shifted from one hip to the other. 'You'd best come in, then,' she said after a moment. She moved back into the shadowy interior so that the doorway was clear.

I stepped across the threshold.

What I always remembered about being in the front hall for the first time were the paintings. I stopped inside the door, clutching my bundle, and stared. I had seen paintings before, but never so many in one room. I counted eleven. The largest painting was of two men, almost naked, wrestling each other. I did not recognise it as a story from the Bible, and wondered if it was a Catholic subject. Other paintings were of more familiar things — piles of fruit, landscapes, ships on the sea, portraits. They seemed to be by several painters. I wondered which of them were my new master's. None was what I had expected of him.

Later I discovered they were all by other painters — he rarely kept his own finished paintings in the house. He was an art dealer as well as an artist, and paintings hung in almost every room, even where I slept. There were more than fifty in all, though the number varied over time as he traded and sold them.

'Come now, no need to idle and gape.' The woman hurried down a lengthy hallway, which ran along one side of the house all the way to the back. I followed as she turned abruptly into a room on the left. On the wall directly opposite hung a painting that was larger than me. It was of Christ on the Cross, surrounded by the Virgin Mary, Mary Magdalene and St John. I tried not to stare but I was amazed by its size and subject. 'Catholics are not so different from us,' my father had said. But we did not have such pictures in our houses, or our churches, or anywhere. Now I would see this painting every day.

I was always to think of that room as the Crucifixion room. I was never comfortable in it.

The painting surprised me so much that I did not notice the woman in the corner until she spoke. 'Well, girl,' she said, 'that is something new for you to see.' She sat in a comfortable chair, smoking a pipe. Her teeth gripping the stem had gone brown, and her fingers were stained with ink. The rest of her was spotless – her black dress, lace collar, stiff white cap. Though her lined face was stern her light brown eyes seemed amused.

She was the kind of old woman who looked as if she would outlive everyone.

She is Catharina's mother, I thought suddenly. It was not just the colour of her eyes and the wisp of grey curl that escaped her cap in the same way as her daughter's. She had the manner of someone used to looking after those less able than she – of looking after Catharina. I understood now why I had been brought to her rather than her daughter.

Though she seemed to look at me casually, her gaze was watchful. When she narrowed her eyes I realised she knew everything I was thinking. I turned my head so that my cap hid my face.

Maria Thins puffed on her pipe and chuckled. 'That's right, girl. You keep your thoughts to yourself here. So, you're to work for my daughter. She's out now, at the shops. Tanneke here will show you around and explain your duties.'

I nodded. 'Yes, madam.'

Tanneke, who had been standing at the old woman's side, pushed past me. I followed, Maria Thins' eyes branding my back. I heard her chuckling again.

Tanneke took me first to the back of the house, where there were cooking and washing kitchens and two storage rooms. The washing kitchen led out to a tiny courtyard full of drying white laundry.

'This needs ironing, for a start,' Tanneke said. I said nothing, though it looked as if the laundry had not yet been bleached properly by the midday sun.

She led me back inside and pointed to a hole in the floor of one of the storage rooms, a ladder leading down into it. 'You're to sleep there,' she announced. 'Drop your things there now and you can sort yourself out later.'

I reluctantly let my bundle drop into the dim hole, thinking of the stones Agnes and Frans and I had thrown into the canal to seek out the monsters. My things thudded on to the dirt floor. I felt like an apple tree losing its fruit.

I followed Tanneke back along the hallway, which all the rooms opened off – many more rooms than in our house. Next to the Crucifixion room where Maria Thins sat, towards the front of the house, was a smaller room with children's beds, chamberpots, small chairs and a table, on it various earthenware, candlesticks, snuffers and clothing, all in a jumble.

'The girls sleep here,' Tanneke mumbled, perhaps embarrassed by the mess.

She turned up the hallway again and opened a door into a large room, where light streamed in from the front windows and across the red and grey tiled floor. 'The great hall,' she muttered. 'Master and mistress sleep here.'

Their bed was hung with green silk curtains. There was other furniture in the room — a large cupboard inlaid with ebony, a whitewood table pushed up to the windows with several Spanish leather chairs arranged around it. But again it was the paintings that struck me. More hung in this room than anywhere else. I counted to nineteen silently. Most were portraits — they appeared to be members of both families. There was also a painting of the Virgin Mary, and one of the three kings worshipping the Christ Child. I gazed at both uneasily.

'Now, upstairs.' Tanneke went first up the steep stairs, then put a finger to her lips. I climbed as quietly as I could. At the top I looked around and saw the closed door. Behind it was a silence that I knew was him.

I stood, my eyes fixed on the door, not daring to move in case it opened and he came out.

Tanneke leaned towards me and whispered, 'You'll be cleaning in there, which the young mistress will explain to you later. And these rooms —' she pointed to doors towards the back of the house — 'are *my* mistress' rooms. Only I go in there to clean.'

We crept downstairs again. When we were back in the washing kitchen Tanneke said, 'You're to take on the laundry for the house.' She pointed to a great mound of clothes — they had fallen far behind with their washing. I would struggle to catch up. 'There's a cistern in the cooking kitchen but you'd best get your water for washing from the canal – it's clean enough in this part of town.'

'Tanneke,' I said in a low voice, 'have you been doing all this yourself? The cooking and cleaning and washing for the house?'

I had chosen the right words. '*And* some of the shopping.' Tanneke puffed up with pride at her own industry. 'Young mistress does most of it, of course, but she goes off raw meat and fish when she's carrying a child. And that's *often*,' she added in a whisper. 'You're to go to the Meat Hall and the fish stalls too. That will be another of your duties.'

With that she left me to the laundry. Including me there were ten of us now in the house, one a baby who would dirty more clothes than the rest. I would be laundering every day, my hands chapped and cracked from the soap and water, my face red from standing over the steam, my back aching from lifting wet cloth, my arms burned by the iron. But I was new and I was young – it was to be expected I would have the hardest tasks.

The laundry needed to soak for a day before I could wash it. In the storage room that led down to the cellar I found two pewter waterpots and a copper kettle. I took the pots with me and walked up the long hallway to the front door.

The girls were still sitting on the bench. Now Lisbeth had the bubble blower while Maertge fed baby Johannes bread softened with milk. Cornelia and Aleydis were chasing bubbles. When I appeared they all stopped what they were doing and looked at me expectantly.

'You're the new maid,' the girl with the bright red hair declared.

'Yes, Cornelia.'

Cornelia picked up a pebble and threw it across the road into the canal. There were long scratches up and down her arm — she must have been bothering the house cat.

'Where will you sleep?' Maertge asked, wiping mushy fingers on her apron.

'In the cellar.'

'We like it down there,' Cornelia said. 'Let's go and play there now!'

She darted inside but did not go far. When no one followed her she came back out, her face cross.

'Aleydis,' I said, extending my hand to the youngest girl, 'will you show me where to get water from the canal?'

She took my hand and looked up at me. Her eyes were like two shiny grey coins. We crossed the street, Cornelia and Lisbeth following. Aleydis led me to stairs that descended to the water. As we peeked over I tightened my grip on her hand, as I had done years before with Frans and Agnes whenever we stood next to water.

'You stand back from the edge,' I ordered. Aleydis obediently took a step back. But Cornelia followed close behind me as I carried the pots down the steps.

'Cornelia, are you going to help me carry the water? If not, go back up to your sisters.'

She looked at me, and then she did the worst thing. If she had sulked or shouted, I would know I had mastered her. Instead she laughed.

I reached over and slapped her. Her face turned red, but she did not cry. She ran back up the steps. Aleydis and Lisbeth peered down at me solemnly.

I had a feeling then. This is how it will be with her mother, I thought, except that I will not be able to slap her.

I filled the pots and carried them to the top of the steps. Cornelia had disappeared. Maertge was still sitting with Johannes. I took one of the pots inside and back to the cooking kitchen, where I built up the fire, filled the copper kettle, and put it on to heat.

When I came back Cornelia was outside again, her face still flushed. The girls were playing with tops on the grey and white tiles. None of them looked up at me.

The pot I had left was missing. I looked into the canal and saw it floating, upside down, just out of reach of the stairs.

'Yes, you will be a handful,' I murmured. I looked around for a stick to fish it out with but could find none. I filled the other pot again and carried it inside, turning my head so that the girls could not see my face. I set the pot next to the kettle on the fire. Then I went outside again, this time with a broom.

Cornelia was throwing stones at the pot, probably hoping to sink it.

'I'll slap you again if you don't stop.'

'I'll tell our mother. Maids don't slap us.' Cornelia threw another stone.

'Shall I tell your grandmother what you've done?'

A fearful look crossed Cornelia's face. She dropped the stones she held.

A boat was moving along the canal from the direction of the Town Hall. I recognised the man poling from earlier that day – he had delivered his load of bricks and the boat was riding much higher. He grinned when he saw me.

23

I blushed. 'Please, sir,' I began, 'can you help me get that pot?'

'Oh, you're looking at me now that you want something from me, are you? There's a change!'

Cornelia was watching me curiously.

I swallowed. 'I can't reach the pot from here. Perhaps you could —'

The man leaned over, fished out the pot, dumped the water from it, and held it out to me. I ran down the steps and took it from him. 'Thank you. I'm most grateful.'

He did not let go of the pot. 'Is that all I get? No kiss?' He reached over and pulled my sleeve. I jerked my arm away and wrestled the pot from him.

'Not this time,' I said as lightly as I could. I was never good at that sort of talk.

He laughed. 'I'll be looking for pots every time I pass here now, won't I, young miss?' He winked at Cornelia. 'Pots and kisses.' He took up his pole and pushed off.

As I climbed the steps back to the street I thought I saw a movement in the middle window on the first floor, the room where he was. I stared but could see nothing except the reflected sky.

Catharina returned while I was taking down laundry in the courtyard. I first heard her keys jangling in the hallway. They hung in a great bunch just below her waist, bouncing against her hip. Although they looked uncomfortable to me, she wore them with great pride. I then heard her in the cooking kitchen, ordering about Tanneke and the boy who had carried things from the shops for her. She spoke harshly to both.

I continued to pull down and fold bedsheets, napkins, pillowcases, tablecloths, shirts, chemises, aprons, handkerchiefs, collars, caps. They had been hung carelessly, bunched in places so that patches of cloth were still damp. And they had not been shaken first, so there were creases everywhere. I would be ironing much of the day to make them presentable.

Catharina appeared at the door, looking hot and tired, though the sun was not yet at its highest. Her chemise puffed out messily from the top of her blue dress, and the green housecoat she wore over it was already crumpled. Her blonde hair was frizzier than ever, especially as she wore no cap to smooth it. The curls fought against the combs that held them in a bun.

She looked as if she needed to sit quietly for a moment by the canal, where the sight of the water might calm and cool her.

I was not sure how I should be with her – I had never been a maid, nor had we ever had one in our house. There were no servants on our street. No one could afford one. I placed the laundry I was folding in a basket, then nodded at her. 'Good morning, madam.'

She frowned and I realised I should have let her speak first. I would have to take more care with her.

'Tanneke has taken you around the house?' she said.

'Yes, madam.'

'Well, then, you will know what to do and you will do it.' She hesitated, as if at a loss for words, and it came to me that she knew little more about being my mistress than I did about being her maid. Tanneke had probably been trained by Maria Thins and still followed her orders, whatever Catharina said to her.

I would have to help her without seeming to.

'Tanneke has explained that besides the laundry you want me to go for the meat and fish, madam,' I suggested gently.

Catharina brightened. 'Yes. She will take you when you finish with the washing here. After that you will go every day yourself. And on other errands as I need you,' she added.

'Yes, madam.' I waited. When she said nothing else I reached up to pull a man's linen shirt from the line.

Catharina stared at the shirt. 'Tomorrow,' she announced as I was folding it, 'I will show you upstairs where you are to clean. Early — first thing in the morning.' Before I could reply she disappeared inside.

After I brought in the laundry I found the iron, cleaned it, and set it in the fire to heat. I had just begun ironing when Tanneke came and handed me a shopping pail. 'We're going to the butcher's now,' she said. 'I'll need the meat soon.' I had heard her clattering in the cooking kitchen and had smelled parsnips roasting.

Out in front Catharina sat on the bench, with Lisbeth on a stool by her feet and Johannes asleep in a cradle. She was combing Lisbeth's hair and searching for lice. Next to her Cornelia and Aleydis were sewing. 'No, Aleydis,' Catharina was saying, 'pull the thread tight, that's too loose. You show her, Cornelia.'

I had not thought they could all be so calm together.

Maertge ran over from the canal. 'Are you going to the butcher's? May I go too, Mama?'

'Only if you stay with Tanneke and mind her.'

I was glad that Maertge came with us. Tanneke was still wary of me, but Maertge was merry and quick and that made it easier for us to be friendly.

I asked Tanneke how long she had worked for Maria Thins.

'Oh, many years,' she said. 'A few before master and young mistress were married and came to live here. I started when I was no older than you. How old are you, then?'

'Sixteen.'

'I began when I was fourteen,' Tanneke countered triumphantly. 'Half my life I've worked here.'

I would not have said such a thing with pride. Her work had worn her so that she looked older than her twenty-eight years.

The Meat Hall was just behind the Town Hall, south and to the west of Market Square. Inside were thirty-two stalls — there had been thirty-two butchers in Delft for generations. It was busy with housewives and maids choosing, bartering and buying for their families, and men carrying carcasses back and forth. Sawdust on the floor soaked up blood and clung to shoes and hems of dresses. There was a tang of blood in the air that always made me shiver, though at one time I had gone there every week and ought to have grown used to the smell. Still, I was pleased to be in a familiar place. As we passed between the stalls the butcher we used to buy our meat from before my father's accident called out to me. I smiled at him, relieved to see a face I knew. It was the first time I had smiled all day.

It was strange to meet so many new people and see so many new things in one morning, and to do so apart from all the familiar things that made up my life. Before, if I met someone new I was always surrounded by family and neighbours. If I went to a new place I was with Frans or my

27

mother or father and felt no threat. The new was woven in with the old, like the darning in a sock.

Frans told me not long after he began his apprenticeship that he had almost run away, not from the hard work, but because he could not face the strangeness day after day. What kept him there was knowing that our father had spent all his savings on the apprentice fee, and would have sent him right back if he had come home. Besides, he would find much more strangeness out in the world if he went elsewhere.

'I will come and see you,' I whispered to the butcher, 'when I am alone.' Then I hurried to catch up with Tanneke and Maertge.

They had stopped at a stall further along. The butcher there was a handsome man, with greying blond curls and bright blue eyes.

'Pieter, this is Griet,' Tanneke said. 'She will be fetching the meat for us now. You're to add it to our account as usual.'

I tried to keep my eyes on his face, but I could not help glancing down at his blood-splattered apron. Our butcher always wore a clean apron when he was selling, changing it whenever he got blood on it.

'Ah.' Pieter looked me over as if I were a plump chicken he was considering roasting. 'What would you like today, Griet?'

I turned to Tanneke. 'Four pounds of chops and a pound of tongue,' she ordered.

Pieter smiled. 'And what do you think of that, miss?' he addressed Maertge. 'Don't I sell the best tongue in Delft?'

Maertge nodded and giggled as she gazed at the display of joints, chops, tongue, pigs' feet, sausages.

'You'll find, Griet, that I have the best meat and the most honest scales in the hall,' Pieter remarked as he weighed the tongue. 'You'll have no complaints about me.'

I stared at his apron and swallowed. Pieter put the chops and tongue into the pail I carried, winked at me and turned to serve the next customer.

We went next to the fish stalls, just beside the Meat Hall. Seagulls hovered above the stalls, waiting for the fishheads and innards the fishmongers threw into the canal. Tanneke introduced me to their fishmonger — also different from ours. I was to alternate each day between meat and fish.

When we left I did not want to go back to the house, to Catharina and the children on the bench. I wanted to walk home. I wanted to step into my mother's kitchen and hand her the pailful of chops. We had not eaten meat in months.

Catharina was combing through Cornelia's hair when we returned. They paid no attention to me. I helped Tanneke with dinner, turning the meat on the grill, fetching things for the table in the great hall, cutting the bread.

When the meal was ready the girls came in, Maertge joining Tanneke in the cooking kitchen while the others sat down in the great hall. I had just placed the tongue in the meat barrel in one of the storage rooms — Tanneke had left it out and the cat had almost got to it — when he appeared from outside, standing in the doorway at the end of the long hall, wearing his hat and cloak. I stood still and he paused, the light behind him so that I could not see his face. I did not know if he was looking down the hallway at me. After a moment he disappeared into the great hall.

Tanneke and Maertge served while I looked after the baby in the Crucifixion room. When Tanneke was done she joined me and we ate and drank what the family did – chops, parsnips, bread, and mugs of beer. Although Pieter's meat was no better than our family butcher's, it was a welcome taste after going so long without. The bread was rye rather than the cheaper brown bread we had been eating, and the beer was not so watery either.

I did not wait on the family at that dinner and so I did not see him. Occasionally I heard his voice, usually along with Maria Thins'. From their tones it was clear they got on well.

After dinner Tanneke and I cleared up, then mopped the floors of the kitchens and storage rooms. The walls of each kitchen were tiled in white, and the fireplace in blue and white Delft tiles painted with birds in one section, ships in another, and soldiers in another. I studied them carefully, but none had been painted by my father.

I spent most of the rest of the day ironing in the washing kitchen, occasionally stopping to build up the fire, fetch wood, or step into the courtyard to escape the heat. The girls played in and out of the house, sometimes coming in to watch me and poke at the fire, another time to tease Tanneke when they found her asleep next door in the cooking kitchen, Johannes crawling around her feet. They were a little uneasy with me – perhaps they thought I might slap them. Cornelia scowled at me and did not stay long in the room, but Maertge and Lisbeth took the clothes I had ironed and put them away for me in the cupboard in the great hall. Their mother was asleep there. 'The last month before the baby comes she'll stay in bed much of the day,' Tanneke confided, 'propped up with pillows all around her.'

Maria Thins had gone to her upstairs rooms after dinner. Once, though, I heard her in the hallway and when I looked up she was standing in the doorway, watching me. She said nothing, so I turned back to my ironing and pretended she wasn't there. After a moment out of the corner of my eye I saw her nod and shuffle off.

He had a guest upstairs – I heard two male voices as they climbed up. Later when I heard them coming down I peeked around the door to watch them go out. The man with him was plump and wore a long white feather in his hat.

When it got dark we lit candles, and Tanneke and I had bread and cheese and beer with the children in the Crucifixion room while the others ate tongue in the great hall. I was careful to sit with my back to the Crucifixion scene. I was so exhausted I could hardly think. At home I had worked just as hard but it was never so tiring as in a strange house where everything was new and I was always tense and serious. At home I had been able to laugh with my mother or Agnes or Frans. Here there was no one to laugh with.

I had not yet been down to the cellar where I was to sleep. I took a candle with me but was too tired to look around beyond finding a bed, pillow and blanket. Leaving the trap door of the cellar open so that cool, fresh air could reach me, I took off my shoes, cap, apron and dress, prayed briefly, and lay down. I was about to blow out the candle when I noticed the painting hanging at the foot of my bed. I sat up, wide awake now. It was another picture of Christ on the Cross, smaller than the one upstairs but even more disturbing. Christ had thrown his head back in pain, and Mary Magdalene's eyes were rolling. I lay back gingerly, unable to take my eyes off it. I could not imagine sleeping in the room with the painting. I wanted to take it down but did not dare. Finally I blew out the candle — I could not afford to waste candles on my first day in the new house. I lay back again, my eyes fixed to the place where I knew the painting hung.

I slept badly that night, tired as I was. I woke often and looked for the painting. Though I could see nothing on the wall, every detail was fixed in my mind. Finally, when it was beginning to grow light, the painting appeared again and I was sure the Virgin Mary was looking down at me.

When I got up in the morning I tried not to look at the painting, instead studying the contents of the cellar in the dim light that fell through the window in the storage room above me. There was not much to see — several tapestry-covered chairs piled up, a few other broken chairs, a mirror, and two more paintings, both still lifes, leaning against the wall. Would anyone notice if I replaced the Crucifixion with a still life?

Cornelia would. And she would tell her mother.

I did not know what Catharina — or any of them — thought of my being Protestant. It was a curious feeling, having to be aware of it myself. I had never before been outnumbered.

I turned my back on the painting and climbed the ladder. Catharina's keys were clinking at the front of the house and

I went to find her. She moved slowly, as if she were half asleep, but she made an effort to draw herself up when she saw me. She led me up the stairs, climbing slowly, holding tightly to the rail to pull her bulk up.

At the studio she searched among the keys, then unlocked and pushed open the door. The room was dark, the shutters closed — I could make out only a little from the cracks of light streaming in between them. The room gave off a clean, sharp odour of linseed oil that reminded me of my father's clothes when he had returned from the tile factory at night. It smelled like wood and fresh-cut hay mixed together.

Catharina remained on the threshold. I did not dare enter before her. After an awkward moment she ordered, 'Open the shutters, then. Not the window on the left. Just the middle and far windows. And only the lower part of the middle window.'

I crossed the room, edging around an easel and chair to the middle window. I pulled open the lower window, then opened out the shutters. I did not look at the painting on the easel, not while Catharina was watching me from the doorway.

A table had been pushed up against the window on the right, with a chair set in the corner. The chair's back and seat were of leather tooled with yellow flowers and leaves.

'Don't move anything over there,' Catharina reminded me. 'That is what he is painting.'

Even if I stood on my toes I was too small to reach the upper window and shutters. I would have to stand on the chair, but did not want to do so in front of her. She made me nervous, waiting in the doorway for me to make a mistake.

I considered what to do.

It was the baby who saved me – he began wailing downstairs. Catharina shifted from one hip to the other. As I hesitated she grew impatient and finally left to tend to Johannes.

I quickly climbed up and stood carefully on the wooden frame of the chair, pulled open the upper window, leaned out and pushed the shutters open. Peeking down at the street below, I spied Tanneke scrubbing the tiles in front of the house. She did not see me, but a cat padding across the wet tiles behind her paused and looked up.

I opened the lower window and shutters and got down from the chair. Something moved in front of me and I froze. The movement stopped. It was me, reflected in a mirror that hung on the wall between the two windows. I gazed at myself. Although I had an anxious, guilty expression, my face was also bathed in light, making my skin glow. I stared, surprised, then stepped away.

Now that I had a moment I surveyed the room. It was a large, square space, not as long as the great hall downstairs. With the windows open it was bright and airy, with whitewashed walls, and grey and white marble tiles on the floor, the darker tiles set in a pattern of square crosses. A row of Delft tiles painted with cupids lined the bottom of the walls to protect the whitewash from our mops. They were not my father's.

Though it was a big room, it held little furniture. There was the easel and chair set in front of the middle window, and the table placed in front of the window in the right corner. Besides the chair I had stood on there was another by the table, of plain leather nailed on with brass studs, and two lion heads carved into the tops of the posts. Against the far wall, behind the chair and easel, was a small cupboard, its drawers closed, several brushes and a knife with a diamond-shaped blade arranged on top next to clean palettes. Beside the cupboard was a desk on which were papers and books and prints. Two more lion-head chairs had been set against the wall near the doorway.

It was an orderly room, empty of the clutter of everyday life. It felt different from the rest of the house, almost as if it were in another house altogether. When the door was closed it would be difficult to hear the shouts of the children, the jangle of Catharina's keys, the sweeping of our brooms.

I took up my broom, bucket of water and dustcloth and began to clean. I started in the corner where the scene of the painting had been set up, where I knew I must not move a thing. I kneeled on the chair to dust the window I had struggled to open, and the yellow curtain that hung to one side of it in the corner, touching it lightly so that I would not disturb its folds. The panes of glass were dirty and needed scrubbing with warm water, but I was not sure if he wanted them clean. I would have to ask Catharina.

I dusted the chairs, polishing the brass studs and lion heads. The table had not been cleaned properly in some time. Someone had wiped around the objects placed there – a powderbrush, a pewter bowl, a letter, a black ceramic pot, blue cloth heaped to one side and hanging over the edge – but they had to be moved for the table really to be cleaned. As my mother had said, I would have to find a way to move things yet put them back exactly as if they had not been touched.

The letter lay close to the corner of the table. If I placed

35

my thumb along one edge of the paper, my second finger along another, and anchored my hand with my smallest finger hooked to the table edge, I should be able to move the letter, dust there, and replace it where my hand indicated.

I laid my fingers against the edges and drew in my breath, then removed the letter, dusted, and replaced it all in one quick movement. I was not sure why I felt I had to do it quickly. I stood back from the table. The letter seemed to be in the right place, though only he would really know.

Still, if this was to be my test, I had best get it done.

From the letter I measured with my hand to the powderbrush, then placed my fingers at various points around one side of the brush. I removed it, dusted, replaced it, and measured the space between it and the letter. I did the same with the bowl.

This was how I cleaned without seeming to move anything. I measured each thing in relation to the objects around it and the space between them. The small things on the table were easy, the furniture harder — I used my feet, my knees, sometimes my shoulders and chin with the chairs.

I did not know what to do with the blue cloth heaped messily on the table. I would not be able to get the folds exact if I moved the cloth. For now I left it alone, hoping that for a day or two he would not notice until I had found a way to clean it.

With the rest of the room I could be less careful. I dusted and swept and mopped — the floor, the walls, the windows, the furniture — with the satisfaction of tackling a room in need of a good cleaning. In the far corner, opposite the table and window, a door led to a storeroom, filled with paintings and canvases, chairs, chests, dishes, bedpans, a coat rack and a row of books. I cleaned in there too, tidying the things away so that there was more order to the room.

All the while I had avoided cleaning around the easel. I did not know why, but I was nervous about seeing the painting that sat on it. At last, though, there was nothing left to do. I dusted the chair in front of the easel, then began to dust the easel itself, trying not to look at the painting.

When I glimpsed the yellow satin, however, I had to stop.

I was still staring at the painting when Maria Thins spoke. 'Not a common sight, now, is it?'

I had not heard her come in. She stood inside the door-way, slightly stooped, wearing a fine black dress and lace collar.

I did not know what to say, and I couldn't help it – I turned back to the painting.

Maria Thins laughed. 'You're not the only one to forget your manners in front of one of his paintings, girl.' She came over to stand beside me. 'Yes, he's managed this one well. That's van Ruijven's wife.' I recognised the name as the patron my father had mentioned. 'She's not beautiful but he makes her so,' she added. 'It will fetch a good price.'

Because it was the first painting of his I was to see, I always remembered it better than the others, even those I saw grow from the first layer of underpaint to the final highlights.

A woman stood in front of a table, turned towards a mirror on the wall so that she was in profile. She wore a mantle of rich yellow satin trimmed with white ermine, and a fashionable five-pointed red ribbon in her hair. A window lit her from the left, falling across her face and tracing the delicate curve of her forehead and nose. She was tying a string of pearls round her neck, holding the ribbons up, her hands suspended in the air. Entranced with herself in the mirror, she did not seem to be aware that anyone was looking at her. Behind her on a bright white wall was an old map, in the dark foreground the table with the letter on it, the powderbrush and the other things I had dusted around.

I wanted to wear the mantle and the pearls. I wanted to know the man who painted her like that.

I thought of me looking at my reflection in the mirror earlier and was ashamed.

Maria Thins seemed content to stand with me and contemplate the painting. It was odd to look at it with the setting just behind it. Already from my dusting I knew all of the objects on the table, and their relation to one another – the letter by the corner, the powderbrush lying casually next to the pewter bowl, the blue cloth bunched around the dark pot. Everything seemed to be exactly the same, except cleaner and purer. It made a mockery of my own cleaning.

Then I saw a difference. I drew in my breath.

'What is it, girl?'

'In the painting there are no lion heads on the chair next to the woman,' I said.

'No. There was once a lute sitting on that chair as well. He makes plenty of changes. He doesn't paint just what he sees, but what will suit. Tell me, girl, do you think this painting is done?'

I stared at her. Her question must be a trick but I could not imagine any change that would make it better.

'Isn't it?' I faltered.

Maria Thins snorted. 'He's been working on it for three

months. I expect he'll do so for two more months. He will change things. You'll see.' She looked around. 'Done your cleaning, have you? Well, then, go on, girl — go to your other tasks. He'll come soon to see how you've done.'

I looked at the painting one last time, but by studying it so hard I felt something slip away. It was like looking at a star in the night sky — if I looked at one directly I could barely see it, but if I looked from the corner of my eye it became much brighter.

I gathered my broom and bucket and cloth. When I left the room, Maria Thins was still standing in front of the painting.

I filled the pots from the canal and set them on the fire, then went to find Tanneke. She was in the room where the girls slept, helping Cornelia to dress while Maertge helped Aleydis and Lisbeth helped herself. Tanneke was not in good spirits, glancing at me only to ignore me as I tried to speak to her. Finally I stood directly in front of her so that she had to look at me. 'Tanneke, I'll go to the fish stalls now. What would you like today?'

'Going so early? We always go later in the day.' Tanneke still did not look at me. She was tying white ribbons into five-pointed stars in Cornelia's hair.

'I'm free while the water is heating and thought I would go now,' I replied simply. I did not add that the best cuts were to be had early, even if the butcher or fishmonger promised to set aside things for the family. She should know that. 'What would you like?'

'Don't fancy fish today. Go to the butcher's for a mutton

joint.' Tanneke finished with the ribbons and Cornelia jumped up and pushed past me. Tanneke turned away and opened a chest to search for something. I watched her broad back for a moment, the greyish-brown dress pulled tight across it.

She was jealous of me. I had cleaned the studio, where she was not allowed, where no one, it seemed, could go except me and Maria Thins.

When Tanneke straightened, a bonnet in her hand, she said, 'The master painted me once, you know. Painted me pouring milk. Everyone said it was his best painting.'

'I'd like to see it,' I responded. 'Is it still here?'

'Oh no, van Ruijven bought it.'

I thought for a moment. 'So one of Delft's wealthiest men takes pleasure in looking at you each day.'

Tanneke grinned, her pocked face growing even wider. The right words changed her mood in a moment. It was simply up to me to find the words.

I turned to go before her mood could sour. 'May I come with you?' Maertge asked.

'And me?' Lisbeth added.

'Not today,' I said firmly. 'You have something to eat and help Tanneke.' I did not want it to become habit for the girls to accompany me. I would use it as a reward for minding me.

I was also longing to walk in familiar streets on my own, not to have a constant reminder of my new life chattering at my side. As I stepped into Market Square, leaving Papists' Corner behind, I breathed in deeply. I had not realised that I had been holding myself in tight all the time I was with the family.

Before going to Pieter's stall I stopped at the butcher I

knew, who beamed when he saw me. 'At last you decide to say hello! What, yesterday you were too grand for the likes of me?' he teased.

I started to explain my new situation but he interrupted me. 'Of course I know. Everyone is talking — Jan the tiler's daughter has gone to work for the painter Vermeer. And then I see after one day she is already too proud to speak to old friends!'

'I have nothing to be so proud of, becoming a maid. My father is ashamed.'

'Your father was simply unlucky. No one is blaming him. There is no need for you to be ashamed, my dear. Except of course that you are not buying your meat from me.'

'I have no choice, I'm afraid. That's for my mistress to decide.'

'Oh, it is, is it? So your buying from Pieter has nothing to do with his handsome son?'

I frowned. 'I have not seen his son.'

The butcher laughed. 'You will, you will. Off you go. When you see your mother next tell her to come and see me. I will set aside something for her.'

I thanked him and passed along the stalls to Pieter's. He seemed surprised to see me. 'Here already, are you? Couldn't wait to get here for more of that tongue?'

'I'd like a joint of mutton today, please.'

'Now tell me, Griet, was that not the best tongue you have had?'

I refused to give him the compliment he craved. 'The master and mistress ate it. They did not remark on it.'

Behind Pieter a young man turned round — he had been cutting into a side of beef at a table behind the stall. He must have been the son, for though he was taller than his father, he had the same bright blue eyes. His blond hair was long and thick with curls, framing a face that made me think of apricots. Only his bloody apron was displeasing to the eye.

His eyes came to rest on me like a butterfly on a flower and I could not keep from blushing. I repeated my request for mutton, keeping my eyes on his father. Pieter rummaged through his meat and pulled out a joint for me, laying it on the counter. Two sets of eyes watched me.

The joint was grey at the edges. I sniffed the meat. 'This is not fresh,' I said bluntly. 'Mistress will be none too pleased that you expect her family to eat meat such as this.' My tone was haughtier than I had intended. Perhaps it needed to be.

Father and son stared at me. I held the gaze of the father, trying to ignore the son.

At last Pieter turned to his son. 'Pieter, get me that joint set aside on the cart.'

'But that's meant for –' Pieter the son stopped. He disappeared, returning with another joint, which I could immediately see was superior. I nodded. 'That's better.'

Pieter the son wrapped the joint and placed it in my pail. I thanked him. As I turned to go I caught the glance that passed between father and son. Even then I knew somehow what it meant, and what it would mean for me.

Catharina was sitting on the bench when I got back, feeding Johannes. I showed her the joint and she nodded. As I was about to go in she said in a low voice, 'My husband has

inspected the studio and found the cleaning suited him.'
She did not look at me.

'Thank you, madam.' I stepped inside, glanced at a still
life of fruits and a lobster, and thought, So, I really am to
stay.

The rest of the day passed much as the first had, and as
the days to follow would. Once I had cleaned the studio
and gone to the fish stalls or the Meat Hall I began again
on the laundry, one day sorting, soaking and working on
stains, another day scrubbing, rinsing, boiling and wringing
before hanging things to dry and be bleached in the noon
sun, another day ironing and mending and folding. At some
point I always stopped to help Tanneke with the midday
meal. Afterwards we cleaned up, and then I had a little time
free to rest and sew on the bench out front, or back in the
courtyard. After that I finished whatever I had been doing
in the morning, then helped Tanneke with the late meal.
The last thing we did was to mop the floors once more so
that they would be fresh and clean for the morning.

At night I covered the Crucifixion hanging at the foot of
my bed with the apron I had worn that day. I slept better
then. The next day I added the apron to the day's wash.

While Catharina was unlocking the studio door on the
second morning I asked her if I should clean the windows.

'Why not?' she answered sharply. 'You do not need to
ask me such petty things.'

'Because of the light, madam,' I explained. 'It might
change the painting if I clean them. You see?'

She did not see. She would not or could not come into

43

the room to look at the painting. It seemed she never entered the studio. When Tanneke was in the right mood I would have to ask her why. Catharina went downstairs to ask him and called up to me to leave the windows.

When I cleaned the studio I saw nothing to indicate that he had been there at all. Nothing had been moved, the palettes were clean, the painting itself appeared no different. But I could feel that he had been there.

I had seen very little of him the first two days I was in the house on the Oude Langendijck. I heard him sometimes, on the stairs, in the hallway, chuckling with his children, talking softly to Catharina. Hearing his voice made me feel as if I were walking along the edge of a canal and unsure of my steps. I did not know how he would treat me in his own house, whether or not he would pay attention to the vegetables I chopped in his kitchen.

No gentleman had ever taken such an interest in me before.

I came face to face with him on my third day in the house. Just before dinner I went to find a plate that Lisbeth had left outside and almost ran into him as he carried Aleydis in his arms down the hallway.

I stepped back. He and Aleydis regarded me with the same grey eyes. He neither smiled nor did not smile at me. It was hard to meet his eyes. I thought of the woman looking at herself in the painting upstairs, of wearing pearls and yellow satin. She would have no trouble meeting the gaze of a gentleman. When I managed to lift my eyes to his he was no longer looking at me.

The next day I saw the woman herself. On my way back from the butcher a man and woman walked ahead of me on the Oude Langendijck. At our door he turned to her and bowed, then walked on. There was a long white feather in his hat — he must have been the visitor from a few days earlier. From the brief glimpse I caught of his profile I saw that he had a moustache, and a plump face to match his body. He smiled as if he were about to pay a flattering but false compliment. The woman turned into the house before I could see her face but I did see the five-pointed red ribbon in her hair. I held back, waiting by the doorway until I heard her go up the stairs.

Later I was putting away some clothes in the cupboard in the great hall when she came back down. I stood up as she entered. She was carrying the yellow mantle in her arms. The ribbon was still in her hair.

'Oh!' she said. 'Where is Catharina?'

'She's gone with her mother to the Town Hall, madam. Family business.'

'I see. Never mind, I'll see her another day. I'll leave this here for her.' She draped the mantle across the bed and dropped the pearl necklace on top of it.

'Yes, madam.'

I could not take my eyes off her. I felt as if I were seeing her and yet not seeing her. It was a strange sensation. She was, as Maria Thins had said, not as beautiful as when the light struck her in the painting. Yet she was beautiful, if only because I was remembering her so. She gazed at me with a puzzled look on her face, as if she ought to know me since I was staring at her with such familiarity. I managed to lower my eyes. 'I will tell her you called, madam.'

She nodded but looked troubled. She glanced at the pearls she had laid on top of the mantle. 'I think I shall leave these up in the studio with him,' she announced, picking up the necklace. She did not look at me, but I knew she was thinking that maids were not to be trusted with pearls. After she had gone her face lingered like perfume.

On Saturday Catharina and Maria Thins took Tanneke and Maertge with them to the market in the square, where they would buy vegetables to last the week, staples and other things for the house. I longed to go with them, thinking I might see my mother and sister, but I was told to stay at the house with the younger girls and the baby. It was difficult to keep them from running off to the market. I would have taken them there myself but I did not dare leave the house unattended. Instead we watched the boats go up and down the canal, full on their way to the market with cabbages, pigs, flowers, wood, flour, strawberries, horseshoes. They were empty on the way back, the boatmen counting money or drinking. I taught the girls games I had played with Agnes and Frans, and they taught me games they had made up. They blew bubbles, played with their dolls, ran with their hoops while I sat on the bench with Johannes in my lap.

Cornelia seemed to have forgotten about the slap. She was cheerful and friendly, helpful with Johannes, obedient to me. 'Will you help me?' she asked me as she tried to climb on to a barrel the neighbours had left out in the street. Her light brown eyes were wide and innocent. I found myself warming to her sweetness, yet knowing I could not trust her. She could be the most interesting of the girls, but also the most changeable – the best and the worst at the same time.

They were sorting through a collection of shells they had

brought outside, dividing them into piles of different colours, when he came out of the house. I squeezed the baby round his middle, feeling his ribs under my hands. He squealed and I buried my nose in his ear to hide my face.

'Papa, can I go with you?' Cornelia cried, jumping up and grabbing his hand. I could not see the expression on his face – the tilt of his head and the brim of his hat hid it.

Lisbeth and Aleydis abandoned their shells. 'I want to go too!' they shouted in unison, grabbing his other hand.

He shook his head and then I could see his bemused expression. 'Not today – I'm going to the apothecary's.'

'Will you buy paint things, Papa?' Cornelia asked, still holding on to his hand.

'Among other things.'

Baby Johannes began to cry and he glanced down at me. I bounced the baby, feeling awkward.

He looked as if he would say something, but instead he shook off the girls and strode down the Oude Langendijck.

He had not said a word to me since we discussed the colour and shape of vegetables.

I woke very early on Sunday, for I was excited about going home. I had to wait for Catharina to unlock the front door, but when I heard it swing open I came out to find Maria Thins with the key.

'My daughter is tired today,' she said as she stood aside to let me out. 'She will rest for a few days. Can you manage without her?'

'Of course, madam,' I replied, then added, 'and I may always ask you if I have questions.'

47

Maria Thins chuckled. 'Ah, you're a cunning one, girl. You know whose pot to spoon from. Never mind, we can do with a bit of cleverness around here.' She handed me some coins, my wages for the days I had worked. 'Off you go now, to tell your mother all about us, I suspect.'

I slipped away before she could say more, crossed Market Square, past those going to early services at the New Church, and hurried up the streets and canals that led me home. When I turned into my street I thought how different it felt already after less than a week away. The light seemed brighter and flatter, the canal wider. The plane trees lining the canal stood perfectly still, like sentries waiting for me.

Agnes was sitting on the bench in front of our house. When she saw me she called inside, 'She's here!' then ran to me and took my arm. 'How is it?' she asked, not even saying hello. 'Are they nice? Do you work hard? Are there any girls there? Is the house very grand? Where do you sleep? Do you eat off fine plates?'

I laughed and would not answer any of her questions until I had hugged my mother and greeted my father. Although it was not very much, I felt proud to hand over to my mother the few coins in my hand. This was, after all, why I was working.

My father came to sit outside with us and hear about my new life. I gave my hands to him to guide him over the front stoop. As he sat down on the bench he rubbed my palms with his thumb. 'Your hands are chapped,' he said. 'So rough and worn. Already you have the scars of hard work.'

'Don't worry,' I answered lightly. 'There was so much

laundry waiting for me because they didn't have enough help before. It will get easier soon.'

My mother studied my hands. 'I'll soak some mallow in oil,' she said. 'That will keep your hands soft. Agnes and I will go into the country to pick some.'

'Tell us!' Agnes cried. 'Tell us about them.'

I told them. Only a few things I didn't mention – how tired I was at night; how the Crucifixion scene hung at the foot of my bed; how I had slapped Cornelia; how Maertge and Agnes were the same age. Otherwise I told them everything.

I passed on the message from our butcher to my mother. 'That is kind of him,' she said, 'but he knows we have no money for meat and will not take such charity.'

'I don't think he meant it as charity,' I explained. 'I think he meant it out of friendship.'

She did not answer, but I knew she would not go back to the butcher.

When I mentioned the new butchers, Pieter the father and son, she raised her eyebrows but said nothing.

Afterwards we went to services at our church, where I was surrounded by familiar faces and familiar words. Sitting between Agnes and my mother, I felt my back relaxing into the pew, and my face softening from the mask I had worn all week. I thought I might cry.

Mother and Agnes would not let me help them with dinner when we came back home. I sat with my father on the bench in the sun. He held his face up to the warmth and kept his head cocked that way all the time we talked.

'Now, Griet,' he said, 'tell me about your new master. You hardly said a word about him.'

'I haven't seen much of him,' I was able to reply truthfully. 'He is either in his studio, where no one is to disturb him, or he is out.'

'Taking care of Guild business, I expect. But you have been in his studio – you told us about the cleaning and the measurements, but nothing about the painting he is working on. Describe it to me.'

'I don't know if I can in such a way that you will be able to see it.'

'Try. I have little to think of now except for memories. It will give me pleasure to imagine a painting by a master, even if my mind creates only a poor imitation.'

So I tried to describe the woman tying pearls around her neck, her hands suspended, gazing at herself in the mirror, the light from the window bathing her face and her yellow mantle, the dark foreground that separated her from us.

My father listened intently, but his own face was not illuminated until I said, 'The light on the back wall is so warm that looking at it feels the way the sun feels on your face.'

He nodded and smiled, pleased now that he understood.

'This is what you like best about your new life,' he said presently. 'Being in the studio.'

The only thing, I thought, but did not say.

When we ate dinner I tried not to compare it with that in the house at Papists' Corner, but already I had become accustomed to meat and good rye bread. Although my mother was a better cook than Tanneke, the brown bread was dry, the vegetable stew tasteless with no fat to flavour it. The room, too, was different – no marble tiles, no thick silk curtains, no tooled leather chairs. Everything was simple and clean, without ornamentation. I loved it because I knew it, but I was aware now of its dullness.

At the end of the day it was hard saying goodbye to my parents – harder than when I had first left, because this time I knew what I was going back to. Agnes walked with me as far as Market Square. When we were alone, I asked her how she was.

'Lonely,' she replied, a sad word from a ten-year-old. She had been lively all day but had now grown subdued.

'I'll come every Sunday,' I promised. 'And perhaps during the week I can come quickly to say hello after I've gone for the meat or fish.'

'Or I can come to see you when you are out buying things,' she suggested, brightening.

We did manage to meet in the Meat Hall several times. I was always glad to see her – as long as I was alone.

I began to find my place at the house on the Oude Langendijck. Catharina, Tanneke and Cornelia were all difficult at times, but usually I was left alone to my work. This may have been Maria Thins' influence. She had decided, for her own reasons, that I was a useful addition, and the others, even the children, followed her example.

Perhaps she felt the clothes were cleaner and better bleached now that I had taken on the laundry. Or that the meat was more tender now that I chose it. Or that he was happier with a clean studio. These first two things were true. The last, I did not know. When he and I finally spoke it was not about my cleaning.

I was careful to deflect any praise for better housekeeping

from myself. I did not want to make enemies. If Maria Thins liked the meat, I suggested it was Tanneke's cooking that made it so. If Maertge said her apron was whiter than before, I said it was because the summer sun was particularly strong now.

I avoided Catharina when I could. It had been clear from the moment she'd seen me chopping vegetables in my mother's kitchen that she disliked me. Her mood was not improved by the baby she carried, which made her ungainly and nothing like the graceful lady of the house she felt herself to be. It was a hot summer, too, and the baby was especially active. It began to kick whenever she walked, or so she said. As she grew bigger she went about the house with a tired, pained look. She took to staying in bed later and later, so that Maria Thins took over her keys and unlocked the studio door for me in the mornings. Tanneke and I began to do more and more of her work – looking after the girls, buying things for the house, changing the baby.

One day when Tanneke was in a good mood, I asked her why they did not take on more servants to make things easier. 'With a big house like this, and your mistress' wealth, and the master's paintings,' I added, 'could they not afford another maid? Or a cook?'

'Huh,' Tanneke snorted. 'They can barely manage to pay you.'

I was surprised – the coins amounted to so little in my hand each week. It would take me years of work to be able to buy something as fine as the yellow mantle that Catharina kept so carelessly folded in her cupboard. It did not seem possible that they could be short of money.

52

'Of course they'll find a way to pay for a nurse for a few months when the baby comes,' Tanneke added. She sounded disapproving.

'Why?'

'So she can feed the baby.'

'The mistress won't feed her own baby?' I asked stupidly.

'She couldn't have so many children if she fed her own. It stops you having them, you know, if you feed your own.'

'Oh.' I felt very ignorant of such things. 'Does she want more children?'

Tanneke chuckled. 'Sometimes I think she's filling the house with children because she can't fill it with servants as she'd like.' She lowered her voice. 'The master doesn't paint enough to make the money for servants, you see. Three paintings a year he does, usually. Sometimes only two. You don't get rich from that.'

'Can he not paint faster?' I knew even as I said it that he would not. He would always paint at his own pace.

'Mistress and young mistress disagree sometimes. Young mistress wants him to paint more, but my mistress says speed would ruin him.'

'Maria Thins is very wise.' I had learned that I could voice opinions in front of Tanneke as long as Maria Thins was in some way praised. Tanneke was fiercely loyal to her mistress. She had little patience with Catharina, however, and when she was in the right mood she advised me on how to handle her. 'Take no notice of what she says,' she counselled. 'Keep your face empty when she speaks, then do things your own way, or how my mistress or I tell you to do them. She never checks, she never notices. She just orders us about because

53

she feels she has to. But we know who our real mistress is, and so does she.'

Although Tanneke was often bad-tempered with me, I learned not to take it to heart, as she never remained so for long. She was fickle in her moods, perhaps from being caught between Catharina and Maria Thins for so many years. Despite her confident words about ignoring what Catharina said, Tanneke did not follow her own advice. Catharina's harsh tone upset her. And Maria Thins, for all her fairness, did not defend Tanneke from Catharina. I never once heard Maria Thins berate her daughter for anything, though Catharina needed it at times.

There was also the matter of Tanneke's housekeeping. Perhaps her loyalty made up for her sloppiness about the house — corners unmopped, meat burned on the outside and raw on the inside, pots not scrubbed thoroughly. I could not imagine what she had done to his studio when she tried to clean it. Though Maria Thins rarely scolded Tanneke, they both knew she ought to, and this kept Tanneke uncertain and quick to defend herself.

It became clear to me that in spite of her shrewd ways, Maria Thins was soft on the people closest to her. Her judgement was not as sound as it appeared.

Of the four girls, Cornelia was, as she had shown the first morning, the most unpredictable. Both Lisbeth and Aleydis were good, quiet girls, and Maertge was old enough to begin learning the ways of the house, which steadied her — though occasionally she would have a fit of temper and shout at me much like her mother. Cornelia did not shout but she was at times ungovernable. Even the threat of Maria Thins' anger that I had used on the first day did not always work.

She could be funny and playful one moment, then turn the next, like a purring cat who bites the hand stroking it. While loyal to her sisters, she did not hesitate to make them cry by pinching them hard. I was wary of Cornelia, and could not be fond of her in the way I came to be of the others.

I escaped from them all when I cleaned the studio. Maria Thins unlocked the door for me and sometimes stayed a few minutes to check on the painting, as if it were a sick child she was nursing. Once she left, though, I had the room to myself. I looked around to see if anything had changed. At first it seemed to remain the same, day after day, but after my eyes grew accustomed to the details of the room I began to notice small things – the brushes rearranged on top of the cupboard, one of the cupboard's drawers left ajar, the palette knife balanced on the easel's ledge, a chair moved a little from its place by the door.

Nothing, however, changed in the corner he was painting. I was careful not to displace any of it, quickly adjusting to my way of measuring so that I was able to clean that area almost as quickly and confidently as the rest of the room. And after experimenting on other bits of cloth, I began to clean the dark blue cloth and yellow curtain with a damp rag, pressing it carefully so that it picked up dust without disturbing the folds.

There seemed to be no changes to the painting, as hard as I looked for them. At last one day I discovered that another pearl had been added to the woman's necklace. Another day the shadow of the yellow curtain had grown bigger. I thought too that some of the fingers on her right hand had been moved.

The satin mantle began to look so real I wanted to reach out and touch it.

I had almost touched the real one the day van Ruijven's wife left it on the bed. I had just been reaching over to stroke the fur collar when I had looked up to see Cornelia in the door, watching me. One of the other girls would have asked me what I was doing, but Cornelia had just watched. That was worse than any questions. I had dropped my hand and she'd smiled.

Maertge insisted on coming with me to the fish stalls one morning several weeks after I had begun working at the house. She loved to run through Market Square, looking at things, petting the horses, joining other children in their games, sampling smoked fish from various stalls. She poked me in the ribs as I was buying herring and shouted, 'Look, Griet, look at that kite!'

The kite above our heads was shaped like a fish with a long tail, the wind making it look as if it were swimming through the air, with seagulls wheeling around it. As I smiled I saw Agnes hovering near us, her eyes fixed on Maertge. I still had not told Agnes there was a girl her age in the house – I thought it might upset her, that she would feel she was being replaced.

Sometimes when I visited my family at home I felt awkward telling them anything. My new life was taking over the old.

When Agnes looked at me I shook my head slightly so that Maertge would not see, and turned away to put the fish in my pail. I took my time – I could not bear to see the hurt on her face. I did not know what Maertge would do if Agnes spoke to me.

When I turned around Agnes had gone.

I shall have to explain to her when I see her Sunday, I thought. I have two families now, and they must not mix.

I was always ashamed afterwards that I had turned my back on my own sister.

I was hanging out washing in the courtyard, shaking out each piece before hanging it taut from the line, when Catharina appeared, breathing heavily. She sat down on a chair by the door, closed her eyes and sighed. I continued what I was doing as if it were natural for her to sit with me, but my jaw tightened.

'Are they gone yet?' she asked suddenly.

'Who, madam?'

'Them, you silly girl. My husband and – go and see if they've gone upstairs yet.'

I stepped cautiously into the hallway. Two sets of feet were climbing the stairs.

'Can you manage it?' I heard him say.

'Yes, yes, of course. You know it's not very heavy,' another man replied, in a voice deep like a well. 'Just a bit cumbersome.'

They reached the top of the stairs and entered the studio. I heard the door close.

'Have they gone?' Catharina hissed.

'They are in the studio, madam,' I responded.

'Good. Now help me up. ' Catharina held out her hands and I pulled her to her feet. I did not think she could grow much bigger and still manage to walk. She moved down the hallway like a ship with its sails full, holding on to her bunch of keys so that they wouldn't clink, and disappeared into the great hall.

Later I asked Tanneke why Catharina had been hiding.

'Oh, van Leeuwenhoek was here,' she answered, chuckling. 'A friend of the master's. She's afraid of him.'

'Why?'

Tanneke laughed harder. 'She broke his box! She was looking in it and knocked it over. You know how clumsy she is.'

I thought of my mother's knife spinning across the floor. 'What box?'

'He has a wooden box that you look in and – see things.'

'What things?'

'All sorts of things!' Tanneke replied impatiently. She clearly did not want to talk about the box. 'Young mistress broke it, and van Leeuwenhoek won't see her now. That's why master won't allow her in his room unless he's there. Perhaps he thinks she'll knock over a painting!'

I discovered what the box was the next morning, the day he spoke to me about things that took me many months to understand.

When I arrived to clean the studio, the easel and chair had been moved to one side. The desk was in their place, cleared of papers and prints. On it sat a wooden box about the size of a chest for storing clothes in. A smaller box was attached to one side, with a round object protruding from it.

I did not understand what it was, but I did not dare touch it. I went about my cleaning, glancing over at it now and then as if its use would suddenly become clear to me. I cleaned the corner, then the rest of the room, dusting the box so that I hardly touched it with my cloth. I cleaned the storeroom and mopped the floor. When I was done I stood in front of the box, arms crossed, moving around to study it.

My back was to the door but I knew suddenly that he was standing there. I wasn't sure whether to turn round or wait for him to speak.

He must have made the door creak, for then I was able to turn and face him. He was leaning against the threshold, wearing a long black robe over his daily clothes. He was watching me curiously, but he did not seem anxious that I might damage his box.

'Do you want to look in it?' he asked. It was the first time he had spoken directly to me since he asked about the vegetables many weeks before.

'Yes, sir. I do,' I replied without knowing what I was agreeing to. 'What is it?'

'It is called a camera obscura.'

The words meant nothing to me. I stood aside and watched him unhook a catch and lift up part of the box's top, which had been divided in two and hinged together. He propped up the lid at an angle so that the box was partly open. There was a bit of glass underneath. He leaned over and peered into the space between the lid and box, then touched the round piece at the end of the smaller box. He seemed to be looking at something, though I didn't think there could be much in the box to take such interest in.

He stood up and gazed at the corner I had cleaned so

59

carefully, then reached over and closed the middle window's shutters, so that the room was lit only by the window in the corner.

Then he took off his robe.

I shifted uneasily from one foot to the other.

He removed his hat, placing it on the chair by the easel, and pulled the robe over his head as he leaned over the box again.

I took a step back and glanced at the doorway behind me. Catharina had little will to climb the stairs these days, but I wondered what Maria Thins, or Cornelia, or anyone would think if they saw us. When I turned back I kept my eyes fixed on his shoes, which were gleaming from the polish I had given them the day before.

He stood up at last and pulled the robe from his head, his hair ruffled. 'There, Griet, it is ready. Now you look.' He stepped away from the box and gestured me towards it. I stood rooted to my place.

'Sir —'

'Place the robe over your head as I did. Then the image will be stronger. And look at it from this angle so it will not be upside down.'

I did not know what to do. The thought of me covered with his robe, unable to see, and him looking at me all the while, made me feel faint.

But he was my master. I was meant to do as he said.

I pressed my lips together, then stepped up to the box, to the end where the lid had been lifted. I bent over and looked in at the square of milky glass fixed inside. There was a faint drawing of something on it.

He draped his robe gently over my head so that it blocked

out all light. It was still warm from him, and smelled of the way brick feels when it has been baked by the sun. I placed my hands on the table to steady myself and closed my eyes for a moment. I felt as if I had drunk my evening beer too quickly.

'What do you see?' I heard him say.

I opened my eyes and saw the painting, without the woman in it.

'Oh!' I stood up so suddenly that the robe dropped from my head to the floor. I stepped back from the box, treading on the cloth.

I moved my foot. 'I'm sorry, sir. I will wash the robe this morning.'

'Never mind about the robe, Griet. What did you see?'

I swallowed. I was terribly confused, and a little frightened. What was in the box was a trick of the devil, or something Catholic I did not understand. 'I saw the painting, sir. Except that the woman wasn't in it, and it was smaller. And things were — switched around.'

'Yes, the image is projected upside down, and left and right are reversed. There are mirrors that can fix that.'

I did not understand what he was saying.

'But —'

'What is it?'

'I don't understand, sir. How did it get there?'

He picked up the robe and brushed it off. He was smiling. When he smiled his face was like an open window.

'Do you see this?' He pointed to the round object at the end of the smaller box. 'This is called a lens. It is made of a piece of glass cut in a certain way. When light from that scene — ' he pointed to the corner — 'goes through it and

into the box it projects the image so that we can see it here.'
He tapped the cloudy glass.

I was staring at him so hard, trying to understand, that
my eyes began to water.

'What is an image, sir? It is not a word I know.'

Something changed in his face, as if he had been looking
over my shoulder but was now looking at me. 'It is a picture,
like a painting.'

I nodded. More than anything I wanted him to think I
could follow what he said.

'Your eyes are very wide,' he said then.

I blushed. 'So I have been told, sir.'

'Do you want to look again?'

I did not, but I knew I could not say so. I thought for a
moment. 'I will look again, sir, but only if I am left alone.'

He looked surprised, then amused. 'All right,' he said. He
handed me his robe. 'I'll return in a few minutes, and tap
on the door before I enter.'

He left, closing the door behind him. I grasped his robe,
my hands shaking.

For a moment I thought of simply pretending to look,
and saying that I had. But he would know I was lying.

And I was curious. It became easier to consider it without
him watching me. I took a deep breath and gazed down
into the box. I could see on the glass a faint trace of the
scene in the corner. As I brought the robe over my head
the image, as he called it, became clearer and clearer – the
table, the chairs, the yellow curtain in the corner, the back
wall with the map hanging on it, the ceramic pot gleaming
on the table, the pewter basin, the powderbrush, the letter.
They were all there, assembled before my eyes on a flat

62

surface, a painting that was not a painting. I cautiously touched the glass – it was smooth and cold, with no traces of paint on it. I removed the robe and the image went faint again, though it was still there. I put the robe over me once more, closing out the light, and watched the jewelled colours appear again. They seemed to be even brighter and more colourful on the glass than they were in the corner.

It became as hard to stop looking into the box as it had been to take my eyes from the painting of the woman with the pearl necklace the first time I'd seen it. When I heard the tap on the door I just had time to straighten up and let the robe drop to my shoulders before he walked in.

'Have you looked again, Griet? Have you looked properly?'

'I have looked, sir, but I am not at all sure of what I have seen.' I smoothed my cap.

'It is surprising, isn't it? I was as amazed as you the first time my friend showed it to me.'

'But why do you look at it, sir, when you can look at your own painting?'

'You do not understand.' He tapped the box. 'This is a tool. I use it to help me see, so that I am able to make the painting.'

'But – you use your eyes to see.'

'True, but my eyes do not always see everything.'

My eyes darted to the corner, as if they would discover something unexpected that had been hidden from me before, behind the powderbrush, emerging from the shadows of the blue cloth.

'Tell me, Griet,' he continued, 'do you think I simply paint what is there in that corner?'

I glanced at the painting, unable to answer. I felt as if I

were being tricked. Whatever I answered would be wrong.

'The camera obscura helps me to see in a different way,' he explained. 'To see more of what is there.'

When he saw the baffled expression on my face he must have regretted saying so much to someone like me. He turned and snapped the box shut. I slipped off his robe and held it out to him.

'Sir —'

'Thank you, Griet,' he said as he took it from me. 'Have you finished with the cleaning here?'

'Yes, sir.'

'You may go, then.'

'Thank you, sir.' I quickly gathered my cleaning things and left, the door clicking shut behind me.

I thought about what he had said, about how the box helped him to see more. Although I did not understand why, I knew he was right because I could see it in his painting of the woman, and also what I remembered of the painting of Delft. He saw things in a way that others did not, so that a city I had lived in all my life seemed a different place, so that a woman became beautiful with the light on her face.

The day after I looked in the box I went to the studio and it was gone. The easel was back in its place. I glanced at the painting. Previously I had found only tiny changes in it. Now there was one easily seen — the map hanging on the wall behind the woman had been removed from both the painting and the scene itself. The wall was now bare. The painting looked the better for it — simpler, the lines of the woman clearer now against the brownish-white background of the wall. But the change upset me – it was so sudden. I would not have expected it of him.

I felt uneasy after I left the studio, and as I walked to the Meat Hall I did not look about me as I usually did. Though I waved hello to the old butcher I did not stop, even when he called out to me.

Pieter the son was minding the stall alone. I had seen him a few times since that first day, but always in the presence of his father, standing in the background while Pieter the father took charge. Now he said, 'Hello, Griet. I wondered when you would come.'

I thought that a silly thing to say, as I had been buying meat at the same time each day.

His eyes did not meet mine.

I decided not to remark on his words. 'Three pounds of stewing beef, please. And do you have more of those sausages your father sold me the other day? The girls liked them.'

'There are none left, I'm afraid.'

A woman came to stand behind me, waiting her turn. Pieter the son glanced at her. 'Can you wait for a moment?' he said to me in a low voice.

'Wait?'

'I want to ask you something.'

I stood aside so that he could serve the woman. I did not like doing so when I was feeling so unsettled, but I had little choice.

When he was done and we were alone again he asked, 'Where does your family live?'

'The Oude Langendijck, at Papists' Corner.'

'No, no, *your* family.'

I flushed at my mistake. 'Off the Rietveld Canal, not far from the Koe Gate. Why do you ask?'

His eyes fully met mine at last. 'There have been reports of the plague in that quarter.'

I took a step back, my eyes widening. 'Has a quarantine been set?'

'Not yet. They expect to today.'

Afterwards I realised he must have been asking others about me. If he hadn't already known where my family lived, he would never have known to tell me about the plague.

I do not remember getting back from there. Pieter the son must have placed the meat in my pail but all I knew was that I arrived at the house, dropped the pail at Tanneke's feet and said, 'I must see the mistress.'

Tanneke rummaged through the pail. 'No sausages, and nothing to take their place! What's the matter with you? Go straight back to the Meat Hall.'

'I must see the mistress,' I repeated.

'What is it?' Tanneke grew suspicious. 'Have you done something wrong?'

'My family may be quarantined. I must go to them.'

'Oh.' Tanneke shifted uncertainly. 'I wouldn't know about that. You'll have to ask. She's in with my mistress.'

Catharina and Maria Thins were in the Crucifixion room. Maria Thins was smoking her pipe. They stopped talking when I entered.

'What is it, girl?' Maria Thins grunted.

'Please, madam,' I addressed Catharina, 'I have heard that my family's street may be quarantined. I would like to go and see them.'

'What, and bring the plague back with you?' she snapped. 'Certainly not. Are you mad?'

I looked at Maria Thins, which made Catharina angrier. 'I have said no,' she announced. 'It is *I* who decide what you can and cannot do. Have you forgotten that?'

'No, madam.' I lowered my eyes.

'You won't be going home Sundays until it's safe. Now go, we have things to discuss without you hanging about.'

I took the washing to the courtyard and sat outside with my back to the door so that I would not have to see anyone. I wept as I scrubbed one of Maertge's dresses. When I smelled Maria Thins' pipe I wiped my eyes but did not turn round.

'Don't be silly, girl,' Maria Thins said quietly to my back. 'You can't do anything for them and you have to save yourself. You're a clever girl, you can work that out.'

I did not answer. After a while I could no longer smell her pipe.

The next morning he came in while I was sweeping the studio.

'Griet, I am sorry to hear of your family's misfortune,' he said.

I looked up from my broom. There was kindness in his eyes, and I felt I could ask him. 'Will you tell me, sir, if the quarantine has been set?'

'It was, yesterday morning.'

'Thank you for telling me, sir.'

He nodded, and was about to leave when I said, 'May I ask you something else, sir? About the painting.'

He stopped in the doorway. 'What is it?'

'When you looked in the box, did it tell you to remove the map from the painting?'

'Yes, it did.' His face became intent like a stork's when it sees a fish it can catch. 'Does it please you that the map is gone?'

'It is a better painting now.' I did not think I would have dared to say such a thing at another time, but the danger to my family had made me reckless.

His smile made me grip my broom tightly.

I was not able to work well then. I was worried about my family, not about how clean I could get the floors or how white the sheets. No one may have remarked on my good housekeeping before, but everyone noticed how careless I was now. Lisbeth complained of a spotted apron. Tanneke grumbled that my sweeping caused dust to settle on the dishes. Catharina shouted at me several times – for forgetting to iron the sleeves of her chemise, for buying cod when I was meant to get herring, for letting the fire go out.

Maria Thins muttered, 'Steady yourself, girl,' as she passed me in the hallway.

Only in the studio was I able to clean as I had before, maintaining the precision he needed.

I did not know what to do that first Sunday I was not allowed to go home. I could not go to our church either, as it was in the quarantined area as well. I did not want to remain at the house, though – whatever Catholics did on Sundays, I did not want to be among them.

They left together to go to the Jesuit church around the corner in the Molenpoort, the girls wearing good dresses, even Tanneke changed into a yellowish brown wool dress, and carrying Johannes. Catharina walked slowly, holding on to her husband's arm. Maria Thins locked the door behind her. I stood on the tiles in front of the house as they disappeared and considered what to do. The bells in the New Church tower in front of me began to sound the hour.

I was baptised there, I thought. Surely they will allow me inside for the service.

I crept into the vast place, feeling like a mouse hiding in a rich man's house. It was cool and dim inside, the smooth round pillars reaching up, the ceiling so high above me it could almost be the sky. Behind the minister's altar was the grand marble tomb of William of Orange.

I saw no one I knew, only people dressed in sober clothes much finer in their cloth and cut than any I would ever wear. I hid behind a pillar for the service, which I could hardly listen to, I was so nervous that someone would come along and ask me what I was doing there. At the end of the service I slipped out quickly before anyone approached me. I walked round the church and looked across the canal at the house. The door was still shut and locked. Catholic services must last longer than ours, I thought.

I walked as far as I could towards my family's house, stopping only where a barrier manned by a soldier blocked the way. The streets looked very quiet beyond it.

'How is it,' I asked the soldier, 'back there?'

He shrugged and did not reply. He looked hot in his cloak and hat, for though the sun was not out the air was warm and close.

'Is there a list? Of those who have died?' I could barely say the words.

'Not yet.'

I was not surprised — the lists were always delayed, and usually incomplete. Word of mouth was often more accurate. 'Do you know — have you heard if Jan the tiler —'

'I know nothing of anyone in there. You'll have to wait.' The soldier turned away as others approached him with similar queries.

I tried to speak to another soldier on a barrier at a different street. Though friendlier, he too could tell me nothing about my family. 'I could ask around, but not for nothing,' he added, smiling and looking me up and down so I would know he didn't mean money.

'Shame on you,' I snapped, 'for seeking to take advantage of those in misery.'

But he did not seem ashamed. I had forgotten that soldiers think of just one thing when they see a young woman.

When I got back to the Oude Langendijck I was relieved to find the house open. I slipped inside and spent the afternoon hiding in the courtyard with my prayer book. In the evening I crept into bed without eating, telling Tanneke my stomach hurt.

At the butcher's Pieter the son pulled me to one side while his father was busy with someone else. 'Have you had news of your family?'

I shook my head. 'No one could tell me anything.' I did not meet his gaze. His concern made me feel as if I had just stepped off a boat and the ground was wobbling under my feet.

'I will find out for you,' Pieter stated. From his tone it was clear that I was not to argue with him.

'Thank you,' I said after a long pause. I wondered what

70

I would do if he did find out something. He was not demanding anything the way the soldier had, but I would be obliged to him. I did not want to be obliged to anyone.

'It may take a few days,' Pieter murmured before he turned to hand his father a cow's liver. He wiped his hands on his apron. I nodded, my eyes on his hands. The creases between his nails and his fingers were filled with blood.

I expect I will have to get used to that sight, I thought.

I began to look forward to my daily errand even more than to cleaning the studio. I dreaded it too, though, especially the moment Pieter the son looked up from his work and saw me, and I searched his eyes for clues. I wanted to know, yet as long as I didn't, it was possible to hope.

Several days passed when I bought meat from him, or passed by his stall after I had bought fish, and he simply shook his head. Then one day he looked up and looked away, and I knew what he would say. I just did not know who.

I had to wait until he finished with several customers. I felt so sick I wanted to sit down, but the floor was speckled with blood.

At last Pieter the son took off his apron and came over. 'It is your sister, Agnes,' he said softly. 'She is very ill.'

'And my parents?'

'They stay well, so far.'

I did not ask what risk he had gone to in order to find out for me. 'Thank you, Pieter,' I whispered. It was the first time I had spoken his name.

I looked into his eyes and saw kindness there. I also saw what I had feared — expectation.

*   *   *

On Sunday I decided to visit my brother. I did not know how much he knew of the quarantine or of Agnes. I left the house early and walked to his factory, which was outside the city walls not far from the Rotterdam Gate. Frans was still asleep when I arrived. The woman who answered at the gate laughed when I asked for him. 'He'll be asleep for hours yet,' she said. 'They sleep all day on Sundays, the apprentices. It's their day off.'

I did not like her tone, nor what she said. 'Please wake him and tell him his sister is here,' I demanded. I sounded a bit like Catharina.

The woman raised her eyebrows. 'I didn't know Frans came from a family so high on their throne you can see up their noses.' She disappeared and I wondered if she would bother to wake Frans. I sat on a low wall to wait. A family passed me on their way to church. The children, two girls and two boys, ran ahead of their parents, just as we had ours. I watched them until they passed from sight.

Frans appeared at last, rubbing sleep from his face. 'Oh, Griet,' he said. 'I didn't know if it would be you or Agnes. I suppose Agnes wouldn't come so far on her own.'

He didn't know. I couldn't keep it from him, not even to tell him gently.

'Agnes has been struck by the plague,' I blurted out. 'God help her and our parents.'

Frans stopped rubbing his face. His eyes were red.

'Agnes?' he repeated in confusion. 'How do you know this?'

'Someone found out for me.'

'You haven't seen them?'

'There is a quarantine.'

'A quarantine? How long has there been one?'

'Ten days so far.'

Frans shook his head angrily. 'I heard nothing of this! Stuck in this factory day after day, nothing but white tiles as far as I can see. I think I may go mad.'

'It's Agnes you should be thinking of now.'

Frans hung his head unhappily. He had grown taller since I'd seen him months before. His voice had deepened as well.

'Frans, have you been going to church?'

He shrugged. I could not bring myself to question him further.

'I'm going now to pray for them all,' I said instead. 'Will you come with me?'

He did not want to, but I managed to persuade him – I did not want to face a strange church alone again. We found one not far away, and although the service did not comfort me, I prayed hard for our family.

Afterwards Frans and I walked along the Schie River. We said little, but we each knew what the other was thinking – neither of us had heard of anyone recovering from the plague.

One morning when Maria Thins was unlocking the studio for me she said, 'All right, girl. Clear that corner today.' She pointed to the area that he was painting. I did not understand what she meant. 'All the things on the table should go into the chests in the storeroom,' she continued, 'except the bowl and Catharina's powderbrush. I'll take them with me.' She crossed to the table and picked up two of the

73

objects I had spent so many weeks setting carefully in their places.

When she saw my face Maria Thins laughed. 'Don't worry. He's finished. He doesn't need this now. When you're done here make sure you dust all the chairs and set them out by the middle window. And open all the shutters.' She left, cradling the pewter bowl in her arms.

Without the bowl and brush the tabletop was transformed into a picture I did not recognise. The letter, the cloth, the ceramic pot lay without meaning, as if someone had simply dropped them on to the table. Still, I could not imagine moving them.

I put off doing so by going about my other duties. I opened all the shutters, which made the room very bright and strange, then dusted and mopped everywhere but the table. I looked at the painting for some time, trying to discover what was different about it that now made it complete. I had seen no changes in it over the past several days.

I was still pondering when he entered. 'Griet, you've not yet cleared up. Be quick about it — I've come to help you move the table.'

'I'm sorry for being so slow, sir. It's just —' He seemed surprised that I wanted to say something — 'I'm so used to the objects where they are that I hate to move them.'

'I see. I will help you, then.' He plucked the blue cloth from the table and held it out. His hands were very clean. I took the cloth from him without touching them and brought it to the window to shake out. Then I folded it and placed it in a chest in the storeroom. When I came back he had gathered up the letter and the black ceramic pot and stored them away. We moved the table to the side of the room and I set up the chairs by the middle window while he moved the easel and painting to the corner where the scene had been set.

It was odd to see the painting in the place of the setting. It all felt strange, this sudden movement and change after weeks of stillness and quiet. It was not like him. I did not ask him why. I wanted to look at him, to guess what he was thinking, but I kept my eyes on my broom, cleaning up the dust disturbed by the blue cloth.

He left me and I finished up quickly, not wanting to linger in the studio. It was no longer comforting there.

That afternoon van Ruijven and his wife visited. Tanneke and I were sitting on the bench in front while she showed me how to mend some lace cuffs. The girls had gone over to Market Square and were flying a kite near the New Church where we could see them, Maertge holding the end of the string while Cornelia tugged the kite up into the sky.

I saw the van Ruijvens coming from a long way off. As they approached I recognised her from the painting and my brief meeting with her, and him as the moustached man with the white feather in his hat and the oily smile, who had once escorted her to the door.

'Look, Tanneke,' I whispered, 'it's the gentleman who admires the painting of you every day.'

'Oh!' Tanneke blushed when she saw them. Straightening her cap and apron, she hissed, 'Go and tell mistress they're here!'

I ran inside and found Maria Thins and Catharina with the sleeping baby in the Crucifixion room. 'The van Ruijvens have come,' I announced.

Catharina and Maria Thins removed their caps and

smoothed their collars. Catharina held on to the table and pulled herself up. As they were leaving the room Maria Thins reached up and straightened one of Catharina's tortoiseshell combs, which she wore only on special occasions.

They greeted their guests in the front hall while I hovered in the hallway. As they moved to the stairs van Ruijven caught sight of me and paused for a moment.

'Who's this, then?'

Catharina frowned at me. 'Just one of the maids. Tanneke, bring us up some wine, please.'

'Have the wide-eyed maid bring it to us,' van Ruijven commanded. 'Come, my dear,' he said to his wife, who began climbing the stairs.

Tanneke and I stood side by side, she annoyed, me dismayed by his attention.

'Go on, then!' Catharina cried to me. 'You heard what he said. Bring the wine.' She pulled herself heavily up the stairs after Maria Thins.

I went to the little room where the girls slept, found glasses stored there, polished five of them with my apron and set them on a tray. Then I searched the kitchen for wine. I did not know where it was kept, for they did not drink wine often. Tanneke had disappeared in a huff. I feared the wine was kept locked away in one of the cupboards, and that I would have to ask Catharina for the key in front of everyone.

Fortunately, Maria Thins must have anticipated this. In the Crucifixion room she had left out a white jug with a pewter top, filled with wine. I set it on the tray and carried it up to the studio, first straightening my cap, collar and apron as the others had done.

When I entered they were standing by the painting. 'A jewel once again,' van Ruijven was saying. 'Are you happy with it, my dear?' he addressed his wife.

'Of course,' she answered. The light was shining through the windows on to her face and she looked almost beautiful.

As I set the tray down on the table my master and I had moved that morning Maria Thins came over. 'I'll take that,' she whispered. 'Off you go. Quickly, now.'

I was on the stairs when I heard van Ruijven say, 'Where's that wide-eyed maid? Gone already? I wanted to have a proper look at her.'

'Now, now, she's nothing!' Catharina cried gaily. 'It's the painting you want to look at.'

I went back to the front bench and took my seat next to Tanneke, who wouldn't say a word to me. We sat in silence, working on the cuffs, listening to the voices floating out from the windows above.

When they came down again I slipped around the corner and waited, leaning against the warm bricks of a wall in the Molenpoort, until they were gone.

Later a man servant from their house came and disappeared up to the studio. I did not see him go, as the girls had come back and wanted me to build up the fire so they could bake apples in it.

The next morning the painting was gone. I had not had a chance to look at it one last time.

That morning as I arrived at the Meat Hall I heard a man ahead of me say the quarantine had been lifted. I hurried to Pieter's stall. Father and son were both there, and several

77

people were waiting to be served. I ignored them and went straight up to Pieter the son. 'Can you serve me quickly?' I said. 'I must go to my family's house. Just three pounds of tongue and three of sausages.'

He stopped what he had been doing, ignoring the indignant sounds from the old woman he had been helping. 'I suppose if I were young and smiled at you you'd do anything for me too,' she scolded as he handed the packages to me.

'She's not smiling,' Pieter replied. He glanced at his father, then handed me a smaller package. 'For your family,' he said in a low voice.

I did not even thank him — I snatched the package and ran.

Only thieves and children run.

I ran all the way home.

My parents were sitting side by side on the bench, heads bowed. When I reached them I took my father's hand and raised it to my wet cheek. I sat next to them and said nothing.

There was nothing to be said.

There followed a time when everything was dull. The things that had meant something — the cleanliness of the laundry, the daily walk on errands, the quiet studio — lost importance, though they were still there, like bruises on the body that fade to hard lumps under the skin.

It was at the end of the summer that my sister died. That autumn was rainy. I spent much of my time hanging laundry on racks indoors, shifting them closer to the fire, trying to dry the clothes before mildew took over but without scorching them.

Tanneke and Maria Thins treated me kindly enough when they found out about Agnes. Tanneke managed to check her irritation for several days, though soon she began again to scold and sulk, leaving it to me to placate her. Maria Thins said little but took to cutting off her daughter when Catharina became sharp with me.

Catharina herself seemed to know nothing of my sister, or did not show it. She was nearing her confinement, and as Tanneke had predicted she spent most of her time in bed, leaving the baby Johannes to Maertge's charge. He was beginning to toddle about, and kept the girls busy.

The girls did not know I had a sister and so would not understand that I could lose one. Only Aleydis seemed to sense that something was wrong. She sometimes came to sit by me, pushing her body close to mine like a pup burrowing into its mother's fur for warmth. She comforted me in a simple way that no one else could.

One day Cornelia came out to the courtyard where I was hanging up clothes. She held out an old doll to me. 'We don't play with this any more,' she announced. 'Not even Aleydis. Would you like to give it to your sister?' She made her eyes wide and innocent, and I knew she must have overheard someone mention Agnes' death.

'No, thank you,' was all I could say, almost choking on the words.

She smiled and skipped away.

The studio remained empty. He did not start another painting. He spent much of his time away from the house, either at the Guild or at Mechelen, his mother's inn across the square. I still cleaned the studio, but it became like any other task, just another room to mop and dust.

When I visited the Meat Hall I found it hard to meet Pieter the son's eye. His kindness pained me. I should have returned it but did not. I should have been flattered but was not. I did not want his attention. I came to prefer being served by his father, who teased me but did not demand anything from me but to be critical of his meat. We ate fine meat that autumn.

On Sundays I sometimes went to Frans' factory and urged him to come home with me. He did twice, cheering my parents a little. Until a year before they'd had three children at home. Now they had none. When Frans and I were both there we reminded them of better times. Once my mother even laughed, before stopping herself with a shake of her head. 'God has punished us for taking for granted our good fortune,' she said. 'We must not forget that.'

It was not easy visiting home. I found that after staying away those few Sundays during the quarantine, home had come to feel like a strange place. I was beginning to forget where my mother kept things, what kind of tiles lined the fireplace, how the sun shone in the rooms at different times of the day. After only a few months I could describe the house in Papists' Corner better than my family's.

Frans especially found it hard to visit. After long days and nights at the factory he wanted to smile and laugh and tease, or at least to sleep. I suppose I coaxed him there hoping to knit our family together again. It was impossible, though. Since my father's accident we had become a different family.

*   *   *

When I came back one Sunday from my parents', Catharina had begun her labour. I heard her groaning when I stepped inside the front door. I peeked into the great hall, which was darker than usual — the lower windows had been shuttered to give her privacy. Maria Thins was there with Tanneke and the midwife. When Maria Thins saw me she said, 'Go look for the girls — I've sent them out to play. It won't be long now. Come back in an hour.'

I was glad to leave. Catharina was making a great deal of noise, and it did not seem right to listen to her in that state. I knew too that she would not want me there.

I looked for the girls in their favourite place, the Beast Market round the corner from us, where livestock was sold. When I found them they were playing marbles and chasing one another. Baby Johannes tumbled after them — unsteady on his feet, he half walked, half crawled. It was not the kind of play we would have been allowed on a Sunday, but Catholics held different views.

When Aleydis grew tired she came to sit with me. 'Will Mama have the baby soon?' she asked.

'Your grandmother said she would. We'll go back in a bit and see them.'

'Will Papa be pleased?'

'I should think so.'

'Will he paint more quickly now there's another baby?'

I did not answer. Catharina's words were coming from a little girl's mouth. I did not want to hear more.

When we returned he was standing in the doorway. 'Papa, your cap!' cried Cornelia. The girls ran up to him and tried to snatch off the quilted paternity cap he wore, its ribbons dangling below his ears. He looked both proud and embarrassed. I was surprised — he had become a father five times before, and I thought he would be used to it. There was no reason for him to be embarrassed.

It is Catharina who wants many children, I thought then. He would rather be alone in his studio.

But that could not be quite right. I knew how babies were made. He had his part to play, and he must have played it willingly. And as difficult as Catharina could be, I had often seen him look at her, touch her shoulder, speak to her in a low voice laced with honey.

I did not like to think of him in that way, with his wife and children. I preferred to think of him alone in his studio. Or not alone, but with only me.

'You have another brother, girls,' he said. 'His name is Franciscus. Would you like to see him?' He led them inside while I hung back in the street, holding Johannes.

Tanneke opened the shutters of the great hall's lower windows and leaned out.

'Is the mistress all right?' I asked.

'Oh, yes. She makes a racket but there's nothing behind it. She's made to have babies — pops them out like a chestnut from its shell. Now come, master wants to say a prayer of thanks.'

Though uncomfortable, I could not refuse to pray with them. Protestants would have done the same after a good birth. I carried Johannes into the great hall, which was much lighter now and full of people. When I set him down he tottered over to his sisters, who were gathered around the bed. The curtains had been drawn back and Catharina lay propped against pillows, cradling the baby. Though exhausted, she was smiling, happy for once. My master stood near her, gazing down at his new son. Aleydis was holding his hand. Tanneke and the midwife were clearing away basins and bloody sheets while the new nurse waited near the bed.

Maria Thins came in from one of the kitchens with some wine and three glasses on a tray. When she set them down he let go of Aleydis' hand, stepped away from the bed, and he and Maria Thins kneeled. Tanneke and the midwife stopped what they were doing and kneeled as well. Then the nurse and children and I kneeled, Johannes squirming and crying out as Lisbeth forced him to sit.

My master said a prayer to God, thanking Him for the safe delivery of Franciscus and for sparing Catharina. He added some Catholic phrases in Latin which I did not understand, but I did not mind much – he had a low, soothing voice that I liked to listen to.

When he was done Maria Thins poured three glasses of wine and she and he and Catharina drank good health to the baby. Then Catharina handed the baby to the nurse, who put him to her breast.

Tanneke signalled to me and we left the room to get bread and smoked herring for the midwife and the girls. 'We'll begin preparing for the birth feast now,' Tanneke remarked as we were setting things out. 'Young mistress likes a big one. We'll be run off our feet as usual.'

The birth feast was the biggest celebration I was to witness in that house. We had ten days to prepare for it, ten days of cleaning and cooking. Maria Thins hired two girls for a week to help Tanneke with the food and me with the cleaning. My girl was slow-witted but worked well as long as I told her exactly what to do and kept a close eye on her. One day we washed, whether they were clean already or not, all the tablecloths and napkins that would be needed for the feast, as well as all the clothes in the house – shirts, robes, bonnets, collars, handkerchiefs, caps, aprons. The linens took another day. Then we washed all the tankards, glasses, earthenware plates, jugs, copper pots, pancake pans, iron grills and spits, spoons, ladles, as well as those from the neighbours who lent them for the occasion. We polished the brass and the copper and the silver. We took curtains down and shook them outside, and beat all the cushions and rugs. We polished the wood of the beds, the cupboards, the chairs and tables, the windowsills, until everything gleamed.

By the end my hands were cracked and bleeding.

It was very clean for the feast.

Maria Thins placed special orders for lamb and veal and tongue, for a whole pig, for hare and pheasant and capons, for oysters and lobsters and caviar and herring, for sweet wine and the best ale, for sweet cakes prepared specially by the baker.

When I placed the meat order for Maria Thins with Pieter the father, he rubbed his hands. 'So, yet another mouth to feed,' he proclaimed. 'All the better for us!'

Great wheels of Gouda and Edam arrived, and artichokes, and oranges and lemons and grapes and plums, and almonds and hazelnuts. Even a pineapple was sent, gift of a wealthy cousin of Maria Thins. I had never seen one before, and was not tempted by its rough, prickly skin. It was not for me to eat anyway. None of the food was, except for the odd taste Tanneke allowed us. She let me try a tiny bit of caviar, which I liked less than I admitted, for all its luxury, and some of the sweet wine, which was wonderfully spiced with cinnamon.

Extra peat and wood were piled in the courtyard, and spits borrowed from a neighbour. Barrels of ale were also kept in the courtyard, and the pig was roasted there. Maria Thins hired a young boy to look after all the fires, which were in use all night once we began roasting the pig.

Throughout the preparations Catharina remained in bed with Franciscus, tended by the nurse, serene as a swan. Like a swan too, though, she had a long neck and sharp beak. I kept away from her.

'This is how she would like the house to be every day,' Tanneke grumbled to me as she was preparing jugged hare and I was boiling water to wash the windows with. 'She wants everything to be in a state around her. Queen of the bedcovers!' I chuckled with her, knowing I shouldn't encourage her to be disloyal but cheered none the less when she was.

He stayed away during the preparations, locked in his studio or escaping to the Guild. I saw him only once, three days before the feast. The hired girl and I were polishing candlesticks in the kitchen when Lisbeth came to find me. 'Butcher's asking for you,' she said. 'Out front.'

I dropped the polishing cloth, wiped my hands on my apron and followed her up the hallway. I knew it would be the son. He had never seen me in Papists' Corner. At least my face was not chapped and red as it normally was from hanging over the steaming laundry.

Pieter the son had pulled up a cart in front of the house, loaded with the meat Maria Thins had ordered. The girls were peering into it. Only Cornelia looked round. When I appeared in the doorway Pieter smiled at me. I remained calm and did not blush. Cornelia was watching us.

She was not the only one. I felt his presence at my back – he had come down the hallway behind me. I turned to look at him, and saw that he had seen Pieter's smile, and the expectation there as well.

He transferred his grey eyes to me. They were cold. I felt dizzy, as if I had stood up too quickly. I turned back round. Pieter's smile was not so wide now. He had seen my dizziness.

I felt caught between the two men. It was not a pleasant feeling.

I stood aside to let my master pass. He turned into the Molenpoort without a word or glance. Pieter and I watched him go in silence.

'I have your order,' Pieter said then. 'Where would you like it?'

That Sunday when I went home to my parents I did not want to tell them that another child had been born. I thought it would remind them of losing Agnes. But my mother had heard of it at the market and so I was made to describe to them the birth and praying with the family and all the preparations that had been made so far for the feast. My mother was concerned about the state of my hands, but I promised her the worst was done.

'And a painting?' my father asked. 'Has he begun another painting?' He always hoped that I would describe a new painting to him.

'Nothing,' I replied. I had spent little time in the studio that week. Nothing there had changed.

'Perhaps he is idle,' my mother said.

'He is not that,' I answered quickly.

'Perhaps he does not want to see,' my father said.

'I don't know what he wants,' I said more sharply than I had intended. My mother gazed at me. My father shifted in his seat.

I said nothing more about him.

The guests began to arrive around noon on the feast day. By evening there were perhaps a hundred people in and out of the house, spilling into the courtyard and the street. All sorts had been invited – wealthy merchants as well as our baker, tailor, cobbler, apothecary. Neighbours were there, and my master's mother and sister, and Maria Thins' cousins. Painters were there, and other Guild members. Van Leeuwenhoek was there, and van Ruijven and his wife.

Even Pieter the father was there, without his blood-stained apron, nodding and smiling at me as I passed with a jug of spiced wine. 'Well, Griet,' he said as I poured him some, 'my son will be jealous that I'm spending the evening with you.'

'I think not,' I murmured, pulling away from him, embarrassed.

Catharina was the centre of attention. She had on a green silk dress altered to accommodate her belly, which had not yet shrunk. Over it she wore the ermine-trimmed yellow mantle van Ruijven's wife had worn for the painting. It was odd to see it around another woman's shoulders. I didn't like her wearing it, though it was of course hers to wear. She also wore a pearl necklace and earrings, and her blonde curls were dressed prettily. She had recovered quickly from the birth, and was very merry and graceful, her body relieved of some of the burden it had been carrying over the months. She moved easily through the rooms, drinking and laughing with her guests, lighting candles, calling for food, bringing people together. She stopped only to make a fuss over Franciscus when he was being fed by the nurse.

My master was much quieter. He spent most of his time in one corner of the great hall, talking to van Leeuwenhoek, though his eyes often followed Catharina around the room as she moved among her guests. He wore a smart black velvet jacket and his paternity cap, and looked comfortable though not much interested in the party. Large crowds did not appeal to him as they did his wife.

Late in the evening, van Ruijven managed to corner me in the hallway as I was passing along it with a lighted candle and a wine jug. 'Ah, the wide-eyed maid,' he cried, leaning into me. 'Hello, my girl.' He grabbed my chin in his hand, his other hand pulling the candle up to light my face. I did not like the way he looked at me.

'You should paint her,' he said over his shoulder.

My master was there. He was frowning. He looked as if he wanted to say something to his patron but could not.

'Griet, get me some more wine.' Pieter the father had popped out from the Crucifixion room and was holding a cup towards me.

'Yes, sir.' I pulled my chin from van Ruijven's grasp and quickly crossed to Pieter the father. I could feel two pairs of eyes on my back.

'Oh, I'm sorry, sir, the jug's empty. I'll just get some more from the kitchen.' I hurried away, holding the jug close so they would not discover that it was full.

When I returned a few minutes later only Pieter the father remained, leaning against the wall. 'Thank you,' I said in a low voice as I filled his glass.

He winked at me. 'It was worth it just to hear you call me sir. I'll never hear that again, will I?' He raised his glass in a mock toast and drank.

After the feast winter descended on us, and the house became cold and flat. Besides a great deal of cleaning up, there was no longer something to look forward to. The girls, even Aleydis, became difficult, demanding attention, rarely helping. Maria Thins spent longer in her own rooms upstairs than she had before. Franciscus, who had remained quiet all the way through the feast, suffered from wind and began to cry almost constantly. He made a piercing sound that could be heard throughout the house – in the courtyard, in the studio, in the cellar. Given her nature, Catharina was surprisingly patient with the baby, but snapped at everyone else, even her husband.

I had managed to put Agnes from my mind while preparing for the feast, but memories of her returned even more strongly than before. Now that I had time to think, I thought too much. I was like a dog licking its wounds to clean them but making them worse.

Worst of all, he was angry with me. Since the night van Ruijven cornered me, perhaps even since Pieter the son smiled at me, he had become more distant. I seemed also to cross paths with him more often than before. Although he went out a great deal – in part to escape Franciscus' crying – I always seemed to be coming in the front door as he was leaving, or coming down the stairs as he was going up, or sweeping the Crucifixion room when he was looking for Maria Thins there. One day on an errand for Catharina I even met him in Market Square. Each time he nodded politely, then stepped aside to let me pass without looking at me.

I had offended him, but I did not know how.

The studio had become cold and flat as well. Before it had felt busy and full of purpose – it was where paintings were being made. Now, though I quickly swept away any dust that settled, it was simply an empty room, waiting for nothing but dust. I did not want it to be a sad place. I wanted to take refuge there, as I had before.

One morning Maria Thins came to open the door for me and found it already unlocked. We peered into the semidarkness. He was asleep at the table, his head on his arms, his back to the door. Maria Thins backed out. 'Must have come up here because of the baby's cries,' she muttered. I tried to look again but she was blocking the way. She shut the door softly. 'Leave him be. You can clean there later.'

The next morning in the studio I opened all the shutters and looked around the room for something I could do, something I could touch that would not offend him, something I could move that he would not notice. Everything was in its place – the table, the chairs, the desk covered with books and papers, the cupboard with the brushes and knife carefully arranged on top, the easel propped against the wall, the clean palettes next to it. The objects he had painted were packed away in the storeroom or back in use in the house.

One of the bells of the New Church began to toll the

hour. I went to the window to look out. By the time the bell had finished its sixth stroke I knew what I would do.

I got some water heated on the fire, some soap and clean rags and brought them back to the studio, where I began cleaning the windows. I had to stand on the table to reach the top panes.

I was washing the last window when I heard him enter the room. I turned to look at him over my left shoulder, my eyes wide. 'Sir,' I began nervously. I was not sure how to explain my impulse to clean.

'Stop.'

I froze, horrified that I had gone against his wishes.

'Don't move.'

He was staring at me as if a ghost had suddenly appeared in his studio.

'I'm sorry, sir,' I said, dropping the rag into the bucket of water. 'I should have asked you first. But you are not painting anything at the moment and —'

He looked puzzled, then shook his head. 'Oh, the windows. No, you may continue what you were doing.'

I would rather not have cleaned in front of him, but as he continued to stand there I had no choice. I swished the rag in the water, wrung it out and began wiping the panes again, inside and out.

I finished the window and stepped back to view the effect. The light that shone in was pure.

He was still standing behind me. 'Does that please you, sir?' I asked.

'Look over your shoulder at me again.'

I did as he commanded. He was studying me. He was interested in me again.

'The light,' I said. 'It's cleaner now.'

'Yes,' he said. 'Yes.'

The next morning the table had been moved back to the painting corner and covered with a red, yellow and blue table-rug. A chair was set against the back wall, and a map hung over it.

He had begun again.

1665

My father wanted me to describe the painting once
more.

'But nothing has changed since the last time,'
I said.

'I want to hear it again,' he insisted, hunching over in
his chair to get nearer to the fire. He sounded like Frans
when he was a little boy and had been told there was nothing
left to eat in the hotpot. My father was often impatient
during March, waiting for winter to end, the cold to ease,
the sun to reappear. March was an unpredictable month,
when it was never clear what might happen. Warm days
raised hopes until ice and grey skies shut over the town
again.

March was the month I was born.

Being blind seemed to make my father hate winter even
more. His other senses strengthened, he felt the cold acutely,
smelled the stale air in the house, tasted the blandness of
the vegetable stew more than my mother. He suffered when
the winter was long.

I felt sorry for him. When I could I smuggled to him treats
from Tanneke's kitchen — stewed cherries, dried apricots, a
cold sausage, once a handful of dried rose petals I had found
in Catharina's cupboard.

95

'The baker's daughter stands in a bright corner by a window,' I began patiently. 'She is facing us, but is looking out the window, down to her right. She is wearing a yellow and black fitted bodice of silk and velvet, a dark blue skirt, and a white cap that hangs down in two points below her chin.'

'As you wear yours?' my father asked. He had never asked this before, though I had described the cap the same way each time.

'Yes, like mine. When you look at the cap long enough,' I added hurriedly, 'you see that he has not really painted it white, but blue, and violet, and yellow.'

'But it's a white cap, you said.'

'Yes, that's what is so strange. It's painted many colours, but when you look at it, you think it's white.'

'Tile painting is much simpler,' my father grumbled. 'You use blue and that's all. A dark blue for the outlines, a light blue for the shadows. Blue is blue.'

And a tile is a tile, I thought, and nothing like his paintings. I wanted him to understand that white was not simply white. It was a lesson my master had taught me.

'What is she doing?' he asked after a moment.

'She has one hand on a pewter pitcher sitting on a table and one on a window she's partly opened. She's about to pick up the pitcher and dump the water from it out the window, but she's stopped in the middle of what she's doing and is either dreaming or looking at something in the street.'

'Which is she doing?'

'I don't know. Sometimes it seems one thing, sometimes the other.'

My father sat back in his seat, frowning. 'First you say

the cap is white but not painted white. Then you say the girl is doing one thing or maybe another. You're confusing me.' He rubbed his brow as if his head ached.

'I'm sorry, Father. I'm trying to describe it accurately.'

'But what is the story in the painting?'

'His paintings don't tell stories.'

He did not respond. He had been difficult all winter. If Agnes had been there she would have been able to cheer him. She had always known how to make him laugh.

'Mother, shall I light the footwarmers?' I asked, turning from my father to hide my irritation. Now that he was blind, he could easily sense the moods of others, when he wanted to. I did not like him being critical of the painting without having seen it, or comparing it to the tiles he had once painted. I wanted to tell him that if he could only see the painting he would understand that there was nothing confusing about it. It may not have told a story, but it was still a painting you could not stop looking at.

All the time my father and I talked, my mother had been busy around us, stirring the stew, feeding the fire, setting out plates and mugs, sharpening a knife to cut the bread. Without waiting for her to answer I gathered the footwarmers and took them to the back room where the peat was stored. As I filled them I chided myself for being angry with my father.

I brought the footwarmers back and lit them from the fire. When I had placed them under our seats at the table I led my father over to his chair while my mother spooned out the stew and poured the beer. My father took a bite and made a face. 'Didn't you bring anything from Papists' Corner to sweeten this mush?' he muttered.

'I couldn't. Tanneke has been difficult with me and I've stayed away from her kitchen.' I regretted it the moment the words left my mouth.

'Why? What did you do?' More and more my father was looking to find fault with me, at times even siding with Tanneke.

I thought quickly. 'I spilled some of their best ale. A whole jug.'

My mother looked at me reproachfully. She knew when I lied. If my father hadn't been feeling so miserable he might have noticed from my voice as well.

I was getting better at it, though.

When I left to go back my mother insisted on accompanying me part of the way, even though it was raining, a cold, hard rain. As we reached the Rietveld Canal and turned right towards Market Square, she said, 'You will be seventeen soon.'

'Next week,' I agreed.

'Not long now until you are a woman.'

'Not long.' I kept my eyes on the raindrops pebbling the canal. I did not like to think about the future.

'I have heard that the butcher's son is paying you attention.'

'Who told you that?'

In answer she simply brushed raindrops from her cap and shook out her shawl.

I shrugged. 'I'm sure he's paying me no more attention than he is other girls.'

I expected her to warn me, to tell me to be a good girl, to protect our family name. Instead she said, 'Don't be rude to him. Smile at him and be pleasant.'

Her words surprised me, but when I looked in her eyes and saw there the hunger for meat that a butcher's son could provide, I understood why she had set aside her pride.

At least she did not ask me about the lie I had told earlier. I could not tell them why Tanneke was angry at me. That lie hid a much greater lie. I would have too much to explain.

Tanneke had discovered what I was doing during the afternoons when I was meant to be sewing.

I was assisting him.

It had begun two months before, one afternoon in January not long after Franciscus was born. It was very cold. Franciscus and Johannes were both poorly, with chesty coughs and trouble breathing. Catharina and the nurse were tending them by the fire in the washing kitchen while the rest of us sat close to the fire in the cooking kitchen.

Only he was not there. He was upstairs. The cold did not seem to affect him.

Catharina came to stand in the doorway between the two kitchens. 'Someone must go to the apothecary,' she announced, her face flushed. 'I need some things for the boys.' She looked pointedly at me.

Usually I would be the last chosen for such an errand. Visiting the apothecary was not like going to the butcher's or fishmonger's – tasks Catharina continued to leave to me after the birth of Franciscus. The apothecary was a respected doctor, and Catharina or Maria Thins liked to go to him. I was not allowed such a luxury. When it was so cold, however, any errand was given to the least important member of the house.

For once Maertge and Lisbeth did not ask to come with me. I wrapped myself in a woollen mantle and shawls while Catharina told me I was to ask for dried elderflowers and a coltsfoot elixir. Cornelia hung about, watching me tuck in the loose ends of the shawls.

'May I come with you?' she asked, smiling at me with well-practised innocence. Sometimes I wondered if I judged her too harshly.

'No,' Catharina replied for me. 'It's far too cold. I won't have another of my children getting sick. Off you go, then,' she said to me. 'Quick as you can.'

I pulled the front door shut and stepped into the street. It was very quiet – people were sensibly huddled in their houses. The canal was frozen, the sky an angry grey. As the wind blew through me and I drew my nose further into the wool folds around my face, I heard my name being called. I looked around, thinking Cornelia had followed me. The front door was shut.

I looked up. He had opened a window and poked his head out.

'Sir?'

'Where are you going, Griet?'

'To the apothecary, sir. Mistress asked me. For the boys.'

'Will you get me something as well?'

'Of course, sir.' Suddenly the wind did not seem so bitter.

'Wait, I'll write it down.' He disappeared and I waited. After a moment he reappeared and tossed down a small leather pouch. 'Give the apothecary the paper inside and bring what he gives you back to me.'

I nodded and tucked the pouch into a fold of my shawl, pleased with this secret request.

The apothecary's was along the Koornmarkt, towards the Rotterdam Gate. Although it was not far, each breath I took seemed to freeze inside me so that by the time I pushed into the shop I was unable to speak.

I had never been to an apothecary, not even before I became a maid – my mother had made all of our remedies. His shop was a small room, with shelves lining the walls from floor to ceiling. They held all sizes of bottles, basins and earthenware jars, each one neatly labelled. I suspected that even if I could read the words I would not understand what each vessel held. Although the cold killed most smells, here there lingered an odour I did not recognise, like something in the forest, hidden under rotting leaves.

I had seen the apothecary himself only once, when he came to Franciscus' birth feast a few weeks before. A bald, slight man, he reminded me of a baby bird. He was surprised to see me. Few people ventured out in such cold. He sat behind a table, a set of scales at his elbow, and waited for me to speak.

'I've come for my master and mistress,' I gasped at last when my throat had warmed enough for me to speak. He looked blank and I added, 'The Vermeers.'

'Ah. How is the growing family?'

'The babies are ill. My mistress needs dried elderflowers and an elixir of coltsfoot. And my master –' I handed him the pouch. He took it with a puzzled expression, but when he read the slip of paper he nodded. 'Run out of bone black and ochre,' he murmured. 'That's easily repaired. He's never had anyone fetch the makings of colours for him before, though.' He squinted over the slip of paper at me. 'He always gets them himself. This is a surprise.'

I said nothing.

'Have a seat, then. Back here by the fire while I get your things together.' He became busy, opening jars and weighing small mounds of dried flower buds, measuring syrup into a bottle, wrapping things carefully in paper and string. He placed some things in the leather pouch. The other packages he left loose.

'Does he need any canvases?' he asked over his shoulder as he replaced a jar on a high shelf.

'I wouldn't know, sir. He asked me to get only what was on that paper.'

'This is very surprising, very surprising indeed.' He looked me up and down. I drew myself up – his attention made me wish I were taller. 'Well, it is cold, after all. He wouldn't go out unless he had to.' He handed me the packages and pouch and held the door open for me. Out in the street I looked back to see him still peering at me through a tiny window in the door.

Back at the house I went first to Catharina to give her the loose packages. Then I hurried to the stairs. He had come down and was waiting. I pulled the pouch from my shawl and handed it to him.

'Thank you, Griet,' he said.

'What are you doing?' Cornelia was watching us from further along the hallway.

To my surprise he didn't answer her. He simply turned and climbed the stairs again, leaving me alone to face her.

The truth was the easiest answer, though I often felt

uneasy telling Cornelia the truth. I was never sure what she would do with it. 'I've bought some paint things for your father,' I explained.

'Did he ask you to?'

To that question I responded as her father had – I walked away from her towards the kitchens, removing my shawls as I went. I was afraid to answer, for I did not want to cause him harm. I knew already that it was best if no one knew I had run an errand for him.

I wondered if Cornelia would tell her mother what she had seen. Although young she was also shrewd, like her grandmother. She might horde her information, carefully choosing when to reveal it.

She gave me her own answer a few days later.

It was a Sunday and I was in the cellar, looking in the chest where I kept my things for a collar to wear that my mother had embroidered for me. I saw immediately that my few belongings had been disturbed – collars not refolded, one of my chemises balled up and pushed into a corner, the tortoiseshell comb shaken from its handkerchief. The handkerchief around my father's tile was folded so neatly that I became suspicious. When I opened it the tile came apart in two pieces. It had been broken so that the girl and boy were separated from each other, the boy now looking behind him at nothing, the girl all alone, her face hidden by her cap.

I wept then. Cornelia could not have guessed how that would hurt me. I would have been less upset if she had broken our heads from our bodies.

*　　*　　*

He began to ask me to do other things. One day he asked me to buy linseed oil at the apothecary's on my way back from the fish stalls. I was to leave it at the bottom of the stairs for him so that he and the model would not be disturbed. So he said. Perhaps he was aware that Maria Thins or Catharina or Tanneke – or Cornelia – might notice if I went up to the studio at an unusual time.

It was not a house where secrets could be kept easily.

Another day he had me ask the butcher for a pig's bladder. I did not understand why he wanted one until he later asked me to lay out the paints he needed each morning when I had finished cleaning. He opened the drawers to the cupboard near his easel and showed me which paints were kept where, naming the colours as he went. I had not heard of many of the words – ultramarine, vermilion, massicot. The brown and yellow earth colours and the bone black and lead white were stored in little earthenware pots, covered with parchment to keep them from drying out. The more valuable colours – the blues and reds and yellows – were kept in small amounts in pigs' bladders. A hole was punched in them so the paint could be squeezed out, with a nail plugging it shut.

One morning while I was cleaning he came in and asked me to stand in for the baker's daughter, who had taken ill and could not come. 'I want to look for a moment,' he explained. 'Someone must stand there.'

I obediently took her place, one hand on the handle of the water pitcher, the other on the window frame, opened slightly so that a chilly draught brushed my face and chest.

Perhaps this is why the baker's daughter is ill, I thought.

He had opened all of the shutters. I had never seen the room so bright.

'Tilt your chin down,' he said. 'And look down, not at me. Yes, that's it. Don't move.'

He was sitting by the easel. He did not pick up his palette or his knife or his brushes. He simply sat, hands in his lap, and looked.

My face turned red. I had not realised that he would stare at me so intently.

I tried to think of something else. I looked out the window and watched a boat moving along the canal. The man poling it was the man who had helped me get the pot from the canal my first day. How much has changed since that morning, I thought. I had not even seen one of his paintings then. Now I am standing in one.

'Don't look at what you are looking at,' he said. 'I can see it in your face. It is distracting you.'

I tried not to look at anything, but to think of other things. I thought of a day when our family went out into the countryside to pick herbs. I thought of a hanging I had seen in Market Square the year before, of a woman who had killed her daughter in a drunken rage. I thought of the look on Agnes' face the last time I had seen her.

'You are thinking too much,' he said, shifting in his seat.

I felt as if I had washed a tub full of sheets but not got them clean. 'I'm sorry, sir. I don't know what to do.'

'Try closing your eyes.'

I closed them. After a moment I felt the window frame and the pitcher in my hands, anchoring me. Then I could sense the wall behind me, and the table to my left, and the cold air from the window.

This must be how my father feels, I thought, with the space all around him, and his body knowing where it is.

'Good,' he said. 'That is good. Thank you, Griet. You may continue cleaning.'

I had never seen a painting made from the beginning. I thought that you painted what you saw, using the colours you saw.

He taught me.

He began the painting of the baker's daughter with a layer of pale grey on the white canvas. Then he made reddish-brown marks all over it to indicate where the girl and the table and pitcher and window and map would go. After that I thought he would begin to paint what he saw — a girl's face, a blue skirt, a yellow and black bodice, a brown map, a silver pitcher and basin, a white wall. Instead he painted patches of colour — black where her skirt would be, ochre for the bodice and the map on the wall, red for the pitcher and the basin it sat in, another grey for the wall. They were the wrong colours — none was the colour of the thing itself. He spent a long time on these false colours, as I called them.

Sometimes the girl came and spent hour after hour standing in place, yet when I looked at the painting the next day nothing had been added or taken away. There were just areas of colour that did not make things, no matter how long I studied them. I only knew what they were meant to be because I cleaned the objects themselves, and had seen what the girl was wearing when I peeked at her one day as she changed into Catharina's yellow and black bodice in the great hall.

I reluctantly set out the colours he asked for each morning. One day I put out a blue as well. The second time I laid it out he said to me, 'No ultramarine, Griet. Only the colours I asked for. Why did you set it out when I did not ask for it?' He was annoyed.

'I'm sorry, sir. It's just —' I took a deep breath — 'she is wearing a blue skirt. I thought you would want it, rather than leaving it black.'

'When I am ready, I will ask.'

I nodded and turned back to polishing the lion-head chair. My chest hurt. I did not want him to be angry at me.

He opened the middle window, filling the room with cold air.

'Come here, Griet.'

I set my rag on the sill and went to him.

'Look out the window.'

I looked out. It was a breezy day, with clouds disappearing behind the New Church tower.

'What colour are those clouds?'

'Why, white, sir.'

He raised his eyebrows slightly. 'Are they?'

I glanced at them. 'And grey. Perhaps it will snow.'

'Come, Griet, you can do better than that. Think of your vegetables.'

'My vegetables, sir?'

He moved his head slightly. I was annoying him again. My jaw tightened.

'Think of how you separated the whites. Your turnips and your onions — are they the same white?'

Suddenly I understood. 'No. The turnip has green in it, the onion yellow.'

'Exactly. Now, what colours do you see in the clouds?'

'There is some blue in them,' I said after studying them

107

for a few minutes. 'And — yellow as well. And there is some green!' I became so excited I actually pointed. I had been looking at clouds all my life, but I felt as if I saw them for the first time at that moment.

He smiled. 'You will find there is little pure white in clouds, yet people say they are white. Now do you understand why I do not need the blue yet?'

'Yes, sir.' I did not really understand, but did not want to admit it. I felt I almost knew.

When at last he began to add colours on top of the false colours, I saw what he meant. He painted a light blue over the girl's skirt, and it became a blue through which bits of black could be seen, darker in the shadow of the table, lighter closer to the window. To the wall areas he added yellow ochre, through which some of the grey showed. It became a bright but not a white wall. When the light shone on the wall, I discovered, it was not white, but many colours.

The pitcher and basin were the most complicated — they became yellow, and brown, and green, and blue. They reflected the pattern of the rug, the girl's bodice, the blue cloth draped over the chair — everything but their true silver colour. And yet they looked as they should, like a pitcher and a basin.

After that I could not stop looking at things.

It became harder to hide what I was doing when he wanted me to help him make the paints. One morning he took me up to the attic, reached by a ladder in the storeroom next to the studio. I had never been there before. It was a small room, with a steeply slanted roof and a window that let in light and a view of the New Church. There was little there apart from a small cupboard and a stone table with a hollow place in it, holding a stone shaped like an egg with one end cut off. I had seen a similar table once at my father's tile factory. There were also some vessels — basins and shallow earthenware plates — as well as tongs by the tiny fireplace.

'I would like you to grind some things here for me, Griet,' he said. He opened a cupboard drawer and took out a black stick the length of my little finger. 'This is a piece of ivory, charred in the fire,' he explained. 'For making black paint.'

Dropping it in the bowl of the table, he added a gummy substance that smelled of animal. Then he picked up the stone, which he called a muller, and showed me how to hold it, and how to lean over the table and use my weight against the stone to crush the bone. After a few minutes he had ground it into a fine paste.

'Now you try.' He scooped the black paste into a small pot and got out another piece of ivory. I took up the muller and tried to imitate his stance as I leaned over the table.

'No, your hand needs to do this.' He placed his hand over mine. The shock of his touch made me drop the muller, which rolled off the table and fell on the floor.

I jumped away from him and bent down to pick it up. 'I'm sorry, sir,' I muttered, placing the muller in the bowl.

He did not try to touch me again.

'Move your hand up a little,' he commanded instead. 'That's right. Now use your shoulder to turn, your wrist to finish.'

It took me much longer to grind my piece, for I was clumsy and flustered from his touch. And I was smaller than him, and unused to the movement I was meant to make. At least my arms were strong from wringing out laundry.

'A little finer,' he suggested when he inspected the bowl. I ground for a few more minutes before he decided it was ready, having me rub the paste between my fingers so I would know how fine he wanted it. Then he laid several more pieces of bone on the table. 'Tomorrow I will show you how to grind white lead. It is much easier than bone.'

I stared at the ivory.

'What is it, Griet? You're not frightened of a few bones, are you? They are no different from the ivory comb you use to tidy your hair.'

I would never be rich enough to own such a comb. I tidied my hair with my fingers.

'It's not that, sir.' All the other things he had asked of me I was able to do while cleaning or running errands. No one but Cornelia had become suspicious. But grinding things would take time — I could not do it while I was meant to be cleaning the studio, and I could not explain to others why I must go to the attic at times, leaving my other tasks. 'This will take some time to grind,' I said feebly.

'Once you are used to it, it will not take as long as today.'

I hated to question or disobey him — he was my master. But I feared the anger of the women downstairs. 'I'm meant to go to the butcher's now, and to do the ironing, sir. For the mistress.' My words sounded petty.

He did not move. 'To the butcher's?' He was frowning.

'Yes, sir. The mistress will want to know why I cannot do my other work. She will want to know that I am helping you, up here. It's not easy for me to come up for no reason.'

There was a long silence. The bell in the New Church tower struck seven times.

'I see,' he murmured when it had stopped. 'Let me consider this.' He removed some of the ivory, putting it back in a drawer. 'Do this bit now.' He gestured at what was left. 'It shouldn't take long. I must go out. Leave it here when you are done.'

He would have to speak to Catharina and tell her about my work. Then it would be easier for me to do things for him.

I waited, but he said nothing to Catharina.

The solution to the problem of the colours came unexpectedly from Tanneke. Since Franciscus' birth the nurse had been sleeping in the Crucifixion room with Tanneke. From there she could get easily to the great hall to feed the baby when he woke. Although Catharina was not feeding him herself, she insisted that Franciscus sleep in a cradle next to her. I thought this a strange arrangement, but when I came to know Catharina better I understood that she wanted to hold on to the appearance of motherhood, if not the tasks themselves.

Tanneke was not happy sharing her room with the nurse, complaining that the nurse got up too often to tend to the baby, and when she did remain in bed she snored. She spoke of it to everyone, whether they listened or not. Tanneke began to slacken her work, and blamed it on not getting enough sleep. Maria Thins told her there was nothing they could do, but Tanneke continued to grumble. She often threw black looks at me – before I came to live in the house

Tanneke had slept where I did in the cellar whenever a nurse was needed. It was almost as if she blamed me for the nurse's snores.

One evening she even appealed to Catharina. Catharina was preparing herself for an evening at the van Ruijvens', despite the cold. She was in a good mood — wearing her pearls and yellow mantle always made her happy. Over her mantle she had tied a wide linen collar that covered her shoulders and protected the cloth from the powder she was dusting on her face. As Tanneke listed her woes, Catharina continued to powder herself, holding up a mirror to inspect the results. Her hair had been dressed in braids and ribbons, and as long as she kept her happy expression she was very beautiful, the combination of her blonde hair and light brown eyes making her look exotic.

At last she waved the powderbrush at Tanneke. 'Stop!' she cried with a laugh. 'We need the nurse and she must sleep near me. There's no space in the girls' room, but there is in yours, so she is there. There's nothing to be done. Why do you bother me about it?'

'Perhaps there is one thing that may be done,' he said. I glanced up from the cupboard where I was searching for an apron for Lisbeth. He was standing in the doorway. Catharina gazed up at her husband in surprise. He rarely showed interest in domestic affairs. 'Put a bed up in the attic and let someone sleep there. Griet, perhaps.'

'Griet in the attic? Why?' Catharina cried.

'Then Tanneke may sleep in the cellar, as she prefers,' he explained mildly.

'But —' Catharina stopped, confused. She seemed to disapprove of the idea but could not say why.

'Oh yes, madam,' Tanneke broke in eagerly. 'That would certainly help.' She glanced at me.

I busied myself refolding the children's clothes, though they were already tidy.

'What about the key to the studio?' Catharina finally found an argument. There was only one entrance to the attic, by the ladder in the studio's storeroom. To get to my bed I would have to pass through the studio, which was kept locked at night. 'We can't give a maid the key.'

'She won't need a key,' he countered. 'You may lock the studio door once she has gone to bed. Then in the morning she may clean the studio before you come and unlock the door.'

I paused with my folding. I did not like the idea of being locked into my room at night.

Unfortunately this notion seemed to please Catharina. Perhaps she thought locking me away would keep me both safely in one place and out of her sight. 'All right, then,' she decided. She made most decisions quickly. She turned to Tanneke and me. 'Tomorrow you two move a bed to the attic. This is only temporary,' she added, 'until the nurse is no longer needed.'

Temporary as my trips to the butcher and fishmonger were meant to be temporary, I thought.

'Come with me to the studio for a moment,' he said. He was looking at her in a way I had begun to recognise — a painter's way.

'Me?' Catharina smiled at her husband. Invitations to his studio were rare. She set down her powderbrush with a flourish and began to remove the wide collar, now covered with dust.

He reached out and grasped her hand. 'Leave that.'

This was almost as surprising as his suggestion to move me to the attic. As he led Catharina upstairs, Tanneke and I exchanged looks.

The next day the baker's daughter began to wear the wide white collar while modelling for the painting.

Maria Thins was not so easily fooled. When she heard from a gleeful Tanneke about her move to the cellar and mine to the attic she puffed on her pipe and frowned. 'You two could just switch —' she pointed at us with the pipe — 'so that Griet sleeps with the nurse and you go in the cellar. Then there is no need for anyone to move to the attic.'

Tanneke was not listening — she was too full of her victory to notice the logic in her mistress' words.

'Mistress has agreed to it,' I said simply.

Maria Thins gave me a long sideways look.

Sleeping in the attic made it easier for me to work there, but I still had little time to do so. I could get up earlier and go to bed later, but sometimes he gave me so much work that I had to find a way to go up in the afternoons, when I normally sat by the fire and sewed. I began to complain of not being able to see my stitching in the dim kitchen, and needing the light of my bright attic room. Or I said my stomach hurt and I wanted to lie down. Maria Thins gave me that same sideways look each time I made an excuse, but did not comment.

I began to get used to lying.

Once he had suggested that I sleep in the attic he left it to me to arrange my duties so that I could work for him.

He never helped by lying for me, or asking me if I had time to spare for him. He gave me instructions in the morning and expected them to be done by the next day.

The colours themselves made up for the troubles I had hiding what I was doing. I came to love grinding the things he brought from the apothecary — bones, white lead, madder, massicot — to see how bright and pure I could get the colours. I learned that the finer the materials were ground, the deeper the colour. From rough, dull grains madder became a fine bright red powder and, mixed with linseed oil, a sparkling paint. Making it and the other colours was magical.

From him I learned too how to wash substances to rid them of impurities and bring out the true colours. I used a series of shells as shallow bowls, and rinsed and rerinsed colours, sometimes thirty times, to get out the chalk or sand or gravel. It was long and tedious work, but very satisfying to see the colour grow cleaner with each wash, and closer to what was needed.

The only colour he did not allow me to handle was ultramarine. Lapis lazuli was so expensive, and the process of extracting a pure blue from the stone so difficult, that he worked with it himself.

I grew used to being around him. Sometimes we stood side by side in the small room, me grinding white lead, him washing lapis or burning ochres in the fire. He said little to me. He was a quiet man. I did not speak either. It was peaceful then, with the light coming in through the window. When we were done we poured water from a pitcher over each other's hands and scrubbed ourselves clean.

It was very cold in the attic — although there was the

little fire he used for heating linseed oil or burning colours, I did not dare light it unless he wanted me to. Otherwise I would have to explain to Catharina and Maria Thins why peat and wood were disappearing so fast.

I did not mind the cold so much when he was there. When he stood close to me I could feel the warmth of his body.

I was washing a bit of massicot I had just ground one afternoon when I heard Maria Thins' voice in the studio below. He was working on the painting, the baker's daughter sighing occasionally as she stood.

'Are you cold, girl?' Maria Thins asked.

'A little,' came the faint reply.

'Why doesn't she have a footwarmer?'

His voice was so low that I didn't hear his answer.

'It won't show in the painting, not by her feet. We don't want her getting sick again.'

Again I could not hear what he said.

'Griet can get one for her,' Maria Thins suggested. 'She should be in the attic for she's meant to have a stomach ache. I'll just find her.'

She was quicker than I had thought an old woman could be. By the time I put my foot on the top rung she was halfway up the ladder. I stepped back into the attic. I could not escape her, and there was no time to hide anything.

When Maria Thins climbed into the room, she quickly took in the shells laid in rows on the table, the jug of water, the apron I wore speckled with yellow from the massicot.

'So this is what you've been up to, eh, girl? I thought as much.'

I lowered my eyes. I did not know what to say.

'Stomach ache, sore eyes. We are not all idiots around here, you know.'

Ask him, I longed to tell her. He is my master. This is his doing.

But she did not call to him. Nor did he appear at the bottom of the ladder to explain.

There was a long silence. Then Maria Thins said, 'How long have you been assisting him, girl?'

'A few weeks, madam.'

'He's been painting faster these last weeks, I've noticed.'

I raised my eyes. Her face was calculating.

'You help him to paint faster, girl,' she said in a low voice, 'and you'll keep your place here. Not a word to my daughter or Tanneke, now.'

'Yes, madam.'

She chuckled. 'I might have known, clever one that you are. You almost fooled even me. Now, get that poor girl down there a footwarmer.'

I liked sleeping in the attic. There was no Crucifixion scene hanging at the foot of the bed to trouble me. There were no paintings at all, but the clean scent of linseed oil and the musk of the earth pigments. I liked my view of the New Church, and the quiet. No one came up except him. The girls did not visit me as they sometimes had in the cellar, or secretly search through my things. I felt alone there, perched high above the noisy household, able to see it from a distance.

Rather like him.

The best part, however, was that I could spend more time

in the studio. Sometimes I wrapped myself in a blanket and crept down late at night when the house was still. I looked at the painting he was working on by candlelight, or opened a shutter a little to let in moonlight. Sometimes I sat in the dark in one of the lion-head chairs pulled up to the table and rested my elbow on the blue and red table-rug that covered it. I imagined wearing the yellow and black bodice and pearls, holding a glass of wine, sitting across the table from him.

There was one thing I did not like about the attic, however. I did not like being locked in at night.

Catharina had got the studio key back from Maria Thins and began to lock and unlock the door. She must have felt it gave her some control over me. She was not happy about my being in the attic – it meant I was closer to him, to the place she was not allowed in but where I could wander freely.

It must have been hard for a wife to accept such an arrangement.

It worked for a time, however. For a time I was able to slip away in the afternoons and wash and grind colours for him. Catharina often slept then – Franciscus had not settled, and woke her most nights so that she needed sleep during the day. Tanneke usually fell asleep by the fire as well, and I could leave the kitchen without always having to make up an excuse. The girls were busy with Johannes, teaching him to walk and talk, and rarely noticed my absence. If they did Maria Thins said I was running an errand for her, fetching things from her rooms, or sewing something for her that needed bright attic light to work by. They were children, after all, absorbed in their own world, indifferent to the adult lives around them except when it directly affected them.

Or so I thought.

One afternoon I was washing white lead when Cornelia called my name from downstairs. I quickly wiped my hands, removed the apron I wore for attic work and changed into my daily apron before climbing down the ladder to her. She stood on the threshold of the studio, looking as if she were standing at the edge of a puddle and tempted to step in it.

'What is it?' I spoke rather sharply.

'Tanneke wants you.' Cornelia turned and led the way to the stairs. She hesitated at the top. 'Will you help me, Griet?' she asked plaintively. 'Go first so that if I fall you will catch me. The stairs are so steep.'

It was unlike her to be scared, even on stairs she did not use much. I was touched, or perhaps I was simply feeling guilty for being sharp with her. I descended the stairs, then turned and held out my arms. 'Now you.'

Cornelia was standing at the top, hands in her pockets. She started down the stairs, one hand on the banister, the other balled into a tight fist. When she was most of the way down she let go and jumped so that she fell against me, sliding down my front, pressing painfully into my stomach. Once she regained her feet she began to laugh, head thrown up, brown eyes narrowed to slits.

'Naughty girl,' I muttered, regretting my softness.

I found Tanneke in the cooking kitchen, Johannes in her lap.

'Cornelia said you wanted me.'

'Yes, she's torn one of her collars and wants you to

mend it. Wouldn't let me touch it — I don't know why, she knows I mend collars best.' As Tanneke handed it to me her eyes strayed to my apron. 'What's that there? Are you bleeding?'

I looked down. A slash of red dust crossed my stomach like a streak on a window pane. For a moment I thought of the aprons of Pieter the father and son.

Tanneke leaned closer. 'That's not blood. It looks like powder. How did that get there?'

I gazed at the streak. Madder, I thought. I ground this a few weeks ago.

Only I heard the stifled giggle from the hallway.

Cornelia had been waiting some time for this mischief. She had even managed somehow to get up to the attic to steal the powder.

I did not make up an answer fast enough. As I hesitated, Tanneke's suspicion grew. 'Have you been in the master's things?' she said in an accusing tone. She had, after all, modelled for him and knew what he kept in the studio.

'No, it was —' I stopped. If I tattled on Cornelia I would sound petty and it would probably not stop Tanneke from discovering what I did in the attic.

'I think young mistress had better see this,' she decided.

'No,' I said quickly.

Tanneke drew herself up as much as she could with a sleeping child in her lap. 'Take off your apron,' she commanded, 'so I can show it to the young mistress.'

'Tanneke,' I said, gazing levelly at her, 'if you know what's best for you, you'll not disturb Catharina, you'll speak to Maria Thins. Alone, not in front of the girls.'

It was those words, with their bullying tone, that caused

the most damage between Tanneke and me. I did not think to sound like that — I was simply desperate to stop her from telling Catharina any way I could. But she would never forgive me for treating her as if she were below me.

My words at least had their effect. Tanneke gave me a hard, angry look, but behind it was uncertainty, and the desire indeed to tell her own beloved mistress. She hung between that desire and the wish to punish my impudence by disobeying me.

'Speak to your mistress,' I said softly. 'But speak to her alone.'

Though my back was to the door, I sensed Cornelia slipping away from it.

Tanneke's own instincts won. With a stony face she handed Johannes to me and went to find Maria Thins. Before I settled him on my lap I carefully wiped away the red pigment with a rag, then threw it in the fire. It still left a stain. I sat with my arms around the little boy and waited for my fate to be decided.

I never found out what Maria Thins said to Tanneke, what threats or promises she made to keep her quiet. But it worked — Tanneke said nothing about my attic work to Catharina or the girls, or to me. She became much harder with me, though — deliberately difficult rather than unthinkingly so. She sent me back to the fish stalls with the cod I knew she had asked for, swearing she had told me to buy plaice. When she cooked she became sloppier, spilling as much grease as she could on her apron so that I would have to soak the cloth longer and scrub harder to get the grease out. She left buckets for me to empty, and stopped bringing water to fill the kitchen cistern or mopping the floors. She sat and watched me balefully, refusing to move her feet so that I had to mop around them, to find afterwards that one foot had covered a sticky puddle of grease.

She did not talk kindly to me any longer. She made me feel alone in a house full of people.

So I did not dare to take nice things from her kitchen to cheer my father with. And I did not tell my parents how hard things were for me at the Oude Langendijck, how careful I had to be to keep my place. Nor could I tell them about the few good things — the colours I made, the nights when I sat alone in the studio, the moments when he and I worked side by side and I was warmed by his presence.

All I could tell them about were his paintings.

One April morning when the cold at last had gone, I was walking along the Koornmarkt to the apothecary when Pieter the son appeared at my side and wished me good day. I had not seen him earlier. He wore a clean apron and carried a bundle, which he said he was delivering further along the Koornmarkt. He was going the same way as me and asked if he could walk with me. I nodded — I did not feel I could say no. Through the winter I had seen him once or twice a week at the Meat Hall. I always found it hard to meet his gaze — his eyes felt like needles pricking my skin. His attention worried me.

'You look tired,' he said now. 'Your eyes are red. They are working you too hard.'

Indeed, they were working me hard. My master had given me so much bone to grind that I had to get up very early

122

to finish it. And the night before Tanneke had made me stay up late to rewash the kitchen floor after she spilled a pan of grease all over it.

I did not want to blame my master. 'Tanneke has taken against me,' I said instead, 'and gives me more to do. Then, of course, it's getting warmer as well and we are cleaning the winter out of the house.' I added this so that he would not think I was complaining about her.

'Tanneke is an odd one,' he said, 'but loyal.'

'To Maria Thins, yes.'

'To the family as well. Remember how she defended Catharina from her mad brother?'

I shook my head. 'I don't know what you mean.'

Pieter looked surprised. 'It was the talk of the Meat Hall for days. Ah, but you don't gossip, do you? You keep your eyes open but you don't tell tales, or listen to them.' He seemed to approve. 'Me, I hear it all day from the old ones waiting for meat. Can't help but some of it sticks.'

'What did Tanneke do?' I asked despite myself.

Pieter smiled. 'When your mistress was carrying the last child but one — what's its name?'

'Johannes. Like his father.'

Pieter's smile dimmed like a cloud crossing the sun. 'Yes, like his father.' He took up the tale again. 'One day Catharina's brother, Willem, came around to the Oude Langendijck, when she was big with child, and began to beat her, right in the street.'

'Why?'

'He's missing a brick or two, they say. He's always been violent. His father as well. You know the father and Maria Thins separated many years ago? He used to beat her.'

123

'Beat Maria Thins?' I repeated in wonder. I would never have guessed that anyone could beat Maria Thins.

'So when Willem began hitting Catharina it seems Tanneke got in between them to protect her. Even thumped him soundly.'

Where was my master when this happened? I thought. He could not have remained in his studio. He could not have. He must have been out at the Guild, or with van Leeuwenhoek, or at Mechelen, his mother's inn.

'Maria Thins and Catharina managed to have Willem confined last year,' Pieter continued. 'Can't leave the house he's lodged in. That's why you haven't seen him. Have you really heard nothing of this? Don't they talk in your house?'

'Not to me.' I thought of all the times Catharina and her mother put their heads together in the Crucifixion room, falling silent when I entered. 'And I don't listen behind doorways.'

'Of course you don't.' Pieter was smiling again as if I had told a joke. Like everyone else, he thought all maids eavesdropped. There were many assumptions about maids that people made about me.

I was silent the rest of the way. I had not known that Tanneke could be so loyal and brave, despite all she said behind Catharina's back, or that Catharina had suffered such blows, or that Maria Thins could have such a son. I tried to imagine my own brother beating me in the street but could not.

Pieter said no more – he could see my confusion. When he left me in front of the apothecary he simply touched my elbow and continued on his way. I had to stand for a moment looking into the dark green water of the canal before I shook my head to clear it and turned to the apothecary's door.

I was shaking from my thoughts a picture of the knife spinning on my mother's kitchen floor.

One Sunday Pieter the son came to services at our church. He must have slipped in after my parents and me, and sat in the back, for I did not see him until afterwards when we were outside speaking to our neighbours. He was standing off to one side, watching me. When I caught sight of him I drew in my breath sharply. At least, I thought, he is Protestant. I had not been certain before. Since working in the house at Papists' Corner I was no longer certain of many things.

My mother followed my gaze. 'Who is that?'

'The butcher's son.'

She gave me a curious look, part surprise, part fear. 'Go to him,' she whispered, 'and bring him to us.'

I obeyed her and went up to Pieter. 'Why are you here?' I asked, knowing I should be more polite.

He smiled. 'Hello, Griet. No pleasant words for me?'

'Why are you here?'

'I'm going to services in every church in Delft, to see which I like best. It may take some time.' When he saw my face he dropped his tone — joking was not the way with me. 'I came to see you, and to meet your parents.'

I blushed so hot I felt feverish. 'I would rather you did not,' I said softly.

'Why not?'

125

'I'm only seventeen. I don't — I'm not thinking of such things yet.'

'There's no rush,' Pieter said.

I looked down at his hands — they were clean, but there were still traces of blood around his nails. I thought of my master's hand over mine as he showed me how to grind bone, and shivered.

People were staring at us, for he was a stranger to the church. And he was a handsome man — even I could see that, with his long blond curls, bright eyes and ready smile. Several young women were trying to catch his eye.

'Will you introduce me to your parents?'

Reluctantly I led him to them. Pieter nodded to my mother and grasped my father's hand, who stepped back nervously. Since he had lost his eyes he was shy of meeting strangers. And he had never before met a man who showed interest in me.

'Don't worry, Father,' I whispered to him while my mother was introducing Pieter to a neighbour, 'you aren't losing me.'

'We've already lost you, Griet. We lost you the moment you became a maid.'

I was glad he could not see the tears that pricked my eyes.

Pieter the son did not come every week to our church, but he came often enough that each Sunday I grew nervous, smoothing my skirt more than it needed, pressing my lips together as we sat in our pew.

'Has he come? Is he here?' my father would ask each Sunday, turning his head this way and that.

I let my mother answer. 'Yes,' she would say, 'he is here,' or 'No, he has not come.'

Pieter always said hello to my parents before greeting me. At first they were uneasy with him. However, Pieter chatted easily to them, ignoring their awkward responses and long silences. He knew how to talk to people, meeting so many at his father's stall. After several Sundays my parents became used to him. The first time my father laughed at something Pieter said he was so surprised at himself that he immediately frowned, until Pieter said something else to make him laugh again.

There was always a moment after they had been speaking when my parents stepped back and left us alone. Pieter wisely let them decide when. The first few times it did not happen at all. Then one Sunday my mother pointedly took my father's arm and said, 'Let us go and speak to the minister.'

For several Sundays I dreaded that moment until I too became used to being on my own with him in front of so many watchful eyes. Pieter sometimes teased me gently, but more often he asked me what I had been doing during the week, or told me stories he had heard in the Meat Hall, or described auctions at the Beast Market. He was patient with me when I became tongue-tied or sharp or dismissive.

He never asked me about my master. I never told him I was working with the colours. I was glad he did not ask me.

On those Sundays I felt very confused. When I should be listening to Pieter I found myself thinking about my master.

One Sunday in May, when I had been working at the house on the Oude Langendijck for almost a year, my mother said to Pieter just before she and my father left us alone, 'Will you come back to eat with us after next Sunday's service?'

Pieter smiled as I gaped at her. 'I'll come.'

I barely heard what he said after that. When he finally left and my parents and I went home I had to bite my lips so that I would not shout. 'Why didn't you tell me you were going to invite Pieter?' I muttered.

My mother glanced at me sideways. 'It's time we asked him,' was all she said.

She was right — it would be rude of us not to invite him to our house. I had not played this game with a man before, but I had seen what went on with others. If Pieter was serious, then my parents would have to treat him seriously.

I also knew what a hardship it would be to them to have him come. My parents had very little now. Despite my wages and what my mother made from spinning wool for others, they could barely feed themselves, much less another mouth — and a butcher's mouth at that. I could do little to help them — take what I could from Tanneke's kitchen, a bit of wood, perhaps, some onions, some bread. They would eat less that week and light the fire less, just so that they could feed him properly.

But they insisted that he come. They would not say so to me, but they must have seen feeding him as a way of filling our own stomachs in the future. A butcher's wife — and her parents — would always eat well. A little hunger now would bring a heavy stomach eventually.

Later, when he began coming regularly, Pieter sent them gifts of meat which my mother would cook for the Sunday. At that first Sunday dinner, however, she sensibly did not serve meat to a butcher's son. He would have been able to judge exactly how poor they were by the cut of the joint. Instead she made a fish stew, even adding shrimps and lobster, never telling me how she managed to pay for them.

The house, though shabby, gleamed from her attentions. She had got out some of my father's best tiles, those she had not had to sell, and polished and lined them up along the wall so Pieter could look at them as he ate. He praised my mother's stew, and his words were genuine. She was pleased, and blushed and smiled and gave him more. Afterwards he asked my father about the tiles, describing each one until my father recognised it and could complete the description.

'Griet has the best one,' he said after they had gone through all those in the room. 'It's of her and her brother.'

'I'd like to see it,' Pieter murmured.

I studied my chapped hands in my lap and swallowed. I had not told them what Cornelia had done to my tile.

As Pieter was leaving my mother whispered to me to see him to the end of the street. I walked beside him, sure that our neighbours were staring, though in truth it was a rainy day and there were few people out. I felt as if my parents had pushed me into the street, that a deal had been made and I was being passed into the hands of a man. At least he is a good man, I thought, even if his hands are not as clean as they could be.

Close to the Rietveld Canal there was an alley that Pieter guided me to, his hand at the small of my back. Agnes used to hide there during our games as children. I stood against the wall and let Pieter kiss me. He was so eager that he bit my lips. I did not cry out — I licked away the salty blood

129

and looked over his shoulder at the wet brick wall opposite as he pushed himself against me. A raindrop fell into my eye.

I would not let him do all he wanted. After a time Pieter stepped back. He reached a hand towards my head. I moved away.

'You favour your caps, don't you?' he said.

'I'm not rich enough to dress my hair and go without a cap,' I snapped. 'Nor am I a —' I did not finish. I did not need to tell him what other kind of woman left her head bare.

'But your cap covers all your hair. Why is that? Most women show some of their hair.'

I did not answer.

'What colour is your hair?'

'Brown.'

'Light or dark?'

'Dark.'

Pieter smiled as if he were indulging a child in a game. 'Straight or curly?'

'Neither. Both.' I winced at my confusion.

'Long or short?'

I hesitated. 'Below my shoulders.'

He continued to smile at me, then kissed me once more and turned back towards Market Square.

I had hesitated because I did not want to lie but did not want him to know. My hair was long and could not be tamed. When it was uncovered it seemed to belong to another Griet — a Griet who would stand in an alley alone with a man, who was not so calm and quiet and clean. A Griet like the women who dared to bare their heads. That was why I kept my hair completely hidden — so that there would be no trace of that Griet.

He finished the painting of the baker's daughter. This time I had warning, for he stopped asking me to grind and wash colours. He did not use much paint now, nor did he make sudden changes at the end as he had with the woman with the pearl necklace. He had made changes earlier, removing one of the chairs from the painting, and moving the map along the wall. I was less surprised by such changes, for I'd had the chance to think of them myself, and knew that what he did made the painting better.

He borrowed van Leeuwenhoek's camera obscura again to look at the scene one last time. When he had set it up he allowed me to look through it as well. Although I still did not understand how it worked, I came to admire the scenes the camera painted inside itself, the miniature, reversed pictures of things in the room. The colours of ordinary objects became more intense — the table-rug a deeper red, the wall map a glowing brown like a glass of ale held up to the sun. I was not sure how the camera helped him to paint, but I was becoming more like Maria Thins — if it made him paint better, I did not question it.

He was not painting faster, however. He spent five months on the girl with the water pitcher. I often worried that Maria Thins would remind me that I had not helped him to work faster, and tell me to pack my things and leave.

She did not. She knew that he had been very busy at the Guild that winter, as well as at Mechelen. Perhaps she had decided to wait and see if things would change in the summer.

Or perhaps she found it hard to chide him since she liked the painting so much.

'It's a shame such a fine painting is to go only to the baker,' she said one day. 'We could have charged more if it were for van Ruijven.' It was clear that while he painted the works, it was she who struck the deals.

The baker liked the painting too. The day he came to see it was very different from the formal visit van Ruijven and his wife had made several months before to view their painting. The baker brought his whole family, including several children and a sister or two. He was a merry man, with a face permanently flushed from the heat of his ovens and hair that looked as if it had been dipped in flour. He refused the wine Maria Thins offered, preferring a mug of beer. He loved children, and insisted that the four girls and Johannes be allowed into the studio. They loved him as well – each time he visited he brought them another shell for their collection. This time it was a conch as big as my hand, rough and spiky and white with pale yellow marks on the outside, a polished pink and orange on the inside. The girls were delighted, and ran to get their other shells. They brought them upstairs and they and the baker's children played together in the storeroom while Tanneke and I served the guests in the studio.

The baker announced he was satisfied with the painting. 'My daughter looks well, and that's enough for me,' he said.

Afterwards, Maria Thins lamented that he had not looked at it as closely as van Ruijven would have, that his senses were dulled by the beer he drank and the disorder he surrounded himself with. I did not agree, though I did not say so. It seemed to me that the baker had an honest response to the painting. Van Ruijven tried too hard when he looked at paintings, with his honeyed words and studied expressions. He was too aware of having an audience to perform for, whereas the baker merely said what he thought.

I checked on the children in the storeroom. They had spread across the floor, sorting shells and getting sand everywhere. The chests and books and dishes and cushions kept there did not interest them.

Cornelia was climbing down the ladder from the attic. She jumped from three rungs up and shouted triumphantly as she crashed to the floor. When she looked at me briefly, her eyes were a challenge. One of the baker's sons, about Aleydis' age, climbed partway up the ladder and jumped to the floor. Then Aleydis tried it, and another child, and another.

I had never known how Cornelia managed to get to the attic to steal the madder that stained my apron red. It was in her nature to be sly, to slip away when no one was looking. I had said nothing to Maria Thins or him about her pilfering. I was not sure they would believe me. Instead I had made sure the colours were locked away whenever he and I were not there.

I said nothing to her now as she sprawled on the floor next to Maertge. But that night I checked my things. Everything was there — my broken tile, my tortoiseshell comb, my prayer book, my embroidered handkerchiefs, my collars, my chemises, my aprons and caps. I counted and sorted and refolded them.

Then I checked the colours, just to be sure. They too were in order, and the cupboard did not look as if it had been tampered with.

Perhaps she was just being a child after all, climbing a ladder to jump from it, looking for a game rather than mischief.

The baker took away his painting in May, but my master did not begin setting up the next painting until July. I grew anxious about this delay, expecting Maria Thins to blame me, even though we both knew that it was not my fault. Then one day I overheard her tell Catharina that a friend of van Ruijven's saw the painting of his wife with the pearl necklace and thought she should be looking out rather than at a mirror. Van Ruijven had thus decided that he wanted a painting with his wife's face turned towards the painter. 'He doesn't paint that pose often,' she remarked.

I could not hear Catharina's response. I stopped sweeping the floor of the girls' room for a moment.

'You remember the last one,' Maria Thins reminded her. 'The maid. Remember van Ruijven and the maid in the red dress?'

Catharina snorted with muffled laughter.

'That was the last time anyone looked out from one of his paintings,' Maria Thins continued, 'and what a scandal that was! I was sure he would say no when van Ruijven suggested it this time, but he has agreed to do it.'

I could not ask Maria Thins, who would know I had been listening to them. I could not ask Tanneke, who would never repeat gossip to me now. So one day when there were few people at his stall I asked Pieter the son if he had heard about the maid in the red dress.

'Oh yes, that story went all around the Meat Hall,' he

134

answered, chuckling. He leaned over and began rearranging the cows' tongues on display. 'It was several years ago now. It seems van Ruijven wanted one of his kitchen maids to sit for a painting with him. They dressed her in one of his wife's gowns, a red one, and van Ruijven made sure there was wine in the painting so he could get her to drink every time they sat together. Sure enough, before the painting was finished she was carrying van Ruijven's child.'

'What happened to her?'

Pieter shrugged. 'What happens to girls like that?'

His words froze my blood. Of course I had heard such stories before, but never one so close to me. I thought about my dreams of wearing Catharina's clothes, of van Ruijven grasping my chin in the hallway, of him saying 'You should paint her' to my master.

Pieter had stopped what he was doing, a frown on his face. 'Why do you want to know about her?'

'It's nothing,' I answered lightly. 'Just something I overheard. It means nothing.'

I had not been present when he set up the scene for the painting of the baker's daughter – I had not yet been assisting him. Now, however, the first time van Ruijven's wife came to sit for him I was up in the attic working, and could hear what he said. She was a quiet woman. She did what was asked of her without a sound. Even her fine shoes did not tap across the tiled floor. He had her stand by the unshuttered window, then sit in one of the two lion-head chairs placed around the table. I heard him close some shutters. 'This painting will be darker than the last,' he declared.

She did not respond. It was as if he were talking to himself. After a moment he called up to me. When I appeared he said, 'Griet, get my wife's yellow mantle, and her pearl necklace and earrings.'

Catharina was visiting friends that afternoon so I could not ask her for her jewels. I would have been frightened to anyway. Instead I went to Maria Thins in the Crucifixion room, who unlocked Catharina's jewellery box and handed me the necklace and earrings. Then I got out the mantle from the cupboard in the great hall, shook it out and folded it carefully over my arm. I had never touched it before. I let my nose sink into the fur – it was very soft, like a baby rabbit's.

As I walked down the hallway to the stairs I had the sudden desire to run out the door with the riches in my arms. I could go to the star in the middle of Market Square, choose a direction to follow, and never come back.

Instead I returned to van Ruijven's wife and helped her into the mantle. She wore it as if it were her own skin. After sliding the earring wires through the holes in her lobes, she looped the pearls around her neck. I had taken up the ribbons to tie the necklace for her when he said, 'Don't wear the necklace. Leave it on the table.'

She sat again. He sat in his chair and studied her. She did not seem to mind – she gazed into space, seeing nothing, as he had tried to get me to do.

'Look at me,' he said.

She looked at him. Her eyes were large and dark, almost black.

He laid a table-rug on the table, then changed it for the blue cloth. He laid the pearls in a line on the table, then in

136

a heap, then in a line again. He asked her to stand, to sit, then to sit back, then to sit forward.

I thought he had forgotten that I was watching from the corner until he said, 'Griet, get me Catharina's powder-brush.'

He had her hold the brush up to her face, lay it on the table with her hand still grasping it, leave it to one side. He handed it to me. 'Take it back.'

When I returned he had given her a quill and paper. She sat in the chair, leaning forward, and wrote, an inkwell at her right. He opened a pair of the upper shutters and closed the bottom pair. The room became darker but the light shone on her high round forehead, on her arm resting on the table, on the sleeve of the yellow mantle.

'Move your left hand forward slightly,' he said. 'There.'

She wrote.

'Look at me,' he said.

She looked at him.

He got a map from the storeroom and hung it on the wall behind her. He took it down again. He tried a small landscape, a painting of a ship, the bare wall. Then he disappeared downstairs.

While he was gone I watched van Ruijven's wife closely. It was perhaps rude of me, but I wanted to see what she would do. She did not move. She seemed to settle into the pose more completely. By the time he returned, with a still life of musical instruments, she looked as if she had always been sitting at the table, writing her letter. I had heard he painted her once before the previous necklace painting, playing a lute. She must have learned by now what he wanted from a model. Perhaps she simply was what he wanted.

He hung the painting behind her, then sat down again to study her. As they gazed at each other I felt as if I were not there. I wanted to leave, to go back to my colours, but I did not dare disturb the moment.

'The next time you come, wear white ribbons in your hair instead of pink, and a yellow ribbon where you tie your hair at the back.'

She nodded so slightly that her head hardly moved.

'You may sit back.'

As he released her, I felt free to go.

The next day he pulled up another chair to the table. The day after that he brought up Catharina's jewellery box and set it on the table. Its drawers were studded with pearls around the keyholes.

Van Leeuwenhoek arrived with his camera obscura while I was working in the attic. 'You will have to get one of your own some day,' I heard him say in his deep voice. 'Though I admit it gives me the opportunity to see what you're painting. Where is the model?'

'She could not come.'

'That is a problem.'

'No. Griet,' he called.

I climbed down the ladder. When I entered the studio van Leeuwenhoek gazed at me in astonishment. He had very clear brown eyes, with large lids that made him look sleepy. He was far from sleepy, though, but alert and puzzled, his mouth drawn in tightly at the corners. Despite his surprise at seeing me, he had a kindly look about him, and when he recovered he even bowed.

No gentleman had ever bowed to me before. I could not stop myself — I smiled.

Van Leeuwenhoek laughed. 'What were you doing up there, my dear?'

'Grinding colours, sir.'

He turned to my master. 'An assistant! What other surprises do you have for me? Next you'll be teaching her to paint your women for you.'

My master was not amused. 'Griet,' he said, 'sit as you saw van Ruijven's wife do the other day.'

I stepped nervously to the chair and sat, leaning forward as she had done.

'Take up the quill.'

I picked it up, my hand trembling and making the feather shake, and placed my hands as I had remembered hers. I prayed he would not ask me to write something, as he had van Ruijven's wife. My father had taught me to write my name, but little else. At least I knew how to hold the quill. I glanced at the sheets on the table and wondered what van Ruijven's wife had written on them. I could read a little, from familiar things like my prayer book, but not a lady's hand.

'Look at me.'

I looked at him. I tried to be van Ruijven's wife.

He cleared his throat. 'She will be wearing the yellow mantle,' he said to van Leeuwenhoek, who nodded.

My master stood, and they set up the camera obscura so that it pointed at me. Then they took turns looking. When they were bent over the box with the black robe over their heads, it became easier for me to sit and think of nothing, as I knew he wanted me to.

He had van Leeuwenhoek move the painting on the back wall several times before he was satisfied with its position, then open and shut shutters while he kept his head under the robe. At last he seemed satisfied. He stood up and folded the robe over the back of the chair, then stepped over to the desk, picked up a piece of paper, and handed it to van Leeuwenhoek. They began discussing its contents – Guild business he wanted advice about. They talked for a long time.

Van Leeuwenhoek glanced up. 'For the mercy of God, man, let the girl get back to her work.'

My master looked at me as if surprised that I was still sitting at the table, quill in hand. 'Griet, you may go.'

As I left I thought I saw a look of pity cross van Leeuwenhoek's face.

He left the camera set up in the studio for some days. I was able to look through it several times on my own, lingering on the objects on the table. Something about the scene he was to paint bothered me. It was like looking at a painting that has been hung crookedly. I wanted to change something, but I did not know what. The box gave me no answers.

One day van Ruijven's wife came again and he looked at her for a long time in the camera. I was passing through the studio while his head was covered, and walked as quietly as I could so I would not disturb them. I stood behind him for a moment to look at the setting with her in it. She must have seen me but gave no sign, continuing to gaze straight at him with her dark eyes.

It came to me then that the scene was too neat. Although

I valued tidiness over most things, I knew from his other paintings that there should be some disorder on the table, something to snag the eye. I pondered each object — the jewellery box, the blue table-rug, the pearls, the letter, the inkwell — and decided what I would change. I returned quietly to the attic, surprised by my bold thoughts.

Once it was clear to me what he should do to the scene, I waited for him to make the change.

He did not move anything on the table. He adjusted the shutters slightly, the tilt of her head, the angle of her quill. But he did not change what I had expected him to.

I thought about it while I was wringing out sheets, while I was turning the spit for Tanneke, while I was wiping the kitchen tiles, while I was rinsing colours. While I lay in bed at night I thought about it. Sometimes I got up to look again. No, I was not mistaken.

He returned the camera to van Leeuwenhoek.

Whenever I looked at the scene my chest grew tight, as if something were pressing on it.

He set a canvas on the easel and painted a coat of lead white and chalk mixed with a bit of burnt sienna and yellow ochre.

My chest grew tighter, waiting for him.

He sketched lightly in reddish brown the outline of the woman and of each object.

When he began to paint great blocks of false colours, I thought my chest would burst like a sack that has been filled with too much flour.

As I lay in bed one night I decided I would have to make the change myself.

The next morning I cleaned, setting the jewellery box

back carefully, relining the pearls, replacing the letter, polishing and replacing the inkwell. I took a deep breath to ease the pressure in my chest. Then in one quick movement I pulled the front part of the blue cloth on to the table so that it flowed out of the dark shadows under the table and up in a slant on to the table in front of the jewellery box. I made a few adjustments to the lines of the folds, then stepped back. It echoed the shape of van Ruijven's wife's arm as she rested it on the table.

Yes, I thought, and pressed my lips together. He may send me away for changing it, but it is better now.

That afternoon I did not go up to the attic, although there was plenty of work for me there. I sat outside on the bench with Tanneke and mended shirts. He had not gone to his studio that morning, but to the Guild, and had dined at van Leeuwenhoek's. He had not yet seen the change.

I waited anxiously on the bench. Even Tanneke, who tried to ignore me these days, noted my mood. 'What's the matter with you, girl?' she asked. She had taken to calling me girl like her mistress. 'You're acting like a chicken that knows it's for the slaughter.'

'Nothing,' I said. 'Tell me about what happened when Catharina's brother came here last. I heard about it at the market. They still mention you,' I added, hoping to distract and flatter her, and to cover up how clumsily I moved away from her question.

For a moment Tanneke sat up straighter, until she remembered who was asking. 'That's not your business,' she snapped. 'That's family business, not for the likes of you.'

A few months before she would have delighted in telling a story that set her in the best light. But it was me who was asking, and I was not to be trusted or humoured or favoured with her words, though it must have pained her to pass up the chance to boast.

Then I saw him — he was walking towards us up the Oude Langendijck, his hat tilted to shield his face from the spring sunlight, his dark cloak pushed back from his shoulders. As he drew up to us I could not look at him.

'Afternoon, sir,' Tanneke sang out in a completely different tone.

'Hello, Tanneke. Are you enjoying the sun?'

'Oh yes, sir. I do like the sun on my face.'

I kept my eyes on the stitches I had made. I could feel him looking at me.

After he went inside Tanneke hissed, 'Say hello to the master when he speaks to you, girl. Your manners are a disgrace.'

'It was you he spoke to.'

'And so he should. But you needn't be so rude or you'll end up in the street, with no place here.'

He must be upstairs now, I thought. He must have seen what I've done.

I waited, barely able to hold my needle. I did not know exactly what I expected. Would he berate me in front of Tanneke? Would he raise his voice for the first time since I had come to live in his house? Would he say the painting was ruined?

Perhaps he would simply pull down the blue cloth so that it hung as it had before. Perhaps he would say nothing to me.

Later that night I saw him briefly as he came down for supper. He did not appear to be one thing or the other, happy or angry, unconcerned or anxious. He did not ignore me but he did not look at me either.

When I went up to bed I checked to see if he had pulled the cloth to hang as it had before I touched it.

He had not. I held up my candle to the easel — he had resketched in reddish brown the folds of the blue cloth. He had made my change.

I lay in bed that night smiling in the dark.

The next morning he came in as I was cleaning around the jewellery box. He had never before seen me making my measurements. I had laid my arm along one edge and moved the box to dust under and around it. When I looked over he was watching me. He did not say anything. Nor did I — I was concerned to set the box back exactly as it had been. Then I sponged the blue cloth with a damp rag, especially careful with the new folds I had made. My hands shook a little as I cleaned.

When I was done I looked up at him.

'Tell me, Griet, why did you change the tablecloth?' His tone was the same as when he had asked me about the vegetables at my parents' house.

I thought for a moment. 'There needs to be some disorder in the scene, to contrast with her tranquillity,' I explained. 'Something to tease the eye. And yet it must be something pleasing to the eye as well, and it is, because the cloth and her arm are in a similar position.'

There was a long pause. He was gazing at the table. I waited, wiping my hands against my apron.

'I had not thought I would learn something from a maid,' he said at last.

*　　*　　*

On Sunday my mother joined us as I described the new painting to my father. Pieter was with us, and had fixed his eyes on a patch of sunlight on the floor. He was always quiet when we talked about my master's paintings.

I did not tell them about the change I had made that my master approved of.

'I think his paintings are not good for the soul,' my mother announced suddenly. She was frowning. She had never before spoken of his work.

My father turned his face towards her in surprise.

'Good for the purse, more like,' Frans quipped. It was one of the rare Sundays when he was visiting. Lately he had become obsessed with money. He questioned me about the value of things in the house on the Oude Langendijck, of the pearls and mantle in the painting, of the pearl-encrusted jewellery box and what it held, of the number and size of paintings that hung on the walls. I did not tell him much. I was sorry to think it of my own brother, but I feared his thoughts had turned to easier ways of making a living than as an apprentice in a tile factory. I suspected he was only dreaming, but I did not want to fuel those dreams with visions of expensive objects within his – or his sister's – reach.

'What do you mean, Mother?' I asked, ignoring Frans.

'There is something dangerous about your description of his paintings,' she explained. 'From the way you talk they could be of religious scenes. It is as if the woman you describe is the Virgin Mary when she is just a woman, writing a letter. You give the painting meaning that it does not have or deserve. There are thousands of paintings in Delft. You can see them everywhere, hanging in a tavern as readily as in a rich man's house. You could take two weeks' maid's wages and buy one at the market.'

'If I did that,' I replied, 'you and Father would not eat for two weeks, and you would die without seeing what I bought.'

My father winced. Frans, who had been tying knots in a length of string, went very still. Pieter glanced at me.

My mother remained impassive. She did not speak her mind often. When she did her words were worth gold.

'I'm sorry, Mother,' I stammered. 'I didn't mean —'

'Working for them has turned your head,' she interrupted. 'It's made you forget who you are and where you come from. We're a decent Protestant family whose needs are not ruled by riches or fashions.'

I looked down, stung by her words. They were a mother's words, words I would say to my own daughter if I were concerned for her. Although I resented her speaking them, as I resented her questioning the value of his painting, I knew they held truth.

Pieter did not spend so long with me in the alley that Sunday.

The next morning it was painful to look at the painting. The blocks of false colours had been painted, and he had built up her eyes, and the high dome of her forehead, and part of the folds of the mantle sleeve. The rich yellow in particular filled me with the guilty pleasure that my mother's words had condemned. I tried instead to picture the finished painting hanging at Pieter the father's stall, for sale for ten guilders, a simple picture of a woman writing a letter.

I could not do it.

He was in a good mood that afternoon, or else I would

not have asked him. I had learned to gauge his mood, not from the little he said or the expression on his face — he did not show much — but from the way he moved about the studio and attic. When he was happy, when he was working well, he strode purposefully back and forth, no hesitation in his stride, no movement wasted. If he had been a musical man, he would have been humming or singing or whistling under his breath. When things did not go well, he stopped, stared out the window, shifted abruptly, started up the attic ladder only to climb back down before he was halfway up.

'Sir,' I began when he came up to the attic to mix linseed oil into the white lead I had finished grinding. He was working on the fur of the sleeve. She had not come that day, but I had discovered he was able to paint parts of her without her being there.

He raised his eyebrows. 'Yes, Griet?'

He and Maertge were the only people in the house who always called me by my name.

'Are your paintings Catholic paintings?'

He paused, the bottle of linseed oil poised over the shell that held the white lead. 'Catholic paintings,' he repeated. He lowered his hand, tapping the bottle against the table top. 'What do you mean by a Catholic painting?'

I had spoken before thinking. Now I did not know what to say. I tried a different question. 'Why are there paintings in Catholic churches?'

'Have you ever been inside a Catholic church, Griet?'

'No, sir.'

'Then you have not seen paintings in a church, or statues or stained glass?'

'No.'

'You have seen paintings only in houses, or shops, or inns?'

'And at the market.'

'Yes, at the market. Do you like looking at paintings?'

'I do, sir.' I began to think he would not answer me, that he would simply ask me endless questions.

'What do you see when you look at one?'

'Why, what the painter has painted, sir.'

Although he nodded, I felt I had not answered as he wished.

'So when you look at the painting down in the studio, what do you see?'

'I do not see the Virgin Mary, that is certain.' I said this more in defiance of my mother than in answer to him.

He gazed at me in surprise. 'Did you expect to see the Virgin Mary?'

'Oh no, sir,' I replied, flustered.

'Do you think the painting is Catholic?'

'I don't know, sir. My mother said —'

'Your mother has not seen the painting, has she?'

'No.'

'Then she cannot tell you what it is that you see or do not see.'

'No.' Although he was right, I did not like him to be critical of my mother.

'It's not the painting that is Catholic or Protestant,' he said, 'but the people who look at it, and what they expect to see. A painting in a church is like a candle in a dark room — we use it to see better. It is the bridge between ourselves and God. But it is not a Protestant candle or a Catholic candle. It is simply a candle.'

'We do not need such things to help us to see God,' I countered. 'We have His Word, and that is enough.'

He smiled. 'Did you know, Griet, that I was brought up as a Protestant? I converted when I married. So you do not need to preach to me. I have heard such words before.'

I stared at him. I had never known anyone to decide no longer to be a Protestant. I did not believe you really could switch. And yet he had.

He seemed to be waiting for me to speak.

'Though I have never been inside a Catholic church,' I began slowly, 'I think that if I saw a painting there, it would be like yours. Even though they are not scenes from the Bible, or the Virgin and Child, or the Crucifixion.' I shivered, thinking of the painting that had hung over my bed in the cellar.

He picked up the bottle again and carefully poured a few drops of oil into the shell. With his palette knife he began to mix the oil and white lead together until the paint was like butter that has been left out in a warm kitchen. I was bewitched by the movement of the silvery knife in the creamy white paint.

'There is a difference between Catholic and Protestant attitudes to painting,' he explained as he worked, 'but it is not necessarily as great as you may think. Paintings may serve a spiritual purpose for Catholics, but remember too that Protestants see God everywhere, in everything. By painting everyday things — tables and chairs, bowls and pitchers, soldiers and maids — are they not celebrating God's creation as well?'

I wished my mother could hear him. He would have made even her understand.

Catharina did not like to have her jewellery box left in the studio, where she could not get to it. She was suspicious of me, in part because she did not like me, but also because she was influenced by the stories we had all heard of maids stealing silver spoons from their mistresses. Stealing and tempting the master of the house – that was what mistresses were always looking for in maids.

As I had discovered with van Ruijven, however, it was more often the man pursuing the maid than the other way round. To him a maid came free.

Although she rarely consulted him about household things, Catharina went to her husband to ask that something be done. I did not hear them talk of it myself – Maertge told me one morning. Maertge and I got on well at that time. She had grown older suddenly, losing interest in the other children, preferring to be with me in the mornings as I went about my work. From me she learned to sprinkle clothes with water to bleach them in the sun, to apply a mixture of salt and wine to grease stains to get them out, to scrub the flatiron with coarse salt so that it would not stick and scorch. Her hands were too fine to work in water, however – she could watch me but I would not let her wet her hands. My own were ruined by now – hard and red and cracked, despite my mother's remedies to soften them. I had work hands and I was not yet eighteen.

Maertge was a little like my sister, Agnes, had been – lively, questioning, quick to decide what she thought. But she was also the eldest, with the eldest's seriousness of purpose. She had looked after her sisters, as I had looked after my brother and sister. That made a girl cautious and wary of change.

'Mama wants her jewellery box back,' she announced as we passed around the star in Market Square on our way to the Meat Hall. 'She has spoken to Papa about it.'

'What did she say?' I tried to sound unconcerned as I eyed the points of the star. I had noticed recently that when Catharina unlocked the studio door for me each morning she peered into the room at the table where her jewels lay.

Maertge hesitated. 'Mama doesn't like it that you are locked up with her jewellery at night,' she said at last. She did not add what Catharina was worried about — that I might pick up the pearls from the table, tuck the box under my arm, and climb from the window to the street, to escape to another city and another life.

In her way Maertge was trying to warn me. 'She wants you to sleep downstairs again,' she continued. 'The nurse is leaving soon and there is no reason for you to remain in the attic. She said either you or the jewellery box must go.'

'And what did your father say?'

'He didn't say anything. He will think about it.'

My heart grew heavy like a stone in my chest. Catharina had asked him to choose between me and the jewellery box. He could not have both. But I knew he would not remove the box and pearls from the painting to keep me in the attic. He would remove me. I would no longer assist him.

I slowed my pace. Years of hauling water, wringing out clothes, scrubbing floors, emptying chamberpots, with no chance of beauty or colour or light in my life, stretched before me like a landscape of flat land where, a long way off, the sea is visible but can never be reached. If I could not work with the colours, if I could not be near him, I did not know how I could continue to work in that house.

When we arrived at the butcher's stall and Pieter the son was not there, my eyes unexpectedly filled with tears. I had not realised that I had wanted to see his kind, handsome face. Confused as I felt about him, he was my escape, my reminder that there was another world I could join. Perhaps I was not so different from my parents, who looked on him to save them, to put meat on their table.

Pieter the father was delighted by my tears. 'I will tell my son you wept to find him gone,' he declared, scrubbing his chopping board clean of blood.

'You will do no such thing,' I muttered. 'Maertge, what do we want today?'

'Stewing beef,' she answered promptly. 'Four pounds.'

I wiped my eyes with a corner of my apron. 'There's a fly in my eye,' I said briskly. 'Perhaps it is not so clean around here. The dirt attracts flies.'

Pieter the father laughed heartily. 'Fly in her eye, she says! Dirt here. Of course there are flies — they come for the blood, not the dirt. The best meat is the bloodiest and attracts the most flies. You'll find out for yourself someday. No need to put on airs with us, madam.' He winked at Maertge. 'What do you think, miss? Should young Griet condemn a place when she'll be serving there herself in a few years?'

Maertge tried not to look shocked, but she was clearly surprised by his suggestion that I might not be with her family for always. She had the sense not to answer him — instead she took a sudden interest in the baby a woman at the next stall was holding.

'Please,' I said in a low voice to Pieter the father, 'don't say such things to her, or any of the family, even in jest. I am their maid. That is what I am. To suggest otherwise is to show them disrespect.'

Pieter the father regarded me. His eyes changed colour with every shift in the light. I did not think even my master could have captured them in paint. 'Perhaps you're right,' he conceded. 'I can see I'll have to be more careful when I tease you. But I'll tell you one thing, my dear — you'd best get used to flies.'

He did not remove the jewellery box, and he did not ask me to leave. Instead he brought the box and pearls and earrings to Catharina every evening, and she locked them away in the cupboard in the great hall where she kept the yellow mantle. In the morning when she unlocked the studio door to let me out she handed me the box and jewels. My first task in the studio became to place the box and pearls back on the table, and set out the earrings if van Ruijven's wife was coming to model. Catharina watched from the doorway as I made the measurements with my arms and hands. My gestures would have looked odd to anyone, but she never asked what I was doing. She did not dare.

Cornelia must have known about the problem with the jewellery box. Perhaps like Maertge she had overheard her parents discussing it. She may have seen Catharina bringing up the box in the morning and him carrying it down again at night, and guessed something was wrong. Whatever she saw or understood, she decided it was time to stir the pot once more.

For no particular reason but a vague distrust, she did not like me. She was very like her mother in that way.

She began it, as she had with the torn collar and the red paint on my apron, with a request. Catharina was dressing her hair one rainy morning, Cornelia idling at her side, watching. I was starching clothes in the washing kitchen so I did not hear them. But it was probably she who suggested that her mother wear tortoiseshell combs in her hair.

A few minutes later Catharina came to the doorway separating the washing and cooking kitchens and announced, 'One of my combs is missing. Has either of you seen it?' Although she was speaking to both Tanneke and me, she was staring hard at me.

'No, madam,' Tanneke replied solemnly, coming from the cooking kitchen to stand in the doorway as well so she could look at me.

'No, madam,' I echoed. When I saw Cornelia peeking in from the hallway, with the mischievous look so natural to her, I knew she had begun something that would once again lead to me.

She will do this until she drives me away, I thought.

'Someone must know where it is,' Catharina said.

'Shall I help you search the cupboard again, madam?' Tanneke asked. 'Or shall we look elsewhere?' she added pointedly.

'Perhaps it is in your jewellery box,' I suggested.

'Perhaps.'

Catharina passed into the hallway. Cornelia turned and followed her.

I thought she would pay no attention to my suggestion, since it came from me. When I heard her on the stairs, however, I realised she was heading to the studio, and hurried to join her — she would need me. She was waiting, furious, in the studio doorway, Cornelia lingering behind her.

'Bring the box to me,' Catharina ordered quietly, the humiliation of not being able to enter the room tingeing her words with an edge I had not heard before. She had often spoken sharply and loudly. The quiet control of her tone this time was much more frightening.

I could hear him in the attic. I knew what he was doing — he was grinding lapis for paint for the tablecloth.

I picked up the box and brought it to Catharina, leaving the pearls on the table. Without a word she carried it downstairs, Cornelia once again trailing behind her like a cat thinking it is about to be fed. She would go to the great hall and sort through all her jewels, to see if anything else was missing. Perhaps other things were — it was hard to guess what a seven-year-old determined to make mischief might do.

She would not find the comb in her box. I knew exactly where it was.

I did not follow her, but climbed up to the attic.

He looked at me in surprise, his hand holding the muller suspended above the bowl, but he did not ask me why I had come upstairs. He began grinding again.

I opened the chest where I kept my things and unwrapped the comb from its handkerchief. I rarely looked at the comb

— in that house I had no reason to wear it or even to admire it. It reminded me too much of the kind of life I could never have as a maid. Now that I knew to look at it closely, I could see it was not my grandmother's, though very similar. The scallop shape at the end of it was longer and more curved, and there were tiny serrated marks on each panel of the scallop. It was finer than my grandmother's, though not so much finer.

I wonder if I will ever see my grandmother's comb again, I thought.

I sat for so long on the bed, the comb in my lap, that he stopped grinding again.

'What is wrong, Griet?'

His tone was gentle. That made it easier to say what I had no choice but to say.

'Sir,' I declared at last, 'I need your help.'

I remained in my attic room, sitting on my bed, hands in my lap, while he spoke to Catharina and Maria Thins, while they searched Cornelia, then searched among the girls' things for my grandmother's comb. Maertge finally found it, hidden in the large shell the baker had given them when he came to see his painting. That was probably when Cornelia had switched the combs, climbing down from the attic while the children were all playing in the storeroom and hiding my comb inside the first thing she could find.

It was Maria Thins who had to beat Cornelia — he made it clear it was not his duty, and Catharina refused to, even when she knew that Cornelia should be punished. Maertge told me later that Cornelia did not cry, but sneered throughout the beating.

It was Maria Thins too who came to see me in the attic.

'Well, girl,' she said, leaning against the grinding table, 'you have set the cat loose in the poultry house now.'

'I did nothing,' I protested.

'No, but you have managed to make a few enemies. Why is that? We've never had so much trouble with other help.' She chuckled, but behind her laugh she was sober. 'But he has backed you, in his way,' she continued, 'and that is more powerful than anything Catharina or Cornelia or Tanneke or even I may say against you.'

She tossed my grandmother's comb in my lap. I wrapped it in a handkerchief and replaced it in the chest. Then I turned to Maria Thins. If I did not ask her now, I would never know. This might be the only time she would be willing to answer me. 'Please, madam, what did he say? About me?'

Maria Thins gave me a knowing look. 'Don't flatter yourself, girl. He said very little about you. But it was clear enough. That he came downstairs at all and concerned himself – my daughter knew then that he was taking your side. No, he charged her with failing to raise her children properly. Much cleverer, you see, to criticise her than to praise you.'

'Did he explain that I was – assisting him?'

'No.'

I tried not to let my face show what I felt, but the very question must have made my feelings clear.

'But *I* told her, once he had gone,' Maria Thins added. 'It's nonsense, you sneaking around, keeping secrets from her in her own house.' She sounded as if she were blaming me, but then she muttered, 'I would have thought better of him.' She stopped, looking as if she wished she hadn't revealed so much of her own mind.

157

'What did she say when you told her?'

'She's not happy, of course, but she's more afraid of his anger.' Maria Thins hesitated. 'There's another reason why she's not so concerned. I may as well tell you now. She's carrying a child again.'

'Another?' I let slip. I was surprised that Catharina would want another child when they were so short of money.

Maria Thins frowned at me. 'Watch yourself, girl.'

'I'm sorry, madam.' I instantly regretted having spoken even that one word. It was not for me to say how big their family should be. 'Has the doctor been?' I asked, trying to make amends.

'Doesn't need to. She knows the signs, she's been through it enough.' For a moment Maria Thins' face made clear her thoughts – she too wondered about so many children. Then she became stern again. 'You go about your duties, stay out of her way, and help him, but don't parade it in front of the house. Your place here is not so secure.'

I nodded and let my eyes rest on her gnarled hands as they fumbled with a pipe. She lit it and puffed for a moment. Then she chuckled. 'Never so much trouble with a maid before. Lord love us!'

On Sunday I took the comb back to my mother. I did not tell her what had happened – I simply said it was too fine for a maid to keep.

Some things changed for me in the house after the trouble with the comb. Catharina's treatment of me was the greatest surprise. I had expected that she would be even more difficult than before – give me more work, berate me whenever she could, make me as uncomfortable as possible. Instead she seemed to fear me. She removed the studio key from the precious bunch at her hip and handed it back to Maria Thins, never locking or unlocking the door again. She left her jewellery box in the studio, sending her mother to fetch what she needed from it. She avoided me as much as she could. Once I understood this, I kept out of her way as well.

She did not say anything about my afternoon work in the attic. Maria Thins must have impressed upon her the notion that my help would make him paint more, and support the child she carried as well as those she had already. She had taken to heart his words about her care of the children, who were after all her main charge, and began to spend more time with them than she had before. With the encouragement of Maria Thins, she even began to teach Maertge and Lisbeth to read and write.

Maria Thins was more subtle, but she too changed towards me, treating me with more respect. I was still clearly a maid, but she did not dismiss me so readily, or ignore me, as she did sometimes with Tanneke. She would not go so far as to ask my opinion, but she made me feel less excluded from the household.

I was also surprised when Tanneke softened towards me. I had thought she enjoyed being angry and bearing me a grudge, but perhaps it had worn her out. Or perhaps once it was clear that he took my side, she felt it best not to appear to be opposed to me. Perhaps they all felt like that. Whatever the reason, she stopped creating extra work for me by spilling things, stopped muttering about me under her breath and giving me hard sideways looks. She did not befriend me, but it became easier to work with her.

It was cruel, perhaps, but I felt I had won a battle against her. She was older and had been a part of the household for much longer, but his favouring me clearly carried more weight than her loyalty and experience. She could have felt this slight deeply, but she accepted defeat more easily than I would have expected. Tanneke was a simple creature underneath, and wanted an easy time of it. The easiest way was to accept me.

Although her mother took closer charge of her, Cornelia did not change. She was Catharina's favourite, perhaps because she most resembled her in spirit, and Catharina would do little to tame her ways. Sometimes she looked at me with her light brown eyes, her head tilted so that her red curls dangled about her face, and I thought of the sneer Maertge had described as Cornelia's expression while she was being beaten. And I thought again, as I had on my first day: She will be a handful.

Though I did not make a show of it, I avoided Cornelia as I did her mother. I did not wish to encourage her. I hid the broken tile, my best lace collar which my mother had made for me and my finest embroidered handkerchief, so that she could not use them against me.

He did not treat me differently after the affair of the comb. When I thanked him for speaking up for me, he shook his head as if shooing away a fly that buzzed about him.

It was I who felt differently about him. I felt indebted. I felt that if he asked me to do something I could not say no. I did not know what he would ask that I would want to say no to, but none the less I did not like the position I had come to be in.

I was disappointed in him as well, though I did not like to think about it. I had wanted him to tell Catharina himself about my assisting him, to show that he was not afraid to tell her, that he supported me.

That is what I wanted.

Maria Thins came to see him in his studio one afternoon in the middle of October, when the painting of van Ruijven's wife was nearly complete. She must have known I was working in the attic and could hear her, but nevertheless she spoke directly to him.

She asked him what he intended to paint next. When he did not reply she said, 'You must paint a larger painting, with more figures in it, as you used to. Not another woman alone with only her thoughts. When van Ruijven comes to see his painting you must suggest another to him. Perhaps a companion piece to something you've already painted for him. He will agree – he usually does. And he will pay more for it.'

He still did not respond.

'We're further in debt,' Maria Thins said bluntly. 'We need the money.'

'He may ask that she be in it,' he said. His voice was low but I was able to hear what he said, though only later did I understand what he meant.

'So?'

'No. Not like that.'

'We'll worry about that when it happens, not before.'

A few days later van Ruijven and his wife came to see the finished painting. In the morning my master and I prepared the room for their visit. He took the pearls and jewellery box down to Catharina while I put away everything else and set out chairs. Then he moved the easel and painting into the place where the setting had been and had me open all the shutters.

That morning I helped Tanneke prepare a special dinner for them. I did not think I would have to see them, and when they came at noon it was Tanneke who took up wine as they gathered in the studio. When she returned, however, she announced that I was to help her serve dinner rather than Maertge, who was old enough to join them at the table. 'My mistress has decided this,' she added.

I was surprised – the last time they viewed their painting Maria Thins had tried to keep me away from van Ruijven. I did not say so to Tanneke, though. 'Is van Leeuwenhoek there too?' I asked instead. 'I thought I heard his voice in the hallway.'

Tanneke nodded absently. She was tasting the roasted pheasant. 'Not bad,' she murmured. 'I can hold my head as high as any cook of van Ruijven's.'

While she was upstairs I had basted the pheasant and sprinkled it with salt, which Tanneke used too sparingly.

When they came down to dinner and everyone was seated, Tanneke and I began to bring in the dishes. Catharina glared at me. Never good at concealing her thoughts, she was horrified to see that I was serving.

My master too looked as if he had cracked his tooth on a stone. He stared coldly at Maria Thins, who feigned indifference behind her glass of wine.

Van Ruijven, however, grinned. 'Ah, the wide-eyed maid!' he cried. 'I wondered where you'd got to. How are you, my girl?'

'Very well, sir, thank you,' I murmured, placing a slice of pheasant on his plate and moving away as quickly as I could. Not quickly enough, however – he managed to slide his hand along my thigh. I could still feel the ghost of it a few minutes later.

While van Ruijven's wife and Maertge remained oblivious, van Leeuwenhoek noted everything – Catharina's fury, my master's irritation, Maria Thins' shrug, van Ruijven's lingering hand. When I served him he searched my face as if looking there for the answer to how a simple maid could cause so much trouble. I was grateful to him – there was no blame in his expression.

Tanneke too had noticed the stir I caused, and for once was helpful. We said nothing in the kitchen, but it was she who made the trips back to the table to bring out the gravy, to refill the wine, to serve more food, while I looked after things in the kitchen. I had to go back only once, when we were both to clear away the plates. Tanneke went directly to van Ruijven's place while I took up plates at the other end of the table. Van Ruijven's eyes followed me everywhere.

So did my master's.

I tried to ignore them, instead listening to Maria Thins. She was discussing the next painting. 'You were pleased with the one of the music lesson, weren't you?' she said. 'What better to follow such a painting than another with a musical setting? After a lesson, a concert, perhaps with more people in it, three or four musicians, an audience –'

'No audience,' my master interrupted. 'I do not paint audiences.'

Maria Thins regarded him sceptically.

'Come, come,' van Leeuwenhoek interjected genially,

'surely an audience is less interesting than the musicians themselves.'

I was glad he defended my master.

'I don't care about audiences,' van Ruijven announced, 'but I would like to be in the painting. I will play the lute.' After a pause he added, 'I want her in it too.' I did not have to look at him to know he had gestured at me.

Tanneke jerked her head slightly towards the kitchen and I escaped with the little I had cleared, leaving her to gather the rest. I wanted to look at my master but did not dare. As I was leaving I heard Catharina say in a gay voice, 'What a fine idea! Like that painting with you and the maid in the red dress. Do you remember her?'

On Sunday my mother spoke to me when we were alone in her kitchen. My father was sitting out in the late October sun while we prepared dinner. 'You know I don't listen to market gossip,' she began, 'but it is hard not to hear it when my daughter's name is mentioned.'

I immediately thought of Pieter the son. Nothing we did in the alley was worthy of gossip. I had insisted on that. 'I don't know what you mean, Mother,' I answered honestly.

My mother pulled in the corners of her mouth. 'They are saying your master is going to paint you.' It was as if the words themselves made her mouth purse.

I stopped stirring the pot I had been tending. 'Who says this?'

My mother sighed, reluctant to pass along overheard tales. 'Some women selling apples.'

When I did not respond she took my silence to mean the worst. 'Why didn't you tell me, Griet?'

'Mother, I haven't even heard this myself. No one has said anything to me!'

She did not believe me.

'It's true,' I insisted. 'My master has said nothing, Maria Thins has said nothing. I simply clean his studio. That's as close as I get to his paintings.' I had never told her about my attic work. 'How can you believe old women selling apples rather than me?'

'When there's talk about someone at the market, there's usually a reason for it, even if it's not what's actually being said.' My mother left the kitchen to call my father. She would say no more about the subject that day, but I began to fear she might be right – I would be the last to be told.

The next day at the Meat Hall I decided to ask Pieter the father about the rumour. I did not dare speak of it to Pieter the son. If my mother had heard the gossip, he would have as well. I knew he would not be pleased. Although he had never said so to me, it was clear he was jealous of my master.

Pieter the son was not at the stall. I did not have to wait long for Pieter the father to say something himself. 'What's this I hear?' he smirked as I approached. 'Going to have your picture painted, are you? Soon you'll be too grand for the likes of my son. He's gone off in a sulk to the Beast Market because of you.'

'Tell me what you have heard.'

'Oh, you want it told again, do you?' He raised his voice. 'Shall I make it into a fine tale for a few others?'

'Hush,' I hissed. Underneath his bravado I sensed he was angry with me. 'Just tell me what you have heard.'

165

Pieter the father lowered his voice. 'Only that van Ruijven's cook was saying you are to sit with her master for a painting.'

'I know nothing of this,' I stated firmly, aware even as I said it that, as with my mother, my words had little effect. Pieter the father scooped up a handful of pigs' kidneys. 'It's not me you should be talking to,' he said, weighing them in his hand.

I waited a few days before speaking to Maria Thins. I wanted to see if anyone would tell me first. I found her in the Crucifixion room one afternoon when Catharina was asleep and Maertge had taken the girls to the Beast Market. Tanneke was in the kitchen sewing and watching Johannes and Franciscus.

'May I speak to you, madam?' I said in a low voice.

'What is it, girl?' She lit her pipe and regarded me through the smoke. 'Trouble again?' She sounded weary.

'I don't know, madam. But I have heard a strange thing.'

'So have we all heard strange things.'

'I have heard that – that I am to be in a painting. With van Ruijven.'

Maria Thins chuckled. 'Yes, that is a strange thing. They've been talking in the market, have they?'

I nodded.

She leaned back in her chair and puffed on her pipe. 'Tell me, what would you think of being in such a painting?'

I did not know what to answer. 'What would I think, madam?' I repeated dumbly.

'I wouldn't bother to ask some people that. Tanneke, for instance. When he painted her she stood there happily pouring milk for months without a thought passing through

166

that head, God love her. But you – no, there's all manner of things you think but don't say. I wonder what they are?'

I said the one sensible thing I knew she would understand. 'I do not wish to sit with van Ruijven, madam. I do not think his intentions are honourable.' My words were stiff.

'His intentions are never honourable when it comes to young women.'

I nervously wiped my hands on my apron.

'It seems you have a champion to defend your honour,' she continued. 'My son-in-law is no more willing to paint you with van Ruijven than you are willing to sit with him.'

I did not try to hide my relief.

'But,' Maria Thins warned, 'van Ruijven is his patron, and a wealthy and powerful man. We cannot afford to offend him.'

'What will you say to him, madam?'

'I'm still trying to decide. In the meantime, you will have to put up with the rumours. Don't answer them – we don't want van Ruijven hearing from the market gossips that you are refusing to sit with him.'

I must have looked uncomfortable. 'Don't worry, girl,' Maria Thins growled, tapping her pipe on the table to loosen the ash. 'We'll take care of this. You keep your head down and go about your work, and not a word to anyone.'

'Yes, madam.'

I did tell one person, though. I felt I had to.

It had been easy enough to avoid Pieter the son – there were auctions all that week at the Beast Market, of animals that had been fattening all summer and autumn in the countryside and were ready for slaughter just before winter began. Pieter had gone every day to the sales.

The afternoon after Maria Thins and I spoke I slipped out to look for him at the market, just around the corner from the Oude Langendijck. It was quieter there in the afternoon than in the morning, when the auctions took place. By now many of the beasts had been driven away by their new owners, and men stood about under the plane trees that lined the square, counting their money and discussing the deals that had been made. The leaves on the trees had turned yellow and fallen to mingle with the dung and urine I could smell long before I reached the market.

Pieter the son was sitting with another man outside one of the taverns on the square, a tankard of beer in front of him. Deep in conversation, he did not see me as I stood silently near his table. It was his companion who looked up, then nudged Pieter.

'I would like to speak to you for a moment,' I said quickly, before Pieter had a chance even to look surprised.

His companion immediately jumped up and offered me his chair.

'Could we walk?' I gestured to the square.

'Of course,' Pieter said. He nodded to his friend and followed me across the street. From his expression it was not clear whether or not he was pleased to see me.

'How were the auctions today?' I asked awkwardly. I was never good at making everyday talk.

Pieter shrugged. He took my elbow to steer me around a pile of dung, then dropped his hand.

I gave up. 'There has been gossip about me in the market,' I said bluntly.

'There is gossip about everyone at one time or another,' he replied neutrally.

'It's not true what they say. I'm not going to be in a painting with van Ruijven.'

'Van Ruijven likes you. My father told me.'

'But I'm not going to be in a painting with him.'

'He is very powerful.'

'You must believe me, Pieter.'

'He is very powerful,' he repeated, 'and you are but a maid. Who do you think will win that round of cards?'

'You think I will become like the maid in the red dress.'

'Only if you drink his wine.' Pieter gazed at me levelly.

'My master does not want to paint me with van Ruijven,' I said reluctantly after a moment. I had not wanted to mention him.

'That's good. I don't want him to paint you either.'

I stopped and closed my eyes. The close animal smell was beginning to make me feel faint.

'You're getting caught where you should not be, Griet,' Pieter said more kindly. 'Theirs is not your world.'

I opened my eyes and took a step back from him. 'I came here to explain that the rumour is false, not to be accused by you. Now I'm sorry I bothered.'

'Don't be. I do believe you.' He sighed. 'But you have little power over what happens to you. Surely you can see that?'

When I did not answer he added, 'If your master did want to paint a picture of you and van Ruijven, do you really think you could say no?'

It was a question I had asked myself but found no answer to. 'Thank you for reminding me of how helpless I am,' I replied tartly.

'You wouldn't be with me. We would run our own

business, earn our own money, rule our own lives. Isn't that what you want?'

I looked at him, at his bright blue eyes, his yellow curls, his eager face. I was a fool even to hesitate.

'I didn't come here to talk about this. I'm too young yet.' I used the old excuse. Some day I would be too old to use it.

'I never know what you're thinking, Griet,' he tried again. 'You're so calm and quiet, you never say. But there are things inside you. I see them sometimes, hiding in your eyes.'

I smoothed my cap, checking with my fingers for stray hairs. 'All I mean to say is that there is no painting,' I declared, ignoring what he had just said. 'Maria Thins has promised me. But you're not to tell anyone. If they speak to you of me in the market, say nothing. Don't try to defend me. Otherwise van Ruijven may hear and your words will work against us.'

Pieter nodded unhappily and kicked at a bit of dirty straw.

He will not always be so reasonable, I thought. One day he will give up.

To reward him for his reasonableness, I let him take me into a space between two houses off the Beast Market and run his hands down my body, cupping them where there were curves. I tried to take pleasure in it, but I was still feeling sick from the animal smell.

Whatever I said to Pieter the son, I myself did not feel reassured by Maria Thins' promise to keep me out of the painting. She was a formidable woman, astute in business, certain of her place, but she was not van Ruijven. I did not see how they could refuse him what he wanted. He had wanted a painting of his wife looking directly at the painter, and my master had made it. He had wanted a painting of the maid in the red dress, and had got that. If he wanted me, why should he not get me?

One day three men I had not seen before came with a harpsichord tied securely in a cart. A boy followed them carrying a bass viol that was bigger than he. They were not van Ruijven's instruments, but from one of his relations who was fond of music. The whole house gathered to watch the men struggle with the harpsichord on the steep stairs. Cornelia stood right at the bottom — if they were to drop the instrument it would fall directly on her. I wanted to reach out and pull her back, and if it had been one of the other children I would not have hesitated. Instead I remained where I was. It was Catharina who finally insisted she move to a safer spot.

When they got it up the stairs they took it to the studio, my master supervising them. After the men left, he called down to Catharina. Maria Thins followed her up. A moment later we heard the sound of the harpsichord being played. The girls sat on the stairs while Tanneke and I stood in the hallway, listening.

'Is that the mistress playing? Or your mistress?' I asked Tanneke. It seemed so unlike either of them that I thought perhaps he was playing and simply wanted Catharina to be his audience.

'It's the young mistress, of course,' Tanneke hissed. 'Why would he have asked her up otherwise? She's very good, is the young mistress. She played when she was a girl. But her father kept their harpsichord when he and my mistress separated. Have you never heard young mistress complain about not being able to afford an instrument?'

'No.' I thought for a moment. 'Do you think he will paint her? For this painting with van Ruijven?' Tanneke must have heard the market gossip but had said nothing of it to me.

'Oh, the master never paints her. She can't sit still!'

Over the next few days he moved a table and chairs into the setting, and lifted the harpsichord's lid, which was painted with a landscape of rocks and trees and sky. He spread a table-rug on the table in the foreground, and set the bass viol under it.

One day Maria Thins called me to the Crucifixion room. 'Now, girl,' she said, 'this afternoon I want you to go on some errands for me. To the apothecary's for some elderflowers and hyssop — Franciscus has a cough now it's cold again. And then to Old Mary the spinner for some wool, just enough for a collar for Aleydis. Did you notice hers is unravelling?' She paused, as if calculating how long it would take me to get from place to place. 'And then go to Jan Mayer's house to ask when his brother is expected in Delft. He lives by the Rietveld Tower. That's near your parents, isn't it? You may stop in and visit them.'

Maria Thins had never allowed me to see my parents apart from Sundays. Then I guessed. 'Is van Ruijven coming today, madam?'

'Don't let him see you,' she answered grimly. 'It's best if you're not here at all. Then if he asks for you we can say you're out.'

For a moment I wanted to laugh. Van Ruijven had us

all — even Maria Thins — running like rabbits before dogs.

My mother was surprised to see me that afternoon. Luckily a neighbour was visiting and she could not question me closely. My father was not so interested. He had changed much since I'd left home, since Agnes had died. He was no longer so curious about the world outside his street, rarely asking me about the goings-on at the Oude Langendijck or in the market. Only the paintings still interested him.

'Mother,' I announced as we sat by the fire, 'my master is beginning the painting that you were asking about. Van Ruijven has come over and he is setting it up today. Everyone who is to be in the painting is there now.'

Our neighbour, a bright-eyed old woman who loved market talk, gazed at me as if I had just set a roast capon in front of her. My mother frowned — she knew what I was doing.

There, I thought. That will take care of the rumours.

He was not himself that evening. I heard him snap at Maria Thins at supper, and he went out later and came back smelling of the tavern. I was climbing the stairs to bed when he came in. He looked up at me, his face tired and red. His expression was not angry, but weary, as of a man who has just seen all the wood he must chop, or a maid faced with a mountain of laundry.

The next morning the studio gave few clues about what had happened the afternoon before. Two chairs had been placed, one at the harpsichord, the other with its back to the painter. There was a lute on the chair, and a violin on the table to the left. The bass viol still lay in the shadows under the table. It was hard to tell from the arrangement how many people were to be in the painting.

Later Maertge told me that van Ruijven had come with his sister and one of his daughters.

'How old is the daughter?' I could not help asking.

'Seventeen, I think.'

My age.

They came around again a few days later. Maria Thins sent me on more errands and told me to amuse myself elsewhere for the morning. I wanted to remind her that I could not stay away every day they came to be painted – it was getting too cold to idle in the streets, and there was too much work to do. But I did not say anything. I could not explain it, but I felt something was to change soon. I just did not know how.

I could not go to my parents again – they would think something was wrong, and explaining otherwise would make them believe even worse things were happening. Instead I went to Frans' factory. I had not seen him since he had asked me about the valuables in the house. His questions had angered me and I had made no effort to visit him.

The woman at the gate did not recognise me. When I asked to see Frans she shrugged and stepped aside, disappearing without showing me where to go. I walked into a low building where boys Frans' age sat on benches at long tables, painting tiles. They were working on simple designs, with nothing of the graceful style of my father's tiles. Many were not even painting the main figures, but only the flourishes in the corners of the tiles, the leaves and curlicues, leaving a blank centre for a more skilled master to fill.

When they saw me a chorus of high whistles erupted that

made me want to stop my ears. I went up to the nearest boy and asked him where my brother was. He turned red and ducked his head. Though I was a welcome distraction, no one would answer my question.

I found another building, smaller and hotter, housing the kiln. Frans was there alone, with his shirt off and the sweat pouring from him and a grim look on his face. The muscles in his arms and chest had grown. He was becoming a man.

He had tied quilted material around his forearms and hands that made him look clumsy, but when he pulled trays full of tiles in and out of the kiln, he skilfully wielded the flat sheets so that he did not burn himself. I was afraid to call to him because he would be startled and might drop a tray. But he saw me before I spoke, and immediately set down the tray he held.

'Griet, what are you doing here? Is something wrong with Mother or Father?'

'No, no, they're fine. I've just come to visit.'

'Oh.' Frans pulled the cloths from his arms, wiped his face with a rag and gulped beer from a mug. He leaned against the wall and rolled his shoulders the way men do who have finished unloading cargo from a canal boat and are easing and stretching their muscles. I had never seen him make such a gesture before.

'Are you still working the kiln? They have not moved you to something else? Glazing, or painting like those boys in the other building?'

Frans shrugged.

'But those boys are the same age as you. Shouldn't you be —' I could not finish my sentence when I saw the look on his face.

175

'It's punishment,' he said in a low voice.

'Why? Punishment for what?'

Frans did not answer.

'Frans, you must tell me or I'll tell our parents you're in trouble.'

'I'm not in trouble,' he said quickly. 'I made the owner angry, is all.'

'How?'

'I did something his wife didn't like.'

'What did you do?'

Frans hesitated. 'It was she who started it,' he said softly. 'She showed her interest, you see. But when I showed mine she told her husband. He didn't throw me out because he's a friend of Father's. So I'm on the kiln until his humour improves.'

'Frans! How could you be so stupid? You know she's not for the likes of you. To endanger your place here for something like that!'

'You don't understand what it's like,' Frans muttered. 'Working here, it's exhausting, it's boring. It was something to think about, that's all. *You* have no right to judge, you with your butcher you'll marry and have a fine life with. Easy for you to say what my life should be like when all I can see are endless tiles and long days. Why shouldn't I admire a pretty face when I see one?'

I wanted to protest, to tell him that I understood. At night I sometimes dreamed of piles of laundry that never got smaller no matter how much I scrubbed and boiled and ironed.

'Was she the woman at the gate?' I asked instead.

Frans shrugged and drank more beer. I pictured her sour

expression and wondered how such a face could ever tempt him.

'Why are you here, anyway?' he asked. 'Shouldn't you be at Papists' Corner?'

I had prepared an excuse for why I had come, that an errand had taken me to that part of the Delft. But I felt so sorry for my brother that I found myself telling him about van Ruijven and the painting. It was a relief to confide in him.

He listened carefully. When I finished he declared, 'You see, we're not so different, with the attentions we've had from those above us.'

'But I haven't responded to van Ruijven, and have no intention to.'

'I didn't mean van Ruijven,' Frans said, his look suddenly sly. 'No, not him. I meant your master.'

'What about my master?' I cried.

Frans smiled. 'Now, Griet, don't work yourself into a state.'

'Stop that! What are you suggesting? He has never —'

'He doesn't have to. It's clear from your face. You want him. You can hide it from our parents and your butcher man, but you can't hide it from me. I know you better than that.'

He did. He did know me better.

I opened my mouth but no words came out.

Although it was December, and cold, I walked so fast and fretted so much over Frans that I got back to Papists' Corner long before I should have. I grew hot and began to loosen my shawls to cool my face. As I was walking up the Oude Langendijck I saw van Ruijven and my master coming towards me. I bowed my head and crossed over so that I would pass by my master's side rather than van Ruijven's, but the crossing only drew van Ruijven's attention to me. He stopped, forcing my master to halt with him.

'You — the wide-eyed maid,' he called, turning towards me. 'They told me you were out. I think you've been avoiding me. What's your name, my girl?'

'Griet, sir.' I kept my eyes fixed on my master's shoes. They were shiny and black — Maertge had polished them under my guidance earlier that day.

'Well, Griet, have you been avoiding me?'

'Oh no, sir. I've been on errands.' I held up a pail of things I had been to get for Maria Thins before I visited Frans.

'I hope I will see more of you, then.'

'Yes, sir.' Two women were standing behind the men. I peeked at their faces and guessed they were the daughter and sister who were sitting for the painting. The daughter was staring at me.

'You have not forgotten your promise, I hope,' van Ruijven said to my master.

My master jerked his head like a puppet. 'No,' he replied after a moment.

'Good. I expect you'll want to make a start on that before you ask us to come again.' Van Ruijven's smile made me shiver.

There was a long silence. I glanced at my master. He was struggling to maintain a calm expression, but I knew he was angry.

'Yes,' he said at last, his eyes on the house opposite. He did not look at me.

I did not understand that conversation in the street, but I knew it was to do with me. The next day I discovered how.

In the morning he asked me to come up in the afternoon. I assumed he wanted me to work with the colours, that he was starting the concert painting. When I got to the studio he was not there. I went straight to the attic. The grinding table was clear – nothing had been laid out for me. I climbed back down the ladder, feeling foolish.

He had come in and was standing in the studio, looking out a window.

'Take a seat, please, Griet,' he said, his back to me.

I sat in the chair by the harpsichord. I did not touch it – I had never touched an instrument except to clean it. As I waited I studied the paintings he had hung on the back wall that would form part of the concert painting. There was a landscape on the left, and on the right a picture of three people – a woman playing a lute, wearing a dress that revealed much of her bosom, a gentleman with his arm around her, and an old woman. The man was buying the young woman's favours, the old woman reaching to take the coin he held out. Maria Thins owned the painting and had told me it was called *The Procuress*.

'Not that chair.' He had turned from the window. 'That is where van Ruijven's daughter sits.'

Where I would have sat, I thought, if I were to be in the painting.

He got another of the lion-head chairs and set it close to his easel but sideways so it faced the window. 'Sit here.'

'What do you want, sir?' I asked, sitting. I was puzzled — we never sat together. I shivered, although I was not cold.

'Don't talk.' He opened a shutter so that the light fell directly on my face. 'Look out the window.' He sat down in his chair by the easel.

I gazed at the New Church tower and swallowed. I could feel my jaw tightening and my eyes widening.

'Now look at me.'

I turned my head and looked at him over my left shoulder.

His eyes locked with mine. I could think of nothing except how their grey was like the inside of an oyster shell.

He seemed to be waiting for something. My face began to strain with the fear that I was not giving him what he wanted.

'Griet,' he said softly. It was all he had to say. My eyes filled with tears I did not shed. I knew now.

'Yes. Don't move.'

He was going to paint me.

1666

'You smell of linseed oil.'

My father spoke in a baffled tone. He did not believe that simply cleaning a painter's studio would make the smell linger on my clothes, my skin, my hair. He was right. It was as if he guessed that I now slept with the oil in my room, that I sat for hours being painted and absorbing the scent. He guessed and yet he could not say. His blindness took away his confidence so that he did not trust the thoughts in his mind.

A year before I might have tried to help him, suggest what he was thinking, humour him into speaking his mind. Now, however, I simply watched him struggle silently, like a beetle that has fallen on to its back and cannot turn itself over.

My mother had also guessed, though she did not know what she had guessed. Sometimes I could not meet her eye. When I did her look was a puzzle of anger held back, of curiosity, of hurt. She was trying to understand what had happened to her daughter.

I had grown used to the smell of linseed oil. I even kept a small bottle of it by my bed. In the mornings when I was getting dressed I held it up to the window to admire the colour, which was like lemon juice with a drop of lead-tin yellow in it.

I wear that colour now, I wanted to say. He is painting me in that colour.

Instead, to take my father's mind off the smell, I described the other painting my master was working on. 'A young woman sits at a harpsichord, playing. She is wearing a yellow and black bodice – the same the baker's daughter wore for her painting – a white satin skirt and white ribbons in her hair. Standing in the curve of the harpsichord is another woman, who is holding music and singing. She wears a green, fur-trimmed housecoat and a blue dress. In between the women is a man sitting with his back to us –'

'Van Ruijven,' my father interrupted.

'Yes, van Ruijven. All that can be seen of him is his back, his hair, and one hand on the neck of a lute.'

'He plays the lute badly,' my father added eagerly.

'Very badly. That's why his back is to us – so we won't see that he can't even hold his lute properly.'

My father chuckled, his good mood restored. He was always pleased to hear that a rich man could be a poor musician.

It was not always so easy to bring him back into good humour. Sundays had become so uncomfortable with my parents that I began to welcome those times when Pieter the son ate with us. He must have noted the troubled looks my mother gave me, my father's querulous comments, the awkward silences so unexpected between parent and child. He never said anything about them, never winced or stared or became tongue-tied himself. Instead he gently teased my father, flattered my mother, smiled at me.

Pieter did not ask why I smelled of linseed oil. He did not

seem to worry about what I might be hiding. He had decided to trust me.

He was a good man.

I could not help it, though — I always looked to see if there was blood under his fingernails.

He should soak them in salted water, I thought. One day I will tell him so.

He was a good man, but he was becoming impatient. He did not say so, but sometimes on Sundays in the alley off the Rietveld Canal, I could feel the impatience in his hands. He would grip my thighs harder than he needed, press his palm into my back so that I was glued to his groin and would know its bulge, even under many layers of cloth. It was so cold that we did not touch each other's skin — only the bumps and textures of wool, the rough outlines of our limbs.

Pieter's touch did not always repel me. Sometimes, if I looked over his shoulder at the sky, and found the colours besides white in a cloud, or thought of grinding lead white or massicot, my breasts and belly tingled, and I pressed against him. He was always pleased when I responded. He did not notice that I avoided looking at his face and hands.

That Sunday of the linseed oil, when my father and mother looked so puzzled and unhappy, Pieter led me to the alley later. There he began squeezing my breasts and pulling at their nipples through the cloth of my dress. Then he stopped suddenly, gave me a sly look, and ran his hands over my shoulders and up my neck. Before I could stop him his hands were up under my cap and tangled in my hair.

I held my cap down with both hands. 'No!'

Pieter smiled at me, his eyes glazed as if he had looked too long at the sun. He had managed to pull loose a strand of my hair, and tugged it now with his fingers. 'Some day soon, Griet, I will see all of this. You will not always be a secret to me.' He let a hand drop to the lower curve of my belly and pushed against me. 'You will be eighteen next month. I'll speak to your father then.'

I stepped back from him — I felt as if I were in a hot, dark room and could not breathe. 'I am still so young. Too young for that.'

Pieter shrugged. 'Not everyone waits until they're older. And your family needs me.' It was the first time he had referred to my parents' poverty, and their dependence on him — their dependence which became my dependence as well. Because of it they were content to take the gifts of meat and have me stand in an alley with him on a Sunday.

I frowned. I did not like being reminded of his power over us.

Pieter sensed that he should not have said anything. To make amends he tucked the strand of hair back under my cap, then touched my cheek. 'I'll make you happy, Griet,' he said. 'I will.'

After he left I walked along the canal, despite the cold. The ice had been broken so that boats could get through, but a thin layer had formed again on the surface. When we were children Frans and Agnes and I would throw stones to shatter the thin ice until every sliver had disappeared under water. It seemed a long time ago.

*   *   *

A month before he had asked me to come up to the studio.

'I will be in the attic,' I announced to the room that afternoon.

Tanneke did not look up from her sewing. 'Put some more wood on the fire before you go,' she ordered.

The girls were working on their lace, overseen by Maertge and Maria Thins. Lisbeth had patience and nimble fingers, and produced good work, but Aleydis was still too young to manage the delicate weaving, and Cornelia too impatient. The cat sat at Cornelia's feet by the fire, and occasionally the girl reached down and dangled a bit of thread for the creature to paw at. Eventually, she probably hoped, the cat would tear its claws through her work and ruin it.

After feeding the fire I stepped around Johannes, who was playing with a top on the cold kitchen tiles. As I left he spun it wildly, and it hopped straight into the fire. He began to cry while Cornelia shrieked with laughter and Maertge tried to haul the toy from the flames with a pair of tongs.

'Hush, you'll wake Catharina and Franciscus,' Maria Thins warned the children. They did not hear her.

I crept out, relieved to escape the noise, no matter how cold it would be in the studio.

The studio door was shut. As I approached it I pressed my lips together, smoothed my eyebrows, and ran my fingers down the sides of my cheeks to my chin, as if I were testing an apple to see if it was firm. I hesitated in front of the heavy wooden door, then knocked softly. There was no answer, though I knew he must be there – he was expecting me.

It was the first day of the new year. He had painted the ground layer of my painting almost a month before, but

187

nothing since — no reddish marks to indicate the shapes, no false colours, no overlaid colours, no highlights. The canvas was a blank yellowish white. I saw it every morning as I cleaned.

I knocked louder.

When the door opened he was frowning, his eyes not catching mine. 'Don't knock, Griet, just come in quietly,' he said, turning away and going back to the easel, where the blank canvas sat waiting for its colours.

I closed the door softly behind me, blotting out the noise of the children downstairs, and stepped to the middle of the room. Now that the moment had come at last I was surprisingly calm. 'You wanted me, sir.'

'Yes. Stand over there.' He gestured to the corner where he had painted the other women. The table he was using for the concert painting was set there, but he had cleared away the musical instruments. He handed me a letter. 'Read that,' he said.

I unfolded the sheet of paper and bowed my head over it, worried that he would discover I was only pretending to read an unfamiliar hand.

Nothing was written on the paper.

I looked up to tell him so, but stopped. With him it was often better to say nothing. I bowed my head again over the letter.

'Try this instead,' he suggested, handing me a book. It was bound in worn leather and the spine was broken in several places. I opened it at random and studied a page. I did not recognise any of the words.

He had me sit with the book, then stand holding it while looking at him. He took away the book, handed me the white jug with the pewter top and had me pretend to pour a glass of wine. He asked me to stand and simply look out the window. All the while he seemed perplexed, as if someone had told him a story and he couldn't recall the ending.

'It is the clothes,' he murmured. 'That is the problem.'

I understood. He was having me do things a lady would do, but I was wearing a maid's clothes. I thought of the yellow mantle and the yellow and black bodice, and wondered which he would ask me to wear. Instead of being excited by the idea, though, I felt uneasy. It was not just that it would be impossible to hide from Catharina that I was wearing her clothes. I did not feel right holding books and letters, pouring myself wine, doing things I never did. As much as I wanted to feel the soft fur of the mantle around my neck, it was not what I normally wore.

'Sir,' I spoke finally, 'perhaps you should have me do other things. Things that a maid does.'

'What does a maid do?' he asked softly, folding his arms and raising his eyebrows.

I had to wait a moment before I could answer – my jaw was trembling. I thought of Pieter and me in the alley and swallowed. 'Sewing,' I replied. 'Mopping and sweeping. Carrying water. Washing sheets. Cutting bread. Polishing windowpanes.'

'You would like me to paint you with your mop?'

'It's not for me to say, sir. It is not my painting.'

He frowned. 'No, it is not yours.' He sounded as if he were speaking to himself.

'I do not want you to paint me with my mop.' I said it without knowing that I would.

189

'No. No, you're right, Griet. I would not paint you with a mop in your hand.'

'But I cannot wear your wife's clothes.'

There was a long silence. 'No, I expect not,' he said. 'But I will not paint you as a maid.'

'What, then, sir?'

'I will paint you as I first saw you, Griet. Just you.'

He set a chair near his easel, facing the middle window, and I sat down. I knew it was to be my place. He was going to find the pose he had put me in a month before, when he had decided to paint me.

'Look out the window,' he said.

I looked out at the grey winter day and, remembering when I stood in for the baker's daughter, tried not to see anything but to let my thoughts become quiet. It was hard because I was thinking of him, and of me sitting in front of him.

The New Church bell struck twice.

'Now turn your head very slowly towards me. No, not your shoulders. Keep your body turned towards the window. Move only your head. Slow, slow. Stop. A little more, so that – stop. Now sit still.'

I sat still.

At first I could not meet his eyes. When I did it was like sitting close to a fire that suddenly blazes up. Instead I studied his firm chin, his thin lips.

'Griet, you are not looking at me.'

I forced my gaze up to his eyes. Again I felt as if I were burning, but I endured it – he wanted me to.

Soon it became easier to keep my eyes on his. He looked at me as if he were not seeing me, but someone else, or something else – as if he were looking at a painting.

He is looking at the light that falls on my face, I thought, not at my face itself. That is the difference.

It was almost as if I were not there. Once I felt this I was able to relax a little. As he was not seeing me, I did not see him. My mind began to wander – over the jugged hare we had eaten for dinner, the lace collar Lisbeth had given me, a story Pieter the son had told me the day before. After that I thought of nothing. Twice he got up to change the position of one of the shutters. He went to his cupboard several times to choose different brushes and colours. I viewed his movements as if I were standing in the street, looking in through the window.

The church bell struck three times. I blinked. I had not felt so much time pass. It was as if I had fallen under a spell.

I looked at him – his eyes were with me now. He was looking at me. As we gazed at each other a ripple of heat passed through my body. I kept my eyes on his, though, until at last he looked away and cleared his throat.

'That will be all, Griet. There is some bone for you to grind upstairs.'

I nodded and slipped from the room, my heart pounding. He was painting me.

'Pull your cap back from your face,' he said one day.

'Back from my face, sir?' I repeated dumbly, and regretted it. He preferred me not to speak, but to do as he said. If I did speak, I should say something worth the words.

He did not answer. I pulled the side of my cap that was closest to him back from my cheek. The starched tip grazed my neck.

'More,' he said. 'I want to see the line of your cheek.'

I hesitated, then pulled it back further. His eyes moved down my cheek.

'Show me your ear.'

I did not want to. I had no choice.

I felt under the cap to make sure no hair was loose, tucking a few strands behind my ear. Then I pulled it back to reveal the lower part of my ear.

The look on his face was like a sigh, though he did not make a sound. I caught a noise in my own throat and pushed it down so that it would not escape.

'Your cap,' he said. 'Take it off.'

'No, sir.'

'No?'

'Please do not ask me to, sir.' I let the cloth of the cap drop so that my ear and cheek were covered again. I looked at the floor, the grey and white tiles extending away from me, clean and straight.

'You do not want to bare your head?'

'No.'

'Yet you do not want to be painted as a maid, with your mop and your cap, nor as a lady, with satin and fur and dressed hair.'

I did not answer. I could not show him my hair. I was not the sort of girl who left her head bare.

He shifted in his chair, then got up. I heard him go into the storeroom. When he returned, his arms were full of cloth, which he dropped in my lap.

'Well, Griet, see what you can do with this. Find something here to wrap your head in, so that you are neither a lady nor a maid.' I could not tell if he was angry or amused. He left the room, shutting the door behind him.

I sorted through the cloth. There were three caps, all too fine for me, and too small to cover my head fully. There were pieces of cloth, left over from dresses and jackets Catharina had made, in yellows and browns, blues and greys.

I did not know what to do. I looked around as if I would find an answer in the studio. My eyes fell on the painting of *The Procuress* – the young woman's head was bare, her hair held back with ribbons, but the old woman wore a piece of cloth wrapped around her head, crisscrossing in and out of itself. Perhaps that is what he wants, I thought. Perhaps that is what women who are neither ladies nor maids nor the other do with their hair.

I chose a piece of brown cloth and took it into the store-room, where there was a mirror. I removed my cap and wound the cloth around my head as best I could, checking the painting to try to imitate the old woman's. I looked very peculiar.

I *should* let him paint me with a mop, I thought. Pride has made me vain.

When he returned and saw what I had done, he laughed. I had not heard him laugh often – sometimes with the children, once with van Leeuwenhoek. I frowned. I did not like being laughed at.

'I have only done what you asked, sir,' I muttered.

He stopped chuckling. 'You're right, Griet. I'm sorry. And your face, now that I can see more of it, it is –' He stopped, never finishing his sentence. I always wondered what he would have said.

He turned to the pile of cloth I had left on my chair. 'Why did you choose brown,' he asked, 'when there are other colours?'

I did not want to speak of maids and ladies again. I did not want to remind him that blues and yellows were ladies' colours. 'Brown is the colour I usually wear,' I said simply.

He seemed to guess what I was thinking. 'Tanneke wore blue and yellow when I painted her some years ago,' he countered.

'I am not Tanneke, sir.'

'No, that you certainly are not.' He pulled out a long, narrow band of blue cloth. 'None the less, I want you to try this.'

I studied it. 'That is not enough cloth to cover my head.'

'Use this as well, then.' He picked up a piece of yellow cloth that had a border of the same blue and held it out to me.

Reluctantly I took the two pieces of cloth back to the storeroom and tried again in front of the mirror. I tied the blue cloth over my forehead, with the yellow piece wound round and round, covering the crown of my head. I tucked the end into a fold at the side of my head, adjusted folds here and there, smoothed the blue cloth round my head, and stepped back into the studio.

He was looking at a book and did not notice as I slipped into my chair. I arranged myself as I had been sitting before. As I turned my head to look over my left shoulder, he glanced up. At the same time the end of the yellow cloth came loose and fell over my shoulder.

'Oh,' I breathed, afraid that the cloth would fall from my head and reveal all my hair. But it held — only the end of the yellow cloth dangled free. My hair remained hidden.

'Yes,' he said then. 'That is it, Griet. Yes.'

*   *   *

He would not let me see the painting. He set it on a second easel, angled away from the door, and told me not to look at it. I promised not to, but some nights I lay in bed and thought about wrapping my blanket around me and stealing downstairs to see it. He would never know.

But he would guess. I did not think I could sit with him looking at me day after day without guessing that I had looked at the painting. I could not hide things from him. I did not want to.

I was reluctant, too, to discover how it was that he saw me. It was better to leave that a mystery.

The colours he asked me to mix gave no clues as to what he was doing. Black, ochre, lead white, lead-tin yellow, ultramarine, red lake — they were all colours I had worked with before, and they could as easily have been used for the concert painting.

It was unusual for him to work on two paintings at once. Although he did not like switching back and forth between the two, it did make it easier to hide from others that he was painting me. A few people knew. Van Ruijven knew — I was sure it was at his request that my master was making the painting. My master must have agreed to paint me alone so that he would not have to paint me with van Ruijven. Van Ruijven would own the painting of me.

I was not pleased by this thought. Nor, I believed, was my master.

Maria Thins knew about the painting as well. It was she who probably made the arrangement with van Ruijven. And besides, she could still go in and out of the studio as she liked, and could look at the painting, as I was not allowed to. Sometimes she looked at me sideways with a curious expression she could not hide.

I suspected Cornelia knew about the painting. I caught her one day where she should not be, on the stairs leading to the studio. She would not say why she was there when I asked her, and I let her go rather than bring her to Maria Thins or Catharina. I did not dare stir things up, not while he was painting me.

Van Leeuwenhoek knew about the painting. One day he brought his camera obscura and set it up so they could look at me. He did not seem surprised to see me sitting in my chair — my master must have warned him. He did glance at my unusual head cloth, but did not comment.

They took turns using the camera. I had learned to sit without moving or thinking, and without being distracted by his gaze. It was harder, though, with the black box pointed at me. With no eyes, no face, no body turned towards me, only a box and a black robe covering a humped back, I became uneasy. I could no longer be sure of how they were looking at me.

I could not deny, however, that it was exciting to be studied so intently by two gentlemen, even if I could not see their faces.

My master left the room to find a soft cloth to polish the lens. Van Leeuwenhoek waited until his tread could be heard on the stairs, then said softly, 'You watch out for yourself, my dear.'

'What do you mean, sir?'

'You must know that he's painting you to satisfy van Ruijven. Van Ruijven's interest in you has made your master protective of you.'

I nodded, secretly pleased to hear what I had suspected.

'Do not get caught in their battle. You could be hurt.'

I was still holding the position I had assumed for the painting. Now my shoulders twitched of their own accord, as if I were shaking off a shawl. 'I do not think he would ever hurt me, sir.'

'Tell me, my dear, how much do you know of men?'

I blushed deeply and turned my head away. I was thinking of being in the alley with Pieter the son.

'You see, competition makes men possessive. He is interested in you in part because van Ruijven is.'

I did not answer.

'He is an exceptional man,' van Leeuwenhoek continued. 'His eyes are worth a room full of gold. But sometimes he sees the world only as he wants it to be, not as it is. He does not understand the consequences for others of his point of view. He thinks only of himself and his work, not of you. You must take care then —' He stopped. My master's footsteps were on the stairs.

'Take care to do what, sir?' I whispered.

'Take care to remain yourself.'

I lifted my chin to him. 'To remain a maid, sir?'

'That is not what I mean. The women in his paintings — he traps them in his world. You can get lost there.'

My master came into the room. 'Griet, you have moved,' he said.

'I am sorry, sir.' I took up my position once more.

Catharina was six months pregnant when he began the painting of me. She was large already, and moved slowly, leaning against walls, grabbing the backs of chairs, sinking heavily into one with a sigh. I was surprised by how hard she made carrying a child seem, given that she had done so several times already. Although she did not complain aloud, once she was big she made every movement seem like a punishment she was being forced to bear. I had not noticed this when she was carrying Franciscus, when I was new to the house and could barely see beyond the pile of laundry waiting for me each morning.

As she grew heavier Catharina became more and more absorbed in herself. She still looked after the children, with Maertge's help. She still concerned herself with the house-keeping, and gave Tanneke and me orders. She still shopped for the house with Maria Thins. But part of her was else-where, with the baby inside. Her harsh manner was rare now, and less deliberate. She slowed down, and though she was clumsy she broke fewer things.

I worried about her discovering the painting of me. Luck-ily the stairs to the studio were becoming awkward for her to climb, so that she was unlikely to fling open the studio door and discover me in my chair, him at his easel. And because it was winter she preferred to sit by the fire with the children and Tanneke and Maria Thins, or doze under a mound of blankets and furs.

The real danger was that she would find out from van Ruijven. Of the people who knew of the painting, he was the worst at keeping a secret. He came to the house regularly to sit for the concert painting. Maria Thins no longer sent me on errands or told me to make myself scarce when he came. It would have been impractical – there were only so many errands I could run. And she must have thought he would be satisfied with the promise of a painting, and would leave me alone.

He did not. Sometimes he sought me out, while I was washing or ironing clothes in the washing kitchen, or working with Tanneke in the cooking kitchen. It was not so bad when others were around – when Maertge was with me, or Tanneke, or even Aleydis, he simply called out, 'Hello, my girl,' in his honeyed voice and left me in peace. If I was alone, however, as I often was in the courtyard, hanging up laundry so it could catch a few minutes of pale winter sunlight, he would step into the enclosed space, and behind a sheet I had just hung, or one of my master's shirts, he would touch me. I pushed him away as politely as a maid can a gentleman. None the less he managed to become familiar with the shape of my breasts and thighs under my clothes. He said things to me that I tried to forget, words I would never repeat to anyone else.

Van Ruijven always visited Catharina for a few minutes after sitting in the studio, his daughter and sister waiting patiently for him to finish gossiping and flirting. Although Maria Thins had told him not to say anything to Catharina about the painting, he was not a man to keep secrets quietly. He was very pleased that he was to have the painting of me, and he sometimes dropped hints about it to Catharina.

One day as I was mopping the hallway I overheard him say to her, 'Who would you have your husband paint, if he could paint anyone in the world?'

'Oh, I don't think about such things,' she laughed in reply. 'He paints what he paints.'

'I don't know about that.' Van Ruijven worked so hard to sound sly that even Catharina could not miss the hint.

'What do you mean?' she demanded.

'Nothing, nothing. But you should ask him for a painting. He might not say no. He could paint one of the children – Maertge, perhaps. Or your own lovely self.'

Catharina was silent. From the way van Ruijven quickly changed the subject he must have realised he had said something that upset her.

Another time when she asked if he enjoyed sitting for the painting he replied, 'Not as much as I would if I had a pretty girl to sit with me. But soon enough I'll have her anyway, and that will have to do, for now.'

Catharina let this remark pass, as she would not have done a few months before. But then, perhaps it did not sound so suspicious to her since she knew nothing of the painting. I was horrified, though, and repeated his words to Maria Thins.

'Have you been listening behind doors, girl?' the old woman asked.

'I –' I could not deny it.

Maria Thins smiled sourly. 'It's about time I caught you doing things maids are meant to do. Next you'll be stealing silver spoons.'

I flinched. It was a harsh thing to say, especially after all the trouble with Cornelia and the combs. I had no choice, though – I owed Maria Thins a great deal. She must be allowed her cruel words.

'But you're right, van Ruijven's mouth is looser than a whore's purse,' she continued. 'I will speak to him again.'

Saying something to him, however, was of little use – it seemed to spur him on even more to make suggestions to Catharina. Maria Thins took to being in the room with her daughter when he visited so that she could try to rein in his tongue.

I did not know what Catharina would do when she discovered the painting of me. And she would, one day — if not in the house, then at van Ruijven's, where she would be dining and look up and see me staring at her from a wall.

He did not work on the painting of me every day. He had the concert to paint as well, with or without van Ruijven and his women. He painted around them when they were not there, or asked me to take the place of one of the women — the girl sitting at the harpsichord, the woman standing next to it singing from a sheet of paper. I did not wear their clothes. He simply wanted a body there. Sometimes the two women came without van Ruijven, and that was when he worked best. Van Ruijven himself was a difficult model. I could hear him when I was working in the attic. He could not sit still, and wanted to talk and play his lute. My master was patient with him, as he would be with a child, but sometimes I could hear a tone creep into his voice and knew that he would go out that night to the tavern, returning with eyes like glittering spoons.

I sat for him for the other painting three or four times a week, for an hour or two each time. It was the part of the week I liked best, with his eyes on only me for those hours. I did not mind that it was not an easy pose to hold, that looking sideways for long periods of time gave me headaches. I did not mind when sometimes he had me move my head again and again so that the yellow cloth swung around, so that he could paint me looking as if I had just turned to face him. I did whatever he asked of me.

He was not happy, though. February passed and March arrived, with its days of ice and sun, and he was not happy. He had been working on the painting for almost two months, and though I had not seen it, I thought it must be close to done. He was no longer having me mix quantities of colour for it, but used tiny amounts and made few movements with his brushes as I sat. I had thought I understood how he wanted me to be, but now I was not sure. Sometimes he simply sat and looked at me as if he were waiting for me to do something. Then he was not like a painter, but like a man, and it was hard to look at him.

One day he announced suddenly, as I was sitting in my chair, 'This will satisfy van Ruijven, but not me.'

I did not know what to say. I could not help him if I had not seen the painting. 'May I look at the painting, sir?'

He gazed at me curiously.

'Perhaps I can help,' I added, then wished I had not. I was afraid I had become too bold.

'All right,' he said after a moment.

I got up and stood behind him. He did not turn round, but sat very still. I could hear him breathing slowly and steadily.

The painting was like none of his others. It was just of me, of my head and shoulders, with no tables or curtains, no windows or powderbrushes to soften and distract. He had painted me with my eyes wide, the light falling across my face but the left side of me in shadow. I was wearing blue and yellow and brown. The cloth wound round my head made me look not like myself, but like Griet from another town, even from another country altogether. The background was black, making me appear very much alone, although I was clearly looking at someone. I seemed to be waiting for something I did not think would ever happen.

He was right – the painting might satisfy van Ruijven, but something was missing from it.

I knew before he did. When I saw what was needed – that point of brightness he had used to catch the eye in other paintings – I shivered. This will be the end, I thought.

I was right.

This time I did not try to help him as I had with the painting of van Ruijven's wife writing a letter. I did not creep into the studio and change things – reposition the chair I sat in or open the shutters wider. I did not wrap the blue and yellow cloth differently or hide the top of my chemise. I did not bite my lips to make them redder, or suck in my cheeks. I did not set out colours I thought he might use.

I simply sat for him, and ground and washed the colours he asked for.

He would find it for himself anyway.

It took longer than I had expected. I sat for him twice more before he discovered what was missing. Each time I sat he painted with a dissatisfied look on his face, and dis- missed me early.

I waited.

Catharina herself gave him the answer. One afternoon Maertge and I were polishing shoes in the washing kitchen while the other girls had gathered in the great hall to watch their mother dress for a birth feast. I heard Aleydis and

Lisbeth squeal, and knew Catharina had brought out her pearls, which the girls loved.

Then I heard his tread in the hallway, silence, then low voices. After a moment he called out, 'Griet, bring my wife a glass of wine.'

I set the white jug and two glasses on a tray, in case he chose to join her, and took them to the great hall. As I entered I bumped against Cornelia, who had been standing in the doorway. I managed to catch the jug, and the glasses clattered against my chest without breaking. Cornelia smirked and stepped out of my way.

Catharina was sitting at the table with her powderbrush and jar, her combs and jewellery box. She was wearing her pearls and her green silk dress, altered to cover her belly. I placed a glass near her and poured.

'Would you like some wine too, sir?' I asked, glancing up. He was leaning against the cupboard that surrounded the bed, pressed against the silk curtains, which I noticed for the first time were made of the same cloth as Catharina's dress. He looked back and forth between Catharina and me. On his face was his painter's look.

'Silly girl, you've spilled wine on me!' Catharina pushed away from the table and brushed at her belly with her hand. A few drops of red had splashed there.

'I'm sorry, madam. I'll get a damp cloth to sponge it.'

'Oh, never mind. I can't bear to have you fussing about me. Just go.'

I stole a look at him as I picked up the tray. His eyes were fixed on his wife's pearl earring. As she turned her head to brush more powder on her face the earring swung back and forth, caught in the light from the front windows.

It made us all look at her face, and reflected light as her eyes did.

'I must go upstairs for a moment,' he said to Catharina. 'I won't be long.'

That is it, then, I thought. He has his answer.

When he asked me to come to the studio the next afternoon, I did not feel excited as I usually did when I knew I was to sit for him. For the first time I dreaded it. That morning the clothes I washed felt particularly heavy and sodden, and my hands not strong enough to wring them well. I moved slowly between the kitchen and the courtyard, and sat down to rest more than once. Maria Thins caught me sitting when she came in for a copper pancake pan. 'What's the matter, girl? Are you ill?' she asked.

I jumped up. 'No, madam. Just a little tired.'

'Tired, eh? That's no way for a maid to be, especially not in the morning.' She looked as if she did not believe me.

I plunged my hands into the cooling water and pulled out one of Catharina's chemises. 'Are there any errands you would like me to run this afternoon, madam?'

'Errands? This afternoon? I don't think so. That's a funny thing to ask if you're feeling tired.' She narrowed her eyes. 'You aren't in trouble, are you, girl? Van Ruijven didn't catch you alone, did he?'

'No, madam.' In fact he had, just two days before, but I had managed to pull away from him.

'Has someone discovered you upstairs?' Maria Thins asked in a low voice, jerking her head up to indicate the studio.

'No, madam.' For a moment I was tempted to tell her about the earring. Instead I said, 'I ate something that did not agree with me, that is all.'

Maria Thins shrugged and turned away. She still did not believe me, but had decided it did not matter.

That afternoon I plodded up the stairs, and paused before the studio door. This would not be like other times when I sat for him. He was going to ask me for something, and I was beholden to him.

I pushed open the door. He sat at his easel, studying the tip of one of his brushes. When he looked up at me I saw something I had never before seen in his face. He was nervous.

That was what gave me the courage to say what I said. I went to stand by my chair and placed my hand on one of the lion heads. 'Sir,' I began, gripping the hard, cool carving, 'I cannot do it.'

'Do what, Griet?' He was genuinely surprised.

'What you are going to ask me to do. I cannot wear it. Maids do not wear pearls.'

He stared at me for a long moment, then shook his head a few times. 'How unexpected you are. You always surprise me.'

I ran my fingers around the lion's nose and mouth and up its muzzle to its mane, smooth and knobbled. His eyes followed my fingers.

'You know,' he murmured, 'that the painting needs it, the light that the pearl reflects. It won't be complete otherwise.'

I did know. I had not looked at the painting long – it was too strange seeing myself – but I had known immediately that it needed the pearl earring. Without it there were only my eyes, my mouth, the band of my chemise, the dark space behind my ear, all separate. The earring would bring them together. It would complete the painting.

It would also put me on the street. I knew that he would not borrow an earring from van Ruijven or van Leeuwenhoek or anyone else. He had seen Catharina's pearl and that was what he would make me wear. He used what he wanted for his paintings, without considering the result. It was as van Leeuwenhoek had warned me.

When Catharina saw her earring in the painting she would explode.

I should have begged him not to ruin me.

'You are painting it for van Ruijven,' I argued instead, 'not for yourself. Does it matter so much? You said yourself that he would be satisfied with it.'

His face hardened and I knew I had said the wrong thing.

'I would never stop working on a painting if I knew it was not complete, no matter who was to get it,' he muttered. 'That is not how I work.'

'No, sir.' I swallowed and gazed at the tiled floor. Stupid girl, I thought, my jaw tightening.

'Go and prepare yourself.'

Bowing my head, I hurried to the storeroom where I kept the blue and yellow cloths. I had never felt his disapproval so strongly. I did not think I could bear it. I removed my cap and, feeling the ribbon that tied up my hair was coming undone, I pulled it off. I was reaching back to gather up my hair again when I heard one of the loose floor tiles in the studio clink. I froze. He had never come into the storeroom while I was changing. He had never asked that of me.

I turned round, my hands still in my hair. He stood on the threshold, gazing at me.

I lowered my hands. My hair fell in waves over my shoulders, brown like fields in the autumn. No one ever saw it but me.

'Your hair,' he said. He was no longer angry.

At last he let me go with his eyes.

Now that he had seen my hair, now that he had seen me revealed, I no longer felt I had something precious to hide and keep to myself. I could be freer, if not with him, then with someone else. It no longer mattered what I did and did not do.

That evening I slipped from the house and found Pieter the son at one of the taverns where the butchers drank, near the Meat Hall. Ignoring the whistles and remarks, I went up to him and asked him to come with me. He set down his beer, his eyes wide, and followed me outside, where I took his hand and led him to a nearby alley. There I pulled up my skirt and let him do as he liked. Clasping my hands around his neck, I held on while he found his way into me and began to push rhythmically. He gave me pain, but when I remembered my hair loose around my shoulders in the studio, I felt something like pleasure too.

Afterwards, back at Papists' Corner, I washed myself with vinegar.

When I next looked at the painting he had added a wisp of hair peeking out from the blue cloth above my left eye.

The next time I sat for him he did not mention the earring. He did not hand it to me, as I had feared, or change how I sat, or stop painting.

He did not come into the storeroom again to see my hair either.

He sat for a long time, mixing colours on his palette with his palette knife. There was red and ochre there, but the paint he was mixing was mostly white, to which he added daubs of black, working them together slowly and carefully, the silver diamond of the knife flashing in the grey paint.

'Sir?' I began.

He looked up at me, his knife stilled.

'I have seen you paint sometimes without the model being here. Could you not paint the earring without me wearing it?'

The palette knife remained still. 'You would like me to imagine you wearing the pearl, and paint what I imagine?'

'Yes, sir.'

He looked down at the paint, the palette knife moving again. I think he smiled a little. 'I want to see you wear the earring.'

'But you know what will happen then, sir.'

'I know the painting will be complete.'

You will ruin me, I thought. Again I could not bring myself to say it. 'What will your wife say when she sees the finished painting?' I asked instead, as boldly as I dared.

'She will not see it. I will give it directly to van Ruijven.' It was the first time he had admitted he was painting me secretly, that Catharina would disapprove.

'You need only wear it once,' he added, as if to placate me. 'The next time I paint you I will bring it. Next week. Catharina will not miss it for an afternoon.'

'But, sir,' I said, 'my ear is not pierced.'

He frowned slightly. 'Well, then, you will need to take care of that.' This was clearly a woman's detail, not something he felt he need concern himself with. He tapped the knife and wiped it with a rag. 'Now, let us begin. Chin down a bit.' He gazed at me. 'Lick your lips, Griet.'

I licked my lips.

'Leave your mouth open.'

I was so surprised by this request that my mouth remained open of its own will. I blinked back tears. Virtuous women did not open their mouths in paintings.

It was as if he had been in the alley with Pieter and me. You have ruined me, I thought. I licked my lips again.

'Good,' he said.

I did not want to do it to myself. I was not afraid of pain, but I did not want to take a needle to my own ear.

If I could have chosen someone to do it for me, it would have been my mother. But she would never have understood, nor agreed to it without knowing why. And if she had been told why, she would have been horrified.

I could not ask Tanneke, or Maertge.

I considered asking Maria Thins. She may not yet have known about the earring, but she would find out soon enough. I could not bring myself to ask her, though, to have her take part in my humiliation.

The only person who might do it and understand was Frans. I slipped out the next afternoon, carrying a needlecase Maria Thins had given me. The woman with the sour face at the factory gate smirked when I asked to see him.

'He's long gone and good riddance,' she answered, relishing the words.

'Gone? Gone where?'

The woman shrugged. 'Towards Rotterdam, they say. And then, who knows? Perhaps he'll make his fortune on the seas, if he doesn't die between the legs of some Rotterdam whore.' These last bitter words made me look at her more closely. She was with child.

Cornelia had not known when she broke the tile of Frans and me that she would come to be right — that he would split from me and from the family. Will I ever see him again? I thought. And what will our parents say? I felt more alone than ever.

The next day I stopped at the apothecary's on my way back from the fish stalls. The apothecary knew me now, even greeting me by name. 'And what is it that he wants today?' he asked. 'Canvas? Vermilion? Ochre? Linseed oil?'

'He does not need anything,' I answered nervously. 'Nor my mistress. I have come —' For a moment I considered asking him to pierce my ear. He seemed a discreet man, who might do it without telling anyone or demanding to know why.

I could not ask a stranger such a thing. 'I need something to numb the skin,' I said.

'Numb the skin?'

'Yes. As ice does.'

'Why do you want to numb the skin?'

I shrugged and did not answer, studying the bottles on the shelves behind him.

'Clove oil,' he said at last with a sigh. He reached behind him for a flask. 'Rub a little on the spot and leave it for a few minutes. It doesn't last long, though.'

'I would like some, please.'

'And who is to pay for this? Your master? It is very dear, you know. It comes from far away.' In his voice was a mixture of disapproval and curiosity.

'I will pay. I only want a little.' I removed a pouch from my apron and counted the precious stuivers on to the table. A tiny bottle of it cost me two days' wages. I had borrowed some money from Tanneke, promising to repay her when I was paid on Sunday.

When I handed over my reduced wages to my mother that Sunday I told her I had broken a hand mirror and had to pay for it.

'It will cost more than two days' wages to replace that,' she scolded. 'What were you doing, looking at yourself in a mirror? How careless.'

'Yes,' I agreed. 'I have been very careless.'

I waited until late, when I was sure everyone in the house was asleep. Although usually no one came up to the studio after it was locked for the night, I was still fearful of someone catching me, with my needle and mirror and clove oil. I stood by the locked studio door, listening. I could hear Catharina pacing up and down the hallway below. She was having a hard time sleeping now — her body had become too cumbersome to find a position she could lie in comfortably. Then I heard a child's voice, a girl's, trying to speak low but unable to hide its bright ring. Cornelia was with her mother. I could not hear what they said, and because I was locked into the studio, I could not creep to the top of the stairs to listen more closely.

Maria Thins was also moving about in her rooms next

to the storeroom. It was a restless house, and it made me restless too. I made myself sit in my lion-head chair to wait. I was not sleepy. I had never felt so awake.

Finally Catharina and Cornelia went back to bed, and Maria Thins stopped rustling next door. As the house grew still, I remained in my chair. It was easier to sit there than do what I had to do. When I could not delay any longer, I got up and first peeked at the painting. All I could really see now was the great hole where the earring should go, which I would have to fill.

I took up my candle, found the mirror in the storeroom, and climbed to the attic. I propped the mirror against the wall on the grinding table and set the candle next to it. I got out my needlecase and, choosing the thinnest needle, set the tip in the flame of the candle. Then I opened the bottle of clove oil, expecting it to smell foul, of mould or rotting leaves, as remedies often do. Instead it was sweet and strange, like honeycakes left out in the sun. It was from far away, from places Frans might get to on his ships. I shook a few drops on to a rag, and swabbed my left earlobe. The apothecary was right — when I touched the lobe a few minutes later it felt as if I had been out in the cold without wrapping a shawl around my ears.

I took the needle out of the flame and let the glowing red tip change to dull orange and then to black. When I leaned towards the mirror I gazed at myself for a moment. My eyes were full of liquid in the candlelight, glittering with fear.

Do this quickly, I thought. It will not help to delay.

I pulled the earlobe taut and in one movement pushed the needle through my flesh.

Just before I fainted I thought, I have always wanted to wear pearls.

Every night I swabbed my ear and pushed a slightly larger needle through the hole to keep it open. It did not hurt too much until the lobe became infected and began to swell. Then no matter how much clove oil I dabbed on the ear, my eyes streamed with tears when I drove the needle through. I did not know how I would manage to wear the earring without fainting again.

I was grateful that I wore my cap over my ears so that no one saw the swollen red lobe. It throbbed as I bent over the steaming laundry, as I ground colours, as I sat in church with Pieter and my parents.

It throbbed when van Ruijven caught me hanging up sheets in the courtyard one morning and tried to pull my chemise down over my shoulders and expose my bosom.

'You shouldn't fight me, my girl,' he murmured as I backed away from him. 'You'll enjoy it more if you don't fight. And you know, I will have you anyway when I get that painting.' He pushed me against the wall and lowered his lips to my chest, pulling at my breasts to free them from the dress.

'Tanneke!' I called desperately, hoping in vain that she had returned early from an errand to the baker's.

'What are you doing?'

Cornelia was watching us from the doorway. I had never expected to be glad to see her.

Van Ruijven raised his head and stepped back. 'We're playing a game, dear girl,' he replied, smiling. 'Just a little game. You'll play it too when you're older.' He straightened his cloak and stepped past her into the house.

I could not meet Cornelia's eye. I tucked in my chemise and smoothed my dress with shaking hands. When finally I looked up she was gone.

The morning of my eighteenth birthday I got up and cleaned the studio as usual. The concert painting was done – in a few days van Ruijven would come to view it and take it away. Although I did not need to now, I still cleaned the studio scene carefully, dusting the harpsichord, the violin, the bass viol, brushing the table-rug with a damp cloth, polishing the chairs, mopping the grey and white floor tiles.

I did not like the painting as much as his others. Although it was meant to be more valuable with three figures in it, I preferred the pictures he had painted of women alone – they were purer, less complicated. I found I did not want to look at the concert for long, or try to understand what the people in it were thinking.

I wondered what he would paint next.

Downstairs I set water on the fire to heat and asked Tanneke what she wanted from the butcher. She was sweeping the steps and tiles in front of the house. 'A rack of beef,' she replied, leaning against her broom. 'Why not have something nice?' She rubbed her lower back and groaned. 'It may take my mind off my aches.'

'Is it your back again?' I tried to sound sympathetic, but Tanneke's back always hurt. A maid's back would always hurt. That was a maid's life.

Maertge came with me to the Meat Hall, and I was glad

of it – since that night in the alley I was embarrassed to be alone with Pieter the son. I was not sure how he would treat me. If I was with Maertge, however, he would have to be careful of what he said or did.

Pieter the son was not there – only his father, who grinned at me. 'Ah, the birthday maid!' he cried. 'An important day for you. '

Maertge looked at me in surprise. I had not mentioned my birthday to the family – there was no reason to.

'There's nothing important about it,' I snapped.

'That's not what my son said. He's off now, on an errand. Someone to see.' Pieter the father winked at me. My blood chilled. He was saying something without saying it, something I was meant to understand.

'Your finest rack of beef,' I ordered, deciding to ignore him.

'In celebration, then?' Pieter the father never let things drop, but pushed them as far as he could.

I did not reply. I simply waited until he served me, then put the beef in my pail and turned away.

'Is it really your birthday, Griet?' Maertge whispered as we left the Meat Hall.

'Yes.'

'How old are you?'

'Eighteen.'

'Why is eighteen so important?'

'It's not. You mustn't listen to what he says – he's a silly man.'

Maertge didn't look convinced. Nor was I. His words had tugged at something in my mind.

I worked all morning rinsing and boiling laundry. My

mind turned to many things while I sat over the tub of steaming water. I wondered where Frans was, and if my parents had heard yet that he had left Delft. I wondered what Pieter the father had meant earlier, and where Pieter the son was. I thought of the night in the alley. I thought of the painting of me, and wondered when it would be done and what would happen to me then. All the while my ear throbbed, stabbing with pain whenever I moved my head.

It was Maria Thins who came to get me.

'Leave your washing, girl,' I heard her say behind me. 'He wants you upstairs.' She was standing in the doorway, shaking something in her hand.

I got up in confusion. 'Now, madam?'

'Yes, now. Don't be coy with me, girl. You know why. Catharina has gone out this morning, and she doesn't do that much these days now her time is closer. Hold out your hand.'

I dried a hand on my apron and held it out. Maria Thins dropped a pair of pearl earrings into my palm.

'Take them up with you now. Quickly.'

I could not move. I was holding two pearls the size of hazelnuts, shaped like drops of water. They were silvery grey, even in the sunlight, except for a dot of fierce white light. I had touched pearls before, when I brought them upstairs for van Ruijven's wife and tied them round her neck or laid them on the table. But I had never held them for myself before.

'Go on, girl,' Maria Thins growled impatiently. 'Catharina may come back sooner than she said.'

I stumbled into the hallway, leaving the laundry un-wrung. I climbed the stairs in full view of Tanneke, who was bringing in water from the canal, and Aleydis and Cornelia, who were rolling marbles in the hallway. They all looked up at me.

'Where are you going?' Aleydis asked, her grey eyes bright with interest.

'To the attic,' I replied softly.

'Can we come with you?' Cornelia said in a taunting voice.

'No.'

'Girls, you're blocking my way.' Tanneke pushed past them, her face dark.

The studio door was ajar. I stepped inside, pressing my lips together, my stomach twisting. I closed the door behind me.

He was waiting for me. I held my hand out to him and dropped the earrings into his palm.

He smiled at me. 'Go and wrap up your hair.'

I changed in the storeroom. He did not come to look at my hair. As I returned I glanced at *The Procuress* on the wall. The man was smiling at the young woman as if he were squeezing pears in the market to see if they were ripe. I shivered.

He was holding up an earring by its wire. It caught the light from the window, capturing it in a tiny panel of bright white.

'Here you are, Griet.' He held out the pearl to me.

'Griet! Griet! Someone is here to see you!' Maertge called from the bottom of the stairs.

I stepped to the window. He came to my side and we looked out.

Pieter the son was standing in the street below, arms crossed. He glanced up and saw us standing together at the window. 'Come down, Griet,' he called. 'I want to speak to you.' He looked as if he would never move from his spot.

I stepped back from the window. 'I'm sorry, sir,' I said in a low voice. 'I won't be long.' I hurried to the storeroom, pulled off the head cloths and changed into my cap. He was still standing at the window, his back to me, as I passed through the studio.

The girls were sitting in a row on the bench, staring openly at Pieter, who stared back at them.

'Let's go around the corner,' I whispered, moving towards the Molenpoort. Pieter did not follow, but continued to stand with his arms crossed.

'What were you wearing up there?' he asked. 'On your head.'

I stopped and turned back. 'My cap.'

'No, it was blue and yellow.'

Five sets of eyes watched us – the girls on the bench, him at the window. Then Tanneke appeared in the doorway, and that made six.

'Please, Pieter,' I hissed. 'Let's go along a little way.'

'What I have to say can be said in front of anyone. I have nothing to hide.' He tossed his head, his blond curls falling around his ears.

I could see he would not be silenced. He would say what I dreaded he would say in front of them all.

Pieter did not raise his voice, but we all heard his words. 'I've spoken to your father this morning, and he has agreed that we may marry now you are eighteen. You can leave here and come to me. Today.'

I felt my face go hot, whether from anger or shame I was not sure. Everyone was waiting for me to speak.

I drew in a deep breath. 'This is not the place to talk about such things,' I replied severely. 'Not in the street like this. You were wrong to come here.' I did not wait for his response, though as I turned to go back inside he looked stricken.

'Griet!' he cried.

I pushed past Tanneke, who spoke so softly that I was not sure I heard her right. 'Whore.'

I ran up the stairs to the studio. He was still standing at the window as I shut the door. 'I am sorry, sir,' I said. 'I'll just change my cap.'

He did not turn round. 'He is still there,' he said.

When I returned, I crossed to the window, though I did not stand too close in case Pieter could see me again with my head wrapped in blue and yellow.

My master was not looking down at the street any longer, but at the New Church tower. I peeked – Pieter was gone.

I took my place in the lion-head chair and waited.

When he turned at last to face me, his eyes were masked. More than ever, I did not know what he was thinking.

'So you will leave us,' he said.

'Oh, sir, I do not know. Do not pay attention to words said in the street like that.'

'Will you marry him?'

'Please do not ask me about him.'

'No, perhaps I should not. Now, let us begin again.' He reached around to the cupboard behind him, picked up an earring, and held it out to me.

'I want you to do it.' I had not thought I could ever be so bold.

Nor had he. He raised his eyebrows and opened his mouth to speak, but did not say anything.

He stepped up to my chair. My jaw tightened but I managed to hold my head steady. He reached over and gently touched my earlobe.

I gasped as if I had been holding my breath under water.

He rubbed the swollen lobe between his thumb and finger, then pulled it taut. With his other hand he inserted the earring wire in the hole and pushed it through. A pain like fire jolted through me and brought tears to my eyes.

He did not remove his hand. His fingers brushed against my neck and along my jaw. He traced the side of my face up to my cheek, then blotted the tears that spilled from my eyes with his thumb. He ran his thumb over my lower lip. I licked it and tasted salt.

I closed my eyes then and he removed his fingers. When I opened them again he had gone back to his easel and taken up his palette.

I sat in my chair and gazed at him over my shoulder. My ear was burning, the weight of the pearl pulling at the lobe. I could not think of anything but his fingers on my neck, his thumb on my lips.

He looked at me but did not begin to paint. I wondered what he was thinking.

Finally he reached behind him again. 'You must wear the other one as well,' he declared, picking up the second earring and holding it out to me.

For a moment I could not speak. I wanted him to think of me, not of the painting.

'Why?' I finally answered. 'It can't be seen in the painting.'

'You must wear both,' he insisted. 'It is a farce to wear only one.'

'But — my other ear is not pierced,' I faltered.

'Then you must tend to it.' He continued to hold it out.

I reached over and took it. I did it for him. I got out my needle and clove oil and pierced my other ear. I did not cry, or faint, or make a sound. Then I sat all morning and he painted the earring he could see, and I felt, stinging like fire in my other ear, the pearl he could not see.

The clothes soaking in the kitchen went cold, the water grey. Tanneke clattered in the kitchen, the girls shouted outside, and we behind our closed door sat and looked at each other. And he painted.

When at last he set down his brush and palette, I did not change position, though my eyes ached from looking sideways. I did not want to move.

'It is done,' he said, his voice muffled. He turned away and began wiping his palette knife with a rag. I gazed at the knife — it had white paint on it.

'Take off the earrings and give them back to Maria Thins when you go down,' he added.

I began to cry silently. Without looking at him, I got up and went into the storeroom, where I removed the blue and yellow cloth from my head. I waited for a moment, my hair out over my shoulders, but he did not come. Now that the painting was finished he no longer wanted me.

I looked at myself in the little mirror, and then I removed the earrings. Both holes in my lobes were bleeding. I blotted them with a bit of cloth, then tied up my hair and covered it and my ears with my cap, leaving the tips to dangle below my chin.

When I came out again he was gone. He had left the studio door open for me. For a moment I thought about looking at the painting to see what he had done, to see it finished, the earring in place. I decided to wait until night, when I could study it without worrying that someone might come in.

I crossed the studio and shut the door behind me.

I always regretted that decision. I never got to have a proper look at the finished painting.

Catharina arrived back only a few minutes after I had handed the earrings to Maria Thins, who immediately replaced them in the jewellery box. I hurried to the cooking kitchen to help Tanneke with dinner. She would not look at me straight, but gave me sideways glances, occasionally shaking her head.

He was not at dinner – he had gone out. After we had cleared up I went back to the courtyard to finish rinsing the laundry. I had to haul in new water and reheat it. While I worked Catharina slept in the great hall. Maria Thins smoked and wrote letters in the Crucifixion room. Tanneke sat in the front doorway and sewed. Maertge perched on the bench and made lace. Next to her Aleydis and Lisbeth sorted their shell collection.

I did not see Cornelia.

I was hanging up an apron when I heard Maria Thins say, 'Where are you going?' It was the tone of her voice rather than what she said that made me pause in my work. She sounded anxious.

I crept inside and along the hallway. Maria Thins was at the foot of the stairs, gazing up. Tanneke had come to stand in the front doorway, as she had earlier that day, but facing in and following the look of her mistress. I heard the stairs creak, and the sound of heavy breathing. Catharina was pulling herself up the stairs.

In that moment I knew what was going to happen – to her, to him, to me.

Cornelia is there, I thought. She is leading her mother to the painting.

I could have cut short the misery of waiting. I could have left then, walked out the door with the laundry not done, and not looked back. But I could not move. I stood frozen, as Maria Thins stood frozen at the bottom of the stairs. She too knew what would happen, and she could not stop it.

I sank to the floor. Maria Thins saw me but did not speak. She continued to gaze up uncertainly. Then the noise on the stairs stopped and we heard Catharina's heavy tread over to the studio door. Maria Thins darted up the stairs. I remained on my knees, too weary to rise. Tanneke stood blocking the light from the front door. She watched me, her arms crossed, her face expressionless.

Soon after there was a shout of rage, then raised voices which were quickly lowered.

Cornelia came down the stairs. 'Mama wants Papa to come home,' she announced to Tanneke.

Tanneke stepped backwards outside and turned towards the bench. 'Maertge, go and find your father at the Guild,' she ordered. 'Quickly. Tell him it's important.'

Cornelia look around. When she saw me her face lit up. I got up from my knees and walked stiffly back to the courtyard. There was nothing I could do but hang up laundry and wait.

When he returned I thought for a moment that he might come and find me in the courtyard, hidden among the hanging sheets. He did not – I heard him on the stairs, then nothing.

I leaned against the warm brick wall and gazed up. It was a bright, cloudless day, the sky a mocking blue. It was the kind of day when children ran up and down the streets and shouted, when couples walked out through the town gates, past the windmills and along the canals, when old women sat in the sun and closed their eyes. My father was probably sitting on the bench in front of his house, his face turned towards the warmth. Tomorrow might be bitterly cold, but today it was spring.

They sent Cornelia to get me. When she appeared between the hanging clothes and looked down at me with a cruel smirk on her face, I wanted to slap her as I had that first day I had come to work at the house. I did not, though – I simply sat, hands in my lap, shoulders slumped, and watched her show off her glee. The sun caught glints of gold – traces of her mother – in her red hair.

'You are wanted upstairs,' she said in a formal voice. 'They want to see you.' She turned and skipped back into the house.

I leaned over and brushed a bit of dust from my shoe. Then I stood, straightened my skirt, smoothed my apron, pulled the tips of my cap tight, and checked for loose strands of hair. I licked my lips and pressed them together, took a deep breath and followed Cornelia.

Catharina had been crying – her nose was red, her eyes puffy. She was sitting in the chair he normally pulled up to his easel – it had been pushed towards the wall and the

225

cupboard that held his brushes and palette knife. When I appeared she heaved herself up so that she was standing, tall and broad. Although she glared at me, she did not speak. She squeezed her arms over her belly and winced.

Maria Thins was standing next to the easel, looking sober but also impatient, as if she had other, more important things to attend to.

He stood next to his wife, his face without expression, hands at his sides, eyes on the painting. He was waiting for someone, for Catharina, or Maria Thins, or me, to begin.

I came to stand just inside the door. Cornelia hovered behind me. I could not see the painting from where I stood.

It was Maria Thins who finally spoke.

'Well, girl, my daughter wants to know how you came to be wearing her earrings.' She said it as if she did not expect me to answer.

I studied her old face. She was not going to admit to helping me get the earrings. Nor would he, I knew. I did not know what to say. So I did not say anything.

'Did you steal the key to my jewellery box and take my earrings?' Catharina spoke as if she were trying to convince herself of what she said. Her voice was shaky.

'No, madam.' Although I knew it would be easier for everyone if I said I had stolen them, I could not lie about myself.

'Don't lie to me. Maids steal all the time. You took my earrings!'

'Are they missing now, madam?'

For a moment Catharina looked confused, as much by my asking a question as by the question itself. She had obviously not checked her jewellery box since seeing the painting. She had no idea if the earrings were gone or not. But she did not like me asking the questions. 'Quiet, thief. They'll throw you in prison,' she hissed, 'and you won't see sunlight for years.' She winced again. Something was wrong with her.

'But, madam —'

'Catharina, you must not get yourself into a state,' he interrupted me. 'Van Ruijven will take the painting away as soon as it is dry and you can put it from your mind.'

He did not want me to speak either. It seemed no one did. I wondered why they had asked me upstairs at all when they were so afraid of what I might say.

I might say, 'What about the way he looked at me for so many hours while he painted this painting?'

I might say, 'What about your mother and your husband, who have gone behind your back and deceived you?'

Or I might simply say, 'Your husband touched me, here, in this room.'

They did not know what I might say.

Catharina was no fool. She knew the real matter was not the earrings. She wanted them to be, she tried to make them be so, but she could not help herself. She turned to her husband. 'Why,' she asked, 'have you never painted me?'

As they gazed at each other it struck me that she was taller than he, and, in a way, more solid.

'You and the children are not a part of this world,' he said. 'You are not meant to be.'

'And she is?' Catharina cried shrilly, jerking her head at me.

He did not answer. I wished that Maria Thins and Cornelia and I were in the kitchen or the Crucifixion room, or out in the market. It was an affair for a man and his wife to discuss alone.

'And with *my* earrings?'

Again he was silent, which stirred Catharina even more than his words had. She began to shake her head so that her blonde curls bounced around her ears. 'I will not have this in my own house,' she declared. 'I will not have it!' She looked around wildly. When her eyes fell on the palette knife a shiver ran through me. I took a step forward at the same time as she moved to the cupboard and grabbed the knife. I stopped, unsure of what she would do next.

He knew, though. He knew his own wife. He moved with Catharina as she stepped up to the painting. She was quick but he was quicker — he caught her by the wrist as she plunged the diamond blade of the knife towards the painting. He stopped it just before the blade touched my eye. From where I stood I could see the wide eye, a flicker of earring he had just added, and the winking of the blade as it hovered before the painting. Catharina struggled but he held her wrist firmly, waiting for her to drop the knife. Suddenly she groaned. Flinging the knife away, she clutched her belly. The knife skidded across the tiles to my feet, then spun and spun, slower and slower, as we all stared at it. It came to a stop with the blade pointed at me.

I was meant to pick it up. That was what maids were meant to do — pick up their master's and mistress' things and put them back in their place.

I looked up and met his eye, holding his grey gaze for a long moment. I knew it was for the last time. I did not look at anyone else.

In his eyes I thought I could see regret.

I did not pick up the knife. I turned and walked from the room, down the stairs and through the doorway, pushing aside Tanneke. When I reached the street I did not look back at the children I knew must be sitting on the bench, nor at Tanneke, who would be frowning because I had pushed her, nor up at the windows, where he might be standing. I got to the street and I began to run. I ran down the Oude Langendijck and across the bridge into Market Square.

Only thieves and children run.

I reached the centre of the square and stopped in the circle of tiles with the eight-pointed star in the middle. Each point indicated a direction I could take.

I could go back to my parents.

I could find Pieter at the Meat Hall and agree to marry him.

I could go to van Ruijven's house – he would take me in with a smile.

I could go to van Leeuwenhoek and ask him to take pity on me.

I could go to Rotterdam and search for Frans.

I could go off on my own somewhere far away.

I could go back to Papists' Corner.

I could go into the New Church and pray to God for guidance.

I stood in the circle, turning round and round as I thought.

When I made my choice, the choice I knew I had to make, I set my feet carefully along the edge of the point and went the way it told me, walking steadily.

1676

When I looked up and saw her I almost dropped my knife. I had not set eyes on her in ten years. She looked almost the same, though she had grown a little broader, and as well as the old pockmarks, her face now carried scars up one side — Maertge, who still came to see me from time to time, had told me of the accident, the mutton joint that spat hot oil.

She had never been good at roasting meat.

She was standing far enough away that it was not clear she had indeed come to see me. I knew, though, that this could be no chance. For ten years she had managed to avoid me in what was not a big town. I had not once run into her in the market or the Meat Hall, or along any of the main canals. But then, I did not walk along the Oude Langendijck.

She approached the stall reluctantly. I set down my knife and wiped my bloody hands on my apron. 'Hello, Tanneke,' I said calmly, as if I had seen her only a few days before. 'How have you been keeping?'

'Mistress wants to see you,' Tanneke said bluntly, frowning. 'You're to come to the house this afternoon.'

It had been many years since someone had ordered me about in that tone. Customers asked for things, but that was different. I could refuse them if I didn't like what I heard.

'How is Maria Thins?' I asked, trying to remain polite. 'And how is Catharina?'

'As well as can be expected, given what's happened.'

'I expect they will manage.'

'My mistress has had to sell some property, but she's being clever with the arrangements. The children will be all right.' As in the past, Tanneke could not resist praising Maria Thins to anyone who would listen, even if it meant being too eager with details.

Two women had come up and were standing behind Tanneke, waiting to be served. Part of me wished they were not there so that I could ask her more questions, lead her to give away other details, to tell me much more about so many things. But another part of me — the sensible part that I had held to now for many years — did not want to have anything to do with her. I did not want to hear.

The women shifted from side to side as Tanneke stood solidly in front of the stall, still frowning but with a softer face. She pondered the cuts of meat laid out before her.

'Would you like to buy something?' I asked.

My question snapped her out of her stupor. 'No,' she muttered.

They bought their meat now from a stall at the far end of the Meat Hall. As soon as I began working alongside Pieter they had switched butchers — so abruptly that they did not even pay their bill. They still owed us fifteen guilders. Pieter never asked them for it. 'It's the price I have paid for you,' he sometimes teased. 'Now I know what a maid is worth.'

I did not laugh when he said this.

I felt a tiny hand tugging at my dress and looked down. Little Frans had found me and was clinging to my skirt. I touched the top of his head, full of blond curls like his father's. 'There you are,' I said. 'Where's Jan and your grandmother?'

He was too young to be able to tell me, but I then saw my mother and elder son coming through the stalls towards me.

Tanneke looked back and forth between my sons and her face hardened. She darted a look at me full of blame, but she did not say what she was thinking. She stepped back, treading on the foot of the woman directly behind her. 'Mind you come this afternoon,' she said, then turned away before I could reply.

They had eleven children now — Maertge and market gossip had kept count for me. Yet Catharina had lost the baby she delivered that day of the painting and the palette knife. She gave birth in the studio itself — she could not get down the stairs to her own bed. The baby had come a month early and was small and sickly. It died not long after its birth feast. I knew that Tanneke blamed me for the death.

Sometimes I pictured his studio with Catharina's blood on the floor and wondered how he was able still to work there.

Jan ran to his little brother and pulled him into a corner, where they began to kick a bone back and forth between them.

'Who was that?' my mother asked. She had never seen Tanneke.

'A customer,' I replied. I often shielded her from things I knew would disturb her. Since my father's death she had become skittish as a wild dog about the new, the different, the changed.

'She didn't buy anything,' my mother remarked.

'No. We didn't have what she wanted.' I turned to wait on the next customer before my mother could ask more questions.

Pieter and his father appeared, carrying a side of beef between them. They flung it on to the table behind the stall and took up their knives. Jan and little Frans left their bone and ran over to watch. My mother stepped back — she had never grown used to the sight of so much meat. 'I'll be getting along,' she said, picking up her shopping pail.

'Can you watch the boys this afternoon? I have some errands to run.'

'Where are you going?'

I raised my eyebrows. I had complained before to my mother that she asked too many questions. She had grown old and suspicious when there was usually nothing to be suspicious of. Now, though, when there was something to hide from her, I found myself strangely calm. I did not answer her question.

It was easier with Pieter. He simply glanced up at me from his work. I nodded at him. He had decided long ago not to ask questions, even though he knew I had thoughts sometimes that I did not speak of. When he removed my cap on our wedding night and saw the holes in my ears he did not ask.

The holes were long healed now. All that was left of them were tiny buds of hard flesh I could feel only if I pressed the lobes hard between my fingers.

*   *   *

236

It had been two months since I had heard the news. For two months now I could walk around Delft without wondering if I would see him. Over the years I had occasionally spotted him in the distance, on his way to or from the Guild, or near his mother's inn, or going to van Leeuwenhoek's house, which was not far from the Meat Hall. I never went near him, and I was not sure if he ever saw me. He strode along the streets or across the square with his eyes fixed on a distant point — not rudely or deliberately, but as if he were in a different world.

At first it was very hard for me. When I saw him I froze wherever I was, my chest tightened, and I could not get my breath. I had to hide my response from Pieter the father and son, from my mother, from the curious market gossips.

For a long time I thought I might still matter to him.

After a while, though, I admitted to myself that he had always cared more for the painting of me than for me.

It grew easier to accept this when Jan was born. My son made me turn inward to my family, as I had done when I was a child, before I became a maid. I was so busy with him that I did not have time to look out and around me. With a baby in my arms I stopped walking round the eight-pointed star in the square and wondering what was at the end of each of its points. When I saw my old master across the square my heart no longer squeezed itself like a fist. I no longer thought of pearls and fur, nor longed to see one of his paintings.

Sometimes on the streets I ran into the others — Catharina, the children, Maria Thins. Catharina and I turned our faces from each other. It was easier that way. Cornelia looked through me with disappointed eyes. I think she had hoped to destroy me completely. Lisbeth was kept busy looking after the boys, who were too young to remember me. And Aleydis was like her father – her grey eyes looked about her without settling on anything near to her. After a time there were other children I did not know, or knew only by their father's eyes or their mother's hair.

Of all of them, only Maria Thins and Maertge acknowledged me, Maria Thins nodding briefly when she saw me, Maertge sneaking away to the Meat Hall to speak with me. It was Maertge who brought me my things from the house – the broken tile, my prayer book, my collars and caps. It was Maertge who told me over the years of his mother's death and of how he had to take over the running of her inn, of their growing debt, of Tanneke's accident with the oil.

It was Maertge who announced gleefully one day, 'Papa has been painting me in the manner in which he painted you. Just me, looking over my shoulder. They are the only paintings he has done like that, you know.'

Not exactly in the manner, I thought. Not exactly. I was surprised, though, that she knew of the painting. I wondered if she had seen it.

I had to be careful with her. For a long time she was but a girl, and I did not feel it right to ask too much about her family. I had to wait patiently for her to pass me tidbits of news. By the time she was old enough to be more frank with me, I was not so interested in her family now that I had my own.

Pieter tolerated her visits but I knew she made him uneasy. He was relieved when Maertge married a silk merchant's son and began to see less of me, and bought her meat from another butcher.

Now after ten years I was being called back to the house I had run from so abruptly.

Two months before, I had been slicing tongue at the stall when I heard a woman waiting her turn say to another, 'Yes, to think of dying and leaving eleven children and the widow in such debt.'

I looked up and the knife cut deep into my palm. I did not feel the pain of it until I had asked, 'Who are you speaking of?' and the woman replied, 'The painter Vermeer is dead.'

I scrubbed my fingernails especially hard when I finished at the stall. I had long ago given up always scrubbing them thoroughly, much to Pieter the father's amusement. 'You see, you've grown used to stained fingers as you got used to the flies,' he liked to say. 'Now you know the world a little better you can see there's no reason always to keep your hands clean. They just get dirty again. Cleanliness is not as important as you thought back when you were a maid, eh?' Sometimes, though, I crushed lavender and hid it under my chemise to mask the smell of meat that seemed to hang about me even when I was far from the Meat Hall.

There were many things I'd had to get used to.

I changed into another dress, a clean apron, and a newly starched cap. I still wore my cap in the same way, and I probably looked much as I had the day I first set out to work as a maid. Only now my eyes were not so wide and innocent.

Although it was February, it was not bitterly cold. Many people were out in Market Square — our customers, our neighbours, people who knew us and would note my first step on to the Oude Langendijck in ten years. I would have to tell Pieter eventually that I had gone there. I did not know yet if I would need to lie to him about why.

I crossed the square, then the bridge leading from it over the canal to the Oude Langendijck. I did not hesitate, for I did not want to bring more attention to myself. I turned briskly and walked up the street. It was not far — in half a minute I was at the house — but it felt long to me, as if I were travelling to a strange city I had not visited for many years.

Because it was a mild day, the door was open and there were children sitting on the bench — four of them, two boys and two girls, lined up as their older sisters had been ten years before when I first arrived. The eldest was blowing bubbles, as Maertge had, though he laid down his pipe the moment he saw me. He looked to be ten or eleven years old. After a moment I realised he must be Franciscus, though I did not see much of the baby in him that I had known. But then, I had not thought much of babies when I was young. The others I did not recognise, except for seeing them occasionally in town with the older girls. They all stared at me.

I addressed myself to Franciscus. 'Please tell your grand-mother that Griet is here to see her.'

Franciscus turned to the older of the two girls. 'Beatrix, go and find Maria Thins.'

The girl jumped up obediently and went inside. I thought of Maertge and Cornelia's scramble to announce me so long ago and smiled to myself.

The children continued to stare at me. 'I know who you are,' Franciscus declared.

'I doubt you can remember me, Franciscus. You were but a baby when I knew you.'

He ignored my remark — he was following his own thought. 'You're the lady in the painting.'

I started, and Franciscus smiled in triumph. 'Yes, you are, though in the painting you're not wearing a cap, but a fancy blue and yellow head cloth.'

'Where is this painting?'

He seemed surprised that I should ask. 'With van Ruijven's daughter, of course. He died last year, you know.'

I had heard this news at the Meat Hall with secret relief. Van Ruijven had never sought me out once I'd left, but I had always feared that he would appear again one day with his oily smile and groping hands.

'How did you see the painting if it is at van Ruijven's?'

'Papa asked to have the painting on a short loan,' Franciscus explained. 'The day after Papa died Mama sent it back to van Ruijven's daughter.'

I rearranged my mantle with shaking hands. 'He wanted to see the painting again?' I managed to say in a small voice.

'Yes, girl.' Maria Thins had come to stand in the doorway. 'It didn't help matters here, I can tell you. But by that time he was in such a state that we didn't dare say no, not even Catharina.' She looked exactly the same — she would never age. One day she would simply go to sleep and not wake up.

I nodded to her. 'I'm sorry for your loss and your troubles, madam.'

'Yes, well, life is a folly. If you live long enough, nothing is surprising.'

I did not know how to respond to such words, so I simply said what I knew to be true. 'You wanted to see me, madam.'

'No, it's Catharina who is to see you.'

'Catharina?' I could not keep the surprise from my voice.

Maria Thins smiled sourly. 'You never did learn to keep your thoughts to yourself, did you, girl? Never mind, I expect you get by well enough with your butcher, if he doesn't ask too much of you.'

I opened my mouth to speak, then shut it.

'That's right. You're learning. Now, Catharina and van Leeuwenhoek are in the great hall. He is the executor of the will, you see.'

I did not see. I wanted to ask her what she meant, and why van Leeuwenhoek was there, but I did not dare. 'Yes, madam,' I said simply.

Maria Thins chuckled briefly. 'The most trouble we've ever had with a maid,' she muttered, shaking her head before disappearing inside.

I stepped into the front hallway. There were still paintings hanging everywhere on the walls, some I recognised, others I did not. I half expected to see myself among the still lifes and seascapes, but of course I was not there.

I glanced at the stairs leading up to his studio and stopped, my chest tightening. To stand in the house again, his room above me, was more than I thought I could bear, even though I knew he was not there. For so many years I had not let myself think of the hours I spent grinding colours at his side, sitting in the light of the windows, watching him look at me. For the first time in two months I became fully aware that he was dead. He was dead and he would paint no more paintings. There were so few — I had heard that he never did paint faster, as Maria Thins and Catharina had wanted him to.

It was only when a girl poked her head out from the Crucifixion room that I forced myself to take a deep breath and walk down the hallway towards her. Cornelia was now about the age I had been when I first became a maid. Her red hair had darkened over the ten years and was simply dressed, without ribbons or braids. She had grown less menacing to me over time. In fact I almost pitied her — her face was twisted by a cunning that gave a girl her age an ugly look.

I wondered what would happen to her, what would happen to them all. Despite Tanneke's confidence in her mistress' ability to arrange things, it was a big family, with a big debt. I had heard in the market that they had not paid their bill to the baker in three years, and after my master's death the baker had taken pity on Catharina and accepted a painting to settle the debt. For a brief moment I wondered if Catharina was going to give me a painting too, to settle her debt with Pieter.

Cornelia pulled her head back into the room and I stepped into the great hall. It had not changed much since I had worked there. The bed still had its green silk curtains, now faded. The ivory-inlaid cupboard was there, and the table and Spanish leather chairs, and the paintings of his family and hers. Everything appeared older, dustier, more battered. The red and brown floor tiles were cracked or missing in places.

Van Leeuwenhoek was standing with his back to the door,

his hands clasped behind him, studying a painting of soldiers drinking in a tavern. He turned around and bowed to me, still the kind gentleman.

Catharina was seated at the table. She was not wearing black as I had expected. I did not know if she meant to taunt me, but she wore the yellow mantle trimmed with ermine. It too had a faded look about it, as if it had been worn too many times. There were badly repaired rents in the sleeves, and the fur had been eaten away in places by moths. None the less, she was playing her part as the elegant lady of the house. She had dressed her hair carefully and was wearing powder and her pearl necklace.

She was not wearing the earrings.

Her face did not match her elegance. No amount of powder could mask her rigid anger, her reluctance, her fear. She did not want to meet with me, but she had to.

'Madam, you wished to see me.' I thought it best to address myself to her, though I looked at van Leeuwenhoek as I spoke.

'Yes.' Catharina did not gesture to a chair, as she would have to another lady. She let me stand.

There was an awkward silence as she sat and I stood, waiting for her to begin. She was clearly struggling to speak. Van Leeuwenhoek shifted from one foot to the other.

I did not try to help her. There seemed to be no way that I could. I watched her hands shuffle some papers on the table, run along the edges of the jewellery box at her elbow, pick up the powderbrush and set it down again. She wiped her hands on a white cloth.

'You know that my husband died two months ago?' she began at last.

244

'I had heard, madam, yes. I was very sorry to hear of it. May God keep him.'

Catharina did not seem to take in my feeble words. Her mind was elsewhere. She picked up the brush again and ran her fingers through its bristles.

'It was the war with France, you see, that brought us to this state. Not even van Ruijven wanted to buy paintings then. And my mother had problems collecting her rents. And he had to take over the mortgage on his mother's inn. So it is no wonder things grew so difficult.'

The last thing I had expected from Catharina was an explanation of why they ran into debt. Fifteen guilders after all this time is not so very much, I wanted to say. Pieter has let it go. Think no more of it. But I dared not interrupt her.

'And then there were the children. Do you know how much bread eleven children eat?' She looked up at me briefly, then back down at the powderbrush.

One painting's worth over three years, I answered silently. One very fine painting, to a sympathetic baker.

I heard the click of a tile in the hallway, and the rustle of a dress being stilled by a hand. Cornelia, I thought, still spying. She too is taking her place in the drama.

I waited, holding back the questions I wanted to ask.

Van Leeuwenhoek finally spoke. 'Griet, when a will has been drawn up,' he began in his deep voice, 'an inventory of the family's possessions must be taken to establish the assets while considering the debts. However, there are private matters that Catharina would like to attend to before this is done.' He glanced at Catharina. She continued to play with the powderbrush.

They do not like each other still, I thought. They would not even be in the same room together if they could help it.

Van Leeuwenhoek picked up a piece of paper from the table. 'He wrote this letter to me ten days before he died,' he said to me. He turned to Catharina. 'You must do this,' he ordered, 'for they are yours to give, not his or mine. As executor of his will I should not even be here to witness this, but he was my friend, and I would like to see his wish granted.'

Catharina snatched the paper from his hand. 'My husband was not a sick man, you know,' she addressed herself to me. 'He was not really ill until a day or two before his death. It was the strain of the debt that drove him into a frenzy.'

I could not imagine my master in a frenzy.

Catharina looked down at the letter, glanced at van Leeuwenhoek, then opened her jewellery box. 'He asked that you have these.' She picked out the earrings and after a moment's hesitation laid them on the table.

I felt faint and closed my eyes, touching the back of the chair lightly with my fingers to steady myself.

'I have not worn them again,' Catharina declared in a bitter tone. 'I could not.'

I opened my eyes. 'I cannot take your earrings, madam.'

'Why not? You took them once before. And besides, it's not for you to decide. He has decided for you, and for me. They are yours now, so take them.'

I hesitated, then reached over and picked them up. They were cool and smooth to the touch, as I had remembered them, and in their grey and white curve a world was reflected.

I took them.

'Now go,' Catharina ordered in a voice muffled with hidden tears. 'I have done what he asked. I will do no more.' She stood up, crumpled the paper and threw it on the fire. She watched it flare up, her back to me.

I felt truly sorry for her. Although she could not see it, I nodded to her respectfully, and then to van Leeuwenhoek, who smiled at me. 'Take care to remain yourself,' he had warned me so long ago. I wondered if I had done so. It was not always easy to know.

I slipped across the floor, clutching my earrings, my feet making loose tiles clink together. I closed the door softly behind me.

Cornelia was standing out in the hallway. The brown dress she wore had been repaired in several places and was not as clean as it could be. As I brushed past her she said in a low, eager voice, 'You could give them to me.' Her greedy eyes were laughing.

I reached over and slapped her.

When I got back to Market Square I stopped by the star in the centre and looked down at the pearls in my hand. I could not keep them. What would I do with them? I could not tell Pieter how I came to have them − it would mean explaining everything that had happened so long ago. I could not wear the earrings anyway − a butcher's wife did not wear such things, no more than a maid did.

I walked around the star several times. Then I set out for a place I had heard of but never been to, tucked away in a back street behind the New Church. I would not have visited such a place ten years before.

The man's trade was keeping secrets. I knew that he would ask me no questions, nor tell anyone that I had gone to him. After seeing so many goods come and go, he was no longer curious about the stories behind them. He held the earrings up to the light, bit them, took them outside to squint at them.

'Twenty guilders,' he said.

I nodded, took the coins he held out, and left without looking back.

There were five extra guilders I would not be able to explain. I separated five coins from the others and held them tight in my fist. I would hide them somewhere that Pieter and my sons would not look, some unexpected place that only I knew of.

I would never spend them.

Pieter would be pleased with the rest of the coins, the debt now settled. I would not have cost him anything. A maid came free.

ACKNOWLEDGEMENTS

One of the most helpful and readable sources on seven-teenth-century Holland is Simon Schama's *The Embarrassment of Riches: An Interpretation of Dutch Culture in the Golden Age* (1987). What little is known about Vermeer's life and family has been thoroughly documented by John Montias in *Vermeer and His Milieu* (1989). The catalogue for the 1996 Vermeer exhibition has beautiful reproductions and clear analyses of the paintings.

I would like to thank Philip Steadman, Nicola Costaras, Humphrey Ocean and Joanna Woodall for talking with me about various aspects of Vermeer's work. Mick Bartram, Ora Dresner, Nina Killham, Dale Reynolds, and Robert and Angela Royston all made helpful and supportive comments about the manuscript in progress. Thanks, finally, to my agent Jonny Geller and my editor Susan Watt for doing what they do so well.

FALLING ANGELS

For Jonathan, again

January 1901

KITTY COLEMAN

I woke this morning with a stranger in my bed. The head of blond hair beside me was decidedly not my husband's. I did not know whether to be shocked or amused.

Well, I thought, here's a novel way to begin the new century.

Then I remembered the evening before and felt rather sick. I wondered where Richard was in this huge house and how we were meant to swap back. Everyone else here – the man beside me included – was far more experienced in the mechanics of these matters than I. Than we. Much as Richard bluffed last night, he was just as much in the dark as me, though he was more keen. Much more keen. It made me wonder.

I nudged the sleeper with my elbow, gently at first and then harder until at last he woke with a snort.

'Out you go,' I said. And he did, without a murmur. Thankfully he didn't try to kiss me. How I stood that beard last night I'll never remember – the claret helped, I suppose. My cheeks are red with scratches.

When Richard came in a few minutes later, clutching his clothes in a bundle, I could barely look at him. I was embarrassed, and angry too – angry that I should feel embarrassed and yet not expect him to feel so as well. It was all the more infuriating that he simply kissed me, said, 'Hello, darling,' and began to dress. I could smell her perfume on his neck.

Yet I could say nothing. As I myself have so often said, I am open-minded – I pride myself on it. Those words bite now.

I lay watching Richard dress, and found myself thinking of my brother. Harry always used to tease me for thinking too much – though he refused to concede that he was at all responsible for encouraging me. But all those evenings spent reviewing with me what his tutors had taught him in the morning – he said it was to help him remember it – what did that do but teach me to think and speak my mind? Perhaps he regretted it later. I shall never know now. I am only just out of mourning for him, but some days it feels as if I am still clutching that telegram.

Harry would be mortified to see where his teaching has led. Not that one has to be clever for this sort of thing – most of them downstairs are stupid as buckets of coal, my blond beard among them. Not one could I have a proper conversation with. I had to resort to the wine.

Frankly I'm relieved not to be of this set – to paddle in its shallows occasionally is quite enough for me. Richard, I suspect, feels differently, but he has married the wrong wife if he wanted that sort of life. Or perhaps it is I who chose badly – though I would never have thought so once, back when we were mad for each other.

I think Richard has made me do this to show me he is not as conventional as I feared. But it has had the opposite

4

effect on me. He has become everything I had not thought he would when we married. He has become ordinary.

I feel so flat this morning. Daddy and Harry would have laughed at me, but I secretly hoped that the change in the century would bring a change in us all; that England would miraculously slough off her shabby black coat to reveal something glittering and new. It is only eleven hours into the twentieth century, but I know very well that nothing has changed but a number.

Enough. They are to ride today, which is not for me — I shall escape with my coffee to the library. It will undoubtedly be empty.

RICHARD COLEMAN

I thought being with another woman would bring Kitty back, that jealousy would open her bedroom door to me again. Yet two weeks later she has not let me in any more than before.

I do not like to think that I am a desperate man, but I do not understand why my wife is being so difficult. I have provided a decent life for her and yet she is still unhappy, though she cannot – or will not – say why.

It is enough to drive any man to change wives, if only for a night.

MAUDE COLEMAN

When Daddy saw the angel on the grave next to ours he cried, 'What the devil!'

Mummy just laughed.

I looked and looked until my neck ached. It hung above us, one foot forward, a hand pointing towards heaven. It was wearing a long robe with a square neck, and it had loose hair that flowed onto its wings. It was looking down towards me, but no matter how hard I stared it did not seem to see me.

Mummy and Daddy began to argue. Daddy does not like the angel. I don't know if Mummy likes it or not – she didn't say. I think the urn Daddy has had placed on our own grave bothers her more.

I wanted to sit down but didn't dare. It was very cold, too cold to sit on stone, and besides, the Queen is dead, which I think means no one can sit down, or play, or do anything comfortable.

I heard the bells ringing last night when I was in bed, and when Nanny came in this morning she told me the Queen died yesterday evening. I ate my porridge very slowly, to see if it tasted different from yesterday's, now that the

Queen is gone. But it tasted just the same – too salty. Mrs Baker always makes it that way.

Everyone we saw on our way to the cemetery was dressed in black. I wore a grey wool dress and a white pinafore, which I might have worn anyway but which Nanny said was fine for a girl to wear when someone died. Girls don't have to wear black. Nanny helped me to dress. She let me wear my black and white plaid coat and matching hat, but she wasn't sure about my rabbit's-fur muff, and I had to ask Mummy, who said it didn't matter what I wore. Mummy wore a blue silk dress and wrap, which did not please Daddy.

While they were arguing about the angel I buried my face in my muff. The fur is very soft. Then I heard a noise, like stone being tapped, and when I raised my head I saw a pair of blue eyes looking at me from over the headstone next to ours. I stared at them, and then the face of a boy appeared from behind the stone. His hair was full of mud, and his cheeks were dirty with it too. He winked at me, then disappeared behind the headstone.

I looked at Mummy and Daddy, who had walked a little way up the path to view the angel from another place. They had not seen the boy. I walked backwards between the graves, my eyes on them. When I was sure they were not looking I ducked behind the stone.

The boy was leaning against it, sitting on his heels.

'Why do you have mud in your hair?' I asked.

'Been down a grave,' he said.

I looked at him closely. There was mud on him everywhere – on his jacket, on his knees, on his shoes. There were even bits of it in his eyelashes.

'Can I touch the fur?' he asked.

'It's a muff,' I said. 'My muff.'

'Can I touch it?'

'No.' Then I felt bad saying that, so I held out the muff.

The boy spit on his fingers and wiped them on his jacket, then reached out and stroked the fur.

'What were you doing down a grave?' I asked.

'Helping our Pa.'

'What does your father do?'

'He digs the graves, of course. I helps him.'

Then we heard a sound, like a kitten mewing. We peeked over the headstone and a girl standing in the path looked straight into my eyes, just as I had with the boy. She was dressed all in black, and was very pretty, with bright brown eyes and long lashes and creamy skin. Her brown hair was long and curly and so much nicer than mine, which hangs flat like laundry and isn't one colour or another. Grandmother calls mine ditch-water blonde, which may be true but isn't very kind. Grandmother always speaks her mind.

The girl reminded me of my favourite chocolates, whipped hazelnut creams, and I knew just from looking at her that I wanted her for my best friend. I don't have a best friend, and have been praying for one. I have often wondered, as I sit in St Anne's getting colder and colder (why are churches always cold?), if prayers really work, but it seems this time God has answered them.

'Use your handkerchief, Livy dear, there's a darling.' The girl's mother was coming up the path, holding the hand of a younger girl. A tall man with a ginger beard followed them. The younger girl was not so pretty. Though she looked like the other girl, her chin was not so pointed, her hair not so curly, her lips not so big. Her eyes were hazel rather than brown, and she looked at everything as if nothing surprised her. She spotted the boy and me immediately.

'Lavinia,' the older girl said, shrugging her shoulders and tossing her head so that her curls bounced. 'Mama, I want you and Papa to call me Lavinia, not Livy.'

I decided then and there that I would never call her Livy.

'Don't be rude to your mother, Livy,' the man said. 'You're Livy to us and that's that. Livy is a fine name. When you're older we'll call you Lavinia.'

Lavinia frowned at the ground.

'Now stop all this crying,' he continued. 'She was a good queen and she lived a long life, but there's no need for a girl of five to weep quite so much. Besides, you'll frighten Ivy May.' He nodded at the sister.

I looked at Lavinia again. As far as I could see she was not crying at all, though she was twisting a handkerchief around her fingers. I waved at her to come.

Lavinia smiled. When her parents turned their backs she stepped off the path and behind the headstone.

'I'm five as well,' I said when she was standing next to us. 'Though I'll be six in March.'

'Is that so?' Lavinia said. 'I'll be six in February.'

'Why do you call your parents Mama and Papa? I call mine Mummy and Daddy.'

'Mama and Papa is much more elegant.' Lavinia stared at the boy, who was kneeling by the headstone. 'What is your name, please?'

'Maude,' I answered before I realised she was speaking to the boy.

'Simon.'

'You are a very dirty boy.'

'Stop,' I said.

Lavinia looked at me. 'Stop what?'

'He's a gravedigger, that's why he's muddy.'

Lavinia took a step backwards.

'An apprentice gravedigger,' Simon said. 'I was a mute for the undertakers first, but our Pa took me on once I could use a spade.'

'There were three mutes at my grandmother's funeral,' Lavinia said. 'One of them was whipped for laughing.'

'My mother says there are not so many funerals like that any more,' I said. 'She says they are too dear and the money should be spent on the living.'

'Our family always has mutes at its funerals. I shall have mutes at mine.'

'Are you dying, then?' Simon asked.

'Of course not!'

'Did you leave your nanny at home as well?' I asked, thinking we should talk about something else before Lavinia got upset and left.

She flushed. 'We don't have a nanny. Mama is perfectly able to look after us herself.'

I didn't know any children who didn't have a nanny.

Lavinia was looking at my muff. 'Do you like my angel, then?' she asked. 'My father let me choose it.'

'My father doesn't like it,' I declared, though I knew I shouldn't repeat what Daddy had said. 'He called it sentimental nonsense.'

Lavinia frowned. 'Well, Papa hates your urn. Anyway, what's wrong with my angel?'

'I like it,' the boy said.

'So do I,' I lied.

'I think it's lovely,' Lavinia sighed. 'When I go to heaven I want to be taken up by an angel just like that.'

'It's the nicest angel in the cemetery,' the boy said. 'And I know 'em all. There's thirty-one of 'em. D'you want me to show 'em to you?'

'Thirty-one is a prime number,' I said. 'It isn't divisible by anything except one and itself.' Daddy had just explained to me about prime numbers, though I hadn't understood it all.

Simon took a piece of coal from his pocket and began to draw on the back of the headstone. Soon he had drawn a skull and crossbones — round eyesockets, a black triangle for a nose, rows of square teeth, and a shadow scratched on one side of the face.

'Don't do that,' I said. He ignored me. 'You can't do that.'

'I have. Lots. Look at the stones all round us.'

I looked at our family grave. At the very bottom of the plinth that held the urn, a tiny skull and crossbones had been scratched. Daddy would be furious if he knew it were there. I saw then that every stone around us had a skull and crossbones on it. I had never seen them before.

'I'm going to draw one on every grave in the cemetery,' he continued.

'Why do you draw them?' I asked. 'Why a skull and crossbones?'

'Reminds you what's underneath, don't it? It's all bones down there, whatever you may put on the grave.'

'Naughty boy,' Lavinia said.

Simon stood up. 'I'll draw one for you,' he said. 'I'll draw one on the back of your angel.'

'Don't you dare,' Lavinia said.

Simon immediately dropped the piece of coal.

Lavinia looked around as if she were about to leave.

'I know a poem,' Simon said suddenly.

'What poem? Tennyson?'

'Dunno whose son. It's like this:

> 'There was a young man at Nunhead
> Who awoke in his coffin of lead;
> > "It is cosy enough,"
> > He remarked in a huff,
> > "But I wasn't aware I was dead."'

'Ugh! That's disgusting!' Lavinia cried. Simon and I laughed.

'Our Pa says lots of people've been buried alive,' Simon said. 'He says he's heard 'em, scrabbling inside their coffins as he's tossing dirt on 'em.'

'Really? Mummy's afraid of being buried alive,' I said.

'I can't bear to hear this,' Lavinia cried, covering her ears. 'I'm going back.' She went through the graves towards her parents. I wanted to follow her but Simon began talking again.

'Our Granpa's buried here in the meadow.'

'He never was.'

'He is.'

'Show me his grave.'

Simon pointed at a row of wooden crosses over the path from us. Paupers' graves – Mummy had told me about them, explaining that land had been set aside for people who had no money to pay for a proper plot.

'Which cross is his?' I asked.

'He don't have one. Cross don't last. We planted a rosebush, there, so we always know where he is. Stole it from one of the gardens down the bottom of the hill.'

I could see a stump of a bush, cut right back for the winter. We live at the bottom of the hill, and we have lots of roses at the front. Perhaps that rosebush was ours.

'He worked here too,' Simon said. 'Same as our Pa and me. Said it's the nicest cemetery in London. Wouldn't have wanted to be buried in any of t'others. He had stories to tell about t'others. Piles of bones everywhere. Bodies buried with just a sack of soil over 'em. Phew, the smell!' Simon waved his hand in front of his nose. 'And men snatching bodies in the night. Here he were at least safe and sound, with the boundary wall being so high, and the spikes on top.'

'I have to go now,' I said. I didn't want to look scared like Lavinia, but I didn't like hearing about the smell of bodies.

Simon shrugged. 'I could show you things.'

'Maybe another time.' I ran to catch up with our families, who were walking along together. Lavinia took my hand and squeezed it and I was so pleased I kissed her.

As we walked hand in hand up the hill I could see out of the corner of my eye a figure like a ghost jumping from stone to stone, following us and then running ahead. I wished we had not left him.

I nudged Lavinia. 'He's a funny boy, isn't he?' I said, nodding at his shadow as he went behind an obelisk.

'I like him,' Lavinia said, 'even if he talks about awful things.'

'Don't you wish we could run off the way he does?'

Lavinia smiled at me. 'Shall we follow him?'

I hadn't expected her to say that. I glanced at the others – only Lavinia's sister was looking at us. 'Let's,' I whispered. She squeezed my hand as we ran off to find him.

KITTY COLEMAN

I don't dare tell anyone or I will be accused of treason, but I was terribly excited to hear the Queen is dead. The dullness I have felt since New Year's vanished, and I had to work very hard to appear appropriately sober. The turning of the century was merely a change in numbers, but now we shall have a true change in leadership, and I can't help thinking Edward is more truly representative of us than his mother.

For now, though, nothing has changed. We were expected to troop up to the cemetery and make a show of mourning, even though none of the Royal Family is buried there, nor is the Queen to be. Death is there, and that is enough, I suppose.

That blasted cemetery. I have never liked it.

To be fair, it is not the fault of the place itself, which has a lugubrious charm, with its banks of graves stacked on top of one another — granite headstones, Egyptian obelisks, gothic spires, plinths topped with columns, weeping ladies, angels, and of course, urns — winding up the hill to the glorious Lebanon Cedar at the top. I am even willing to overlook some of the more preposterous monuments —

ostentatious representations of a family's status. But the sentiments that the place encourages in mourners are too overblown for my taste. Moreover, it is the Colemans' cemetery, not my family's. I miss the little churchyard in Lincolnshire where Mummy and Daddy are buried and where there is now a stone for Harry, even if his body lies somewhere in southern Africa.

The excess of it all – which our own ridiculous urn now contributes to – is too much. How utterly out of scale it is to its surroundings! If only Richard had consulted me first. It was unlike him – for all his faults he is a rational man, and must have seen that the urn was too big. I suspect the hand of his mother in the choosing. Her taste has always been formidable.

It was amusing today to watch him splutter over the angel that has been erected on the grave next to the urn (far too close to it, as it happens – they look as if they may bash each other at any moment). It was all I could do to keep a straight face.

'How dare they inflict their taste on us,' he said. 'The thought of having to look at this sentimental nonsense every time we visit turns my stomach.'

'It is sentimental, but harmless,' I replied. 'At least the marble's Italian.'

'I don't give a hang about the marble! I don't want that angel next to our grave.'

'Have you thought that perhaps they're saying the same about the urn?'

'There's nothing wrong with our urn!'

'And they would say that there's nothing wrong with their angel.'

'The angel looks ridiculous next to the urn. It's far too close, for one thing.'

'Exactly,' I said. 'You didn't leave them room for anything.'

'Of course I did. Another urn would have looked fine. Perhaps a slightly smaller one.'

I raised my eyebrows the way I do when Maude has said something foolish. 'Or even the same size,' Richard conceded. 'Yes, that could have looked quite impressive, a pair of urns. Instead we have this nonsense.'

And on and on we went. While I don't think much of the blank-faced angels dotted around the cemetery, they bother me less than the urns, which seem a peculiar thing to put on a grave when one thinks that they were used by the Romans as receptacles for human ashes. A pagan symbol for a Christian society. But then, so is all the Egyptian symbolism one sees here as well. When I pointed this out to Richard he huffed and puffed but had no response other than to say, 'That urn adds dignity and grace to the Coleman grave.'

I don't know about that. Utter banality and misplaced symbolism are rather more like it. I had the sense not to say so.

He was still going on about the angel when who should appear but its owners, dressed in full mourning. Albert and Gertrude Waterhouse – no relation to the painter, they admitted. (Just as well – I want to scream when I see his overripe paintings at the Tate. The Lady of Shalott in her boat looks as if she has just taken opium.) We had never met them before, though they have owned their grave for several years. They are rather nondescript – he a ginger-

18

bearded, smiling type, she one of those short women whose waists have been ruined by children so that their dresses never fit properly. Her hair is crinkly rather than curly, and escapes its pins.

Her elder daughter, Lavinia, who looks to be Maude's age, has lovely hair, glossy brown and curly. She's a bossy, spoiled little thing — apparently her father bought the angel at her insistence. Richard nearly choked where he heard this. And she was wearing a black dress trimmed with crape — rather vulgar and unnecessary for a child that young.

Of course Maude has taken an instant liking to the girl. When we all took a turn around the cemetery together Lavinia kept dabbing at her eyes with a black-edged handkerchief, weeping as we passed the grave of a little boy dead fifty years. I just hope Maude doesn't begin copying her. I can't bear such nonsense. Maude is very sensible but I could see how attracted she was to the girl's behaviour. They disappeared off together — Lord knows what they got up to. They came back the best of friends.

I think it highly unlikely Gertrude Waterhouse and I would ever be the best of friends. When she said yet again how sad it was about the Queen, I couldn't help but comment that Lavinia seemed to be enjoying her mourning tremendously.

Gertrude Waterhouse said nothing for a moment, then remarked, 'That's a lovely dress. Such an unusual shade of blue.'

Richard snorted. We'd had a fierce argument about my dress. In truth I was now rather embarrassed about my choice — not one adult I'd seen since leaving the house was wearing anything but black. My dress was dark blue, but still I stood out far more than I'd intended.

I decided to be bold. 'Yes, I didn't think black quite the thing to wear for Queen Victoria,' I explained. 'Things are changing now. It will be different with her son. I'm sure Edward will make a fine king. He's been waiting long enough.'

'Too long, if you ask me,' Mr Waterhouse said. 'Poor chap, he's past his prime.' He looked abashed, as if surprised that he had voiced his opinion.

'Not with the ladies, apparently,' I said. I couldn't resist.

'Oh!' Gertrude Waterhouse looked horrified.

'For God's sake, Kitty!' Richard hissed. 'My wife is always saying things she shouldn't,' he said apologetically to Albert Waterhouse, who chuckled uneasily.

'Never mind, I'm sure she makes up for it in other ways,' he said.

There was a silence as we all took-in this remark. For one dizzy moment I wondered if he could possibly be referring to New Year's Eve. But of course he would know nothing about that — that is not his set. I myself have tried hard not to think about it. Richard has not mentioned it since, but I feel now that I died a little death that night, and nothing will ever be quite the same, new King or no.

Then the girls returned, all out of breath, providing a welcome distraction. The Waterhouses quickly made their excuses and left, which I think everyone was relieved about except the girls. Lavinia grew tearful, and I feared Maude would too. Afterwards she wouldn't stop talking about her new friend until at last I promised I would try to arrange for them to meet. I am hoping she will forget eventually, as the Waterhouses are just the kind of family who make me feel worse about myself.

LAVINIA WATERHOUSE

I had an adventure at the cemetery today, with my new friend and a naughty boy. I've been to the cemetery many times before, but I've never been allowed out of Mama's sight. Today, though, Mama and Papa met the family that owns the grave next to ours, and while they were talking about the things grown-ups go on about, Maude and I went off with Simon, the boy who works at the cemetery. We ran up the Egyptian Avenue and all around the vaults circling the cedar of Lebanon. It is so delicious there, I almost fainted from excitement.

Then Simon took us on a tour of the angels. He showed us a wonderful child-angel near the Terrace Catacombs. I had never seen it before. It wore a little tunic and had short wings, and its head was turned away from us as if it were angry and had just stamped its foot. It is so lovely I almost wished I had chosen it for our grave. But it was not in the book of angels at the mason's yard. Anyway I am sure Mama and Papa agree that the one I chose for our grave is the best.

Simon took us to other angels close by and then he said he wanted to show us a grave he and his father had just dug. Well. I didn't want to see it but Maude said she did and I didn't want her to think I was afraid. So we went and looked down into it, and although it was frightening, I also got the strangest feeling that I wanted to lie down in that hole. Of course I didn't do such a thing, not in my lovely dress.

Then as we turned to go a horrid man appeared. He had a very red face and bristles on his cheeks, and he smelled of drink. I couldn't help but scream, even though I knew right away it was Simon's father as they have the same blue eyes like pieces of sky. He began shouting terrible things at Simon about where had he been and why were we there, and he used the most awful words. Papa would whip us if Ivy May or I were to use such words. And Papa is not a whipping man. That's how bad they were.

Then the man chased Simon round and round the grave until Simon jumped right into it! Well. I didn't wait to see more — Maude and I ran like fury all the way down the hill. Maude wondered if we shouldn't go back and see if Simon was all right but I refused, saying our parents would be worried about us. But really I didn't want to see that man again, as he frightened me. The naughty boy can take care of himself. I am sure he spends much of his time down graves.

So Maude is my new friend, and I hers — though I do not see why such a plain girl should have a beautiful muff, and a nanny too, neither of which I have. And a beautiful mother with such a tiny waist and big dark eyes. I could not look at Mama without feeling a little ashamed. It is really so unfair.

GERTRUDE WATERHOUSE

Once we heard the news I lay awake all night, worrying about our clothes. Albert could wear his black work suit, with jet cufflinks and a black band for his hat. Mourning has always been easier for men. And Ivy May is too young for her clothes to be a concern.

But Livy and I were to be dressed properly for our Queen's passing. For myself I did not mind so much what I wore, but Livy is so very particular, and difficult if she doesn't get exactly what she wants. I do hate scenes with her – it is like being led in a dance where I know none of the steps and she all of them, so that I feel tripped up and foolish by the end. And yet she is only five years old! Albert says I am too soft with her, but then he bought her the angel she wanted for the grave when he knows how little money we have for that sort of thing, what with our saving to move house. Still, I can't fault him for it. It is so important that the grave be a proper reflection of the family's sentiments to our loved ones. Livy knows that very well, and she was right – the grave did need some attention, especially after that monstrous urn went up next to it.

I rose very early this morning and managed to find a bit of crape I had saved after my aunt's mourning. I had hidden it away because I was meant to have burned it and knew Livy would be horrified to see it in the house. There was not enough of it to trim both our dresses, so I did hers, with a bit left over for my hat. By the time I had finished sewing, Livy was up, and she was so delighted with the effect of the crape that she didn't ask where I'd got it from.

What with the little sleep and the waking early I was so tired by the time we reached the cemetery that I almost cried to see the blue silk Kitty Coleman was wearing. It was an affront to the eyes, like a peacock spreading its feathers at a funeral. It made me feel quite shabby and I was embarrassed even to stand next to her, as doing so begged comparisons and reminded me that my figure is not what it once was.

The one comfort I could take — and it is a shameful one that I shall ask God's forgiveness for — was that her daughter Maude is so plain. I feel proud to see Livy look so well next to drab little Maude.

I was of course as civil as I could be, but it was clear that Kitty Coleman was bored with me. And then she made cutting remarks about Livy, and said disrespectful things — not exactly about the Queen, but I couldn't help feeling that Victoria had in some way been slighted. And she made my poor Albert so tongue-tied he said something completely out of character. I could not bring myself even to ask him afterwards what he meant.

Never mind — she and I shall not have to see each other again. In all the years we have owned adjacent graves at the cemetery, this is the first time we've met. With luck it won't happen again, though I shall always worry that we will. I shan't enjoy the cemetery so much now, I'm afraid.

ALBERT WATERHOUSE

Damned good-looking woman. I don't know what I was thinking, saying what I said, though. Shall make it up to Trudy tomorrow by getting her some of her favourite violet sweeties.

I was glad to meet Richard Coleman, though, urn and all. (What's done is done, I say to Trudy. It's up and there's no use complaining now.) He's got a rather good position at a bank. They live down the bottom of the hill, and from what he says it could be just the place for us if we do decide to move from Islington. There's a good local cricket team he could introduce me to as well. Useful chap.

I don't envy him his wife, pretty as she is. More of a handful than I'd like. Livy is trouble enough.

SIMON FIELD

I stay down the grave awhile after the girls have gone. There don't seem no reason to come out. Our Pa don't bother to come after me, or stand at the top of the hole and shout. He knows where he can get me when he wants. 'This cemetery has a high wall round it,' he always says. 'You can climb out but in the end you always come back through the front gate, feet first.'

The sky's pretty from eight feet down. It looks the colour of that girl's fur. Her muff, she called it. The fur was so soft. I wanted to put my face in it the way I saw her do.

I lie back on the ground and watch the sky. Sometimes a bird flies across, high above me. Bits of dirt from the sides of the hole crumble and fall on my face. I don't worry about the hole collapsing. For the deeper graves we use grave-boards to shore up the sides, but we don't bother with little ones like this. This one's in clay, good and damp so it holds up. It's happened before, the hole caving in, but mostly in sand, or when the clay's dried out. Men have got killed down graves. Our Pa always tells me to put a hand over my face and stick my other hand up if I'm down a grave and it falls in. Then I'll have an air hole through the dirt and they can see by my fingers where I am.

Someone comes then and looks into the grave. He's black against the light, so I can't see who it is. But I know it's not our Pa — he don't smell of the bottle.

'What are you doing down there, Simon?' the man says.

Then I know who it is. I jump to my feet and brush the dirt off my back and bum and legs.

'Just resting, sir.'

'You're not paid to rest.'

'I'm not paid nothing, sir,' I say before I can stop myself.

'Oh? I should think you earn plenty from all you learn here. You're learning a trade.'

'Learning don't feed me, sir.'

'Enough of your insolence, Simon. You are but a servant of the London Cemetery Company. There are plenty more waiting outside the gate who would gladly take your place. Don't you forget that. Now, have you finished that grave?'

'Yes, sir.'

'Then cover it over and go and find your father. He should be putting away the tools. God knows he needs the help. I don't know why I keep him on.'

I know why. Our Pa knows this place better'n anybody. He can take apart any grave, remember who's buried how far down and whether it's sand or clay. He learned it all from our Granpa. And he's fast digging when he wants to be. His arms are hard as rocks. He's best when he's had a bit of the bottle but not too much. Then he and Joe dig and laugh and I haul up and dump the bucket. But once he's had too much it's Joe and me does all the digging and dumping.

I look round for the long tree branch with the stumps on it what I use to climb out the little graves. Our Pa must've taken it out.

'Mr Jackson,' I call, but he's gone already. I shout again but he don't come back. Our Pa will think I've got out and covered the grave — he won't come back either.

I try to dig toeholds into the sides of the hole so I can climb out, but there's no spade, only my hands, and the ground's too hard. 'Sides, it's firm now but I don't know for sure it'll last. I don't want it to cave in on me.

It's cold in the hole now I'm stuck in it. I squat on my heels and wrap my arms round my legs. Every now and again I call out. There's four other graves being dug today and a couple of monuments going up, but none of them near me. Still, maybe a visitor will hear me, or one of them girls'll come back. Sometimes I hear voices and I call out 'Help! Help!' But no one comes. People stay away from graves just dug. They think something's going to pop out the hole and grab 'em.

The sky over me is going dark grey and I hear the bell ringing to tell visitors the cemetery's shutting. There's a boy goes round every day ringing it. I yell till my throat hurts but the bell drowns me out.

After a time the bell stops and after that it's dark. I jump up and down to get warm and then I crouch down again and hug my knees.

In the dark the hole starts to smell stronger of clay and wet things. There's an underground branch of the Fleet River runs through the cemetery. Feels close by.

The sky goes clear of clouds and I start to see little pricks of stars, more and more appearing till the patch of sky above me is full, like someone's sprinkled flour on the sky and is about to roll out dough on it.

I watch them stars all night. There's nothing else to do in the grave. I see things in 'em – a horse, a pickaxe, a spoon. Sometimes I look away and back again and they've moved a little. After a while the horse disappears off the edge of the sky, then the spoon. Once I see a star streak 'cross the sky. I wonder where it goes when it does that.

I think about them girls, the one with the muff and the one with the pretty face. They're tucked up in their beds, all toasty warm. I wish I was like them.

It's not so bad as long as I don't move. When I move it hurts like someone's hitting me with a plank of wood. After a time I can't move at all. My blood must be frozen.

The hardest part is towards the end of the night, when it might be getting light but it don't yet. Our Pa says that's when most people die 'cause they can't wait any longer for the day to start. I watch the stars. The pickaxe disappears and I cry a little bit and then I must fall asleep because when I look up again the stars are gone and it's light and the tears have frozen on my cheeks.

It gets lighter and lighter but no one comes. My mouth is stuck together I'm so thirsty.

Then I hear the hymn 'Holy, Holy, Holy,' which our Pa likes to whistle when he's working. It's funny 'cause he's not been inside a church in years. The whistling gets closer and closer and I try to call out but it hurts too much to make a noise.

I hear him walking round the hole, laying down boards and then the green carpets what look like grass, to make the ground round the grave look nice and neat. Then he lays the flat ropes across the hole that'll go under the coffin for lowering it, and then the two wooden bearers they lay the coffin on, one each end of the hole. He don't look down and see me. He's dug so many holes he don't need to look in 'em.

I try to open my mouth but can't. Then I hear the horses snorting and their halters creaking and the wheels crunching on the path and I know I have to get out or I never will. I straighten my legs, screaming from the pain 'cept there's no sound 'cause I still can't open my mouth. I manage to stagger to my feet and then I get my mouth working and call out, 'Pa! Pa!' I sound like one of them crows up in the trees. At first nothing happens. I call again and our Pa leans over the hole and squints at me.

'Jesus, boy! Wha're you doing there?'

'Get me out, our Pa! Get me out!'

Our Pa lays himself down the edge of the hole and holds out his arms. 'Hurry, boy! Take my hands.' But I can't reach him. Our Pa looks towards the sound of the horses and shakes his head. 'No time, boy. No time.' He jumps up and goes away and I yell again.

Our Pa comes back with Mr Jackson, who stares down at me with a terrible look on his face. He don't say nothing, but goes away while our Pa just stands there looking after him. Then Mr Jackson is back again and throws down the rope we use to measure how deep we've dug. There's a knot in it every foot. I grab a knot and hold on and he and our Pa pull me up out the hole so I land on the green carpet that's like grass. I jump up, though I hurt all over, and there I am, standing in front of the undertakers in their top hats and the boy mutes in their tiny black coats and the horses nodding so the black feathers strapped to their heads move. Behind the carriage holding the coffin are the mourners in black, all staring at me. I want to laugh at the looks they give me, but I see Mr Jackson's awful face and I run away.

Later, after our Pa's got rum down me and sat me by the fire with a blanket, he knocks me round the ears. 'Don't ever do that again, boy,' he says — like I planned to stay down the hole all night. 'I'll lose my job and then where'll we be?' Then Mr Jackson comes and whips me to make sure I've learned my lesson. I don't care, though, I hardly feel the whip. Nothing can ever hurt so bad as the cold down that grave.

December 1901

RICHARD COLEMAN

I told Kitty we've been invited for New Year's by the same people as last year. She was quiet, looking at me with those dark brown eyes that seduced me years ago but now simply judge me. If she hadn't looked at me like that I might not have added what I did.

'I've already told them we've accepted,' I said, although I hadn't yet. 'With pleasure.'

We shall go on accepting their invitations every year until Kitty becomes my wife again.

March 1903

LAVINIA WATERHOUSE

It was nothing short of a miracle. My best friend at the bottom of our garden! Can anything be more perfect than that?

I was feeling decidedly melancholy this morning as I brushed my hair, looking out of the window into our new garden. Although it is a sweet little patch, and Ivy May and I have a lovely bedroom looking out onto it, I couldn't help feeling a pang for our old house. It was smaller, and on a busy street, and not on the doorstep of a place as lovely as Hampstead Heath. But it was where I was born, and full of memories of my childhood. I wanted to take the bit of wallpaper in the hallway where Papa marked how tall Ivy May and I had grown every year, but he said I mustn't because it would damage the wall. I did cry as we left.

Then out of the corner of my eye I saw a fluttering, and when I looked over at the house backing onto ours, there was a girl hanging out of a window and waving! Well. I squinted and after a moment recognised her — it was Maude, the girl from the cemetery. I knew we had moved close to the cemetery but did not know she was here as well. I picked up my handkerchief and waved until my arm ached. Even

Ivy May, who never pays attention unless I pinch her (and not even then sometimes), got up from her bed to see what the fuss was about.

Maude called out something to me, but she was too far away and I couldn't hear. Then she pointed down at the fence separating our gardens and held up ten fingers. We are such kindred spirits that I understood immediately she meant we should meet there in ten minutes. I blew her a kiss and ducked inside to get dressed as quick as I could.

'Mama! Mama!' I shouted all the way down the stairs. Mama came running from the kitchen, thinking I was ill or had hurt myself. But when I told her about Maude she seemed not the least interested. She has not wanted me to see the Colemans, though she would never say why. Perhaps she has forgot them by now, but I have never forgot Maude, even after all this time. I knew we were destined to be together.

I ran outside and to the garden fence, which was too high to see over. I called to Maude and she answered, and after a moment her face appeared at the top of the fence.

'Oh! How did you get up there?' I cried.

'I'm standing on the birdbath,' said she, wobbling a bit. Then she managed to pull herself up, and before I knew it she'd tumbled over the fence and onto the ground! The poor dear was rather scratched by the rosebushes on the way down. I threw my arms around her and kissed her and brought her to Mama, who I am happy to say was very sweet to her and painted her scratches with iodine.

Then I took her up to my bedroom so that she could see my dollies.

'I didn't forget you,' I said. 'I've looked for you every time we've visited the cemetery, hoping to see you.'

'So have I,' she said.

'But I never did. Only that naughty boy now and then.'

'Simon. Digging with his father.'

'Now that I'm here we can go back together, and he can show us all the other angels. It will be lovely.'

'Yes.'

Then Ivy May tried to spoil it by knocking my dollies' heads together so hard I thought they might burst. I told her to leave but Maude said she didn't mind if Ivy May stayed with us as she didn't have a brother or sister to play with. Well. Ivy May looked pleased as Punch at that – as much as she looks pleased about anything.

Never mind. Then Maude had breakfast with us and we could not stop talking.

It is truly a miracle from heaven that the angels have led us to this house and me to my best friend.

MAUDE COLEMAN

It is funny how things happen. Daddy always says that coincidences are usually nothing of the sort if only one studies them carefully enough. He proved his point today.

I was looking out of my window when I saw a girl standing in hers across the way, brushing her hair. I had never seen her there before; two spinsters used to live in that house but had moved out a few weeks before. Then she tossed her head and shrugged her shoulders, and I realised it was Lavinia. I was so surprised to see her that I simply stood and stared.

I hadn't seen her for so long – not since the Queen's death over two years ago. Although I had asked Mummy several times if we could meet, she always made an excuse. She did promise to ask at the cemetery for the Waterhouses' address, but I don't think she ever did. After a time I stopped asking because I knew it was her way of saying no. I didn't know why she didn't want me to have a best friend, but there was nothing I could do, except to hang about in the cemetery whenever we visited, hoping the Waterhouses would choose to visit then too. But they never did. I had given up on ever having a best friend. And I had not met any other girls who would like to go around the cemetery with me the way Lavinia did.

Now here she was, just across the way. I began to wave, and when at last she saw me she waved too, frantically. It was very gratifying that she was so happy to see me. I signalled to her to meet me in the garden, then ran downstairs to tell my parents about the amazing coincidence.

Mummy and Daddy were already eating breakfast and reading the papers – Daddy the *Mail*, Mummy the *St Pancras Gazette*. When I told them who our new neighbours were, Daddy was not amazed at all but explained he'd told the Waterhouses about that house.

Mummy gave him a peculiar look. 'I didn't know you were so friendly with them,' she said.

'He contacted me at the bank,' Daddy said, 'quite some time ago. Said they were thinking of moving to the area and did I know of any property. When that house came up I told him about it.'

'So now we are to be neighbours in life as well as in death,' Mummy said. She cracked the shell of her egg very hard with a spoon.

'Apparently he's a fine batsman,' Daddy said. 'The team could do with one.'

When it became clear that there was no coincidence, that Daddy had led the Waterhouses here, I felt strangely let down. I wanted to believe in Fate, but Daddy has shown once again that there is no such thing.

GERTRUDE WATERHOUSE

I would not dream of criticising Albert's judgement. He knows best in these matters, and to be sure I am very pleased with our new little house, a storey higher than our Islington house and with a garden full of roses rather than the neighbour's chickens scrabbling in the dirt.

But my heart did sink when I discovered that not only are we neighbours with the Colemans, but their house backs on to ours. And of course it is yet a storey higher than ours and has the most tremendous garden. When no one was about I stood on a chair and peeked over. There is a willow, and a pond, and a bank of rhododendrons, and a lovely long lawn which I am sure the girls will play croquet on all summer.

Kitty Coleman was working in the garden, planting out primroses. Her dress was of the same buttery colour, and she wore a lovely wide-brimmed hat tied on with a chiffon scarf. Even at her gardening she is so well dressed. She didn't see me, I am thankful to say, or I should have been so mortified I might have fallen from the chair. As it was I hopped down quickly and jarred my ankle.

I would not confess this to anyone, not even Albert, but

it irritates me that she keeps such a fine garden. It is south-facing and very sunny, which makes it easier. And she must have a man to help – at the very least with the lawn, which looks rolled. I shall do my best with our roses, but I do kill plants off so easily. I really am hopeless in the garden. It doesn't help that ours is north-facing. And we cannot manage any help with it at present. I hope she does not offer to send her man over – I wouldn't know what to do.

After Maude tumbled over the back fence I felt we should call round, if only to explain the scratches. The front of their house is so elegant – the garden is full of rosebushes, and the steps leading up to the door are tiled in black and white. (The door of our own house opens directly on to the pavement. But I must try not to compare.)

I was hoping just to leave my card, but Kitty Coleman received us very gracefully in her morning room. I blinked at the colours she'd had it done in – mustard yellow with a dark brown trim, which I suppose is fashionable now. She called them 'golden yellow' and 'chocolate brown', which sound much better than they looked. I prefer our own burgundy. There is nothing to compare with a simple burgundy parlour. Mind you, I don't have a morning room – perhaps if I did have such a light room as hers on the first floor I might paint it yellow as well.

But I doubt it.

Her taste is very refined – embroidered silk shawls over the sofas, potted ferns, vases of dried flowers, and a baby grand piano. I was rather shocked by the modern coffee set, which has a pattern of tiny black and yellow checks that made me feel dizzy. I myself prefer a simple rose pattern. But *chacun à son goût*. Oh! I made the mistake of saying so out loud, and she replied in French. I understood not a word of it! It was my own silly fault for trying to show off.

I came away with one secret comfort. No, two. The girls at least are delighted with each other, and Livy could do with a sensible friend. At least Maude will be a steadying influence, unless she too succumbs to Livy's spell as the rest of us have — all but dear Ivy May, who is impervious to her sister's excesses. I am always surprised by her. Quiet as she is, she does not let Livy get the upper hand.

And the other comfort: Kitty Coleman's At Homes are Tuesday afternoons, just as mine are. When we discovered this, she smiled a little and said, 'Oh dear, that is a pity.' I will not switch mine, however — some traditions I will not tamper with. And I know she will not switch hers. In this way we shall be able to avoid that social occasion, at least.

I can't say exactly why I don't like her. She is perfectly civil and has good manners and is lovely to look at. She has a fine house and a handsome husband and a clever daughter. But I would not be her. A vein of discontent runs through her that disturbs everything around her. And I know it is uncharitable of me to think it, but I do doubt her Christian commitment. She thinks too much and prays too little, I suspect. But they are the only people we know close by, and the girls are already so fond of each other, and so I am afraid we are bound to see a great deal of each other.

When we got home and were sitting in our back parlour, I couldn't help but look out of the window at their grand house in the distance. It will always be there to remind me of their superior position. I found this so upsetting that I let my teacup crash into its saucer, and the dear thing cracked. I did weep then, and even Ivy May's arms around my neck (she does not like hugs, as a rule) did little to comfort me.

June 1903

MAUDE COLEMAN

Lavinia and I are desperate to get to the cemetery. Now that we can go together it will be so much more fun than before. But since the Waterhouses have moved to the house at the bottom of the garden, we have not managed to go, what with one thing and another: we went to Auntie Sarah's in the country at Easter, and then Lavinia was ill, and then Mummy or Mrs Waterhouse had a visit to make or an errand to run. What a bother — we live so close yet cannot get anyone to take us and are not allowed to go there on our own. It is a shame Nanny left to look after her old mother, or she could have taken us.

Yesterday I asked Mummy if she would go with us.

'I'm too busy,' she said. She didn't seem busy to me — she was just reading a book. I did not say so, however. She is meant to be looking after me now that Nanny has gone. But mostly I end up with Jenny and Mrs Baker.

I asked her if Jenny could take Lavinia and me.

'Jenny has far too much to do to be dragging you up there.'

'Oh, please, Mummy. Just for a little while.'

'Don't use that wheedling tone with me. You've learned it from Lavinia and it doesn't suit you.'

'Sorry. But perhaps – perhaps Jenny has an errand to run for you up in the Village. Then she could take us.'

'Haven't you lessons to prepare for?'

'Finished them.'

Mummy sighed. 'It's just as well you're going to school in the autumn. Your tutor can't keep up with you.'

I tried to be helpful. 'Perhaps you have books that need returning to the library?'

'I do, in fact. Oh, all right, go and tell Jenny to come here. And she can see if the fabric I've ordered has arrived while she's in the Village.'

Lavinia and I raced up the hill, pulling Jenny with us. She complained the whole way, and was quite puffed at the top, though if she hadn't used her breath for complaining she might have been all right. All our hurrying didn't make any difference anyway – Ivy May refused to run, and Jenny made Lavinia go back and get her. At times it can be a trial having Ivy May with us, but Mrs Waterhouse insisted upon it. Once we got to the cemetery, though, Jenny let us do whatever we liked, as long as we kept Ivy May with us. We immediately ran off to find Simon.

It was such a treat to be in the cemetery without anyone to look after us. Whenever I go with Mummy and Daddy or Grandmother I feel I have to be very quiet and solemn, when really what I want to do is just what Lavinia and I did – rush about and explore. As we looked for Simon we played all sorts of games: jumping from grave to grave without touching the ground (which is not difficult, as the graves are so packed in); taking a side each of a path and scoring points for seeing an obelisk, or a woman leaning on an urn, or an animal; playing tag around the Circle of Lebanon. Lavinia does shriek when she's being chased, and some grown-ups told us to hush and mind our manners. After that we tried to be quiet but we had such fun playing that it was hard.

At last we found Simon, right up the top of the cemetery not far from the north gate. We didn't see him at first, but his Pa was standing next to a new grave, pulling a bucket of soil up using a rope and pulley on a frame set over the hole. He dumped it into what looked like a big wooden box on wheels, several feet high and heaped with soil.

We crept closer and hid behind a headstone, not wanting Simon's Pa to see us, for he is dirty and red-faced and whiskery, and we could smell the drink on him even from where we were. Lavinia says he's just like a character out of Dickens. I suppose all gravediggers are.

We could hear Simon singing in the grave, a song Jenny sometimes sings along with the crowds on the Heath on a Bank Holiday Monday:

> 'Now if you want a 'igh old time
> Just take the tip from me,
> Why 'Ampstead, 'appy 'Ampstead is
> The place to 'ave a spree.'

Simon's Pa wasn't even looking at us, but somehow he knew we were there, for he called out, 'Well, little missies, wha're you wanting?'

Simon stopped singing. His Pa said, 'Come out from there, all three of youse.'

Lavinia and I looked at each other, but before we could

decide what to do, Ivy May had stepped out from behind the headstone, and we had no choice but to follow.

'Please, sir, we want to see Simon.' I was surprised that I called him sir.

He seemed surprised too, looking at us as if he couldn't believe we were there. Then he suddenly shouted into the hole, 'Boy, you got visitors!'

After a moment Simon's head popped out of the grave. He stared at us.

'Well, naughty boy,' Lavinia said, 'aren't you going to say anything?'

'Can we switch places for a bit, our Pa?' he said.

' 'Tain't much room down there for me and Joe,' Simon's Pa said. Simon didn't say anything, and his Pa chuckled. 'Oh well, then, go on there with your girlies.'

Simon climbed out and his Pa climbed in, grinning at us before disappearing into the grave. Simon pulled the bucket up and dumped it into the wooden box. He was very muddy.

'What's that?' I asked, pointing at the box.

'Lamb's box,' Simon said. 'You put what you've dug in it, then when the coffin's in the hole you roll it up and open the side – see, it's got a hinge – and let the dirt go straight into the grave. So as you don't make a mess round the grave, see. There's two more over there, already full.' He waved at the other boxes, pulled up against the boundary wall. 'You just leave a little pile of dirt at the end of the grave for the mourners to drop in.'

'Can we look in the grave?'

Simon nodded and we edged up to the hole. It was deeper than I'd expected. Simon's Pa was at the bottom with another man. I could only see the tops of their heads – Simon's Pa's like steel wool, the other man's completely bald. They were hacking at the sides of the hole with spades. There was hardly room for them to turn around. The bald man looked up at us. He had a long face and a nose like a sausage. He and Simon's Pa seemed to be digging partners, with Simon helping.

Simon hauled up another bucket full of clumps of clay. I could see a worm wriggling on top.

'Do you ever find anything while you're digging?' I asked, 'besides worms?'

Simon dumped the clay into the Lamb's box and lowered the bucket back into the grave. 'Pieces of china. Some fountain pens. A spinning top. This were school grounds before it were a cemetery. And before that it were the gardens of a big house.'

Simon's Pa looked up. 'Need more shoring down here, boy.'

Simon began handing down planks of wood from a pile. I noticed then that wood had been pushed in at regular intervals around the edges of the hole.

'How deep is it?' I asked.

'Twelve feet so far,' Simon said. 'We're going down to seventeen, ain't we, our Pa?'

I stared down. 'That deep?'

'Lots of people to bury over the years. Coffin's eighteen inches, plus a foot 'tween each coffin, makes space for six coffins. That's a family.'

I added it in my head – it was like a puzzle my tutor would give me. 'Seven coffins.'

'No, you leave a bit more than a foot at the top.'

'Of course. Six feet under.'

'Not really,' Simon said. 'That's just a saying. We just leave two feet atop the last coffin.'

'What on earth are you two going on about?' Lavinia said.

Simon's Pa began hammering on a piece of wood with a mallet.

'Are they safe down there?' I asked.

Simon shrugged. 'Safe enough. The wood shores up the grave. And it's clay, so it's not likely to cave in. Holds itself up. It's sand you got to watch out for. Sand's easier to dig but it don't hold. Sand's deadly.'

'Oh, do stop talking about such tedious things!' Lavinia cried. 'We want you to show us some angels.'

'Leave him alone, Lavinia,' I said. 'Can't you see he's working?' While I love Lavinia – she is my best friend, after all – she is rarely interested in what I am. She never wants to look through the telescope Daddy sets up in the garden, for instance, or dig about in the *Encyclopaedia Britannica* at the library. I wanted to ask Simon more about the graves and the digging but Lavinia wouldn't let me.

'Maybe later, when this is done,' Simon said.

'We only have half an hour,' I explained. 'Jenny said.'

'Who's Jenny?'

'Our maid.'

'Where's she now?'

'Up in the Village. We left her by the gate.'

'She met a man,' Ivy May said.

Simon looked at her. 'Who's this, then?'

'Ivy May. My little sister,' Lavinia said. 'But she's wrong. You didn't see any man, did you, Maude?'

I shook my head, but I wasn't sure.

'He had a wheelbarrow and she followed him into the cemetery,' Ivy May insisted.

'Did he have red hair?' Simon asked.

Ivy May nodded.

'Oh, him. He'll be knocking her, then.'

'What, someone's hitting Jenny?' I cried. 'Then we must go and rescue her!'

'Nah, not hitting,' Simon said. 'It's –' He looked at me and Lavinia and stopped. 'Never mind. 'Tis nothing.'

Simon's Pa laughed from down the hole. 'Got yourself all tangled up there, boy! Forgot who you was talking to. Got to be careful what you say if you're going to mix with them girls!'

'Hush, our Pa.'

'We'd best go,' I said, uneasy now about Jenny. 'I'm sure half an hour's gone now. Which is the quickest path back to the main gate?'

Simon pointed at a statue of a horse a little way away. 'Take the path by the horse and follow it down.'

'Not that way!' Lavinia cried. 'That's straight through the Dissenters!'

'So?' Simon said. 'They won't bite you. They're dead.'

The Dissenters' section is where all the people who are not Church of England are buried – Catholics, mostly, as well as Baptists and Methodists and other sorts. I've heard suicides are buried back there, though I didn't say that to Lavinia. I've only walked through it twice. It wasn't so different from the rest of the cemetery, but I did feel peculiar, as if I were in a foreign country. 'Come, Lavinia,' I said, not wanting Simon to think we were judging the Dissenters, 'it doesn't matter. Besides, wasn't your mother Catholic before she married your father?' I'd found a rosary under a cushion at Lavinia's house recently and their char, Elizabeth, had told me.

Lavinia flushed. 'No! And what would it matter if she were?'

'It doesn't matter — that's just what I'm saying.'

'I know,' Simon interrupted. 'If you want you can go back by the sleeping angel. Have you seen it? It's on the main path, not in the Dissenters.'

We shook our heads.

'I'll show you — it's not far. I'm just off for a tick, our Pa,' he called down into the hole.

Simon's Pa grunted.

'C'mon, quick.' Simon ran down the path and we hurried after him. This time even Ivy May ran.

We had never seen the angel he showed us. All the other angels in the cemetery are walking or flying or pointing or at least standing and bowing their heads. This one was lying on its side, wings tucked under it, fast asleep. I didn't know angels needed sleep as humans do.

Lavinia adored it, of course. I preferred to talk more about grave-digging, but when I turned to ask Simon something about the Lamb's box, he was gone. He had run back to his grave without saying goodbye.

At last I managed to drag Lavinia away from the angel, but when we got back to the main gate, Jenny wasn't there. I still didn't understand what Simon had meant about her and the man, and was a little worried. Lavinia wasn't bothered, though.

'Let's go to the mason's yard next door and look at the angels,' she said. 'Just for a minute.'

I had never been to the yard before. It was full of all sorts of stone, big blocks and slabs, blank headstones, plinths, even a stack of obelisks leaning against one another in a corner. It was very dusty and the ground gritty. Everywhere we could hear the 'tink tink tink' of men chipping stone.

Lavinia led the way into the shop. 'May we look at the book of angels, please?' she said to the man behind the counter. I thought she was very bold.

He didn't seem at all surprised, however. He pulled from the shelf behind him a large, dusty book and laid it on the counter.

'This is what we chose our angel from,' Lavinia explained. 'I love to look in it. It's got hundreds of angels. Aren't they lovely?' She began turning the pages. There were drawings of all sorts of angels – standing, kneeling, looking up, looking down, eyes closed, holding wreaths, trumpets, folds of cloth. There were baby angels and twin angels and cherubim and little angel heads with wings.

'They're – nice,' I said. I don't know why, exactly, but I don't much like the cemetery angels. They are very smooth and regular, and their eyes are so blank – even when I stand in their line of sight they never seem to look at me. What is the good of a messenger who doesn't even notice you?

Daddy hates angels because he says they are sentimental. Mummy calls them vapid. I had to look up the word – it means that something is dull or flat or empty. I think she is right. That is certainly what their eyes are like. Mummy says angels get more attention than they deserve. When there is an angel on a grave in the cemetery, everyone looks at it rather than the other monuments around it, but there is really nothing to see.

'Why do you like angels so much?' I asked Lavinia.

She laughed. 'Who couldn't like them? They are God's messengers and they bring love. Whenever I look in their gentle faces they make me feel peaceful and secure.'

That, I suspect, is an example of what Daddy calls sentimental thinking.

'Where is God, exactly?' I asked, thinking about angels flying between us and Him.

Lavinia looked shocked and stopped turning pages. 'Why, up there, of course.' She pointed at the sky outside. 'Don't you listen at Sunday school?'

'But there are stars and planets up there,' I said. 'I know – I've seen them through Daddy's telescope.'

'You watch out, Maude Coleman,' Lavinia said, 'or you'll commit blasphemy.'

'But –'

'Don't!' Lavinia covered her ears. 'I can't bear to listen!'

Ivy May giggled.

I gave up. 'Let's go back to Jenny.'

This time Jenny was waiting for us at the main gate, red and breathless as if she'd just climbed the hill again, but unhurt, I was glad to see.

'Where've you girls been?' she cried. 'I've been worried silly!'

We were all just starting down the hill when I asked her if she'd checked on the fabric for Mummy.

'The book!' she shrieked, and ran back into the cemetery to fetch it. I hate to think where she left it.

JENNY WHITBY

I were none too pleased to be running errands for the missus, I can tell you. She knows very well how busy I am. Six in the blooming morning till nine at night – later if they've a supper party. One day's holiday a year apart from Christmas and Boxing Day. And she wants me to take back books and pick up fabric – things she can very well do herself. Books I've no time to read myself, even if I wanted to – which I don't.

Still, it were a lovely sunny day, and I'll admit 'twas nice to get out, though I don't much like that hill up to the Village. We got to the cemetery and I were going to leave the girls there and nip up to the shops and back. Then I saw him, on his own, pushing a wheelbarrow across the courtyard with a little skip in his step. He looked back at me and smiled, and I thought, Hang on a tick.

So I went in with the girls and told 'em to do what they liked for half an hour, no more. They was wanting to find a little boy they play with, and I said to be careful and not to let him get cheeky. And to keep an eye on the little girl, Ivy May. She's of the habit of getting left behind, it seems – though I bet she likes it that way. I made 'em all hold hands. So they run off one way, and I t'other.

November 1903

KITTY COLEMAN

Tonight we went with the Waterhouses to a bonfire on the Heath. The girls wanted to, and the men get on well enough (though Richard privately mocks Albert Waterhouse as a buffoon), and it's left to Gertrude Waterhouse and me to smile and bear each other's company as best we can. We stood around an enormous bonfire on Parliament Hill, clutching our sausages and baked potatoes, and marvelling that we were gathered on the very hill where Guy Fawkes waited to see Parliament burn. I watched as people moved closer to or farther away from the heat of the flames, trying to find a spot where they were comfortable. But even if our faces were hot, our backs were cold — like the potatoes, charred on the outside, raw inside.

My threshold to heat is much higher than Richard's or Maude's — or most people's, for that matter. I stepped closer and closer until my cheeks flamed. When I looked around, the ring of people was far behind me — I stood alone by the edge of the fire.

Richard wasn't even looking at the fire, but up at the clear sky. That is just like him — his love is not heat, but the cold distance of the universe. When we were first courting he would take me, with Harry as chaperone, to observation parties to look at the stars. I thought it most romantic then. Tonight, though, when I followed his gaze up to the starry sky all I felt was the blank space between those pinpricks and me, and it was like a heavy blanket waiting to drop on me. It was almost as suffocating as my fear of being buried alive.

I cannot see what he sees in the stars — he and now Maude, for he has begun taking her with him when he goes out to the Heath at night with his telescope. I haven't said anything, because there is nothing I can truly complain of, and Maude clearly thrives on his attention. But it brings me low, for I can see him fostering in her the same cold rationality that I discovered in him once we were married.

I am being ridiculous, of course. I too was brought up by my father to be logical, and I despise the sentimentality of the age, as embodied to perfection by the Waterhouses. But I'm secretly glad Maude and Lavinia are friends. Irritating and melodramatic as Lavinia is, she is not cold, and she counterbalances the icy hand of astronomy.

I stood by the fire, everyone around me so cheerful, and thought what an odd creature I am — even I know that. Too much space and I'm frightened, too little and I'm frightened. There is indeed no comfortable place for me — I am too near the fire or too far away.

Behind me, Gertrude Waterhouse stood with an arm around each daughter. Maude stood next to Lavinia, and they were all laughing about something — Maude a little shyly, as if she was not sure she should be sharing the laughter with them. I felt a pang for her.

At times it is painful to be with the Waterhouses. Lavinia

may be bossy with her mother, but there is clearly an affection between them that I cannot muster with Maude. After a few hours with them I come away resolved to link my arm with Maude's when we walk, as Gertrude does with Lavinia. And to be with her more – read to her, help her with her sewing, bring her into the garden with me, take her into town.

It has never been like that with her. Maude's birth was a shock from which I have not recovered. When I came to from the ether and first held her in my arms I felt as if I were nailed to the bed, trapped by her mouth at my breast. Of course I loved her – love her – but my life as I had imagined it ended on that day. It fed a low feeling in me that resurfaces with increasing frequency.

At least I was lucky in my doctor. When he came to see me a few days after the birth I sent the nurse from the room and told him I wanted no more babies. He took pity on me and explained the timing and the signs to look for, and what I might say to my husband to keep him away during those times. It does not work for every woman, but it has for me, and Richard has never guessed – not that he is often in my bed these days. I had to pay the doctor, of course, an ironic fee – 'to make certain you've understood my lesson' was how he put it – just the once when my body had recovered. I kept my eyes closed and it wasn't so bad. It did occur to me that he could use it against me, blackmail me for further payments in the flesh, but he never did. For that and his biology lesson I have always been grateful. I even shed a tear when I later heard he had died. An understanding doctor can come in handy at times.

To be fair to Maude, that trapped feeling had emerged

well before her birth. I first felt it one morning when Richard and I were just back from our honeymoon and newly installed in our London house. He kissed me goodbye in my new morning room – which I had chosen to be at the front of the house, overlooking the street rather than the garden, so that I could keep an eye on the world outside – and left to catch his train to work. I watched from the window as he walked away, and felt the same jealousy I had suffered when seeing my brother go off to school. When he had gone round the corner, I turned and looked at the still, quiet room, just on the edge of the city that is the centre of the world, and I began to cry. I was twenty years old, and my life had settled into a long, slow course over which I had no control.

I recovered, of course. I knew very well that I was lucky in many things: to have had an education and a liberal father, to have a husband who is handsome and well enough off that we can afford a cook as well as a live-in maid, and who does not discourage me from bettering myself, even if he is unable to give me the larger world I long for. I dried my tears that morning, grateful that at least my mother-in-law had not been there to see me cry. Small mercies – I thank my God for them.

My marriage is no longer what it once was. Now I dread Richard's announcement about New Year's Eve. I do not know that he really takes pleasure from the experience itself. Rather he is doing it to punish me. But I do not think I am capable of being what he wants me to be, of becoming once more the lively wife who thinks the world a reasonable place and he a reasonable man.

If I could do that, or even pretend to, we could spend our New Year's at home. But I can't do it.

I tried tonight to quell my black feelings and at least not neglect Maude. As we were leaving the bonfire I went up to her, took her hand and slipped it into the crook of my elbow. Maude jumped as if I had bitten her, then looked guilty for having such a response. She held onto me rather awkwardly, but we managed to remain like that for several minutes before she made an excuse and ran to catch up with her friend. To my shame, I was relieved.

May 1904

MAUDE COLEMAN

I know I shouldn't say this, but Grandmother always manages to ruin our day when she visits, even before she arrives. Until her letter came yesterday we were having such a lovely time, sitting around the table on the patio and reading out bits from the papers to each other. That is my favourite time with Mummy and Daddy. It was a warm spring day, the flowers in Mummy's garden were just beginning to bloom, and Mummy for once seemed happy.

Daddy was reading little snippets out from the *Mail*, and Mummy from the local paper all the crimes committed that week – fraud, wife-beating, and petty theft the most common. She loves the crimes page.

'Listen to this,' she said. ' "James Smithson has appeared before the court charged with stealing his neighbour's cat. In his defence Mr Smithson said the puss had made off with the Sunday joint and he was only reclaiming his property, now inside the cat." '

We all three laughed, but when Jenny arrived with the letter Mummy stopped smiling.

'What on earth am I going to do with her for the day?' she said when she had finished the letter.

Daddy didn't answer, but frowned and kept reading his paper.

That was when I suggested visiting the columbarium. I was not entirely certain what a columbarium was, but one had opened at the cemetery, and it sounded grand enough for Grandmother.

'Good idea, Maude,' Mummy said. 'If she'll agree.'

Daddy looked up from the *Mail*. 'I would be very surprised if she agreed to see such an unsavoury thing.'

'Oh, I don't know,' Mummy said. 'I think it's rather a clever idea. I'm surprised you don't, given how much you like urns.'

When I heard the word urn, I knew they would argue, so I ran down to the bottom of the garden to tell Lavinia that we might go to the cemetery the next day. Daddy and Mr Waterhouse have put up ladders so that we can climb the fence more easily, after I sprained my wrist once from falling.

I am rather frightened of Grandmother. She looks as if she has swallowed a fishbone and can't get it out, and she says things that I would be punished for saying. Today when she arrived she looked at me and said, 'Lord, child, you are plain. No one would guess you were Kitty's daughter. Or my granddaughter, for that matter.' She always likes to remind everyone that she was a beauty when she was younger.

We went up to the morning room, and Grandmother said once again that she did not approve of the colours Mummy had done the room in. I rather like them. They remind me of the workman's café Jenny sometimes takes me to as a treat, where there is a pot of mustard and a

76

bottle of brown sauce on each table. Perhaps Mummy saw them there and decided to use them in her morning room – though it is hard to imagine Mummy in a workman's café, with all the smoke and grease and the men who have not shaved. Mummy has always said she prefers a man with smooth skin like Daddy's.

Mummy ignored Grandmother's remarks. 'Coffee, please, Jenny,' she ordered.

'Not for me,' Grandmother said. 'Just a cup of hot water and a slice of lemon.'

I stood behind them by the window so that I could look out through the venetian blinds. It was dusty outside, what with all the activity in the street – horses pulling carts loaded with milk, coal, ice, the baker's boy going door to door with his basket of bread, boys bringing letters, maids running errands. Jenny always says she is at war with dust and is losing the battle.

I liked looking out. When I turned back to the room, where dust floated in a shaft of sunlight, it seemed very still.

'Why are you lurking back there?' Grandmother said. 'Come out so we can see you. Play us something on the piano.'

I looked at Mummy, horrified. She knew I hated playing.

She was no help. 'Go on, Maude,' she said. 'Play us something from your last lesson.'

I sat down at the piano and wiped my hands on my pinafore. I knew Grandmother would prefer a hymn to Mozart, so I began to play 'Abide with me', which I know Mummy hates. After a few bars Grandmother said, 'Gracious, child, that's terrible. Can't you play better than that?'

I stopped and stared down at the keys; my hands were trembling. I hated Grandmother's visits.

'Come, now, Mother Coleman, she's nine years old,' Mummy at last defended me. 'She hasn't been taking lessons for long.'

'A girl needs to learn these things. How's her sewing?'

'Not good,' Mummy answered frankly. 'She's inherited that from me. But she reads very well. She's reading *Sense and Sensibility*, aren't you, Maude?'

I nodded. 'And *Through the Looking-Glass* again. Daddy and I have been recreating the chess game from it.'

'Reading,' Grandmother said, her fishbone look even stronger. 'That won't get a girl anywhere. It'll just put ideas in her head. Especially rubbish like those Alice books.'

Mummy sat up a little straighter. She read all the time. 'What's the matter with a girl having ideas, Mother Coleman?'

'She won't be satisfied with her life if she has ideas,' Grandmother said. 'Like you. I always said to my son that you wouldn't be happy. "Marry her if you must," I said, "but she'll never be satisfied." I was right. You always want something more, but all your ideas don't tell you what.'

Mummy didn't say anything, but sat with her hands clasped so tightly in her lap I could see the whites of her knuckles.

'But *I* know what you need.'

Mummy glanced at me, then shook her head at Grandmother, which meant Grandmother was about to say something I should not hear. 'You should have more children,' she said, ignoring Mummy. She always ignores Mummy. 'The doctor said there's no physical reason why you can't. You'd like a brother or sister, wouldn't you, Maude?'

I looked from Grandmother to Mummy. 'Yes,' I said, to punish Mummy for making me play the piano. I felt bad the moment I said it, but it was true, after all. I am often jealous of Lavinia because she has Ivy May, even though Ivy May can be a nuisance when she has to come everywhere with us.

Just then Jenny arrived with a tray, and we were all relieved to see her. When she had served them I managed to slip out after her as she left. Mummy was saying something about the Summer Exhibition at the Royal Academy. 'It's sure to be rubbish,' Grandmother was saying as I shut the door.

'*Rubbish*,' Jenny repeated when we were in the kitchen, her head shaking and her nose wrinkling. She sounded so much like Grandmother that I laughed till my stomach hurt.

I sometimes wonder why Grandmother bothers to visit. She and Mummy disagree on almost everything, and Grandmother is not very polite about it. It is always left to Mummy to smooth things over. 'The privilege of age,' Daddy says whenever Mummy complains.

For a moment I felt bad about abandoning Mummy upstairs, but I was still angry that she said my sewing was as bad as my piano. So I stayed in the kitchen and helped Mrs Baker with lunch. We were to have cold cow's tongue and salad, and lady's fingers for pudding. Lunches with Grandmother are never very interesting.

When Jenny came down with the coffee tray she said she

had overheard Grandmother say she does want to visit the columbarium, 'even though it is for *heathens*.' I didn't wait for her to finish, but ran to get Lavinia.

KITTY COLEMAN

Frankly I was surprised that Mrs Coleman was so keen on seeing the columbarium. I expect the idea appeals to her sense of tidiness and economy, though she made it clear it would never be appropriate for Christians.

At any rate I was relieved to have something to do with her. I always dread her visits, though it is easier than when I was first married. It has taken these ten years of marriage to learn to handle her — like a horse, except that I have never managed a horse — they are so big and clumsy.

But handle her I have. The portraits, for example. As a wedding present she gave us several dark oil portraits of various Colemans from the last century or so, all with the same dour expression that she wears as well — which is remarkable given that she married into the family rather than inheriting the look.

They are dreary things, but Mrs Coleman insisted they be hung in the hallway where every visitor could see and admire them; and Richard did nothing to dissuade her. It is rare he will cross her. His one rebellious act has been to marry a doctor's daughter from Lincolnshire, and he will probably spend the rest of his days avoiding other conflicts.

So up went the portraits. After six months I found some botanical watercolours exactly the same size, and hung them instead, replacing them with the portraits whenever Mrs Coleman came to call. Luckily she is not the kind of woman to pay surprise visits – she always announces her arrival the day before, giving me plenty of time to switch paintings.

After several years of swapping I grew more confident, and at last felt able to leave up the watercolours. Of course on arrival she noticed them first thing, before she had even unbuttoned her coat. 'Where are the family portraits?' she demanded. 'Why are they not in their places?'

Luckily I was prepared. 'Oh, Mother Coleman' (how it grates to call her that – she is no mother to me), 'I was concerned that the draughts from the door might damage them, and so I had them rehung in Richard's study, where he can take comfort from his ancestors' presence.'

Her response was typical. 'I myself don't know why you've left them there all that time. I should like to have said something, but this is your home, after all, and far be it from me to tell you how to run it.'

Jenny almost dropped Mrs Coleman's coat on the floor from giggling – she knew all too well the palaver that had gone on over the pictures, for it had been she who'd helped me switch the paintings each time.

I did have one victory over Mrs Coleman early on, and it has seen me through many a grinding afternoon with her when afterwards I have had to lie down with a dose of Beecham's. Mrs Baker was my triumph. I chose her as our cook because of her name – the frivolity of the reason was irresistible. And I could not help it – I told Mrs Coleman as well.

When she heard she spat out her tea, appalled. 'Chosen for her name? Don't be ridiculous! What way is that to run a household?'

To my immense satisfaction, Mrs Baker — a small, self-contained woman who reminds me of a bundle of twigs — has turned out to be a gem, a thrifty, able cook who instinctively understands certain things so that I do not need to spell them out. When I tell her Mrs Coleman is coming for lunch, for example, she serves bouillon rather than mulligatawny, a poached egg rather than an omelette. Yes, she is a gem.

Jenny has been more of a trial, but I like her better than Mrs Baker, who has a way of looking at everyone sideways and so appearing constantly suspicious. Jenny has a big mouth and wide cheeks — a face made for laughing. She is always going about her work with a smirk on her face, as if she is about to burst with some great joke. And she does, too — I can hear her laugh all the way up from the kitchen. I try not to think it but I can't help wondering if the laughter is ever directed at me. I am sure it is.

Mrs Coleman says she is not to be trusted, of course. I suspect she may be right. There is something restless about Jenny that suggests one day she will crash, and we will all suffer the consequences. But I am determined to keep her on, if only to annoy Mrs Coleman.

And she has been good for Maude — she is a warm girl. (Mrs Baker is cold like pewter.) Since Maude's nanny left and I am meant to be looking after her, Jenny has become indispensable in keeping an eye on her. She often takes her to the cemetery — a whim of Lavinia's that Maude has unfortunately adopted and which I did not nip in the bud as I ought to have done. Jenny doesn't complain much — I suspect she welcomes the chance for a rest. She always leaves for the cemetery in high spirits.

Maude said the Waterhouses would like to come along to see the columbarium too, which was just as well. I suspected that Gertrude Waterhouse is, if not the class of woman Mrs Coleman would have had her son marry (not that I was either), then at least more compatible with her. They could talk about their mutual adoration of the late Queen, if nothing else.

The columbarium is housed in one of the vaults in the Circle of Lebanon, where a sort of channel has been dug round a big Lebanon cedar and lined with a double row of family vaults. To get to it one walks up the Egyptian Avenue, a gloomy row of vaults overhung with rhododendrons, the entrance done in the Egyptian style, with elaborate columns decorated with lotus flowers. The whole thing is rather theatrical — I am sure it was very stylish back in the 1840s, and now it makes me want to laugh. The tree is lovely, at least, its branches crooked and almost horizontally spread, like an umbrella of blue-green needles. With the blue sky behind it like today it can make the heart soar.

Perhaps I should have prepared the girls more for what they were about to see. Maude is quite phlegmatic and robust, and Ivy May, the younger Waterhouse girl with the big hazel eyes, keeps her thoughts to herself. But Lavinia is the kind of girl who will find any excuse to fall into a faint, which she promptly did the moment she peered through the iron grillwork into the columbarium. Not that there is much to see, really — it is a small, high vault lined with cubicles of about one foot by eighteen inches. They are all empty except for two quite high up which have been covered over with stone plaques, and another with an urn sitting in it, with no plaque as of yet. Given that there are urns everywhere on graves here, it is hard to see what Lavinia made such a fuss about.

It was secretly gratifying too, I must confess, for up until that moment Gertrude Waterhouse and Mrs Coleman had been getting on very well. I would never say I was jealous, but it did make me feel rather inadequate. However, when Gertrude had to attend to her prone daughter, waving smelling salts under her nose while Ivy May fanned her with a handkerchief, Mrs Coleman grew more disapproving. 'What's wrong with the girl?' she barked.

'She's a bit sensitive, I'm afraid,' poor Gertrude replied. 'She's not meant to see such sights.'

Mrs Coleman humphed. Her humphs are often more damaging than her words.

While we waited for Lavinia to revive, Maude asked me why it was called a columbarium.

'That's Latin for dovecote, where birds live.'

'But birds don't live there.'

'No. The little cubbyholes are for urns, as you can see, like what we have on our grave except much smaller.'

'But why do they keep urns there?'

'Most people when they die are buried in coffins. But some people choose to be burned. The urns hold their ashes and this is where you can put them.'

'Burned?' Maude looked a bit shocked.

'Cremated is the word, actually,' I said. 'There's nothing wrong with it. In a way it's less frightening than being buried. Much quicker, at least. It's becoming a little more popular now. Perhaps I'd like to be cremated.' I threw out the last comment rather flippantly, as I had never really considered it before. But now, staring at the urn in one of the cubby-holes, it began to appeal — though I should not want my ashes placed in an urn. Rather they be scattered somewhere, to help the flowers grow.

'Rubbish!' Mrs Coleman interrupted. 'And it's entirely inappropriate for a girl of Maude's age to be told about such things.' Having said that, however, she couldn't resist continuing. 'Besides, it's un-Christian and illegal. I wonder if it is even legal to build such a thing —' she waved at the columbarium — 'if it encourages criminal activity.'

As she was speaking a man came trotting down the steps next to the columbarium that led from the upper to the lower level of the Circle. He stopped abruptly when he heard her. 'Pardon me, madam,' he said, bowing to Mrs Coleman. 'I couldn't help overhearing your comment. Indeed, crem-ation is not illegal. It has never been illegal in England — it's simply been disapproved of by society, and so it has not been carried out. But there have been crematoria for many years — the first was built at Woking in 1885.'

'Who are you?' Mrs Coleman demanded. 'And what business is it of yours what I say?'

'Pardon me, madam,' the man repeated, with another bow. 'I am Mr Jackson, the superintendent of the cemetery. I simply wished to set you straight on the facts of cremation because I wanted to reassure you that there is nothing illegal about the columbarium. The Cremation Act passed two years ago regulates the procedures and practice throughout all of Britain. The cemetery is simply responding to the public's demand, and reflecting public opinion on the matter.'

'You are certainly not reflecting *my* opinion on the matter, young man,' Mrs Coleman huffed, 'and I am a grave owner here – have been for almost fifty years.'

I smiled at her idea of a young man – he looked to be forty at least, with grey hairs in his rather bushy moustache. He was quite tall, and wore a dark suit with a bowler hat. If he had not introduced himself I would have thought he was a mourner. I had probably seen him before, but could not remember him.

'I am not saying that cremation should never be practised,' Mrs Coleman went on. 'For non-Christians it can be an option: the Hindu and the Jew, atheists and suicides, those sorts who don't care about their souls. But I am truly shocked to see such a thing sited on consecrated ground. It should have been placed in the Dissenters' section, where the ground is not blessed. Here it is an offence to Christianity.'

'Those whose remains lie in the columbarium were certainly Christian, madam,' Mr Jackson said.

'But what about reassembly? How can the body and soul be reunited on the Day of Resurrection if the body has been –' Mrs Coleman did not complete her sentence, but waved a hand at the cubicles.

'Burned to a crisp,' Maude finished for her. I stifled a giggle.

Rather than wilting under her onslaught, Mr Jackson seemed to grow from it. He stood quite calmly, hands clasped behind his back, as if he were discussing a mathematical equation rather than a sticky question of theology. Maude and I, and the Waterhouses – Lavinia having recovered by this time – all stared at him, waiting for him to speak.

'Surely there is no difference between the decomposed

remains of a buried body and the ashes of a burned one,' he said.

'There is all the difference!' Mrs Coleman sputtered. 'But this is a most distasteful argument, especially in front of our girls here, one of whom has just recovered from a fit.'

Mr Jackson looked around as if he were just seeing the rest of us. 'My apologies, ladies,' he bowed (again). 'I did not mean to offend.' But then he did not leave the argument, as Mrs Coleman clearly wanted him to. 'I would simply say that God is capable of all things, and nothing we do with our remains will stop Him if he wishes to reunite our souls with our bodies.'

There was a little silence then, punctuated by a tiny gasp from Gertrude Waterhouse. The implication behind his words — that with her argument Mrs Coleman might be doubting the power of God Himself — was not lost on her. Nor on Mrs Coleman, who, for the first time since I have known her, seemed at a loss for words. It was not a long moment, of course, but it was an immensely satisfying one.

'Young man,' Mrs Coleman said finally, 'if God wanted us to burn our dead he would have said so in the Bible. Come, Maude,' she said, turning her back on him, 'it is time we paid a visit to our grave.'

As she led away a reluctant Maude, Mr Jackson glanced at me and I smiled at him. He bowed for the fourth time, muttered something about having a great deal to do, and rushed off, quite red in the face.

Well, I thought. Well.

LAVINIA WATERHOUSE

I didn't mean to faint, really I didn't. I know Maude thinks I bring it on deliberately, but I didn't – not this time. It was just that when I looked into the columbarium, I was sure I saw a little movement. I thought it might be the ghost of one of the poor souls with their ashes in there, hovering about in search of its body. Then I felt something touch the back of my neck and I knew it must be a ghost, and I fainted.

When I told Maude afterwards what had happened she said it was probably the shadow from the cedar against the back wall of the columbarium. But I know what I saw, and it was not of this world.

Afterwards I felt quite wretched, but no one paid any attention to me, not even to get me a glass of water – they were all agog at that man talking about burning and whatnot. I could not follow what he said at all, it was so tedious.

Then Maude's grandmother dragged her off, and our mothers began to follow, and only Ivy May waited for me. She can be a dear sometimes. I got to my feet and was brushing off my dress when I heard a noise above me and looked up to see Simon on the roof of the columbarium! I couldn't help but scream, what with the ghost and all. I don't think anyone but Ivy May heard me – no one came back to see what was wrong.

When I had recovered I said, 'What are you doing up there, naughty boy?'

'Looking at you,' he said cheekily.

'Do you like me, then?' I asked.

'Sure.'

'Better than Maude? I'm prettier.'

'Her mum's the prettiest of all,' he said.

I frowned. That was not at all what I'd wanted him to say. 'Come, Ivy May,' I said, 'we must find the others.' I held out my hand to her, but she would not take it. She just looked up at Simon, her hands clasped behind her as if she were inspecting something.

'Ivy May don't say much, do she?' he said.

'No, she doesn't.'

'Sometimes I do,' she said.

'There you go,' Simon nodded. He smiled at her, and to my surprise Ivy May smiled back.

That was when the man came back – Mr Jackson, the one who talked about all the burning. He rushed round the corner, saw Simon and me and stopped.

'What are you doing here, Simon? You're meant to be helping your father. And what are you doing with these girls? They're not for the likes of you. Has he been bothering you, young lady?' he said to me.

'Oh, yes, he's been bothering me awfully,' I said.

'Simon! I'll have your father's job for this. Go and tell him to stop digging. That's the end of you, lad.'

I wasn't sure if he was bluffing. But Simon scrambled to his feet and stared at the man. He looked as if he wanted to say something, but he glanced at me and didn't. Then suddenly he took a few steps back and before I knew it he'd jumped clear over our heads from the roof of the columbarium to the Circle with the cedar in it. I was so surprised I just stood there with my mouth open. He must have jumped ten feet.

'Simon!' the man shouted again. Simon scrambled up the cedar and began creeping out along one of the branches. When he was quite a long way up he stopped and sat on the branch with his back to us, swinging his legs. He wore no shoes.

'She was lying. He wasn't bothering us.'

Ivy May often chooses to speak just when I don't want her to. I felt like pinching her.

Mr Jackson raised his eyebrows. 'What was he doing?'

I couldn't think what to say, and looked at Ivy May.

'He was showing us where to go,' Ivy May said.

I nodded. 'We were lost, you see.'

Mr Jackson sighed. His jaw moved about as if he were chewing something. 'Why don't I escort you two young ladies to your mother. Do you know where she is?'

'At our grave,' I said.

'And what is your name?'

'Lavinia Ermyntrude Waterhouse.'

'Ah, in the meadow, with an angel on it.'

'Yes. I chose that angel, you know.'

'Come with me, then.'

As we turned to follow him I did give Ivy May a great

pinch, but it was not very satisfying because she did not cry out. I suppose she thought she had used her mouth enough for one day.

EDITH COLEMAN

I cut short my visit. I had planned to stay to supper and to see Richard, but found the trip to the cemetery so trying that when we returned to my son's house I asked the maid to fetch me a cab. The girl was standing in the hallway with a dose of Beecham's on a tray — the only time she has ever had the sense to anticipate anyone's needs. She had flavoured it with lime water, which was entirely unnecessary, and I told her so, at which point she giggled. Insolent girl. I would have shown her the door in an instant, but Kitty didn't seem to notice.

It was most annoying that Kitty didn't tell me who the Waterhouses were — then I would have avoided an unfortunate moment. (I can't help wondering if she did it deliberately.) When we visited our grave I remarked on the angel on the next grave. Richard has indicated for some time that he intends to ask the grave owners to replace the angel with an urn to match ours. I merely asked Gertrude Waterhouse her opinion — neglecting as I did so to note the name on the grave. I was as surprised to discover it is their angel as she was to find we do not like it. In the interest of getting the truth out into the open — someone must, after all, and these things always seem to come down to me — I set aside any social embarrassment I felt and explained that everyone would prefer the graves to have matching urns. But then Kitty undermined my argument by saying she rather liked the angel now, while at the same time Gertrude Waterhouse confessed they did not at all like our urn. (Fancy that!)

Then that tiresome Waterhouse girl piped up, saying that if the graves had matching urns people would think the two families were related. That remark gave me pause, I must say. I don't think such an association with the Waterhouses would be beneficial to the Colemans in the least.

And I don't think much of the Waterhouse girl's influence over my granddaughter — she has no sense of proportion, and she may well ruin Maude's. Maude could do much better for a friend.

I wash my hands of the affair of the angel and the urn. I have tried, but it is for the men to sort out, while we women bear the consequences. It is unlikely that Richard will do anything now, as it has been over three years since the angel was erected, and apparently he and Albert Waterhouse are quite friendly on the cricket team.

It was all very awkward, and I was furious with Kitty for making it so. It is just like her to embarrass me. She has never been easy, but I was more inclined to be tolerant of her when she and Richard were first married, as I knew she made him happy. These past few years, however, they have clearly been at odds. I could never speak to Richard of it, of course, but frankly I am sure she does not welcome him into her bed — otherwise they would have more children and Richard would not look so grim. I can do nothing but hint to Kitty that things ought to be otherwise, but it has no effect — she no longer makes Richard happy, and she seems unlikely to make me a grandmother again.

Now, to smooth things over with Gertrude Waterhouse, I changed the subject to the upkeep of the cemetery, about which I was sure we would all be in agreement. When my husband and I were married he brought me to the cemetery to show me the Coleman family grave, and I was all the more certain that I had chosen well in a husband. It looked to be a solid, safe and orderly place: the boundary walls were high, the flowerbeds and paths well-tended, the staff unobtrusive and professional. The much-praised landscape design did not interest me, and I didn't care for the excesses of the Egyptian Avenue and Circle of Lebanon, but I recognised them as features that have established the reputation of the cemetery as the preferred burial place of our class. Far be it from me to complain.

Now, however, standards are slipping. Today I saw dead tulips in the flowerbeds. That would never have happened thirty years ago — then a flower was replaced the moment it passed its prime. And it is not just the management. Some grave owners are even choosing to plant wild flowers around their graves! Next they'll bring in a cow to munch the buttercups.

As an example of lowered standards I pointed out some ivy from an adjacent grave (not the Waterhouses') that was creeping up the side of ours. If nothing is done it will soon cover the urn and topple it. Kitty made to pull it off, but I stopped her, saying it was for the cemetery management to make sure other people's ivy doesn't grow onto our property. I insisted that she leave the ivy as evidence, and that the superintendent himself be alerted to the situation.

To my surprise Kitty went off then and there to find the superintendent, leaving Gertrude Waterhouse and me to make awkward conversation until she reappeared — which was a very long time indeed. She must have taken a turn around the entire cemetery.

To be fair, Gertrude Waterhouse is pleasant enough. What she needs is more backbone. She should take some from my daughter-in-law, who has far more than is good for her.

SIMON FIELD

I like it up the tree. You can see all over the cemetery, and down to town. You can sit up there all peaceful and no one else sees you. One of them big black crows comes and sits on the branch near me. I don't throw nothing or yell at it. I let it sit with me.

I don't stay long, though. When the girls are gone a few minutes I climb down to find 'em. I'm running down the main path when I see Mr Jackson coming the other way and I have to dive behind a grave.

He's talking to one of the gardeners. 'Who is that woman with the girls?' he says. 'The one wearing the apple-green dress?'

'Tha's Mrs Coleman, guv. Kitty Coleman. You know that grave down by the paupers with the big urn? Tha's theirs.'

'Yes, of course. The urn and the angel, too close together.'

'Tha's it. She's a looker, ain't she?'

'Watch yourself, man.'

The gardener chuckled. 'Sure, guv. Sure I'll watch myself.'

When they've passed I go down to the graves. I have to hide from the gardeners working in the meadow. It's tidy here, all the grass clipped and the weeds pulled and the paths raked. Some places in the cemetery they don't bother with so much now, but in the meadow there's always someone doing something. Mr Jackson says it has to look good for the visitors, else they won't buy plots and there'll be no money to pay us. Our Pa says that's rubbish — people die every day and need a place to be buried, and they'll pay whether the grass is cut or no. He says all that matters is a grave well dug.

I crouch down behind the grave with the angel on it. Livy's grave. There still ain't no skull 'n' crossbones marked on it, though it makes my fingers itch to see it blank like that. I kept my word.

The ladies are standing in front of the two graves talking, and Livy and Maude are sitting in the grass, making chains out of little daisies. I peek out now and then but they don't see me. Only Ivy May does. She stares straight at me with big greeny-brown eyes like a cat that freezes when it sees you and waits to see what you're going to do — kick it or pat it. She don't say nothing and I put my finger on my mouth to go shhh. I owe her for saving our Pa's job.

Then I hear the lady in the green dress say, 'I'll go and find the superintendent, Mr Jackson. He may be able to get someone to look after things here.'

'It won't make any difference,' the old lady says. 'It's the attitude that's changed. The attitude of this new age which doesn't respect the dead.'

'Nevertheless, he can at least have someone remove the ivy since you won't allow me to,' the lady in green says. She kicks at her skirts. I like it when she does that. It's like she's trying to kick 'em off. 'I'll just go and find him. Won't be a minute.' She goes up the path and I slip from grave to grave, following her.

I'd like to tell her where Mr Jackson is now but I don't know myself. There's three graves being dug today, and four funerals. There's a column being put up near the monkey puzzle tree, and there's some new graves sunk and need more dirt on 'em. Mr Jackson could be any of them places, overseeing the men. Or he could be having a cuppa down the lodge, or selling someone a grave. She don't know that, though.

On the main path she almost gets run down by a team of horses pulling a slab of granite. She jumps back, but she don't shriek like lots of ladies would. She just stands there, all white, and I have to hide behind a yew tree while she takes out a handkerchief and presses it to her forehead and neck.

Near the Egyptian Avenue another lot of diggers comes down towards her with spades over their shoulders. They're hard men – our Pa and me stay away from 'em. But when she stops 'em and says something they look at the ground, both of 'em, like they're under a spell. One points up the path and over to the right and she thanks 'em and walks the way he pointed. When she's past they look at each other and one says something I can't hear and they both laugh.

They don't see me following her. I jump from grave to grave, ducking behind the tombstones. The granite slabs on the graves are warm under my feet where they've been in the sun. Sometimes I just stand still for a minute to feel that warmth. Then I run to catch up with her. Her back from behind looks like an hour-glass. We got hour-glasses on graves here with wings on 'em. Time flies, our Pa says they mean. You think you got long in this world but you don't.

She turns down the path by the horse statue into the Dissenters, and then I remember they're trimming branches off the horse chestnuts back there. We go round a corner and there's Mr Jackson with four gardeners — two on the ground and two who have climbed a big chestnut tree. One of 'em straddles a branch and shinnies out along it, holding tight with his legs. A gardener on the ground makes a joke about the branch being a woman, and everybody laughs 'cept Mr Jackson and the lady, who nobody knows is there yet. She smiles, though.

They've tied ropes round the branch and the two men up the tree are pulling back and forth on a two-man saw. They stop to wipe the sweat off their faces, and to unstick the saw when it gets caught.

Some of the men see the lady in the green dress. They nudge each other but nobody tells Mr Jackson. She looks happier watching the men in the tree than when she was with the other ladies. Her eyes are dark, like there's coal smudged round them, and little bits of her hair are coming out of their pins.

Suddenly there's a crack, and the branch breaks where they're sawing it. The lady cries out, and Mr Jackson turns round and sees her. The men let the branch down with the ropes and when it's on the ground they start sawing it to pieces.

Mr Jackson comes over to the lady. He's red in the face like it's him been sawing the branch all this time instead of telling others what to do.

'I'm sorry, Mrs Coleman, I didn't see you. Have you been here long?'

'Long enough to hear a tree branch compared to a woman.'

Mr Jackson sputters like his beer's gone down the wrong way.

Mrs Coleman laughs. 'That's all right,' she says. 'It was quite refreshing, actually.'

Mr Jackson don't seem to know what to say. Lucky for him one of the men in the tree shouts down, 'Any other branches to cut here, guv?'

'No, just take this one down to the bonfire area. Then we're finished here.'

'Do you have fires here?' Mrs C. asks.

'At night, yes, to burn wood and leaves and other refuse. Now, madam, how may I be of service?'

'I wanted to thank you for speaking to my mother-in-law about cremation,' she says. 'It was very instructive, though I expect she was rather taken aback to be answered so forth-rightly.'

'Those with firm opinions must be dealt with firmly.'

'Whom are you quoting?'

'Myself.'

'Oh.'

They don't say nothing for a minute. Then she says, 'I think I should like to be cremated, now that I know it will be no more of a challenge to God than interment.'

'It is something you must consider carefully and decide for yourself, madam. It is not a decision to be taken lightly.'

'I don't know about that,' she says. 'Sometimes I think it

matters not a jot what I do or don't do, or what is done to me.'

He looks at her shocked, like she's just cursed. Then one of the gatekeepers comes running up the path and says, 'Guv, the Anderson procession's at the bottom of Swain's Lane.'

'Already?' Mr Jackson says. He pulls his watch from his pocket. 'Blast, they're early. Send a boy over to the grave to tell the diggers to stand by. I'll be down in a moment.'

'Right, guv.' The man runs back down the path.

'Is it always this busy?' Mrs C. says. 'So much activity doesn't encourage quiet contemplation. Though I suppose it is a little quieter here in the Dissenters.'

'A cemetery is a business, like any other,' Mr Jackson says. 'People tend to forget that. Today in fact is relatively quiet for burials. But I'm afraid we can't guarantee peace and quiet, except on Sundays. It's the nature of the work – it's impossible to predict when people will pass on. We must be prepared to act swiftly – nothing can be planned in advance. We have had twenty funerals in one day. Other days we've had none. Now, madam, was there something else you wanted? I'm afraid I must be getting on.'

'Oh, it seems so trivial now, compared to all this.' She waves her hand round her. I'll have to ask our Pa what trivial means.

'Nothing is trivial here. What is it?'

'It's about our grave down in the meadow. Some ivy from another grave is growing up the side of it. Though I believe it is our responsibility to cut it, it's rather upset my mother-in-law, who feels the cemetery should complain to the neighbouring grave owner.'

Now I understand what trivial means.

Mr Jackson smiles a smile you only see when he's with visitors, like he's got a pain in his back and is trying to hide it. Mrs C. looks embarrassed.

'I'll have someone remove it at once,' he says, 'and I shall have a word with the other owners.' He looks round as if he's looking for a boy to give orders to, so I step out from the stone I was standing behind. It's risky 'cause I know he's still mad at me for hanging round Livy and Ivy May rather'n working. But I want Mrs C. to see me.

'I'll do it, sir,' I say.

Mr Jackson looks surprised. 'Simon, what are you doing here? Have you been harassing Mrs Coleman?'

'I don't know what harassing means, sir, but I ain't been doing it. I'm just offering to clear off that ivy.'

Mr Jackson is about to say something but Mrs C. interrupts. 'Thank you, Simon. That would be very kind of you.' And she smiles at me.

No lady's ever said such a nice thing to me, nor smiled at me. I can't move, staring at her smile.

'Go, boy. Go,' Mr Jackson says quietly.

I smile back at her. Then I go.

January 1905

JENNY WHITBY

It were a right nuisance, that was sure. We'd got into a routine, he and I. Everyone was happy – the missus, the girls, him and me. (I always come last on the list.) I'd take the girls up the hill once a week or so. I'd my bit of fun, they'd theirs, and her ladyship didn't have to do nothing but sit at home and read.

But then she got it into her head to take them to the cemetery herself. In the summer she started going up there two, three times a week. The girls were in heaven, but me, I were in hell.

Then she stopped, and started sending me again, and I thought: It's back on. But now it's winter the girls don't go so much, and when they do she wants to take them again. Sometimes she even takes them when they ain't so keen on going. It's cold there, with all that stone round the place. They have to run to keep warm. Me, I know how to keep warm when I'm there.

Once or twice I've convinced the missus that I should go instead of her. Rest of the time I've to sneak out of an afternoon. He ain't there evenings. Gardeners work shorter hours than maids, I like to remind him.

'Yep, an' we get paid twice as much,' he said. 'It's a dog's life, innit?'

I asked him what it is with the missus — what she goes to the cemetery so much for.

'Maybe the same reason as you,' he said.

'She never!' I laughed. 'Who would she go for, anyhow — a gravedigger?'

'The guvnor, more like,' he said.

I laughed again, but he were serious — said everyone saw 'em together, talking over in the Dissenters.

'Just talking?'

'Yep, just like us,' he said. 'Fact is, we talk too much, you an' me. Just shut your mouth an' open your legs, now.'

Cheeky sod.

October 1905

GERTRUDE WATERHOUSE

I do like to make an effort with my At Homes. I always have them in the front parlour, and use the rose-pattern tea set, and Elizabeth bakes a cake – lemon this week.

Albert asks sometimes if we oughtn't use the front parlour as the dining room instead, rather than eating in the back parlour, which is a bit cramped when the table is pulled out. Now Albert is right in most things, but when it comes to running a household I do get my way. I always feel better having a 'best' room to show visitors to, even if it's only used once or twice a week. Thus I have insisted that we leave the rooms as they are, though I admit it is a bit inconvenient to fold the table back three times a day.

It is very silly too, and I will never tell Albert, but I also prefer to have my At Homes in the front parlour because it is out of view of the Colemans' house. This is very silly because for one thing, according to Livy, who has been to them a few times with Maude (I have never gone, of course), Kitty Coleman has her At Homes in her morning room, which is on the other side of the house, overlooking the street rather than us. And even if it were on this side, she would hardly have the time to look out of her window over at us. But just the same I do not like to think of her presence at my back, judging what I do. It would make me nervous and unable to attend to my visitors.

I am always a little anxious when Lavinia goes to Kitty Coleman's At Homes, which I'm relieved to say is not very often. Indeed, more often than not the girls come here after school. Maude says it's much more snug here, which on reflection I think is intended as a compliment rather than a comment on the lack of space. At any rate I have decided to take it as such. She is a dear girl and I do try to see her as separate from her mother.

I am quietly pleased that, for all the space and elegance of the Colemans' house, it is here that the girls prefer to be. Livy says their house gets very cold and draughty except in the kitchen, and she fears she'll catch a chill — though really apart from her fainting, she has a robust constitution and a healthy appetite. She also says she prefers our comfortable dark sofas and chairs and the velvet curtains to Kitty Coleman's taste for rattan furniture and Venetian blinds.

Until the girls arrive back from school, Ivy May helps me with the At Homes, passing round the cake and taking the teapot back to the kitchen for Elizabeth to fill. The ladies who come — neighbours from the street and from church, and stalwart friends who make the journey from Islington to see me, bless them — all smile at her, though they are often puzzled by her as well.

She is indeed a funny little thing. At first her refusal to speak very often did upset me, but over time I've grown used to it and now love her the better for it. Ivy May's silence can be a great comfort after Livy's dramas and tears. And there is nothing the matter with her head — she reads and writes well enough for a girl of seven, and her numbers are good. In a year I will send her to school with Livy and Maude, and then it may be harder for her — her teachers may not be so patient with her as we are.

I asked her once why she said so little, and the dear replied, 'When I do speak, you listen.' It is surprising that someone so young should have worked that out for herself. I could have done with the lesson — I do go on and on, from nerves and to fill the silence. Sometimes in front of Kitty Coleman I could just sink into the ground from hearing myself chatter like a performing monkey. Kitty Coleman just smiles as if she's terribly bored but hiding it so civilly.

When the girls get home Livy immediately takes over the passing out of the cake to the ladies and little Ivy May sits quietly in the corner. It breaks my heart sometimes. Still, I am glad to have the girls around me, and I try to make things as comfortable as possible. Here at least I can have some influence over them. I don't know what Kitty Coleman gets up to when they are at Maude's. Mostly she ignores them, according to Livy.

They like to come here, but they love best of all to go to the cemetery. I have had to limit how often Livy may go — else she'd be up there every day. As it is, I do believe she lies to me about it. A neighbour said she thought she saw Livy and Maude running among the graves with a boy one day when she was meant to be playing at Maude's, but when I questioned her she denied it, saying the neighbour must need new spectacles! I did not look convinced, and Livy began to cry to think I suspected her of lying. So really I do not know what to think.

I wanted to have a word with Kitty Coleman about the

frequency of their visits – it being she who most often takes them. What an awkward conversation it was! She does make me feel such a fool. When I suggested that it was perhaps unhealthy for them to visit the cemetery so often, she replied, 'Oh, the girls are getting plenty of fresh air, which is very healthy for them. But really if they want to go there, we have Queen Victoria to blame for it, elevating mourning to such ridiculous heights that girls with romantic notions grow drunk from it.'

Well! I was mortified, and not a little angry too. Apart from the slight on Livy, Kitty Coleman knows how dear the late Queen still is to me, God bless her soul. There is no need to go criticising the dead. I told Kitty Coleman so, straight to her face.

She just smiled and said, 'If we can't criticise her now, when can we? Do so when she was alive and we'd likely have been tried for treason.'

'The monarchy is above criticism,' I responded with as much dignity as I could muster. 'They are our sovereign representatives, and we do well to look up to them or it reflects poorly on us.'

Soon after I made my excuses and left, still furious with her. It was only afterwards that I remembered I had not properly spoken to her about curtailing Livy's cemetery visits. She is impossible – I shall never understand her. If I am honest, nor do I wish to.

February 1906

MAUDE COLEMAN

I know every inch of the cemetery now. I know it better than my own garden. Mummy does take us there all the time, even after school in winter when it is already getting dark and we have not asked to go.

Of course it is great fun playing there. We find Simon first, and if he is free he comes with us for a bit. We play hide and seek, and tour the angels (there are two new ones), and sometimes we sit at our graves and Lavinia tells stories about the people buried in the cemetery. She has an old guide to the cemetery that she likes to read from, about the girl whose dress caught fire, or the lieutenant-colonel killed in the Boer War described as 'brave and kind-hearted', or the man who died in a railway accident. Or she simply makes up stories, which I find rather tedious but which Simon likes. I haven't the imagination she has. I am more interested in the plants and trees, or the kind of stone used for the memorials; or, if Ivy May is with is, I test her reading using words on the graves.

I do not know what Mummy does while we play. She wanders off and I rarely see her until she comes looking for us when it is time to go. She says it is good for us to take the air, and I suppose she is right, but I am sometimes cold and, I admit, a little weary of the place. It is funny to think how desperate I used to be to get to the cemetery when I wasn't allowed to, and yet now that I go there all the time, it is no longer quite so special.

KITTY COLEMAN

He will not have me. I am mad for him but he will not have me.

For almost two years I have visited the cemetery solely for the purpose of seeing him. And yet he will not take me.

I was careful at first — although I sought him out I did not want it to appear so. I always took the girls with me, then let them go off to play and pretended to be looking for them when really I was looking for him. I have paced up and down its paths, appearing to be fascinated by the merits of Roman versus plain crosses, or obelisks in Portland stone versus granite, or the names on graves chiselled into the stone versus fastened on with metal letters. I do not know what the workers there think of me, but they have grown used to my presence, and always nod respectfully.

I have learned a great deal about the cemetery that I did not know before. I know where they dump the extra soil displaced by coffins, and where the timber is kept for shoring up the deep graves, and the green rugs they place round freshly dug graves to look like grass. I know which grave-diggers sing as they work, and where they hide their bottles of spirits. I have seen the ledgers and the detailed maps, each plot numbered, used to record graves. I have grown used to the horses pulling stones about the place. I have come to know the cemetery as an industry rather than as a place of spiritual contemplation.

He runs it as if it were an immaculate passenger ship crossing the ocean. He can be hard and brutal if necessary with the staff — some of the men are very rough indeed. But I think he is fair, too, and he respects good work.

Above all, he is kind to me without making me feel a lesser person.

We talk about all sorts of things — about the world and how it works, and about God and how He works. He asks my opinions, and does not laugh at them, but considers them. He is how I had always hoped Richard would turn out to be. But I made the mistake of thinking my husband would change when we married; instead he became more entrenched.

John Jackson is not a handsome man. He is not a prosperous man, though he is not poor either. He is not from a good family. He does not attend supper parties or the theatre or openings to exhibitions. He is not an educated man, though he is learned; when he showed me Michael Faraday's grave in the Dissenters he was able to explain his experiments with magnetic fields far better than Richard or even my brother could have.

He is a truthful man, a religious man, a principled man, a moral man. It is those last qualities that have undone me.

I am not accustomed to being turned down. Not that I have offered myself as such before, but I enjoy flirting and expect a response, else I would not do it. But he does not flirt. When I tried to with him, early on, he said he does not like coquettes, that he only wants the truth, and I stopped. And so over several months – constantly interrupted by his cemetery duties – I told him what little there is to tell of my small life: of how much I miss my late parents and brother, of my dull despair, of my impossible search for a place by the fire that is neither too hot nor too cold. (Only a few things I have kept from him – my knowledge of how to avoid having a baby, my cold bed, the New Year's Eve Richard insists upon. He would be disgusted by the last. Myself, I am not disgusted so much as resigned.)

When, at last, in the autumn after a summer of what felt like a courtship, I told him in clear terms what I was prepared to do, he said no.

I stopped going to the cemetery for a time then, sending Jenny with the girls when they wanted to go. But I could not keep away. And so for this past year we have again seen each other, but not as often and without the heightened expectations. It is painful, but he has upheld his principles, and I have come to accept that they are more important than me.

So we meet, and he speaks kindly to me. Today he said to me that he has always wanted a sister and now he has one. I did not reply that I have already had a brother and don't want another.

April 1906

LAVINIA WATERHOUSE

It is so nice to have someone to mourn properly. And now I am eleven and old enough to wear a proper mourning dress, it is even better. Dear Auntie would have been so touched to see me dressed like this, and Papa got tears in his eyes when he saw me 'looking so much like my dear sister'.

I have studied *The Queen* and *Cassell's* very carefully so that I will not make any mistakes, and I have even written my own manual to help out other girls in my position who may have questions about the correct etiquette for mourning. I asked Maude to help me but she was not interested. Sometimes she will go on about constellations, or planets, or stones she has found in the Heath, or plants in her mother's garden, until I just want to scream.

So I have had to do it all myself. I think it has turned out very well — at least Mama says so. I have written it in my best script on black-edged paper, and I got Ivy May to draw an angel on the cover. Her drawing is quite good, and the book looks very handsome. I am going to copy the text below so that I shall always have it.

The Complete Guide to Mourning Etiquette
by Miss Lavinia Ermyntrude Waterhouse

It is a very sad thing when someone dies. We mark the occasion with mourning. We wear special black clothes and black jewellery, we use special stationery for letters, and we do not go to parties or concerts.

Mourning lasts different lengths of time depending upon the loved one who has died.

The Widow mourns the longest because she is the saddest. What a terrible thing it is to lose a husband! She mourns for 2 years – 18 months full mourning, 6 months half-mourning. Some ladies mourn for longer. Our own late Queen wore mourning for her husband Albert for the rest of her life – forty years!

How sad it is for a mother to lose her child, or a child her mother. They mourn for 1 year.

> For brothers and sisters – 6 months
> For grandparents – 6 months
> Uncles and aunts – 2 months
> Great-uncles and great-aunts – 6 weeks
> First cousins – 4 weeks
> Second cousins – 3 weeks

Clothing

It is very important to obtain proper mourning clothes. They must be new, and they must be burned after mourning, because it is bad luck to keep them in the house.

Jay's on Regent Street is where all good London families buy their mourning clothes.

Ladies wear dresses made of best paramatta silk and trimmed with crape for full mourning of their husbands, parents, or children. For grandparents and brothers and sisters, ladies wear plain black silk trimmed with crape. For everyone else ladies wear black with no crape.

Ladies wear black gloves and carry white handkerchiefs edged with black.

After a time they can take off the crape. This is called 'slighting' the mourning.

Then there is half-mourning. Ladies wear grey or lavender or violet, or black and white stripes. Their gloves are grey as well.

Jewellery

During full mourning ladies may wear jet brooches and earrings. The brooches may be adorned with the hair of the loved one. In half-mourning ladies may wear a little gold, silver, and pearls and diamonds.

Stationery

Paper for writing must have a black edge. It is very important that the edge should be wide enough to honour the loved one, but not so wide as to be vulgar.

Gentlemen

Gentlemen wear what they normally wear to work but also wear black hatbands, black cravats, and black gloves. They do not wear jewellery.

Children (under ten)

Children may wear black if they wish, but most often they wear white dresses, and sometimes lavender or mauve or grey. They may wear gloves. Children over ten should wear full mourning.

MAUDE COLEMAN

When we went up to the cemetery today they were taking apart the Waterhouse grave. I knew the funeral for Lavinia's aunt was the next day, but I had thought they would be digging the grave later in the day. It was strange to see Simon and his Pa working on one of our graves rather than a stranger's. I had always thought of our graves as solid and indestructible, but now I know that you can take a crowbar to them and pull them apart, and even knock down an angel in the process.

Lavinia took my arm when she saw the group of men around the grave, and I wondered if she was going to make a scene. I was rather weary of her, I must confess. Since her aunt died she has talked of nothing but black clothes and when she can begin wearing jewellery again — even though she is hardly allowed to wear any anyway! The mourning rules of conduct are quite ferocious, from what she says. I don't think I would be very good at it. I would break rules all the time without even knowing it.

Then Mummy suddenly shouted 'John!' I have never heard her shout so loudly. We all jumped, and next thing I knew Simon's Pa had shoved Mr Jackson and sent him flying. And then the Waterhouse angel hit the ground.

It was all very strange. For the longest time I couldn't connect any of the things I saw. I did not understand why Simon's Pa pushed Mr Jackson and why Mr Jackson, looking very pale, then thanked him for it. I did not understand why the angel had fallen. And I did not understand why Mummy knew Mr Jackson's Christian name.

When I saw that the angel's head had broken from its body I found it hard not to laugh. Lavinia fainted, of course. Then Simon ran off with the angel's head under his arm and I did laugh – it made me think of the poem about Isabella burying her lover's head in the pot of basil.

Luckily Lavinia didn't hear me laugh – she had woken up and was busy being sick. Mummy made a surprising fuss over her, putting her arm round her and handing her a handkerchief.

Lavinia stared at Mummy's handkerchief. 'Oh no, I must use my own mourning handkerchief,' she said.

'It doesn't matter,' Mummy said. 'Really it doesn't.'

'Are you sure?'

'God won't strike you dead for using a plain handkerchief.'

'But it's not to do with God,' Lavinia said very earnestly. 'It's about respecting the dead. My auntie would be so hurt if she thought I wasn't thinking of her in everything I do.'

'I shouldn't think your auntie would want to be thought of while you're wiping your mouth after being sick.'

Ivy May giggled. Lavinia frowned at her.

'Things are changing,' Mummy said. 'No one expects you or your father or mother to go through full mourning any longer. You may not remember this, but King Edward limited the mourning period for his mother to three months.'

'I remember. But my mother wore black for longer than anyone else. And I would feel ashamed if I didn't wear black for my auntie.'

'May I be of assistance, madam?' Mr Jackson asked, standing over them.

'Could you order a cab to take us home, please,' Mummy said without looking at him.

Mr Jackson went off to whistle for a cab. By the time he had returned Lavinia was standing, but she was still very pale and shaken.

'Shall we bring her down to the courtyard?' Mr Jackson asked. 'Can you walk, young lady, or would you like me to carry you?'

'I can walk,' Lavinia said. She took a few wobbly steps.

Mummy slipped her arm round Lavinia's shoulders and Mr Jackson took her elbow. They began to go slowly down the path towards the entrance. As Ivy May and I trailed after them, I noticed that Mummy's and Mr Jackson's hands seemed to be touching under Lavinia's upper arm. I wasn't entirely sure, and I thought for a moment of asking Ivy May what she saw, but then decided against it.

Mr Jackson had to carry Lavinia down the steps to the courtyard, and then she insisted she was well enough to walk on her own. When we got to the front gate a hansom was waiting for us, which was not very big for four people, even if three of us were girls. I suppose it was the first cab to be found. Mr Jackson handed Lavinia in — really he had to lift her, she was so weak. Then he turned and handed me in, and then Ivy May. Ivy May sat on my lap so that there would be room for Mummy. She sat very still, without wriggling. She is a solid little bundle, but I liked having her there, and put my arms round her to keep her steady. It made me wish I had a brother or sister to sit on my lap from time to time.

Mr Jackson handed my mother in and shut the door for her. She opened the window, and he leaned in for a moment to say, 'Goodbye, young ladies. I do hope you feel better, miss,' he added, nodding at Lavinia. 'We'll have your angel up again in no time.'

Lavinia hardly looked at him, but leaned back and closed her eyes.

Then, as the wheels began to turn, I heard someone say in a low voice, 'Tomorrow.' I thought it must be Mr Jackson adding that the angel would be ready in time for the funeral the next day.

Mummy must have heard it too, for she sat up suddenly as if Miss Linden at school had come around with her ruler and prodded her in the side the way she does to us during comportment lessons.

Then we were whizzing down the hill, and I spotted Simon coming out of the mason's yard, without the angel's head. He saw us too, and from the corner of my eye I watched him sprint alongside the hansom until he could not keep up any longer.

SIMON FIELD

This is what happens. I see it all.

When we slide the marble slab off the Waterhouse grave, we has to pry it loose from the base of the plinth where the angel stands. Joe and I are doing it, with our Pa and Mr Jackson watching. Mr Jackson's giving advice the way he likes to do. I want to tell him we knows what we're doing, but he's the guvnor — he can say what he likes.

Joe's working at the slab with a crowbar and he leans against the plinth to put his weight behind the bar. Now Joe's a big strong man and his back's pushing that plinth, and before you know it the plinth starts moving. Them masons must've made a mess of the foundation when they put it in for that to happen. I been digging at the cemetery six years and never seen one shift so.

Worse'n that, the mortar holding the angel to the base of the plinth ain't strong. I see the angel wobble back and forth.

'Joe,' I says, 'stop.'

Joe stops with the crowbar but he's still leaning against the plinth, and the angel wobbles again. I can see the crack in the mortar now, but before I can say something the angel starts to topple. I hear a woman shout just as the angel falls sideways and hits the Coleman urn. The head cracks right off, and it falls one way and the body the other. In fact the body falls right where Mr Jackson's standing, 'cept he ain't there now 'cause our Pa's knocked him right out the way.

It all happens slow and fast too. Then Kitty Coleman and the girls run up to us. Livy takes one look at the headless angel and shrieks and faints, which is nothing new. Mrs C. helps up Mr Jackson — his face is all pale and sweaty. He's breathing heavy and he takes out a kerchief and wipes his face. Then he looks at the base of the plinth and the cracked mortar, clears his throat and says, 'I'm going to strangle that mason with my bare hands.'

I know what he means.

Then he says, 'Thank you, Paul,' real quiet and solemn to our Pa. It sounds funny 'cause he never calls our Pa by his name.

Our Pa just shrugs. 'Dunno what they need an angel up there for anyways,' he says. 'Urns and angels and columns and whatnot. Bloody nonsense. When you're dead you're dead. You don't need an angel to tell you that. Give me a pauper's grave any day.' Our Pa taps one of the paupers' wood crosses. 'My Pa were buried in one and that'll suit me too.'

'Just as well,' Mr Jackson says, 'for that's where you're likely to end up.'

You might think our Pa would be offended, but something in the way Mr Jackson says it makes our Pa smile. The guvnor smiles too, and it's a funny sight, given he's just almost been struck down dead. It's like they're mates sitting over a jar in the pub, laughing at a joke.

'Anyhows, best see to the girlie,' our Pa says then, nodding at Livy. Maude's crouching by her, and Mrs C. goes over to her too. Livy sits up. She's all right – she always is.

Ivy May's standing next to me. 'You should have marked that angel,' she says.

Takes me a minute to work out she means the skull 'n' crossbones. 'Can't,' I say. 'Livy won't let me.'

Ivy May shakes her head and I feel bad, like I let her down. No time to say more, though, 'cause Mr Jackson says to me, 'Simon, run to the mason's yard and tell Mr Watson he's wanted here immediately. If he complains, give him this.' He hands me the angel's head, whose nose is broke off. It's heavy and I almost drop it, which makes Livy shriek again. I tuck it under my arm and run.

JENNY WHITBY

I were in the garden beating carpets when he came tumbling over the fence and fell right at my feet. 'Ow!' I shouted. 'What's this boy doing here? You muddy little rascal, jumping the fence like you own the place. Don't you come tracking that mud from the grave into this garden!'

Cheeky boy just grinned at me. 'Why not?' he said. 'You track enough of it here yourself on the bottom of your skirts. Though we ain't seen much of you these days up at the cemetery.'

'Shut your trap,' I said. Oh, he were cheeky, all right. Simon, he's called. Never said much to him at the cemetery but the girls talk about him all the time. He's the brother Maude never had, I always think.

I seen him creeping behind graves to have a look when I been busy with that gardener. He thought he were hidden, but I seen him. Wanted to see the business. I didn't care — I thought it was funny. Not now, though. Gardener don't want no more to do with me. Bastard.

'I never thought much of him,' Simon said now, like he knew exactly what I was thinking. 'You're well clear of him, I'd say.'

'Shut it,' I said. 'No one asked you.' But I weren't really mad at the boy. Talking to him gave me a chance to rest my back – these days beating rugs is a killer. 'Anyways, what you come here for?'

'Want to see where the girls live.'

'How'd you find it?'

'Ran after their cab. Lost it for a bit, so I just walked round till I saw it again, leaving Maude and her mum here. Must've already let out Livy.'

'Sure, she lives right there, Miss Livy and her sister.' I pointed at the house across the way.

Simon had a good look at it. He's a scrawny boy, for all his digging. His face is pinched round the eyes and his wrists are all red and knobbly, busting out of a jacket too small for him.

'Wait here a minute,' I said. I went into the kitchen, where Mrs Baker was cutting up a chicken.

'Who's that boy?' she said right away. She don't miss nothing round here. Can't keep a thing from her. I seen how she looks at me sideways these days, though she don't say nothing.

I ignored her, cut a slice of bread and spread it with butter. Then I took it out to Simon, who looked glad to see it. He ate it fast. I shook my head and went in to get some more. As I was spreading the butter, thicker this time, Mrs Baker said, 'If you give a stray scraps, it'll never leave you alone.'

'Mind your business,' I snapped.

'That bread is my business. I baked it this morning and I'm not baking more today.'

'Then I'll go without.'

'No you won't,' she said. 'If I let you, you'd eat the entire kitchen these days. You watch yourself, Jenny Whitby.'

'Leave me alone,' I said, and ran out before she could say more.

While Simon ate the bread I started to beat the rugs again.

'Look,' he said after a bit, 'there's Livy in the window. What's she doing?'

I looked up. 'They do that all the time, them two. Stand in the windows of their nurseries and make signs at each other. Got their own language no one understands but them.'

'Bet I'd understand it.'

I snorted. 'What's she saying, then?' Miss Livy was pointing up and bowing her head. Then she pulled a finger across her throat and pouted.

'She's talking about the cemetery,' Simon said.

'How'd you know that?'

'That's what the angel on her grave looks like.' Simon bowed his head and pointed. 'Or did, anyway. The head come off – that's why she did that with her throat.'

Then he told me about what happened to the angel and how his Pa saved the guv's life. It were thrilling stuff.

'Look,' Simon said then. 'Livy's seen me.'

Miss Livy was pointing at Simon.

I heard a window open above us and when I looked up Miss Maude was poking her head out to look down.

'I should go,' Simon said. 'I got to help our Pa with the grave.'

'Nah, stay. Miss Maude'll be down to see you.'

'Thanks for the bread,' Simon said, getting up anyway.

'If ever you come there's always bread for you here,' I

said, looking out over the garden and not at him. 'And you don't need to climb the fence to get back here. If the gate's locked the key's hid under the loose stone by the coal chute.'

Simon nodded and went out of the gate.

I should've given him something to take with him. I hate to see a boy go hungry like that. Made me hungry just thinking of it. I went inside to get some of that bread for me. To hell with Mrs Baker.

LAVINIA WATERHOUSE

I went star-gazing on the Heath with Maude and her father tonight. I wasn't sure I ought to do such a thing on the night of the very day of dear Auntie's funeral, but Mama and Papa said I should go. They both seemed very weary — Mama even snapped at me. I looked up in *Cassell's* and *The Queen* under star-gazing, but neither mentioned it, which I took as a sign that I could go, as long as I didn't enjoy it too much.

And I didn't, at first. We went at twilight because Maude's father wanted to see the moon just as it appeared above the horizon. He was looking for something called Copernicus. I thought that was a person, but Maude said it was a crater that used to be a volcano. I am never certain what she and her father mean when they talk about the moon and stars. They let me look through the telescope and asked me if I could see any craters — whatever they are. Really I couldn't see anything but to please them I said I could.

I much preferred looking at the moon without the telescope — I could see it so much better. It was lovely to look at, a half-moon hanging all pale orange just above the horizon.

Then I lay down on a blanket they had brought with them and looked up at the stars, which were just appearing in the sky. I must have fallen asleep because when I woke it was dark and there were many more stars. And then I saw a falling angel, and then another! I pointed them out to Maude, though of course they were gone by the time she looked.

Maude said they are called shooting stars but are actually little pieces of an old comet burning up, and are called meteors. But I know what they really are — they are angels stumbling as they take messages from God to us. Their wings make streaks across the sky until they are able to find their footing again.

When I tried to explain this, Maude and her father looked at me as if I were mad. I lay back down to look for more, and kept it to myself when I saw one.

RICHARD COLEMAN

The moon was magnificent tonight, with Copernicus clearly visible. I was reminded of a night years ago when I took Kitty and her brother out to look at the moon. We were able to see Copernicus then almost as clearly. Kitty looked so lovely in the moonlight and I was happy, even with Harry babbling on in the background about Copernicus the man, trying to impress me. I decided that night I would ask her to marry me.

Tonight, for the first time in a long while, I wished Kitty were with us instead of sitting at home with a book. She never comes star-gazing now. At least Maude is interested. Sometimes I think my daughter is the saving grace of this family.

KITTY COLEMAN

When it came to it at last, he did not hesitate at all. He laid me back on a bank of fading primroses, my body crushing them so that their almond scent filled the air around us. An angel hovered overhead, but he did not want to move. He was daring it to frighten him as the other angel had yesterday. I did not mind it being there, its head bowed so that it looked straight into my eyes — I had cause to thank an angel for driving him into my arms.

I lifted up the skirt of my grey dress and bared my legs. They looked like mushroom stems in the dim light, or the stamens of some exotic flower, an orchid or a lily. He put his hands on me, parted my lips down there, and pushed himself into me. That much was familiar. What was new were his hands remaining there, kneading me insistently. I pulled his head down to my breasts and he bit me through my dress.

At last the heaviness that has resided inside me since I married — perhaps even since I was born — lifted, boiling up slowly in a growing bubble. The angel watched, its gaze blank, and for once I was glad its eyes could not judge me, not even when I cried out as the bubble burst.

As I lay there afterwards with him holding me, I gazed up through the branches of the cypress arching over us. The half-moon was still low in the sky, but above me stars had appeared, and I saw one fall, as if to remind me of the consequences in store. I had seen and felt the signs inside me that day, and I had ignored them. I had had my joy at last, and I knew I would pay for it. I would not tell him, but it would be the end of us.

May 1906

ALBERT WATERHOUSE

Why I have received two invoices from the mason's yard at the cemetery is a mystery. 'For repairs to grave furniture,' one read. This was separate from the invoice for chiselling my sister's name into the plinth. At her funeral I didn't notice anything wrong with the grave. Trudy said she knows nothing of it, but Livy became quite upset when I mentioned it, and ran from the room. Later she said it was because she was having a coughing fit, but I didn't hear any coughing. And Ivy May just looked at me as if she knew the answer but wasn't about to tell me.

My daughters are an even greater mystery to me than the rogue invoice — which I have sent on to the superintendent with a query. Let him sort it out — he seems a capable fellow.

July 1906

EDITH COLEMAN

It has often been the case that I am the one forced to take in hand an unfortunate situation. This age has gone soft. I see it everywhere: in the foolish fashions that pass for women's dress, in the shockingly permissive theatre, in this ludicrous woman's suffrage movement we hear of. Even, dare I say it, in the conduct of our own King. I only hope his mother never got wind of his shenanigans with Mrs Keppel.

The young lack the moral fibre of their elders, and time and again my generation is required at the last to step into the breach. I do not complain of doing so − if I can be of assistance, of course I will do whatever is required, out of Christian charity. When it happens in my own son's house, however, I feel it as a more personal attack − an ill reflection on him and on the Coleman name.

It seems that Kitty is simply blind. It was I who shone the light into the dark corners and illuminated them for her.

I had come to lunch, served on that horrid black and yellow checked service − another example of the frivolities of the day. Far worse, however, was the state of their maid.

After she had banged every dish onto the table and waddled out again, I sat stunned. Kitty did not meet my eye, but pushed the poached fish and new potatoes around her plate. I disapprove of lack of appetite – it is selfish behaviour when there is so much hardship in the world. I would have said so but I was more concerned to address the problem of Jenny.

I tried at first to be gentle. 'My dear,' I said, 'Jenny is not looking her best. Have you spoken to her about it?'

Kitty gave me a puzzled look. 'Jenny?' she repeated vaguely.

'Your maid,' I said more firmly, 'is not well. Surely you can see that.'

'What is wrong with her?'

'Come now, my dear, open your eyes. It is clear as day what the trouble is.'

'Is it?'

I couldn't help but grow a little impatient with Kitty. In truth, I should like to have given her a good shake, as if she were a young girl like Maude. In some ways Maude is more mature than her mother. I had been disappointed that she did not join us for lunch – at times it is easier to speak to her than to Kitty. But I was told she was at her friend's. At least I was able to be more frank with Kitty than I could have if Maude had been with us.

'She has got herself into trouble. With a man,' I added so that there could be no doubt.

Kitty clattered her cutlery most unbecomingly and stared at me with her dark brown eyes that had made my son into a fool years before. She was very pale.

'She is six months gone at least,' I continued, as Kitty seemed

152

incapable of speaking. 'Probably more. I always knew that girl would come to no good. I never liked her – far too insolent. You could see just by looking at her. And she sings as she works – I can't abide that in a servant. I expect the man will not marry her, and even if he does she can't possibly remain here. You don't want a married woman and mother in that position. You need a girl with no attachments.'

My daughter-in-law was still staring at me with a bewildered look. It was very clear that she could not manage – I would have to take charge.

'I shall speak to her after lunch,' I said. 'Leave it with me.'

Kitty didn't say anything for a moment. Finally she nodded.

'Now, eat your fish,' I said.

She pushed it around her plate a bit more, then said she had a headache. I don't like to see such waste, but in this instance I said nothing, as she had clearly had a shock and did look rather ill. Luckily my own constitution is more robust and I finished my fish, which was very good except that the sauce was rather rich. Thank goodness for Mrs Baker – she shall have to hold the house together for the moment until we find a replacement. I'd had my doubts about her when Kitty first hired her, but she is a good plain cook as well as a solid Christian. It does help to hire a widow – like myself she does not have great expectations of life.

Jenny came in to clear and I couldn't help but shake my head at her brazenness. How she thought she could wander about the house with such a thick waist and think no one would notice is quite astonishing. Mind you, I suppose she knows her mistress. If I had not alerted Kitty she might never have noticed until the girl held the babe crying in her arms! I saw Kitty inspect Jenny as she leaned over to gather our plates, and a look like fear crossed her face. She was most certainly not up to dismissing Jenny. I myself felt no fear, but righteous determination.

Kitty said not a word except, 'No coffee for me, Jenny.'

'Nor hot water for me,' I added. There was no point in delaying the proceedings.

The girl grunted, and as she left I thought what a blessing in disguise this was — a chance to get rid of a bad apple.

I told Kitty to go and rest, then waited a short interval before going down to the kitchen, where Mrs Baker was wiping the table clean of flour. I do not go there often, so I suppose she had reason to look surprised. But there was more to her look than that. Mrs Baker is no fool — she knew why I had come.

'The fish was quite good, Mrs Baker,' I said pleasantly. 'Perhaps a little less butter in the sauce next time.'

'Thank you, ma'am,' she replied quite correctly, but managing to sound put out as well.

'Where is Jenny? I want to have a word with her.'

Mrs Baker stopped brushing the table. 'She's in the scullery, ma'am.'

'So you know, then.'

Mrs Baker shrugged and began brushing the table again. 'Anyone with eyes to see would know.'

As I turned towards the scullery, she surprised me by adding, 'Let her be, ma'am. Just let her be.'

'Are you telling me how this house should be run?' I asked.

She did not answer.

'There is no use in being sentimental about it, Mrs Baker. This is for her own good.'

Mrs Baker shrugged again. I was surprised – she is normally a sensible woman. She is from a very different background than myself, of course, but at times I have thought she and I are not so different.

It did not take long. Jenny cried and ran from the room, of course, but it could have been worse. In a way the girl must have been relieved that it was out at last. She knew very well that someone would finally find her out. The waiting must have been excruciating, and I like to think I put the girl out of her misery.

My one regret is that Maude was there. I had thought she was at the Waterhouses', but as I came out of the scullery she was standing in the doorway of the larder. I had spoken to Jenny in a low voice, and I don't think Maude heard what I said, but she heard Jenny's shout, and I would have preferred it if she had not been there.

'Is Jenny ill?' she asked.

'Yes,' I answered, thinking that was the best way to explain it. 'She will have to leave us.'

Maude looked alarmed. 'Is she dying?'

'Don't be silly.' It was exactly the kind of dramatic question her friend Lavinia would ask – Maude was simply parroting her. I knew that girl was a bad influence.

'But what –'

'We missed you at lunch,' I interrupted. 'I thought you were at your friend's.'

Maude turned red. 'I – I was,' she stammered, 'but Lavinia has a – a cough, and so I came back. I've been helping Mrs Baker make soda bread.'

She has never been a good liar. I could have exposed the lie, but I was weary from the business with Jenny, and so I left it. And if I am honest, I didn't want to know. It gave me a pang to think that my own granddaughter would rather bake bread with the cook than have lunch with me.

MAUDE COLEMAN

I had never thought Grandmother would come down to the kitchen. It was the one place where I thought I was safe, and could remain until she was gone — then I would not have to have lunch with her. Even Mummy thought I was at Lavinia's. I would have been, only Lavinia was out visiting her cousins.

As it was I almost managed to hide from Grandmother. I was putting the oats and flour and bicarb in the larder for Mrs Baker when I heard Grandmother come into the kitchen and speak to her. I shrank back into the larder but didn't dare close the door in case she saw it move.

She passed by without looking in and went into the scullery, where she began talking to Jenny in a low voice that sent shivers down my spine. It was the voice she uses when she has something awful to say — that she has discovered you have broken a vase, or not gone to church, or done poorly in school. Jenny began to cry, and though I had a chance to close the larder door then, I didn't — I wanted to hear what they were saying. I crept closer to the open door and heard Grandmother say, '. . . wages until the end of the week, but you must pack your things now.'

Then Jenny cried out and ran from the scullery up the stairs. Grandmother came out of the scullery, and there I was standing in the doorway, my pinafore covered in flour.

I was surprised when Grandmother then told me Jenny was ill, but indeed she had grown slow and fat these days, as if she had a blockage in her stomach. Perhaps she should be taking cod liver oil. Then Grandmother said she would have to leave because of it. I thought she must be terribly ill indeed but Grandmother wouldn't say more about it.

Luckily Grandmother decided to go then, or I might have had a tedious afternoon with her all alone, as she said Mummy had gone to bed with a headache. I saw her to the door, and as she left she said I was to tell Mummy later that everything was sorted out satisfactorily. I knew better than to ask what she meant.

After she had gone I went downstairs again and asked Mrs Baker instead. 'Is Jenny going to leave us?'

There was a pause, then Mrs Baker said, 'I expect she will.'

'Is she very ill, then?'

'Ill? Is that what she's calling it?'

There was a knock on the outside kitchen door. 'Perhaps that's Lavinia,' I said hopefully and ran to the door.

'Don't tell her any of this,' Mrs Baker warned.

'Why not?'

Mrs Baker sighed and shook her head. 'Never mind. Tell her what you like. She'll find out soon enough.'

It was Simon. He did not say hello; he never says hello. He stepped inside and looked around. 'Where's our Jenny? She upstairs?'

I glanced at Mrs Baker, who was gathering up the bowl

and sieve we had used for the bread. She frowned but did not answer.

'She's ill,' I said. 'She may have to go away.'

'She's not ill,' Simon said. 'She's banged up.'

'Banged up – is that like knocking?' I asked uneasily. I hoped no one had hurt Jenny.

'Maude!' Mrs Baker barked, and I jumped. She never shouted at me – only at the butcher's boy if the meat was off, or the baker, whom she once accused of using sawdust in his loaves. She turned to Simon. 'Is it you been teaching her this filthy language? Look at her – she doesn't even know what she's saying. Shame on you, boy!'

Simon gave me a funny look. 'Sorry,' he said. I nodded, though I didn't really know what he was apologising for. In many ways he knew so little – had never been to school, could barely read, and that learned from gravestones. Yet he clearly knew about things in the world that I had no notion of.

Simon turned to Mrs Baker. 'Is there any bread?'

'It's in the oven, little beggar boy,' Mrs Baker snapped. 'You'll have to wait.'

Simon just looked at her. He seemed not the least bothered that she had just called him a beggar. She sighed, then set down the bowl and sieve and went to the sideboard, where she found an end of a loaf. 'Go and put some butter on it,' she said, handing it to him. 'You know where it is.'

Simon disappeared into the larder.

'Make him a cup of tea, Maude,' she ordered, picking up her dishes again and heading for the scullery. 'Just one sugar,' she added over her shoulder.

I gave him two sugars.

Simon had spread the bread with great hunks of butter, as if it were cheese. I watched him eat it at the table, his teeth carving rectangular grooves in the butter.

'Simon,' I whispered. 'What does banged up mean?' It felt wicked saying the words, now that I knew they were shocking.

Simon shook his head. 'Not for me to say. Best to ask your ma.'

I knew I never would.

SIMON FIELD

The sody bread smells good, baking in the oven. I want to wait for it, but I know I was lucky to get anything at all from Mrs Baker. She ain't so generous with the bread as our Jenny is.

I want to see our Jenny. Maude thinks she's in her room upstairs. So when I've finished the bread I pretend to leave, but don't pull the back door closed. I wait and peek through the window till I see Maude and Mrs B. go into the scullery together. Then I sneak back in real quiet and run up the stairs before anyone sees me.

I never been in the rest of the house. It's big, with lots of stairs that I keep stopping on 'cause there's so much to see. On the walls there's paintings and drawings of all sorts of things, buildings and people but mostly birds and flowers. Some of the birds I know from the cemetery, and some of the flowers too. They're proper drawings, with all the bits of the plant as well as the flower. I seen a book of Mr Jackson's at the lodge with pictures like that.

The rugs on the stairs and in the hallways are mostly green, with some yellow and blue and red bits in a pattern.

Each landing has a plant on it, them ones with long thin leaves what wave up and down as I go past. Our Jenny hates 'em 'cause she has to clean all the little leaves and it takes so long. 'No one asked me what plants they should have,' she said once. 'Why don't she get one of them aspidistras with a few big leaves that are easy to wash?'

I go on up until I'm on the top landing. There are two doors up there, both closed. I have to choose, so I open one and go in. It's Maude's room. I stand and look a long time. There's so many toys and books, more than I ever seen in a room. There's a whole shelf of dolls, all different sizes, and another shelf of games — boxes full of things, puzzles and such. There's lots of shelves of books. There's a brown and white hobby horse with a black leather saddle that moves back and forth on rollers. There's a wood dolls' house with fancy furniture in all the rooms, miniature rugs and chairs and tables. There's pictures on the walls of Maude's room, children and dogs and cats, and something that looks like a map of the sky, with all the stars connected up with lines to make pictures like what I saw in the stars that cold night in the grave.

It's toasty warm in the room — there's a fireplace just had a fire burning, and a fender in front of it with clothes hanging on it to air. I want to stay here, but I can't — I has to find our Jenny.

I go out of the room and up to the other door and knock.

'Go away,' she says.

'It's me, our Jenny.'

'Go away.'

I kneel down and look through the keyhole. Our Jenny's lying on her bed, her hands tucked under her cheek. Her eyes are red but she's not crying. Next to her is her corset. I can see the shape of her big belly under her skirt.

I go in anyway. She don't shout at me, so I sit on a chair. There ain't much in the room, just the chair and bed, a chamber pot and a bucket of coal, a green rug on the floor and a row of pegs with her clothes hanging on 'em. On the window ledge are a couple of coloured bottles, blue and green. The room is dark 'cause there's only a little window what faces north over the street.

'Jenny, our Jenny,' I says, 'what're you going to do?'

'I dunno,' she says. 'Go back to me mum, I suppose. I have to leave by the end of the day.'

'You should go to our Ma – that's what she does, delivers babies. Nellie off Leytonstone High Street, next to the Rose and Crown. Everybody knows her. Mind you, you should've gone to her earlier and she'd have got rid of it for you.'

'I couldn't do that!' Our Jenny sounds shocked.

'Why not? You don't want it, do you?'

'It's a sin. It's murder!'

'But you sinned already, ain't you? What difference does it make?'

She don't answer, but shakes her head back and forth and brings her legs up so they're curled round her belly. 'Anyway, it's too late,' she says. 'The baby's coming soon, and that's that.' She starts to cry, big ugly sobs. I look round and see a brown knitted shawl on the chair. I put it over her.

'Oh God, what am I to do?' our Jenny cries. 'Mum'll kill me. I send her most of my pay – how's she to get by without it?'

'You'll have to get another job, and your ma can look after the baby.'

'But no one'll hire me when they find out what's happened. She'll never give me a reference. This is the only job I've had. I need her reference.'

I think for a minute. 'Mrs C. will if you make her,' I say finally. I feel bad saying it, 'cause I like Maude's ma. I still remember how she smiled at me that day she wore the green dress.

Our Jenny looks up at me, curious now. 'How do you mean?'

'You know something about her,' I say. 'About her and Mr Jackson meeting in the cemetery. You could say something about that.'

Our Jenny pushes herself up so that she's sitting. 'That's wicked. Besides, there's no sin in talk. All they did was talk. Didn't they?'

I shrug.

She wipes her hair back from her face where it's stuck to her cheeks. 'What would I say?'

'Tell her you'll tell her husband about her and Mr Jackson meeting if she don't give you a good reference.'

'Ooo, that is wicked.' Our Jenny thinks for a minute. Then she gets a funny look on her face, like a thief who's just spotted an open window in a rich man's house. 'Maybe I could even keep my job. She'll have to keep me on if I'm not to tell her husband.'

I feel sick when she says that. I like our Jenny but she's greedy. 'I dunno,' I say. 'Our Pa always says never ask for too much. Ask for just what you need or you mightn't get any at all.'

'And look where your Pa's got to — a gravedigger all his life,' our Jenny says.

'Don't see as being a gravedigger's any worse'n being a maid.'

'Anyway, get out with you. If I'm to talk to her I'd best try to get my corset back on.'

From the look on her face I know there's nothing I can say will stop her. So I go out and down the stairs. I get to the next landing and there are four closed doors there. I listen for a minute but don't hear no one. I never been in a house like this. Our Ma and me sisters share a back-to-back, two rooms for the five of 'em. Five or six families could live in this house. I look at the doors. They're all oak, with brass handles shining — our Jenny's been at 'em with the polish. I choose one and open it.

I heard about rooms like this but ain't ever seen one. There's tiles everywhere, white tiles on the floor and up the sides of the walls to just over my head. One row of the tiles at the top has flowers on 'em, like tulips, red and green. There's a big white bathtub, and a white sink, with the silver pipes and taps all scrubbed shiny by our Jenny. There's big white towels hanging on a rack, and I touch one. Where I've touched it I leave a black mark and I feel bad 'cause it's so clean in here otherwise.

In a little room off this one is a WC, white too, with a seat made of mahogany, like some of the rich people's coffins I see at the cemetery. I think of the privy and bucket me and our Pa use, and it's so different from this they don't even seem like they're meant for the same thing.

I go out and choose another door, to the room at the front of the house. The walls are yellow, and though it's facing north too like our Jenny's room, there's two big windows, with balconies you can walk out on, and the light that comes in turns gold when it hits the walls. There's two sofas pushed together to make an L, and shawls decorated with butterflies and flowers spread over 'em. There's a piano and little tables with books and magazines on them, and a sideboard with photographs on it, of her and Maude and Maude's Pa and some other people.

Then I hear our Jenny talking out on the landing. There ain't time to get out of the room, and somehow I know she and Mrs C. will come in here. I crouch down quick behind one of the sofas. If I was playing hidey-seek with my sisters that's the first place they would look. But Jenny and Mrs C. ain't looking for me.

JENNY WHITBY

For all my brave face to Simon, I was dreading talking to the missus. She ain't been bad to me over the years, and I do know I've sinned. Nor did I like resorting to blackmail. But I need my place here – I need my wages. It felt like I'd been mopping a room and not been paying attention, and before you know it I was stuck in the corner with a wet floor all round me. I'd have to jump far to get free.

When I'd straightened my clothes and put on my cap and splashed water on my face, I went downstairs. As I got to the landing she came out of her bedroom, and I knew I had to do it then. I opened my mouth but before I could say a word she said, 'Jenny, I would like to speak with you, please. Let's go into the morning room'.

I followed her in. 'Have a seat,' she said. I sat down on a sofa. I clean in here every day but I'd never sat down before. It's a pretty room.'

She went over to one of the windows and looked through the blinds. She was wearing a dress the colour of bone, with a cameo pinned at her throat. The colour don't suit her – she looked tired and pale.

I swallowed 'cause my throat was dry and I couldn't speak yet. I hadn't really thought what I was going to say.

But then it didn't turn out like I thought it would. Not at all. Never in a million years would I have guessed what she was going to say.

She turned from the window. 'I'm sorry to hear of your troubles, Jenny,' she said first. 'And I'm sorry about the way Mrs Coleman must have treated you. She can be very harsh.'

'She's a bitch,' I said before I could stop myself. Saying that made it easier to go on. 'Now I got something to say to you, ma'am.'

'Please listen to me first. We might be able to help each other.'

'Me help you? I don't think so, ma'am. There's nothing –'

'Jenny, I need your help.'

'You need me? After you toss me out in the street like a wore-out broom, after all I done for you and Miss Maude and Mr Coleman, just because I – because I . . .' I couldn't help it. I started to cry.

She let me cry a while. Then she said something real quiet. I couldn't hear it, and she had to say it again. 'I share your predicament.'

I didn't know what that meant, but the fancy word sounded serious enough that I stopped crying.

'It's not so – advanced,' she said. 'And because of that I can still do something about it. But I don't know where to go. I don't know who to ask. I couldn't possibly ask my friends. And so I'm asking you to help me by telling me where to go to – do this. Do you understand what I'm saying to you?'

I looked at her, and I thought of the meals she'd missed,

and the headaches she'd had, and the naps in the afternoon, and the private washing I hadn't had to do for her for a couple months, and the penny dropped. I just hadn't noticed 'cause I'd had my own worries on my mind.

'Yes,' I said, quiet now. 'I understand.'

'I don't want to go anywhere where I'll be known. It must be a place far away, but not too far that I couldn't get there easily. Do you know where I can go?'

Now another penny dropped and I knew what she wanted from me. 'It's a sin,' I said.

She looked out of the window again. 'That will be on my head, not yours.'

I let her wait. She was handing the blackmail to me on a silver plate, just like I bring in the post to her in this room each morning. I wouldn't even have to say nothing about her and Mr Jackson. Just as well, 'cause I hadn't really known what they got up to – till now.

I knew why she was asking me now, too. She thought she was getting rid of me anyway, so I'd never tell nobody. But there was a price to pay for keeping me quiet. That's where the blackmail was.

'It'll cost you,' I said.

'How much do you want?' She said it like she'd been expecting me to name a price. But I surprised her.

'My position here.'

She stared at me. 'What if I gave you some money? For you and the baby, to keep you until you've found another position?'

'No.'

'I'd give you a good reference, of course. We wouldn't have to mention the baby. We could come up with another

169

reason for your leaving — that your mother was ill and you had to look after her.'

'Leave my mum out of this.'

'I'm not suggesting —'

'I want to stay here.'

'But — what will I say to Mrs Coleman? It was she who dismissed you. I can't go back on her decision.' She sounded desperate.

'You're the lady of the house, ma'am. I expect you can do what you like. You done already anyway.'

She didn't say nothing for a bit. The baby moved inside me — I could feel its little foot kicking.

'All right,' she said finally. 'You can come back to your job once you've had the baby. But you must leave today, and you can't bring the baby with you or have anyone bring it here to see you. You can see it Sundays.'

'And Saturday afternoons. I want Saturday afternoons free too.' I was surprised at myself — the success of the blackmail made me bold.

'All right, Saturday afternoons too. But you're not to tell anyone any of this or I will make sure your baby's taken away from you. Are we clear about that?'

'Yes, ma'am.' It was strange to hear her try to sound hard — she wasn't much good at it.

'All right. Where am I to go, then?'

'Leytonstone,' I said. 'To Nellie off the High Street, next to the Rose and Crown.'

I heard a noise behind my sofa then, and I knew someone was back there. She didn't seem to notice, though — she was looking out of the window again. I glanced behind me and saw Simon crouched there. It didn't surprise me that he was eavesdropping – just like the little rascal. He was staring at me all angry for mentioning his mum. I shrugged – what else could I say?

'Go now,' she said then without looking at me. 'Go and pack your things. I'll order a cab for you.'

'Yes, ma'am.' I got up. Now we were done with the business I wanted to say something to her but I didn't know what exactly. So I just said, 'Goodbye, ma'am,' and she said, 'Goodbye, Jenny.' I went to the door and opened it. Just before I went out I looked back at her. She was still standing by the window, her eyes closed, clasping her hands in a fist against her stomach.

'Oh,' she said in a little sigh all to herself.

Simon was still hiding behind the sofa.

I hope his mum is gentle with her.

September 1906

ALBERT WATERHOUSE

Don't know that I'll tell anyone, not even Trudy, but I escorted Kitty Coleman home the other night. I was coming back from nets on the Heath with Richard Coleman when I remembered that Trudy wanted me to leave a message with the vicar at St Anne's – a trifle about altar flowers or some such thing. I try not to attend to that sort of detail – best left to Trudy. But I told Richard I'd catch him up at the Bull and Last, and ran off like a good errand boy.

Afterwards I was heading towards the pub when I looked up Swain's Lane and saw Kitty Coleman, walking along slowly with her head bowed, kicking at her skirts. I thought her a peculiar sight, given it was twilight and she was alone and didn't seem to be walking anywhere in particular.

'Evening, Mrs Coleman,' I said, raising my cap. 'Nice night for a stroll, isn't it? Last spurt of summer, looks like we're having.' My choice of words made me blush. I don't know what it is about Kitty Coleman – she inspires me to say things I shouldn't.

She didn't seem to notice, though – she just stared at me like I was a ghost. I was taken aback by her appearance. Richard had mentioned she'd been ill and was not looking her finest. But it was more than that. Her looks were plainly gone, I am sorry to say.

'Are you on your way somewhere?'

Kitty Coleman hesitated. 'I have been – I wanted to climb the hill but couldn't.'

'It is steep, that hill up to the cemetery. And if you haven't been well it must seem like a mountain. Would you like me to take you to your husband? I was just going to meet him at the pub.'

'I don't want to see Richard,' Kitty Coleman said quickly.

I didn't know what to make of that, but I couldn't leave her there on her own – she seemed so ill and child-like. 'Shall I see you home, then?'

I held out my arm, feeling a little silly and wondering what Trudy would say if she could see us. I know she doesn't think much of Kitty Coleman. Luckily Trudy was safely tucked away at home with our girls. Maude was there too, staying the night.

After a moment Kitty Coleman took my arm. The quickest way to her house was straight past the Bull and Last, but I didn't go that way. It would have felt strange to parade past the pub and have Richard Coleman look out and see me with his wife on my arm when I was meant to be at the vicar's. I could have explained it, but it still didn't look right. So I took the back way, which she didn't remark upon. I tried to make conversation en route, but she didn't say much, just 'Yes' and 'Thank you' when thanks weren't even called for.

Never mind. I saw her home, feeling a little foolish but a little proud too – her face may not be so pretty now but she still carries herself well and wore a nice grey dress, even if it was a bit rumpled. A couple of passers-by stared at us and I couldn't help but hold myself a little straighter.

'Will you be all right, then, Mrs Coleman?' I asked when we got to her door.

'Of course. Thank you.'

'You look after yourself, now. Tuck yourself up with a Horlicks and get an early night.'

She nodded and slipped inside. It was only when I was heading back to the pub that I realised she hadn't said my name at all. I began to wonder if she'd even recognised me.

At the Bull and Last Richard teased me for spending so long at the vicar's. I just nodded and ordered another pint.

October 1906

LAVINIA WATERHOUSE

I was truly shocked when I saw Maude's mother.

We almost didn't see her. We had stopped at Maude's house on our way home from school only because I wanted Maude to lend me a book about plants so that I can copy passages from it for a school essay. Maude was reluctant to get it, and I thought it was because she disapproved of my copying, as our essays are meant to be original. (It is so tedious to think up things to write, especially about 'the life cycle of leaves'!) But now I think it was because she did not want me to see her mother. Indeed, when I think back on it, Maude has been coming to my house almost every day for months – even more than before.

She hurried me up to her room for the book and hurried me down again. Just then Mrs Coleman came out of the morning room. She looked at us so vaguely that I was not even sure she really saw us until Maude said, 'Hello, Mummy,' very softly, and she nodded slightly.

I was so surprised by her appearance that I did not even say anything about it to Maude – which made me rather sad, as I thought we shared all our thoughts. But I could not bring myself to ask her why her mother is so thin, and her hair suddenly has grey in it, and her skin looks like ditch-water. Worse than that — for one can always dye or pull out grey hair (as Mama does) and apply a tonic to dull skin — Mrs Coleman does not sparkle as she used to. Admittedly her sparkle felt a little wicked at times — which is why Mama does not care for her — but without it she is very flat indeed.

Clearly something is wrong at the Colemans'. Not only is Maude's mother not herself, but a few months ago their maid Jenny was suddenly taken ill and had to go away. Perhaps they have the same illness. Maude says Jenny is returning soon. I shall have to look to see if she has grey hairs as well. It is just as well she's coming back, for the temporary chars have been dreadful. Maude hasn't liked any of them, and the house looked none too clean, the little I saw of it. The plants on the landings were terribly dusty.

I said nothing of this to Maude, poor dear. She was very subdued as we went on to my house. I tried to be especially nice to her, even suggesting that we attend the official opening of our local public library. They have been building it on Chester Road all summer, and there is to be a ceremony on Thursday afternoon. I am not keen on going — it will be all tedious speeches — but it may cheer Maude as she is so fond of libraries. And it would mean we could leave early and miss the last class at school, which is maths. I can't abide maths — all those dull numbers. In fact I don't like any of my classes, except for domestic arts and composition, though Miss Johnson says my imagination needs reining in — a compliment, I should think!

Mama will have to get permission for us both to leave school early, as Maude's mother is clearly incapable of making such arrangements. And I expect Mama and Ivy May will have to come with us, although it is only a few minutes away. Maude and I are eleven years old, yet we are still not allowed to go anywhere alone except to walk to school together. Mama says you never know what might happen, and reads all sorts of terrible things out from the newspapers – babies left to freeze on the Heath, or people drowning in the ponds, or rough men looking for girls to prey upon.

When we arrived home I asked Mama if we could all go to the library ceremony. She said yes, the dear. She always says yes to me.

Then Maude asked a funny thing. 'Please, Mrs Waterhouse,' she said, 'could you ask my mother to come with us? She hasn't been well these past months, and she could do with getting a bit of air.'

Well, Mama was nonplussed by this request – surely Maude could ask her own mother! – but she said she would. I was a bit put out, as I am not at all sure I wish to be seen with someone who has clearly let herself go. None the less, I must stand by my friend. Besides, Mama may not be able to convince Mrs Coleman to come with us – it is not as if they are close friends. If she does, though, perhaps I will steal over to their house one night and leave a bottle of hair dye on the doorstep.

GERTRUDE WATERHOUSE

I did not have the heart to say no to Maude. It is horrifying to think a girl cannot even ask her mother to escort her somewhere. I wanted to enquire why she felt she could not, but she looked so meek and sad that I simply said I would do my best and left it at that. I did not think I could do much good, though, even for something as insignificant as arranging an outing. I have never had any influence with Kitty Coleman, and if Maude cannot convince her to come to a little local event, I do not see how I will be able to.

None the less, I called on Kitty the next morning when the girls were at school. The moment I saw her I felt terribly guilty for not having gone there sooner. She did look awful – thin and pinched – and her lovely hair no longer glossy. It is such a surprise to see the lifeblood sapped from someone once so vital. If I were a more spiteful person, it might have made me feel better to see such loveliness brought down. Instead my heart went out to her. I even squeezed her hand, which surprised her, though she did not jerk it away. Her hand was chilly.

'Oh, you're so cold, my dear!' I exclaimed.

'Am I?' she asked absently.

I pulled the yellow silk shawl from the back of the sofa and wrapped it around her. 'I'm so sorry that you have been ill.'

'Did someone say I was?'

'Oh, I . . .' I grew flustered. 'Maude — she said you'd had pneumonia some time ago.' That much at least was true, or so I thought, though from Kitty Coleman's reaction I began to wonder.

'Is that what Maude said?' she asked. I wondered if Kitty would actually answer a question rather than ask one. But then she shrugged. 'I suppose that may as well do,' she muttered, which made no sense, but I did not try to question her.

She rang a bell, but when the girl appeared — it was not their usual maid — Kitty looked at her blankly, as if she had forgotten why she summoned her. The girl stared back just as blankly.

'Perhaps some tea for your mistress,' I suggested.

'Yes,' Kitty murmured. 'That would be good.'

When the girl had left I said, 'Have you seen a doctor recently?'

'Why?'

'Well, for your convalescence. Perhaps there's something you could take — a tonic. Or go to a spa.' I was trying in vain to name remedies for whatever afflicted her. All I could think of were novels I'd read in which the heroine went to spas in Germany, or to the south of France for the climate.

'The doctor said I must build up my strength with plenty of food and fresh air,' Kitty repeated mechanically. She looked as if she ate little more than a mouthful of food a day, and I doubt she went out at all.

'That is just what I was coming to speak to you about. I am proposing to take the girls on a little outing to the new library that is about to open on Chester Road, and I wondered if you and Maude would join us. We could go afterwards for tea up in Waterlow Park.' I felt a little silly, making it sound as if I were suggesting an expedition to Antarctica rather than a trip just around the corner.

'I don't know,' she replied. 'It's a bit far.'

'The library itself is quite close,' I said quickly, 'and we don't have to go all the way up the hill for tea – we could choose some place closer. Or you could come to me.' Kitty had never been to my house. I did not want her to sit in my cramped parlour, but I felt I had to offer.

'I'm not . . .'

I waited for Kitty to finish her sentence, but she did not. Something had happened to her – she was like a little lamb that has lost its way and is wandering aimlessly in a field. I did not relish playing her shepherd, but I also knew that God did not intend for a shepherd to judge His flock. I grasped her hand again. 'What is wrong, my dear? What has distressed you so?'

Kitty gazed at me. Her eyes were so dark it was like looking into a well. 'I have spent my life waiting for something to happen,' she said. 'And I have come to understand that nothing will. Or it already has, and I blinked during that moment and it's gone. I don't know which is worse – to have missed it or to know there is nothing to miss.'

I did not know what to say, for I did not understand her at all. Still, I had to try to answer. 'I think that you are very lucky indeed,' I said, making my voice as stern as I dared. 'You have a fine husband and a good daughter, and a lovely house and garden. You have food on the table and a cook to cook it. To many you have an enviable life.' Though not to me, I added silently.

'Yes, but . . .' Kitty stopped again, scanning my face for something. It appeared she did not find it, for she let her eyes drop.

I let go of her hand. 'I am going to send around a tonic that my mother used to prepare for me when I felt low, with brandy and egg yolk and a little sugar. I'm sure it will be an effective pick-me-up. And do you have any brilliantine? A bit on your brush will do wonders to your hair. And my dear, do come with us to the library ceremony on Thursday.' Kitty opened her mouth to speak, but I bravely talked over her. 'I insist upon it. Maude will be so pleased, as she so wants to go with you. You wouldn't want to disappoint her. She's such a good girl – top of her class.'

'She is?'

Surely Kitty must know how well her daughter was doing in her studies! 'We shall come to collect you at two thirty on Thursday. The fresh air will do you good.' Before she could object I stood up and pulled on my gloves, not even waiting for the tea to arrive (their girl is very slow) before taking my leave.

For the first time since I have known Kitty Coleman, I was in the position to dictate the tone of our relations. Rather than relishing the power, I simply felt miserable.

No one ever said Christian duty would be easy.

MAUDE COLEMAN

I don't know why Lavinia was so keen on going to the library opening. She seemed to think I would be thrilled to go as well, but she has confused celebration with function. While I am, of course, glad we are to have a local public library, I was more interested in borrowing books than in the ceremony. Lavinia is just the opposite — she has always liked parties more than me, but she cannot sit still in a library for five minutes. She does not even like books much — though she is fond of Dickens, of course, and she and her mother like to read aloud Sir Walter Scott. And she can recite some poems — Tennyson's 'Lady of Shalott' and Keats' 'La Belle Dame sans Merci'.

But to please her I said I would go, and Mrs Waterhouse somehow persuaded Mummy to come out with us — the first time she has been out at all since she was ill. I do wish she had worn something a little gayer — she has so many beautiful dresses and hats, but she chose a brown dress and a black felt hat trimmed with three black rosettes. She looked like a mourner among partygoers. Still, at least she came — I was pleased just to walk with her.

I do not think she understood very well where the new

library is. Daddy and I had often gone on a summer evening to inspect the progress of the building, but Mummy had never come with us. Now as we turned into Chester Road from Swain's Lane she grew very agitated at the sight of the southern wall of the cemetery, which is bounded by Chester Road. She even clutched my arm, and without quite knowing why, I said, 'It's all right, Mummy, we aren't going in.' She relaxed a little, though she held on to me until we had passed by the southern gate and reached the crowd outside the library.

The library is a handsome brick building, with tan stone trimmings, a front porch with four Corinthian columns, and side sections with high arched windows. For the opening the front was decked out with white bunting, and a small platform placed on the front steps. Lots of people were milling about on the pavement and spilling into the street. It was a windy day, making the bunting shake and men's bowlers and women's feathers and flowers fly off.

We had not been there long before the speeches began. A man stepped onto the platform and called out, 'Good afternoon, ladies and gentlemen. It is my great pleasure, as Chairman of the Education and Libraries Committee of the St Pancras Borough Council, to welcome you to this most auspicious occasion, the opening of the first free library in the borough as the first step in adopting the Public Libraries' Acts in St Pancras.

'We are indebted to Alderman T. H. W. Idris, MP, and late mayor, for his successful endeavour in getting Mr Andrew Carnegie, of Pittsburgh of the United States, to give £40,000 for the purpose of the adoption of the Acts –'

Just then I felt an elbow in my ribs. 'Look!' Lavinia hissed, pointing. A funeral procession was coming along Chester Road. The Chairman on the platform stopped speaking when he saw the carriages, and the men in the crowd removed their hats while the women bowed their heads. I bowed mine as well but looked up through my lashes, counting five carriages behind the one carrying the coffin.

Then a great gust of wind made all the women grab at their hats. Lavinia and Ivy May and I were wearing our green school berets, which usually stay snug on our heads, but Lavinia pulled hers off as if the wind had loosened it, and tossed her hair and shrugged. I'm sure she did it just to show off her curls.

The undertaker's men walking alongside the front carriage clamped their hands on their top hats; one blew off anyway and the man had to run after it in his long black coat. The horses' black plumes were swaying and one horse whinnied and bucked as the wind got up its nose, so that the driver had to crack his whip, making some ladies scream, and halting the procession. Mummy trembled and clutched my arm.

The wind had loosened the bunting on the library so much that the next gust caught a length of it and blew it up in the air. The long white cloth sailed over our heads and did a kind of dance over the funeral procession, until suddenly the wind dropped and the bunting fell, landing across the carriage that carried the coffin. The crowd gasped – Lavinia of course screamed – and the nervous horse bucked again.

It was all terribly confusing. But above the shouts, the wind and the whinnying horse, I heard a woman laugh. I looked around and saw her standing on the edge of the crowd, dressed entirely in white, with a great deal of lace trim which fluttered so that she looked like a bird. Her laugh was not loud exactly, but it penetrated through everything, like the rag-and-bone man's voice as he walked along our street calling out 'Any old iron!'

Mr Jackson came out from the cemetery gate and ran up to pull the cloth off the carriage. 'Drive on!' he called. 'Quickly, before the horses bolt!' He ran back to the gate and swung it open, beckoning to the lead carriage. After the last carriage had passed inside the cemetery, he swung the gate shut, then picked up the bunting. As he began folding it he gazed at the crowd in front of the library, saw Mummy, and stopped folding the cloth. Mummy jerked as if someone had tapped her on the shoulder, and dropped my arm.

Then the Chairman stepped down from the platform and crossed the road to retrieve the bunting. Mr Jackson was forced to turn to him, and Mummy suddenly drooped. Another gust of wind blew through the crowd and she looked as if she might topple. In a moment the laughing woman was at her side, casually taking my mother's arm and holding her steady.

'Quite a show here, isn't it?' she said with another laugh. 'And the speeches have barely begun!'

She was a small woman, shorter than Mummy but with her shoulders thrown back in a way that made her look as confident as a taller woman. She had big brown eyes that seemed to sit right on the surface of her face so that you could not avoid their stare. When she smiled a tooth showed at the side of her mouth, reminding me of a horse baring its teeth.

I knew immediately that I would not like her.

'I am Caroline Black,' she said, holding out her hand.

Mummy stared at it. After a moment she took it. 'Kitty Coleman,' she said.

I was horrified to recognise the name, though Mummy clearly didn't. Caroline Black was a suffragette who conducted a long-running battle with various sceptical gentlemen about the subject of votes for women on the letters page of the local paper.

Daddy has been very scathing of the suffragettes. He says the word sounds like the term for a sort of bandaging technique developed in the Crimean War. The suffragettes have been chalking signs for their meetings on the pavements near us, and Daddy has occasionally threatened them — possibly even Caroline Black herself — with buckets of water.

The Chairman had begun speaking again. '. . . the Council has provided an open door through which every inhabitant of St Pancras can enter without fee or without challenge to enjoy the treasures of literature enshrined and stored in this building.'

The crowd began to applaud. Caroline Black did not clap, though, and neither did Mummy. I looked round for Lavinia, but couldn't see her. Mrs Waterhouse and Ivy May were still close by, and I followed Ivy May's gaze across the road. Lavinia was standing by the cemetery gate. She saw me and beckoned, pulling at the gate to show me that it was not locked. I hesitated — I did not want to leave Mummy alone with Caroline Black. On the other hand, the speeches were dull, as I had known they would be, and the cemetery would be much more interesting. I took a step towards Lavinia.

'That is all well and good, Mr Ashby,' Caroline Black

called out suddenly. I froze. 'I do applaud the idea of free access to literature and education. But can we honestly celebrate such an occasion when half the population cannot apply its newly available knowledge to that part of life so important to us all? If women do not have the vote, why bother to read the treasures of literature?'

As she spoke, people around her took a few steps back so that she was alone in a circle of spectators apart from Mummy and me standing awkwardly beside her.

Mr Ashby tried to interject, but Caroline Black continued in a smooth voice that carried a long way and would not be interrupted. 'I'm sure if our MP, Mr Dickinson, were here, he would agree with me that the subject of votes for women goes hand in hand with issues like public libraries and education for all. He is even now hoping to present a bill to Parliament about woman's suffrage. I appeal to you –' she gestured at the circle around her – 'as concerned, educated members of the public: each time you enter this building, consider the fact that you yourselves – or, if you are a man, your wives or sisters or daughters – are being denied the chance to be responsible citizens by casting your vote for those who would represent you. But you can do something about this. Come to the meetings of the local WSPU, every Tuesday afternoon at four o'clock, at Birch Cottage, West Hill in Highgate. Votes for women!' She bowed slightly, as if acknowledging applause only she could hear, and took a step back, leaving Mummy and me alone in the circle.

The faces surrounding us stared curiously, probably wondering if we were suffragettes too. Mrs Waterhouse at least gave me a look of horrified sympathy. Next to her Ivy May was staring at my mother. Mummy herself was gazing at Caroline Black, and for the first time in months she was smiling.

I looked across to the cemetery gate, but Lavinia was no longer there. Then I caught a glimpse of her inside the cemetery just before she disappeared between two graves.

KITTY COLEMAN

Her laughter rang out like a clarion call, sending a jolt up my spine that made me open my eyes wide. I had thought it was another foggy, muffled day, but when I looked around for the source of the laughter, I discovered it was one of those crisp, windy autumn days I love, when as a girl I wanted to eat apples and kick at dead leaves.

Then I saw John Jackson across by the gate, and I had to stand very still so that he wouldn't see me. He did none the less. I had tried to walk up the hill a number of times to see him, and to explain. But I had never managed it. I suspected he understood – he understands most things.

I heard the laugh again, right at my side. Caroline took my arm, and I knew nothing would ever be the same.

SIMON FIELD

I'm down the grave standing on the coffin when she comes along. The procession's just left, and I'm shifting dirt so it fills the cracks round the coffin. Then I've to knock out the lowest shoring wood with a hammer and our Pa and Joe'll pull 'em out with a rope. It's twelve feet deep, this one.

Our Pa and Joe are singing:

> 'She's my lady love
> She's my dove, my baby love
> She's no gal for sitting down to dream
> She's the only queen Laguna knows.'

They stop but I keeps on:

> 'I know she likes me
> I know she likes me
> Because she says so
> She is the Lily of Laguna
> She is my Lily, and my Rose.'

Then I look up and see Livy standing at the edge of the grave, laughing down at me.

'Damn, Livy,' I say. 'Wha're you doing there?'

She shakes her hair and shrugs. 'Looking at you, naughty boy,' she says. 'You mustn't say "damn".'

'Sorry.'

'Now, I'm going to get down there with you.'

'You can't do that.'

'Yes, I can.' She turns to our Pa. 'Will you help me down?'

'Oh, no, missie, you don't want to go down there. 'Tain't no place for you. 'Sides, you'll get your nice dress and shoes all dirty.'

'Doesn't matter — I can have them cleaned afterwards. How do you climb down — with a ladder?'

'No, no, no ladder,' our Pa says. 'With a deep un like this we got all this wood stuck in, see, every foot or two, to keep the sides from caving in. We climbs up and down it. But don't you go doing that,' he adds, but too late, 'cause Livy's climbing down already. All I can see of her is her two legs sticking out from a dress and petticoats.

'Don't come down, Livy,' I say, but I don't mean it. She's climbing down the wood frame like she's done it all her life. Then she's down on the coffin with me. 'There,' she says. 'Are you pleased to see me?'

'Course.'

Livy looks round and shivers. 'It's cold down here. And so muddy!'

'What'd you expect? It's a grave, after all.'

Livy scrapes her toe in the clay on the coffin. 'Who's in there?'

I shrug. 'Dunno. Who's in the coffin, our Pa?' I call up.

'No, let me guess,' Livy says. 'It's a little girl who caught pneumonia. Or a man who drowned in one of the Heath ponds trying to save his dog. Or —'

'It's an old man,' our Pa calls down. 'Nat'ral causes.' Our Pa likes to find out something about who we bury, usually from listening to the mourners at the graveside.

Livy looks disappointed. 'I think I shall lie down,' she says.

'You don't want to do that,' I say. 'It's muddy, like you said.'

She don't listen to me. She sits down on the coffin lid and then she stretches out, her hair getting mud in it and all. 'There,' she says, crossing her hands over her chest like she's dead. She looks up at the sky.

I can't believe she don't mind the mud. Maybe she's gone doolally. 'Don't do that, Livy,' I say. 'Get up.'

She still lies there, her eyes closed, and I stare at her face. It's strange seeing something so pretty lying there in the mud. She's got a mouth makes me think of some chocolate-covered cherries Maude gave me once. I wonder if her lips taste like that.

'Where's Maude?' I say to stop thinking of it.

Livy makes a face but keeps her eyes shut. 'Over at the library with her mother.'

'Mrs C.'s out and about?'

I shouldn't have said nothing, nor sounded surprised. Livy opens her eyes, like a dead un suddenly come to life. 'What do you know about Maude's mother?'

'Nothing,' I say quickly. 'Just that she was ill. That's all.'

I've said it too quickly. Livy notices. It's funny – she's not like Ivy May, who sees everything. But when she wants to she notices things.

'Mrs Coleman was ill, but that was over two months ago,' she says. 'She does look dreadful but there's something else wrong. I just know it.' Livy sits up. 'And you know it.'

I shift from one foot to the other. 'I don't know nothing.'

'You do.' Livy smiles. 'You're hopeless at lying, Simon. Now, what do you know about Maude's mother?'

'Nothing I'm going to tell you.'

Livy looks pleased and I wish I hadn't said even that. 'I knew there was something,' she says. 'And I know that you're going to tell me.'

'Why should I tell you anything?'

'Because I'm going to let you kiss me if you do.'

I stare at her mouth. She's just licked her lips and they're all glistening like rain on leaves. She's trapped me. I move towards her, but she pulls her face back.

'Tell me first.'

I shake my head. I hate to say it but I don't trust Livy. I have to have my kiss before I'll say a word. 'I'll only tell you after.'

'No, kiss after.'

I shake my head again, and Livy sees I'm serious. She lies back down on the mud. 'All right, then. But I must pretend I'm Sleeping Beauty and you're the prince who wakes me.' She closes her eyes and crosses her hands over her chest again like she's dead. I look up. Our Pa ain't hanging over the grave — he must've sat down to wait with the bottle. I don't know how long I'll be lucky, so I lean over quick and press my mouth against Livy's. She stays still. Her lips are soft. I touch them with my tongue — they don't taste like chocolate cherries, but like salt. I move back onto my heels and Livy opens her eyes. We look at each other but don't say nothing. She smiles a little.

'Simon, get yourself going, lad. We've another to dig after this,' our Pa calls down. He's standing up top leaning over like he's going to fall in. I don't know if he saw us kissing — he don't say. 'You need help up, missie?' he says.

I don't want him coming down here when Livy's with me. Three people is too much in a grave. 'Leave her 'lone,' I call up. 'I'll bring her out.'

'I'll come up myself as soon as Simon answers my question,' Livy says.

Our Pa looks like he's going to climb down, so I has to say it quick. 'Mrs C. visited our Ma,' I whisper.

'What, on a charity visit?'

'Who says we need charity?'

Livy don't answer.

'Anyhow, it were business, not charity.'

'Your mother is a midwife, isn't she?'

'Yes, but —'

'Do you mean she's had another child?' Livy's eyes get big. 'Maude has a secret brother or sister somewhere? How exciting! I do hope it's a brother.'

'It weren't that,' I say quickly. 'She don't have a brother nor suchlike. It were the other. Getting rid of the brother or sister before it's born. Else it would've been a bastard, see.'

'Oh!' Livy sits up straight and stares at me, her eyes still big. I wish I'd never said a thing. Some people's meant to be innocent of life, and Livy's one of 'em. 'Oh!' she says again, and starts to cry. She lays back down on the mud.

'It's all right, Livy. Our Ma was gentle. But it took her a time to recover.'

'What will I tell Maude?' she sobs.

'Don't tell her nothing,' I say quickly, not wanting it to get worse. 'She don't need to know.'

'But she can't possibly live with her mother in those circumstances.'

'Why not?'

'She can come and live with us. I'll ask Mama. I'm sure she'll say yes, especially when she's heard why.' Livy's stopped crying now.

'Don't tell her nothing, Livy,' I say.

Then I hear a scream overhead and look up. Livy's mother is looking down at us with Maude peeking over her shoulder. Ivy May's standing by herself on the other side of the grave.

'Lavinia, what on earth are you doing lying down there?' her mother cries. 'Get out at once!'

'Hello, Mama,' Livy says calmly, like she ain't just been crying. She sits up. 'Were you looking for me?'

Livy's mum sinks to her feet and starts to cry, not quiet like Livy did, but noisy with lots of gasping.

'It's all right, Mrs Waterhouse,' Maude says, patting her shoulder. 'Lavinia's fine. She's coming right up, aren't you, Lavinia?' She glares at us.

Livy smiles a funny smile, and I know she's thinking about Maude's ma.

'Don't you dare tell her, Livy,' I whisper.

Livy don't say nothing, nor look at me. She just climbs up the wood fast and is gone before I can say more.

Ivy May drops a clod of clay into the grave. It falls at my feet.

It's quiet when they're all gone. I start scraping mud into the cracks round the coffin.

Our Pa comes and sits down at the side of the grave, dangling his legs over the edge. I can smell the bottle.

'You going to help me or what, our Pa?' I say. 'You can bring the Lamb's box over now.'

Our Pa shakes his head. 'It's no use kissing girls like her,' he says.

So he did see. 'Why not?' I say.

Our Pa shakes his head again. 'Them girls is not for you, boy. You know that. They like you 'cause you're different from them, is all. They'll even let you kiss 'em, once. But you won't get nowhere with 'em.'

'I'm not trying to get nowhere with 'em.'

Our Pa starts to chuckle. 'Sure you're not, boy. Sure you're not.'

'Hush, our Pa. You just hush.' I go back to my mud — it's easier than talking to him.

LAVINIA WATERHOUSE

At last I have reached a decision.

I have felt sick ever since Simon told me. Mama thinks I caught a chill down in the grave, but it is not that. I am suffering from Moral Repulsion. Even Simon's kiss – which I shall never tell a soul about – could not make up for the horror of the news about Kitty Coleman.

When they came to get me at the cemetery, I could hardly look at Maude. I knew that she was annoyed with me, but I genuinely felt ill and could not speak. Then we returned to the library and I felt even worse when I saw Maude's mother. Luckily she paid no attention to me – she was in the clutches of a frightening woman who Maude told me is a local suffragette. (I don't understand what all the fuss is about with voting. Politics are so dull – what woman would want to vote anyway?) They walked home arm in arm, talking intimately as if they had known each other for years, and ignored me, which is just as well. It is truly astonishing how brazen Maude's mother is, given what she has done.

I have not been comfortable with Maude since that day,

and, indeed, for a time felt too ill to see her or go to school. I know she thought I was simply pretending, but I felt so burdened. Then, thank goodness, it was half term, and Maude went off to see her aunt in Lincolnshire, and so I could avoid her for a time. Now she is back, though, and the burden of my knowledge is greater than ever. I hate to keep such a secret from her, and indeed, from everyone, and that has made me sick.

I have not told Mama, for I cannot bring myself to shock her. I am feeling quite fond of dear Mama and Papa, and even of Ivy May. They are simple people, unlike myself, who am rather more complicated, but at least I know that they are honest. This is not a House of Secrets.

I must do something. I cannot sit by and watch the contamination at the heart of the Coleman house spread to dear Maude. So, after three weeks of soul-searching, I sat down this afternoon in my room and wrote, in a disguised hand, the following letter:

Dear Mr Coleman,

It is my Christian duty to inform you of Unbecoming Conduct that has taken place in your household concerning your wife. Sir, you are encouraged to ask your wife about the true nature of her illness earlier this year. I think you will be profoundly shocked.

I am writing this as behoves someone concerned with the moral welfare of your daughter, Miss Maude Coleman. I have only her best interests at heart.

With respectful concern,

I wish to remain,
Yours most sincerely,
Anonymous

I shall creep round this evening and slide it under their door. Then I am sure I will begin to feel better.

November 1906

JENNY WHITBY

First thing was, the house were filthy. I had to clean it top to bottom, then clean it again. The only good thing about it was I didn't have time to think about Jack. That and Mrs Baker was actually pleased to see me again. I guess she'd had her fill of the replacements. Them chars was a useless lot.

Then there were my bubbies. Every few hours they'd swell and milk would pour out for Jack, right down my front. I had to wear cotton pads and change 'em all the time, and even then I'd get caught out. Luckily the missus never saw — not that she'd notice anyway. But it happened once when I were cleaning out the coal fire in Miss Maude's room. She come in and I had to quick hug a pile of linens to me, coal dust all over me and all, and make an excuse to get away. She did give me a funny look but didn't say nothing. She's so glad I'm back she's not about to complain.

I dunno how much she knows — Mrs Baker thinks not a lot, that she's still an innocent lamb. But I don't know — sometimes I catch her staring at me or her mother and I think: She's no fool.

Her mother — now there's a strange thing. I come back

on my tippy-toes, dreading to see her after how we parted. I thought she'd be awkward with me, but when I arrived she squeezed my hand and said, 'So lovely to see you again, Jenny. Come in, come in!' She brought me into the morning room, where a fluttery little woman, a Miss Black, jumped up and shook my hand too.

'Jenny is our treasure,' the missus said to Miss Black. Well, I blushed at that, thinking she was teasing me. But she seemed genuine enough, as if she'd forgot all about the blackmail.

'I'll just settle my things in my room and get started,' I said.

'Miss Black and I are plotting great things, aren't we, Caroline?' the missus said like she didn't hear me. 'I'm sure you could be of great help to us.'

'Oh, I don't know, ma'am. Perhaps I'll just fetch you some tea.'

'Tell me, Jenny,' Miss Black said, 'what do you think about woman's suffrage?'

'Well, we all suffer, don't we?' I said carefully, not sure what there was to say.

Miss Black and the missus laughed, though I'd not made a joke.

'No, I mean votes for women,' Miss Black explained.

'But women don't vote,' I said.

'Women *aren't allowed* to vote, but they should have every right to, the same as men. That is what we are fighting for, you see. Don't you feel you have as much right as your father, your brother, your husband to elect who is to govern this country?'

'Haven't got none of them.' She hadn't mentioned sons.

'Jenny, we are fighting for your equality,' the missus said.

'That's very kind of you, ma'am. Now, will you be wanting coffee or tea?'

'Oh, coffee, I think, don't you, Caroline?'

Them two are together all the time now, plotting against the government or some such thing. I should be pleased for the missus, that she seems happier than before. But I ain't. There's something about her don't seem right, like a top that's been wound too tight – it's spinning like it should, but it might just break.

Not that it matters so much to me now – I got others to think of. The first Saturday I went back to Mum's I cried when I saw Jack. Only five days away and he looked like someone else's baby. I'd still a little milk left in me then, but he wouldn't take it – he wanted the girl across the way who's nursing him after losing her own. I cried again to see him at her bubbies.

How I'm to pay her all these months I don't know. Wish I'd thought of that when I were securing my job here with the missus. Four months ago she'd have given me anything, but now if I asked for better wages she'd probably just lecture me about women suffering. One thing I've learned – you've to be scared of blackmail for it to work. I don't think she cares about nothing now except votes for women.

Here's another funny thing – the missus is busy acting like nothing happened to her this summer, but someone ain't forgot. I were putting the shoes out in the hallway, all polished and ready for the next day, when a letter gets slid under the front door, addressed to Mr Coleman. I picked it up and looked at it. It were in a funny hand, like a schoolgirl writing it on a wobbly chair. I opened the front door and looked out. It were a foggy night and I could just make out Miss Lavinia running up the street before she disappeared.

I didn't put the letter on a tray for the master, but kept it with me. Next morning I sat down for a cuppa in the kitchen and showed it to Mrs Baker. Funny how she and I are friendlier since Jack. She don't know about the blackmail, but she must suspect as much. She never asked how I got my job back.

'What would she be writing to the master for except to make trouble?' I said.

Mrs Baker studied the letter, then took it over to the kettle and in a minute had steamed it open. That's what I like about her — she can be horrible mean sometimes, but she's definite.

I read over her shoulder. When we'd finished we looked at each other. 'How does she know about all that?' I wondered aloud, before I realised Mrs Baker mightn't have known about the missus' predicament.

But she did. Mrs Baker's no fool. She must've worked it out for herself.

'That silly girl,' she said now. 'Trying to stir things up.' She opened the door of the range and threw the letter into the flames.

As I said, she's definite.

EDITH COLEMAN

When she opened the door I thought for a moment that I was dreaming. But I knew very well that I was wide awake – I am not the dreaming type. Of course there was a smirk on her face to tell me she knew I was surprised.

'What on earth are you doing here?' I asked. 'Where is the char I hired?' I had taken on the running of the house while Kitty was ill and had been hiring chars until we could find a proper maid.

'I work here again, ma'am,' the impertinent girl replied.

'According to whom?'

'Best ask my mistress, ma'am. May I take your coat, ma'am?'

'Don't you touch my coat. Go and wait in the kitchen. I'll see myself up.'

The girl shrugged and I thought I heard her say, 'Suit yourself.'

I wanted to say something but didn't bother – it was not she I must speak to. Clearly Jenny would not be here if Kitty had not let her come back – behind my back and against my orders.

I walked into the morning room unannounced. Kitty was

sitting with Miss Black, whom I had met briefly on another occasion. I had not thought much of her at the time. She had gone on and on about woman's suffrage, a subject I find intolerable.

They both stood now and Kitty came and kissed me. 'Let me take your coat, Mother Coleman,' she said. 'Why didn't Jenny take it at the door?'

'That is what I should like to discuss with you,' I replied, keeping my coat on for the moment – I was no longer sure that I would be staying. It was unfortunate that Kitty was not alone, as I was reluctant to talk about Jenny in front of others.

'Mother Coleman, you have met Caroline Black before,' Kitty said. 'Caroline, you do remember my mother-in-law, Mrs Coleman.'

'Of course,' Miss Black said. 'It's a pleasure to see you again, Mrs Coleman.'

'Will you sit with us?' Kitty asked, gesturing towards the sofas. 'Jenny's just brought up the tea and Mrs Baker has made some lardy cakes.'

I sat down, feeling very awkward in my coat. Neither woman seemed to notice.

'Caroline and I have been discussing the Women's Social and Political Union,' Kitty said. 'Did you know that they have opened an office in London just off the Aldwych? It's very handy for the newspaper offices, and they can lobby Parliament about woman's suffrage much more effectively from a base here rather than from Manchester.'

'I don't approve of women voting,' I interrupted. 'They don't need to – their husbands are perfectly capable of doing so on their behalf.'

'There are plenty of unmarried women — myself included — deserving of representation,' Miss Black said. 'Besides, a woman doesn't always have the same views as her husband.'

'In any sound marriage the woman is in perfect agreement with her husband. Otherwise they shouldn't have married in the first place.'

'Really? Would you always vote the same way as your husband, Kitty?' Miss Black asked.

'I would most likely vote Conservative,' Kitty said.

'You see?' I said to Miss Black. 'Colemans always vote Conservative.'

'But that is only because a Conservative candidate now seems more likely to agree actively to support woman's suffrage,' Kitty added. 'If a Liberal or even a Labour candidate were openly supportive, I would vote for them.'

I was horrified by such an announcement. 'Don't be silly. Of course you wouldn't.'

'I'm not concerned with the political parties. I'm concerned with a moral issue.'

'You should be concerned with moral issues much closer to home,' I said.

'Whatever do you mean?' I noticed Kitty spoke without looking at me.

'Why is Jenny here? I dismissed her in July.'

Kitty shrugged and smiled at Miss Black as if to apologise for me. 'And I hired her again in October.'

'Kitty, I dismissed your maid four months ago because her conduct was immoral. Such behaviour is irreversible, and she is not fit to work in this house.'

At last my daughter-in-law met my eye. She looked almost bored. 'I asked Jenny to come back because she is a very good maid, she is available, and we need a good maid. The chars you hired were unacceptable.'

Something in her face told me that she was lying, but I did not know what the lie could be.

'Have you forgot what she has gone and done?' I asked.

Kitty sighed. 'No, I have not forgot. I just do not happen to think it is very important. My mind is on other matters, and I simply wanted to hire someone I knew would work well in the house.'

I drew myself up. 'That is ridiculous,' I said. 'You can't have a girl here who has —' I stopped and glanced at Miss Black, who was gazing at me calmly. I did not wish to mince my words but it would be unseemly to be so frank in front of a stranger. I did not complete my sentence, knowing that Kitty could. Instead I said, 'What kind of example does that set for Maude or my son?'

'They don't know of it. They think Jenny was ill.'

'The moral foundation of this house will be undermined by her presence, whether they know of the circumstances or not.'

Kitty smiled, which seemed to me to be a most inappropriate response. 'Mother Coleman,' she said, 'you know that I am so very grateful to you for looking after this house while I was ill. You have been generous with your time and efforts. Now, however, it is time that I took charge of my own house once more. I have decided that Jenny may work for us again, and there is really nothing more to be said about it.'

'What does my son say to this?'

'Richard is blissfully ignorant of household matters. That, I believe, is what you taught me about running a house: never worry your husband.'

I ignored her remark, but I did not forget it. 'I shall have to have a word with him.'

'Do you think he would welcome that?'

'I think any man would want to know if his house is morally threatened.'

'Will you stay for tea?' Kitty said it pleasantly enough, but her words implied that she thought I might wish to go.

I did wish to go. 'I will not stay to tea,' I said, standing up. 'I will not set foot in this house while she is here. Goodbye, Kitty.' I turned and walked out. Kitty did not follow me, and it was just as well that the impertinent maid was not in the hallway to see me out, or I don't know what I might have said to her.

One of the unfortunate consequences of being of what I would call a definite disposition is that occasionally I am caught in a dilemma. I had no qualms about cutting off contact with Kitty if necessary, but I could not say the same for my son and granddaughter. After all, it is not their fault that Kitty is morally lax. However, I was reluctant to involve Richard in what, as Kitty herself reminded me, are women's affairs.

None the less, I did feel he should know something of his wife's impropriety — if not about her decision to take Jenny back, then at least about her friendship with a dubious woman. I invited him over one evening on his own, under the guise of discussing something about his late father's property. The moment I saw him, however, I knew I would not say a word to him either about Jenny or about Caroline Black. He was glowing, even after a day at work, and I was reminded of how he looked when he and Kitty had returned from their honeymoon.

So that is how it is, I thought frankly. She has taken him into her bed again so that she can do what she likes outside of it.

She is no fool, my daughter-in-law. She has come a long way since the day Richard first introduced her to me, a slight, gawky girl from the provinces wearing dresses two years out of fashion. I do not like to play games, and as I looked at my son now, I knew that she had outplayed me.

RICHARD COLEMAN

This year we will be staying at home for New Year's.

February 1907

GERTRUDE WATERHOUSE

Oh dear – I have just returned from one of Kitty Coleman's At Homes with such a headache.

In January something happened that I had always dreaded might one day. Kitty Coleman changed her At Homes to Wednesday afternoons so that she could attend some sort of meeting in Highgate on Tuesdays. (At least that means she will not be coming to my At Homes!) Now I have felt obliged to go – not every week, I should hope, but at least once or twice a month. I managed to get out of the first few, saying I had a chill, or that the girls were unwell, but I couldn't use that excuse every time.

So today I went along, taking Lavinia and Ivy May with me for support. When we arrived the room was already full of women. Kitty Coleman welcomed us and then flitted across the room without making introductions. I must say it was the loudest At Home I have ever attended. Everyone was talking at once, and I am not sure anyone was actually listening. But I listened, and as I did my eyes grew big and my mouth small. I didn't dare say a word. The room was full of suffragettes.

Two were discussing a meeting they were to attend in

Whitechapel. Another was passing around a design for a poster of a woman waving a sign from a train window that read 'Votes for Women'. When I saw it I turned to my daughters. 'Lavinia,' I said, 'go and help Maude.' Maude was serving tea across the room, and looked as miserable as I felt. 'And don't listen to what anyone around you is saying,' I added.

Lavinia was staring hard at Kitty Coleman. 'Did you hear me, Lavinia?' I asked. She shook her head and shrugged, as if to shake away my words, then made a face and crossed the room to Maude.

'Ivy May,' I said, 'would you like to go downstairs and ask the cook if she needs help, please.'

Ivy May nodded and disappeared. She is a good girl.

A woman next to me was saying she had just been speaking at a rally in Manchester and had rotten tomatoes thrown at her.

'At least it wasn't rotten eggs!' another woman cried, and everyone laughed.

Well, almost everyone laughed. A few women like myself were very quiet, and looked just as shocked as I felt. They must have been Kitty's old friends who came to the At Home expecting pleasant conversation and Mrs Baker's excellent scones.

One of them, less timid than me, finally spoke. 'What is it that you speak about at these rallies in Manchester?'

The tomato woman gave her an incredulous look. 'Why, for women to have the vote, of course!'

The poor woman turned bright red, as if she herself had been hit by a tomato, and I was mortified for her.

To her credit, Caroline Black came to her rescue. 'The

Women's Social and Political Union is campaigning to have a bill brought before Parliament that would allow women the right to vote in government elections, just as men do,' she explained. 'We are rallying the support of women and men all over the country by speaking publicly, writing to newspapers, lobbying MPs, and signing petitions. Have you seen the WSPU's pamphlet? Do take one and read it — it is so informative. You can place a donation for it on the table by the door when you go. And don't forget to pass on the pamphlet when you are done — it is really surprising how much life there is in a little pamphlet when you hand it on to others.'

She was in her element, speaking so smoothly and gently and yet also forcefully that several women indeed took away pamphlets and left coins by the door — myself included, I am ashamed to admit. When the pile of pamphlets reached me, Caroline Black was watching me with such a sweet smile on her face that I had to take one. I could not bring myself to hide it down the back of the sofa as I might have liked. I did that later, at home.

Kitty Coleman did not take the floor in quite the same way as Caroline Black, but she was still in an excited state, her eyes glittering, her cheeks flushed as if she were at a ball and had not stopped dancing once. She did not look entirely healthy.

I know I should not say this, but I wish she and Caroline Black had never met. Kitty's transformation has been dramatic, and undoubtedly it has pulled her out of the bad way she was in, but she has not gone back to her old self — she has changed into something altogether more radical. Not that I was greatly enamoured of her old self, but I prefer that to her present state. Even when she is not at her At Homes with suffragettes everywhere, she still talks incessantly about politics and women this and women that till I want to cover my ears. She has bought herself a bicycle and goes around even in the wind and rain, getting grease marks all down her skirts — if they are not already covered in chalk from all the signs she has been drawing on pavements about meetings and rallies and such. Whenever I find her crouched somewhere with a bit of chalk, I cross the road and pretend not to see her.

She is never at home now in the afternoons, but always at a meeting, and neglects poor Maude shamelessly. Sometimes I think of Maude as my third daughter, she is at our house so often. Not that I am complaining — Maude is very thoughtful, helping me with tea or Ivy May with her schoolwork. She sets a good example for Lavinia, who I am sorry to say never seems to take it up. It is very peculiar that one daughter can have a mother who pays her no attention and yet turns out well, while the other gets all the attention in the world and yet is so difficult and selfish.

It was a relief to leave Kitty's At Home. Lavinia seemed eager to come away as well. Back at home she was very kind to me, sending me off to bed to nurse my head while she insisted on making supper. I don't even mind that she burned the soup.

JENNY WHITBY

Lord, I hope these At Homes don't last. Since the missus switched 'em to Wednesdays I'm run off my feet. At least I've got Maude to help — though I don't know that she'll stick it. The whole afternoon she looked like she wanted to bolt, even when Lavinia came to keep her company.

That one makes me laugh. When she's here she watches the missus with an outraged look on her face. And when the master's home, she looks at him all puzzled and sorrowful. She hasn't said nothing, though, nor tried to send another letter — I've kept an eye out. I've no intention of letting her wreck this house — I need my wages. As it is I'm not managing to pay for Jack. Or I am, but I've had to do something I never thought I'd stoop to — taking spoons to sell from an old silver set in the sideboard what the missus' mum left her. They don't use it, and no one but me ever polishes it. It ain't right, I know, but I don't have no choice.

I finally listened to them suffragettes today as I passed round the scones. What I heard made me want to spit. They talk about helping women but it turns out they're choosy about who exactly gets the help. They ain't fighting for my vote — only for women who own property or went to university. But that Caroline Black had the nerve to ask me to donate some of my wages 'for the cause'. I told her I wouldn't give a penny until the cause had anything to do with me!

I were so mad I had to tell Mrs Baker about it when we were washing up afterwards.

'What did she say to that?' Mrs Baker asked.

'Oh, that men would never agree to give the vote to everyone all at once, that they had to start with some women and once they'd secured that they would fight for everyone. But ain't it always the way that they put themselves first? Why can't they fight for us first, I say. Let working women decide what's what.'

Mrs Baker chuckled. 'You wouldn't know who to vote for if they bit you on your arse, and you know it.'

'I would!' I cried. 'I ain't that stupid. Labour, of course. Labour for a labouring woman. But these ladies upstairs won't vote Labour, or even Liberal. They're all Tories like their husbands, and them Tories'll never give the vote to women, no matter what they say.'

Mrs Baker didn't say nothing. Maybe she was surprised I was talking politics. To be honest, I were surprised at myself. I've been round too many suffragettes – they're starting to make me talk a load of rubbish.

July 1907

MAUDE COLEMAN

Daddy and I were on the Heath when I felt it. It was our Friday night together, and we had set up the telescope on Parliament Hill. We had looked at a few stars and were waiting for Mars to appear. I didn't mind the wait. Sometimes we talked, but mostly we simply sat and observed.

As I was sipping a cup of tea from our flask I began to feel a dull ache in my stomach, as if I had eaten too much. Yet I had hardly touched Mrs Baker's welsh rarebit at supper — I am never hungry in hot weather. I shifted on my folding stool and tried to concentrate on what Daddy was saying.

'At the Society meeting recently someone said the opposition of Mars is likely to be very good this month,' he said. 'I don't know if this telescope is powerful enough. We should have borrowed the Society's, though someone else may have it tonight. All this will be a damn sight easier when the observatory is built.'

'*If* it is built,' I reminded him. The Hampstead Scientific Society had been trying to find a site on the Heath where it could build an observatory, but there had been objections to each spot, with a debate raging about it on the letters page of the local paper.

The place between my legs itched: it was damp there, as if I had spilled tea in my lap. Suddenly I understood what was happening. 'Oh,' I said before I could stop myself.

Daddy raised his eyebrows.

'It's nothing. It's —' I stopped, wincing with pain.

'Are you all right, Maude?'

The pain was suddenly so strong I could barely breathe. It ceased for a moment and then began again, like a hand clamped over my stomach, squeezing then letting go.

'Daddy,' I gasped, 'I'm not feeling well, I'm afraid. I'm so sorry, but I have to go back.'

Daddy frowned. 'What is it? What's wrong?'

I was so embarrassed I hardly knew what to say. 'It's — something I need to see Mummy about.' Immediately I wished I had simply said I had a stomach ache. I am not much good at lying.

'Why —' Daddy stopped. I think he understood. At least he did not ask more questions. 'I'll see you back,' he said, reaching for the wing nut that held the telescope to its stand.

'I can go on my own. It's not far, and you don't want to have to set up everything all over again.'

'Of course I'll see you back. I won't have my daughter wandering about alone on the Heath at night.'

I wanted to tell him that since Mummy became so busy with the suffragettes, I'd begun going all over on my own — to the cemetery, up to the Village, even across the Heath to Hampstead. Sometimes Lavinia came with me, but often she was too nervous to go far. But now was not the time to say such things to Daddy. Besides, he did not know how deeply involved Mummy had become – she talked about woman's suffrage with everyone but him, and for the most part confined her WSPU activities to the daytime, and nights when she knew Daddy was busy. For all he knew, she sat at home every day reading and gardening, as she used to.

We packed up in silence. I was glad it was too dark for Daddy to see my face, for I had gone bright red. I trailed down the hill after him, forced to slow down when the pain got too strong. Daddy didn't seem to notice, but continued down the path as if nothing were wrong. When I could I hurried to catch up with him.

We reached the edge of the Heath, where the Bull and Last spilled men with their pints into the street. 'I can walk home from here, Daddy,' I said. 'It's not far and there are plenty of people in the street. I'll be fine.'

'Nonsense.' Daddy kept walking.

When we got home he unlocked the door. A lamp was burning on the hall table. Daddy cleared his throat. 'Your mother is out visiting a friend who's taken ill, but Jenny can see to you.'

'Yes.' I kept my back to the wall in case there was a stain on the back of my dress. I would have died of shame if Daddy had seen.

'Well, then.' Daddy turned to go, pausing at the door. 'Will you be all right now?'

'Yes.'

When the door closed behind him I groaned. My thighs were sticky and chafed and I wanted to lie down. First, though, I needed help. I lit a candle and went upstairs, hesitating outside Mummy's morning room. Perhaps she was there after all, sitting on the sofa reading a book. She would look up and say, 'Hello there, what heavenly sights have you seen?' in the way she used to.

I opened the door. Of course Mummy wasn't there. Sometimes I felt as if the room was no longer Mummy's, but a cause's. The old traces of Mummy — the yellow silk shawl on the sofa, the piano with a vase of dried flowers on it, the prints of plants — were still there. But what I noticed instead was the half-finished banner draped across the sofa that read DEEDS NOT WORDS; the stack of WSPU pamphlets on the piano; the scrapbook on the table, newspaper cuttings, letters, photographs piled next to it along with scissors and a gluepot; the box of chalk, the handbills, the sheets of paper scribbled with lists. Daddy never came in here. If he did he would be very surprised.

I closed the door, climbed the stairs to Jenny's room and tapped on it. 'Jenny?' I called. There was no answer at first, but when I tapped again I heard a grunt, and Jenny opened the door, squinting, a red crease across her cheek where it had pressed against the pillow. She wore a long white nightgown and her feet were bare. 'What's wrong, Miss Maude?' she murmured, rubbing her face.

I stared at Jenny's thick yellow toenails. 'I need your help, please,' I whispered.

'Can it not wait till morning? I was asleep, you know. I have to get up earlier than you lot.'

'I'm sorry. It's — my courses have begun and I don't know what to do.'

'What?'

I repeated myself and turned red again.

Oh, Lord, the curse,' Jenny muttered. She looked me up

and down. 'Blimey, Miss Maude, twelve's young to start — you've not got even a trace of bubbies yet!'

'I'm not so young. I'll be thirteen in — in eight months.' I knew how silly I sounded and began to cry.

Jenny opened her door wide. 'There, now, no need for that.' She put her arm round me. 'You'd best come in — it won't get sorted out with you standing there bawling.'

Jenny's room had been Nanny's room when I was small. Although I had been in it only once or twice since Jenny moved into it, it still felt familiar. It smelled of warm skin and wool blankets and camphorated oil, like the presses Nanny used to heat for my chest when I had a cold. Jenny's dress, apron and cap were hung on pegs. Her hairbrush sat on the small mantel over the fire, and also a photograph of Jenny with a baby in her lap. They were sitting in front of a backdrop of palm fronds, and Jenny wore her best dress. Both looked serious and surprised, as if they had not expected the camera to flash.

'Who's that?' I asked. I had never seen the photograph.

Jenny was wrapping a robe around herself and barely looked up. 'My nephew.'

'I've not heard you mention him. What's his name?'

'Jack.' Jenny crossed her arms. 'Now, has your mum told you anything, or sorted out anything for you?'

I shook my head.

'Of course not. I might've known. Your mother's so busy saving women she don't even look after her own.'

'I know what's happening. I've read about it in books.'

'But you don't know what to do, do you? That's what's important, what you *do* about it. Who cares what it is? "Deeds not words," ain't that what your mum's always saying?'

I frowned.

Jenny pursed her lips. 'Sorry, Miss Maude,' she said. 'All right – I'll lend you some of mine till we've got you what you need.' She kneeled by a small chest where she kept her things and took out a few long thick pieces of cloth and a curious belt I had never seen. She showed me how to fold the cloth in three and fasten it to the belt. She explained about the bucket and salt water to soak the cloths in, to be left under the bed by the chamber pot. Then she went downstairs for a bucket and a hot-water bottle for the pain, while I washed myself and tried on the towel and belt in my room. It felt like my petticoats and bloomers had become all wadded up and caught between my legs, making me waddle like a duck. I was sure everyone would be able to tell.

As awful as it had been having such a thing happen when I was with Daddy, I was glad at least that Lavinia was not there too. She would never forgive me for starting first. She has always been the pretty one, the womanly one – even when we were younger she reminded me of the women in Pre-Raphaelite paintings, with her curly hair and plump figure. Jenny was right – I am flat and, as Grandmother once said, my clothes hang from me like washing from a line. Lavinia and I always assumed that she would get her courses first, would wear a corset first, would marry first, would have children first. Sometimes I've been bothered by this, but often I've been secretly relieved. I have never told her, but I am not so sure that I want to be married and have children.

Now I would have to hide my belts and towels and pain from her. I didn't like keeping secrets from my best friend.

But then, she was keeping one from me. Ever since Mummy took up with Caroline Black, Lavinia has been peculiar about her, but won't say why. When I ask her she simply says that suffragettes are wicked, but I'm sure there's more to it than that. It was something to do with Simon and being down that grave. But she won't say, and neither will Simon. I went to the cemetery on my own and asked him, but he just shrugged and kept on digging.

When Jenny came back with the bucket she gave me a hug. 'You're a woman now, you know. Before you know it you'll be wearing a corset. That's something to tell your mum tomorrow.'

I nodded. But I knew that tomorrow I would say nothing to Mummy. She wasn't here now when she was needed most. Tomorrow did not matter.

February 1908

KITTY COLEMAN

To my surprise, it was harder facing Maude than Richard.

Richard's response was predictable – a rage he contained in front of the police but unleashed in the cab home. He shouted about the family name, about the disgrace to his mother, about the uselessness of the cause. All of this I had known to expect, from hearing of the reactions of other women's husbands. Indeed, I have been lucky to go this long without Richard complaining. He has thought my activities with the WSPU a harmless hobby, to be dabbled in between tea parties. It is only now he truly understands that I too am a suffragette.

One thing he said in the cab did surprise me. 'What about your daughter?' he shouted. 'Now that she's firmly on the road to womanhood, she needs a better example than you are setting.'

I frowned – the phrase he used was so awkward it must be masking something. 'What do you mean?'

Richard stared at me, both incredulous and embarrassed. 'She hasn't told you?'

'Told me what?'

'That she's begun her ... her ...' He waved his hand vaguely at my skirt.

'She has?' I cried. 'When?'

'Months ago.'

'How can you know when I don't?'

'I was with her at the time, that's why! And a humiliating moment it was, for both of us. She had to go to Jenny in the end — you weren't home. I should have guessed then how deeply you were into this ridiculous nonsense.'

Richard could have said more, but must have sensed he didn't need to. I was remembering when my own courses began — how I had run to my mother, crying, and how she had comforted me.

We were silent the rest of the way back. When we got home I took a candle from the hall table and went directly up to Maude's room. I sat on her bed and looked at her in the dim light, wondering what other secrets she was keeping from me, and how to tell her what I must tell her.

She opened her eyes and sat up before I had said anything. 'What is it, Mummy?' she asked so clearly that I am not sure she had been asleep.

It was best to be honest and direct. 'Do you know where I was today while you were at school?'

'At the WSPU headquarters?'

'I was at Caxton Hall for the Women's Parliament. But then I went to Parliament Square with some others to try to get in to the House of Commons.'

'And — did you?'

'No. I was arrested. I've just come back from Cannon Row Police Station with your father. Who is furious, of course.'

'But why were you arrested? What did you do?'

'I didn't do anything. We were simply pushing through the crowd when policemen grabbed us and threw us to the ground. When we got up, they threw us down again and again. The bruises on my shoulders and ribs are quite spectacular. We've all got them.'

I did not add that many of those bruises came from the ride in the Black Maria – how the driver took corners so sharply I was thrown about, or how the cubicles in the van were so small that I felt I had been shut in a coffin standing up, or how it smelled of urine, which I was sure the police had done themselves to punish us further.

'Was Caroline Black arrested too?' Maude asked.

'No. She had fallen back to speak to someone she knew, and by the time she caught up the police had already got us. She was terribly upset not to be taken. She even came down to Cannon Row on her own and sat with us.'

Maude was silent. I wanted to ask her about what Richard had told me in the cab ride home, but found I couldn't. It was easier to talk about what had happened to me.

'I'll be in court early tomorrow,' I continued. 'They may send me straight to Holloway. I wanted to say goodbye now.'

'But – how long would you be in – in prison?'

'I don't know. Possibly up to three months.'

'Three months! What will we do?'

'You? You'll be fine. There is something I want you to do for me, though.'

Maude gazed at me eagerly.

Even before I pulled out the collecting card and began to tell her about self-denial week – a campaign drive the WSPU was initiating to raise money – I knew I was doing the wrong thing. As her mother I should be comforting and reassuring her. Yet even as her face fell I continued to explain that she should ask all our neighbours as well as any visitors to place donations in the card, and that she should send it to the WSPU office at the end of the week.

I don't know why I was so cruel.

DOROTHY BAKER

As a rule I don't involve myself in this family's comings and goings. I arrive at half-seven in the morning, I cook for them, I leave at seven at night – six if the supper's a cold one. I stay out of the way, I don't have opinions. Or if I do I keep them to myself. I have my own little house, my grown children with their dramas – I don't need more. Not like Jenny, who given half a chance pokes her nose into every story going. It's a miracle she's not had it cut right off.

But I do feel sorry for Miss Maude. I was going home the other evening through a thick fog when I saw her walking just ahead of me. I'd never seen her in Tufnell Park before. She's got no reason to come over here – her life goes in other directions, north and west towards Highgate and Hampstead, not east towards Tufnell Park and Holloway. That's to be expected of a family of that class.

The streets here are not so rough, but all the same I didn't like to see her on her own, especially in that peasoup. A person could disappear for good in one. I felt I ought to follow to make sure she came to no harm. It was clear enough where she was headed. Can't say I blame her – I'd have done the same in her shoes, though living near it as I do, I don't feel much draw to see it. But then, I don't have family inside. My children act out their dramas within the bounds of the law.

Miss Maude found her way there easy enough — even with the fog and the strange streets she's got a level head on her. When she got there she stopped and stared. The look of the place when it loomed out of the fog must have thrown her. The Castle, they call it round here. True enough it resembles one, with a big arched entrance and stone towers with ramparts. Most peculiar for a prison. My children used to play knights and maidens in front of it, when they dared. There are also rows of little windows set in a brick wall far back from the road, where the prisoners must be.

Then we both got a surprise — blow me if that Black woman wasn't marching up and down in front of the entrance. She's a little thing, but she wore a long grey coat that flapped round her ankles and made her look taller. She was singing this:

'Sing a song of Christabel's clever little plan
Four and twenty Suffragettes packed in a van
When the van was opened they to the Commons ran
Wasn't that a dainty dish for Campbell-Bannerman?
Asquith was in the treasury, counting out the money
Lloyd George among the Liberal women speaking
    words of honey
And then there came a bright idea to all those little
    men
"Let's give the women votes," they cried, "and all be
    friends again."'

Then she turned to the little windows and shouted, 'Chin

up, my dear – you're halfway through now. Only three weeks to go! And we have so much to do when you come out!' Her voice hardly carried in the fog, though – don't know how she thought anyone inside would hear her.

Miss Maude had seen enough – she turned and ran. I followed but my running days are long over and I lost sight of her. It was dusk now, and I began to worry. The shops were closed, and soon there wouldn't be any decent people out on the street for her to ask directions of.

Then I turned a corner and she was rushing out of the fog towards me, looking very frightened.

'Miss Maude, what on earth are you doing out here?' I said, pretending not to know.

'Mrs Baker!' She was so relieved to see me that she clutched my arm.

'You should be at home,' I scolded, 'not wandering the streets.'

'I've been – for a walk and got lost.'

I looked at her. There was no point in being coy. 'Wanted to see where she is?'

'Yes.' Miss Maude hung her head.

I shuddered. 'Grim place. I've never liked having it on my doorstep. Here, you!' I called to a passing figure.

'Hallo, Mrs Baker.'

'Miss Maude, this is Jimmy, my neighbour's son. See her to the Boston Arms, will you, Jimmy? She'll know her way from there.'

'Thank you, Mrs Baker,' Miss Maude whispered.

I shrugged. 'It's not my business,' I said. 'Not a word of this to anyone. Take care how you go in the fog.'

I keep my word.

March 1908

SIMON FIELD

It's chucking down, so our Jenny lets me in from the rain. Mrs Baker don't say nothing when she sees me – just grunts. Makes me a soft egg, though.

'Lord,' our Jenny says, looking out of the window while I sit at the table eating. 'What a day to be visiting prison.'

'Who's going to prison?' I ask.

Mrs B. bangs a pot of water onto the range and gives our Jenny a look. Jenny ignores her – she says whatever she likes.

'The master and Miss Maude. They ain't been able to visit till now – them suffragettes can't have visitors the first four weeks. First it were to be just the master, but I heard 'em arguing and Miss Maude got her way, bless her. She misses her mum. Though heaven knows why, the woman were hardly round before anyway.'

'That's enough, Jenny,' Mrs B. says.

'It don't matter – it's just Simon.'

'What doesn't matter?' Maude has come down the stairs, and is standing with her arms clutched over her stomach. She looks peaky to me.

Our Jenny and Mrs B. both turn quick to look at her.

'Nothing, Miss Maude,' our Jenny says. 'You had enough to eat?'

'I'm not much hungry, thanks.'

'Terrible luck, getting the curse on top of the rain on your visiting day.'

Maude looks at me then glares at our Jenny.

'For pity's sake, Jenny, leave the girl alone!' Mrs B. don't often shout. 'Get upstairs and clear away the dishes.'

Our Jenny runs off. I've enough sense not to say nothing 'bout the curse. 'Hallo,' is all I says.

'Hello.'

Hard to imagine Maude's ma in prison. Whoever thought she'd end up there? When I first found out from our Jenny, I let it slip real casual one day to Mr Jackson that Mrs C. were in Holloway. He jumped like someone'd pinched him.

'Good Lord. Why is she there?'

I didn't really know why, to be truthful. 'Women's things, sir.'

He stared at me so hard I had to say something more. 'You know, them women what goes round on bicycles, chalking signs on the pavement and shouting at rallies and that.'

'You mean suffragettes?'

'I suppose so, sir.'

'Good Lord,' he said again. 'Prison is a terrible place for a woman. I hope she is not being mistreated.'

'Probably no more'n anyone else in prison, sir. My cousin got out after six months with nothing worse'n flea bites.'

'That is not much comfort, Simon.'

'Sorry, sir.'

I want to say something to Maude now, but can't think of nothing that would help. Then there's a knock at the back door, and Livy comes in dripping wet, and there ain't much chance for me to get a word in. Maude don't look too happy to see her. Livy rushes over and gives her a big hug. She sees me over Maude's shoulder but don't say nothing. She's been funny with me ever since I kissed her. That were over a year ago and she ain't been the same since. Our Pa were right, I guess.

Fact is, this is the first time all three of us has been together in a long while. Not like when the girls was younger and used to visit the cemetery all the time.

'Oh, my dear, you look so pale!' Livy says now. 'You must be terribly upset about your visit.'

The thing about Livy is that she says things like that but she means something else. She don't think it's terribly upsetting Mrs C. is in Holloway – to her it's great fun, though she would never admit it. She looks so excited now, that I know what's to come next.

She sits Maude down at the table. 'Now,' she says, 'I want to suggest something to you.' She's acting like no one else is there – like I'm not sitting at the table too, and Mrs B. ain't peeling potatoes at the sideboard, and our Jenny ain't taking a tray with the breakfast things through to the scullery. But she knows we're there and listening. 'I know you'll say no, so I want you to promise to be quiet until I've finished what I have to say. Do you promise?'

'All right,' Maude says.

'I want to come with you this morning to visit your mother.'

'You can't –'

'I haven't finished yet.'

Maude frowns but stays quiet.

'You know it will be horrid and it will upset you. Don't you want your friend to be there with you, holding your hand and helping you to be as brave as you can in front of your mother?'

We all wait to hear what Maude will say – our Jenny standing in the scullery door, Mrs B. frowning at a potato skin like she's not listening. 'But what about your mother?' Maude says. 'And Daddy? I'm sure he won't let you.'

Livy smiles. 'Mama needn't know, and don't you worry about your father. He'll say yes – I'll make sure of it.'

She will, too. Livy can make a man do anything she likes. I've seen her at the cemetery, rolling her eyes and swirling her skirt, and men do what she says. Even Mr Jackson fetches her a watering can if she wants one – though that may be 'cause he still feels bad about her angel getting broke. Unless you look real hard you can't see the join in the neck where the mason fitted the head back on, but they made a mess of the nose. Probably should've left it chipped. Once I took Livy round the angels and showed her all the chips and scratches on them. I did it to make her feel better but it just seemed to upset her.

'Maude, are you ready?'

Everybody turns to stare at Maude's Pa come down the stairs. The way our Jenny and Mrs B. act – Jenny's eyes get big, and Mrs B. lets her knife slip so she cuts her thumb and has to suck it – it's clear he don't ever come down here. He must be feeling nervous about going to Holloway, or he don't like the whole house above us all empty, and has come looking for people.

Even Maude jumps to see him here. 'Yes, Daddy, I just need to – to get one thing in my room. I'll be right back.' She looks at Livy, then squeezes past her Pa and runs upstairs. He still stands at the bottom of the stairs, looking like he's surprised himself that he's down here.

Livy's getting ready to work her charm. 'Mr Coleman –'

But Mr C. has spotted me. 'Mrs Baker, who is this boy eating our bread?'

Mrs B. don't even flinch. 'Gardener's boy, sir.' She chose well – the garden is Mrs C.'s territory. Mr C. probably don't even set foot in it except to smoke a cig. He won't know which is the gardener's boy.

Mr C. looks out at the rain. 'Well, he certainly picks his days, doesn't he?'

'Yes, he does, sir. Do you hear, Simon? There'll be no gardening for you. Off you go, now.'

I gulp down the rest of my tea, put on my cap and step out into the rain. I don't get to say nothing to Maude, nor hear Livy's sweet talk. Never mind – at least my tum's full.

LAVINIA WATERHOUSE

Really it was not at all difficult. I simply appealed to his softer nature. And he does have a soft nature. He clearly is a broken man with his wife in prison – anyone can see that if they only look. But I am not sure anyone is looking except me. I do feel too that he and I have a special connection, because of the letter. Although he does not know that I wrote it, he must know someone is looking out for him.

For a long time I could not understand why he did not throw his wife out once he had read the letter, but now that I am older and beginning to understand men better, I see that he has quite gallantly set aside his own feelings in order to protect the family name from scandal.

He said yes when I asked to accompany them to Holloway. I repeated more or less what I had said to Maude – that I would be a comfort to her in difficult circumstances – but also suggested he was being an exemplary father and gentleman to consider his daughter's needs in that way.

I cannot help but think that he said yes in part because he prefers my company to Maude's. Certainly I was the livelier one in the cab over. But how could I not be – we were to see the inside of a prison! I couldn't think of anything more deliciously exciting.

The only dampening element (apart from the rain, ha ha!) was that as the cab drove past our house I saw Ivy May had pulled aside the net curtain and was looking out of the window. She seemed to look right at me, and I had to pray that she would not tattle on me – Mama thinks Maude and I were at the library.

I had never seen Holloway prison before. As we walked up to the arched wooden doors of the main entrance, I squeezed Maude's arm. 'It looks like a castle!' I whispered.

To my amazement Maude wrenched her arm away. 'This isn't a fairy tale!' she hissed.

Well. I was a little put out, but soon recovered when I saw the woman who opened the side door to let us in. She was short and fat and wore a grey uniform, with a big bunch of keys hanging at her waist. Best of all, she had a huge mole on her upper lip. She was just like a character out of Dickens, though I didn't say so to Maude. I had to clap my hand over my mouth so the woman wouldn't see me laughing. She did, though, the troll.

We went into a reception room, and Maude and I sat on a narrow bench while Troll opened a ledger book and took down Mr Coleman's details. I was amazed she could read and write.

Troll looked up at us. 'Only one of youse can come in,' she said. 'Only three visitors allowed at one time, an' one's already there. One of youse'll have to wait here.' She fixed a yellow eye on me.

'Another visitor?' Mr Coleman looked puzzled. 'Who?'

Troll put her finger on a page in the ledger. 'Miss C. Black.'

'Damn her! What the devil's she doing here?'

'She arranged a visit, same as you.'

'She's no relation to my wife. Tell her she has to go.'

Troll smiled slyly. 'She's a right to see 'er, same as any-one else. It's your wife decides who she sees an' don't sees.'

Poor Mr Coleman was furious but there was nothing he could do. 'You two wait here for me,' he said to us.

'But I've come to see Mummy!' Maude cried.

'It's best if you stay here with Lavinia. We can't leave her alone.'

He turned to the woman. 'Can the girls wait here for me?'

Troll just grunted.

I smiled, relieved by his chivalry.

'But Lavinia will be fine here on her own,' Maude insisted. 'Won't you, Lavinia?'

I opened my mouth to protest, but that nasty woman jumped in. 'I don't want two of youse cluttering up my bench.' She pointed at Maude. 'You go with your Da, and you –' pointing at me – 'wait where you are.' She went to the door and called out something into the corridor.

I was so shocked I couldn't speak. Being left alone in a prison with a horrid troll? And for such a silly reason as the space needed on a hard bench? Clearly Troll was saying this simply to get at me. I turned to Mr Coleman for help. Unfortunately he then revealed that he is not so gallant as I thought – he simply nodded at Troll.

Another woman came in, tall this time, also wearing the

grey uniform, and jangling her keys in a most irritating manner.

'H15, second division,' Troll said to her. 'Another un's already there.'

The wardress nodded and gestured for Mr Coleman and Maude to follow — which they did, neither of them giving me even a backward glance.

Well. When they were gone, Troll grinned at me from behind her table. I was surprised to see she had a full set of teeth — I would have expected them to be black and falling out. I ignored her and sat very quietly, like a little mouse. For I was rather terrified.

The thing about a little mouse, though, is that it can't help looking around for some crumbs to munch on. There was not much to see in the room — just the table and a few benches, all empty — and I found myself studying Troll. She was sitting behind the table, writing something in the ledger. She really was quite repulsive, even worse than something Dickens would have thought up. Her mole positively gleamed on her lip. I wondered if there were hairs growing out of it. The thought made me giggle. I didn't think she could see me spying on her — I was looking at her through my lashes while pretending to study my fingernails — but she growled, 'What you laughing at, gal?'

'My own little joke,' I said bravely. 'It's nothing to do with you. And really, you had better call me Miss Waterhouse.'

She had the impudence to laugh, so I felt obliged to explain that I was almost certain we were related to the painter J. W. Waterhouse, even though Papa thinks not, and that I had written to him to discover the connection. (I didn't tell her that Mr Waterhouse never responded to my letter.) Of course I was assuming far too much of a prison gatekeeper with a mole on her lip, even if she can write — she clearly had never heard of JWW, not even when I described his painting of the Lady of Shalott that hangs in the Tate. She hadn't even heard of her! Next she would be asking who was Tennyson.

Fortunately this fruitless conversation was interrupted by the arrival back of yet another wardress. Troll said she was glad the other had come because I could 'talk the ear off an elephant, an' all of it rubbish, too.'

I was very tempted to stick out my tongue at her — the longer I sat there the less terrified I was. But then a bell rang, and she went off to answer the door. The other wardress just stood there and stared at me as if I were a piece in a museum exhibition. I glared at her but it didn't seem to put her off. I expect they don't often see girls like me sitting on the bench — no wonder that she stared.

Troll came back with a man in tow, dressed in a dark suit and bowler hat. He stood at the table while Troll looked in her ledger and said, 'She's already got her visitors for today. Popular lady. Did you write ahead to arrange it?'

'No,' the man said.

'You have to write ahead for permission,' Troll said gleefully. She did delight in other's misfortunes. 'And then it's up to her to say she'll see you.'

'I see.' The man turned to leave.

Well. I was rather beyond surprise by that time. So when he glanced over at me and started like a skittish horse, I simply smiled my sweetest smile and said, 'Hello, Mr Jackson'.

Luckily he left before Maude and her father returned or

there would have been an awkward scene. For once Troll held her tongue rather than make everyone's misery worse, and I kept quiet as well. It was very odd indeed that Mr Jackson should want to visit Maude's mother.

It was such a trying day that when I got home I had to have a long nap and a bowl of bread-and-butter pudding to comfort me, as if I were ill. All the while there were thoughts racing around my head that kept trying to fit themselves together. They were to do with Maude's mother and Mr Jackson. I tried very hard not to let them fit together, however, and I think I succeeded.

MAUDE COLEMAN

Daddy and I followed the wardress down a corridor and into a large internal courtyard. From the ground we could see all the way up to the roof. The walls were lined with tier after tier of doors. Outside the rows of doors were gangways of black ironwork, along which other wardresses dressed in grey were walking.

Our wardress led us up two flights of stairs and out along one of the gangways. From the iron railing at my side to the other across the courtyard a wire net had been stretched over the empty space. There were strange things caught in it — a wooden spoon, a white cap, a cracked leather shoe.

In the centre of each cell door hung a leather flap. As I passed one I had an overwhelming urge to lift it. I slowed down so that Daddy and the wardress were several paces ahead, then quickly lifted the flap and put my eye up to the peephole.

The cell was very small — perhaps five feet by seven, not much larger than our scullery. I could see very little — a plank of wood leaning against a wall, a towel hanging from a nail, and a woman sitting on a stool in the corner. She had dark brown hair piled on her head, olive skin, and a strong jaw and mouth set in the manner of a soldier as he marches in a parade. She held herself very straight, as Grandmother is always nagging me to do. She wore a dark green dress with white arrows sewn on it — the badge of a prisoner — a checked apron, and a white cap like the one caught in the net outside the cells. A ball of wool and knitting needles sat in her lap.

I wanted her to look at me. When at last she met my eye, I knew exactly who she was. I had never seen Mrs Pankhurst before — the remarkable Emmeline Pankhurst, leader of the suffragettes. Mummy always hoped she would come to an At Home, but she never did. I heard Caroline Black once describe her leader's eyes as 'deep blue and so penetrating that you would do anything for them — take a spade to Mount Snowdon if she said it ruined her view.'

Mrs Pankhurst smiled at me.

'Maude!'

I jumped back from the peephole. Daddy was staring at me in horror. The wardress was still rushing forward but stopped when she heard Daddy's shout.

I ran to him.

'What in hell's name were you doing?' he whispered, grabbing my arm.

'Sorry,' I whispered.

The wardress grunted. 'Look sharp, keep up with me or you won't see 'er at all.'

Farther along the gangway two women were standing at a cell door — one a wardress, the other Caroline Black. Under her grey coat she was wearing a brilliant white dress with several rows of lace trim across her chest, and a hat trimmed with wilting primroses. She looked as if she should be strolling in Hyde Park. My own plain blue coat and old straw hat were very drab in comparison.

As we approached she was saying into the cell, 'The colours are to be purple for dignity, white for purity, and green for hope. Isn't it a splendid idea? I would've worn them myself today except I wanted to wear primroses for you. Think how striking it will look in public gatherings to see everyone dressed in the same colours!' She glanced at us, smiled, and announced, 'More visitors!'

'Who has come?' I heard from inside the cell.

'Mummy!' I cried. I darted forward, but then stopped – although the door was open, there were still bars across the doorway. I wanted to cry.

Mummy's cell was identical to Mrs Pankhurst's, down to the ball of grey wool sitting on the stool, a grey sock with red stripes at the top almost finished between the knitting needles. Mummy stood against the back wall. 'Hello, Maude,' she said. 'Come to see your old mother locked away, then?' Like Mrs Pankhurst, she too was dressed in dark green serge dotted with white arrows. The dress was too big for her – it covered her feet and hid her waist. Big as it was, I could see from her pinched face that she had lost weight. She had dark circles under her eyes and her skin was blotchy and yellow. Her eyes were bright, as if she had a fever.

'Hello, Richard,' she said to Daddy, who hovered behind me and Caroline Black.

We were all three standing awkwardly in the doorway, stepping from side to side and peeking around each other, as if trying to look at an animal at the zoo. The two wardresses stood on either side of the doorway like sentinels.

'For God's sake, Kitty, haven't you been eating?' Daddy said.

I flinched, and Caroline Black shook her head slightly, the primroses fluttering on her hat. I wished he had said something else instead of blurting out the first thing that popped into his head, but I felt sorry for him, too — he looked so strained and uncomfortable.

Mummy didn't seem bothered, though, but smiled as if he had told a joke. 'If you saw what we get as rations, you wouldn't eat either. I cracked my tooth on a bit of gravel in my bread the other day. It's rather put me off.'

'Mummy, I wrote to you,' I said quickly, 'but the letter was returned.'

'We're not allowed letters for the first four weeks,' Mummy said. 'Caroline could have told you that. And how much did you raise during self-denial week? A good amount, I hope.'

'I — I don't remember,' I whispered.

'You don't remember? Of course you do. It was only four weeks ago, and you've a good memory for figures. Or are you embarrassed that it wasn't much? I don't mind — I didn't expect you to raise what I would have. How much did you get — ten pounds?'

I bowed my head. I had raised barely a tenth of that. I had been meant to ask neighbours and visitors for donations, but couldn't bring myself to do it. Instead I had given up all my pocket money for a month, and Mrs Baker and Mrs Waterhouse had given me a few shillings. I had come to hate that collecting card.

'Did you know,' Caroline Black said, 'that some women ate only brown bread and gruel for the whole week, in tribute to you lot in here? They donated the money they saved from eating a "prison diet" to the WSPU!'

She and Mummy laughed, Caroline Black showing her side tooth.

'How is Mrs Pankhurst?' she asked. 'Have you seen her?'

'We're a bit worried,' Mummy said. 'She didn't come to exercise yesterday, nor to chapel this morning. I do hope she isn't ill.'

'I saw her,' I declared, pleased to be able to say something useful.

'Saw her? When did you see her?' Mummy demanded.

'Just now. A few cells down.'

Mummy and Caroline Black gazed at me with delight. Our wardress, however, frowned.

'How did she look?' Mummy asked eagerly. 'What was she doing?'

'She was knitting.'

'Did she say anything?'

'No, but she smiled at me.'

'Stop this at once!' our wardress cried. 'You're not to talk about such things. I should march you right out of here.'

'That's good news,' Mummy declared, ignoring the wardress. 'Knitting, was she? Just like me.' She glanced at the wool on her stool and laughed. 'The thing I'm worst at they're forcing me to do. By the time I leave I'll be an expert, at knitting socks, anyway.'

'Are those for you?' I had a hard time imagining Mummy wearing grey socks with red stripes.

'No, no! They're for male prisoners. Something to keep us busy. Otherwise it really is agonizingly dull in here. I thought at first I might go mad. But I haven't. Oh, and I've got my Bible to read.' She pointed at a shelf that held two books as well as a tin plate and cup, a wooden salt cellar, a piece of yellow soap, and a small brush and comb. 'And look what they've given us!' She held up the other book. I squinted at the title: *A Healthy Home and How to Keep It*. 'I've read it cover to cover. And d'you know what it tells us — sleep with your window open at night!' Mummy looked up at the small, barred window high above her head and began to laugh again. Caroline Black joined her.

'Kitty,' Daddy said quietly.

To my relief, Mummy stopped laughing.

'Have you learned your lesson in here?' Daddy asked.

Mummy frowned. 'What do you mean by "lesson"?'

'Enough is enough, now. When you get out we can get back to normal.'

'That rather depends on what you mean by "normal"'.

Daddy did not reply.

'Are you suggesting that I give up the fight when I've got out?'

'Surely you're not going to continue?'

'On the contrary, Richard, I think prison has been the making of me. Oddly enough, dullness has made me into a rod of iron. "That which does not defeat me makes me stronger." That's Nietzsche, you know.'

'You read entirely too much,' Daddy said.

Mummy smiled. 'You didn't think that when you first met me. Anyway, when I get out I will have far too much to do to read.'

'We'll discuss this when you are back home,' Daddy said, glancing at Caroline Black. 'You can't be expected to think properly in here.'

'There's nothing to discuss. It's a decision I have made. It has nothing to do with you.'

'It has everything to do with me – I'm your husband!'

'Pardon me, Richard, but nothing I've done in my little life has had any significance whatsoever until I joined the WSPU.'

'How can you say that in front of Maude?'

Mummy looked at me. She seemed genuinely puzzled. 'What about Maude?'

'Are you saying having a child has not been significant?'

'Of course it has. Maude is the reason I'm sitting in this prison cell. I'm doing this so that she will be able to vote.'

'No, you're doing it so that you can swan about town, feeling self-important, making silly speeches and neglecting your home and family.'

'I do feel important,' Mummy replied. 'For perhaps the first time in my life I have something to do, Richard. I'm working! I may not be optimistic like Caroline and the Pankhursts that we'll see suffrage voted in in my lifetime. But our work will one day lead to it. Maude will see those results, even if I don't.'

'Oh, climb down from your soapbox!' Daddy cried. 'You claim to be doing this for your daughter. Have you ever asked Maude what she thinks of you leaving her all alone like this? Have you?'

Five sets of eyes turned on me. Daddy's were furious, Mummy's curious. The two wardresses inspected me without interest. Only Caroline Black's dog-like brown eyes showed any sympathy. I turned red. My stomach was aching.

I took a step backwards and then another, and before I knew it I had turned and started to run.

'Hey! Stop!' I heard a wardress shout.

I continued to run along the gangway, back along the route we had taken – down the stairs, through the courtyard, and along a corridor, accompanied the whole way by shouts from women in grey uniforms, who never managed to catch up with me. I reached a door, opened it, ran to the bench and fell into Lavinia's arms.

'Oh, my poor dear,' Lavinia said, patting me on the back as I sobbed. 'There, now. There, now. It's just as well I came. I suppose.'

RICHARD COLEMAN

When we got back from Holloway I went straight to Kitty's morning room, where she keeps her books. There I saw just how far she has fallen into the black pit that is this cause.

I had been planning to find and burn the Nietzsche, but instead I burned every handbill, every newspaper, every banner I could lay my hands on.

May 1908

ALBERT WATERHOUSE

Poor Richard. I didn't think I would ever be embarrassed for the chap, but I am. I always said his wife would be a handful.

He and I were on the roster to roll the cricket pitch tonight, and were just walking over to the Heath when we saw her. I must say I'm glad Trudy has never asked for a bicycle. Kitty Coleman was riding along merrily, her dress rising to her knees as she pedalled. I caught a good glimpse of an ankle – and a fine one it was, too – before I managed to look away.

Richard made as if he didn't see her, so I pretended not to as well, but then she rang a little bell and we had to raise our hats at her. She waved, then went on her way with a flash of the other ankle.

I thought she was looking remarkably well for having been six weeks in Holloway, but I did not say so to Richard. In fact it seemed best not to say anything at all.

But Richard did, which surprised me, as we're not ones for confidences. 'Tell me, Albert, how do you handle your wife?'

I stumbled over a paving stone. 'How do I handle my wife?'

With firm affection, I thought, as I regained my balance. I did not say so aloud — there are things men do not say aloud.

'Kitty has blackmailed me,' Richard continued.

'How so?'

'She says that if I try to forbid her to work for the suffragettes she will begin giving speeches at rallies. Can you imagine the Coleman name all over those infernal handbills they pass out? Or plastered on posters, or chalked on the pavement? Holloway almost killed my mother from the shame of it — this would finish her off. What would you do in my situation?'

I was trying to picture Trudy making such a threat, but it was impossible to imagine. If anything she is more concerned about the Waterhouse name than I am. And she would rather eat a plate of coal than speak in public. The kinds of threats she makes to me are to do with the colour of the front parlour curtains or which seaside town we are to go to for a holiday.

Richard was looking at me as if he expected a response. 'Perhaps it's just a phase your wife is going through,' I suggested. 'Perhaps the suffragette movement will die out. They're planning a demonstration in Hyde Park in June, aren't they? Even Trudy knows of it, and she's no suffragette. Perhaps that will satisfy them, and afterwards your wife will settle down.'

'Perhaps,' Richard repeated, but I am afraid he did not sound convinced.

KITTY COLEMAN

Maude has been avoiding me for weeks now, ever since I came out of Holloway. At first I didn't notice, as there was so much to do, what with the march to organise for June. It is to be the largest public gathering of people anywhere, ever in the world. We are run off our feet with tasks — booking trains from all over the country, getting permission for the march routes and use of Hyde Park, conferring with the police, finding speakers and marching bands, making banners. It is like planning a battle. No, not just a battle — an entire war.

On that theme, Caroline has had a wonderful idea of what she and I can dress as for the procession. It is to be very dramatic, and I plan to celebrate my liberation from both Holloway and my despair with a liberating costume. It will be a great day.

In the midst of all the activity, though, I did notice that Maude left rooms as soon as I entered them, and was eating more meals at the Waterhouses' than at home.

Richard simply shrugged when I mentioned this to him. 'What did you expect?' he said. It is hard to talk to him now — since I got out of Holloway he has been avoiding me too. Just as well that I have grown a thick skin!

I was not really surprised to see what he had done to my morning room. Other suffragettes' husbands have done worse. To put an end to such behaviour I had to resort to blackmail, which I am not proud of but which was necessary. It worked, too – he may hate what I am doing but he fears his mother more.

On Saturday morning I caught Maude moping in the drawing room and had an idea. 'Come with me into town,' I suggested. 'There's a motor to take us. See?' I pointed out of the window at the Jenkinses' motor-car sitting in front of the house. Mrs Jenkins, a wealthy WSPU member in Highgate, has kindly donated it for WSPU business around town. Her husband doesn't know – we only use it when he's at work or away – and we have had to bribe Fred, the driver, to keep him quiet. It has been worth every penny.

Maude gaped at the car, which was gleaming in the sun. I could see that she wanted to say yes but she felt she shouldn't.

'Do come,' I said. 'It's a lovely day – we can ride with the top down.'

'Where are you going?'

'To Clements Inn. But not for long,' I added quickly, knowing that she did not like the WSPU. 'Then on to Bond Street. Afterwards we could stop at the soda fountain at Fortnum and Mason's – we haven't had an ice-cream there in such a long time.'

I don't know why I was trying so hard. I have never been an attentive mother, but now I feel as if I am fighting for something on Maude's behalf, and want to include her, even if it means bribing her with an ice-cream.

'All right,' she said at last.

I had her and Jenny help bring out the stacks of banners I'd been sewing — or rather, that I'd begun and found I hadn't the time for, and so paid Jenny and Mrs Baker extra to sew. I am still far behind the number I've promised to make. I am going to have to enlist Maude, though her sewing is worse than mine.

It was thrilling to be driven through London. I have done it many times now, but I still love it. Fred wears goggles when he drives, but I refuse to — I feel I never see anything if I have them on. We had tied our hats down with scarves — mine a purple, green and white one that reads 'Votes for Women' (I offered one to Maude but she refused) — but everything flapped like mad in the wind anyway, and dust from the street flew into our clothes and hair. It was terribly exciting. The speed was so exhilarating — we zoomed past milk carts, horse-drawn omnibuses, men on bicycles, and raced alongside motorised cabs and other private cars. Pubs, wash houses, tea shops, all passed by in a blur.

Even Maude enjoyed herself, though she did not say much — not that one can talk over the noise of the engine. For the first time in months she seemed to relax, snug in the back seat between me and the banners. As we drove through an avenue of plane trees, their leaves forming a canopy overhead, she leaned her head back and looked up at the sky.

She helped me unload the banners at Clements Inn — Fred never lifts a finger to help, as he disapproves of suffragettes — but would not stay in the office, preferring to wait outside with Fred. I tried to be quick about it, but there were so many comrades to greet, questions to answer, and points to be raised, that by the time I got back to the car Maude and Fred were both sulking.

'Sorry!' I cried gaily. 'Never mind, let's go on. Colling-wood's on Bond Street, if you please, Fred.' This stop wasn't strictly WSPU business, but it was certainly to do with woman's suffrage.

Maude looked surprised. 'Has Daddy bought you something new?' Collingwood's was where Richard went for jewellery for me.

I laughed. 'In a manner of speaking. You'll see.'

But when she saw the necklace in the black velvet box which the jeweller proudly presented to me, she didn't have quite the response I'd expected. She said nothing.

The necklace was made up of emeralds and amethysts and pearls, clustered together to form purple and white flowers with green leaves. The stones came entirely from necklaces I already owned: pearls I had received for my confirmation, amethysts inherited from my mother, and emeralds from a necklace Mrs Coleman gave me when I got married.

'You've done a marvellous job,' I said to the jeweller. 'It's exquisite!'

Maude was still staring at the necklace.

'Don't you like it?' I asked. 'It's the colours, don't you see? The WSPU colours. Lots of women are having pieces made up in them.'

'I thought . . .' Maude stopped.

'What is it?'

'Well — was I to inherit the necklaces that it is made from?'

'Gracious, is that what the matter is? So now you'll inherit this one instead.'

'Daddy will be furious,' Maude said quietly. 'And Grand-mother. Those were her emeralds.'

'She gave me that necklace to do with what I liked. It's mine now – it's not for her to say.'

Maude was silent, a silence worse than the sulk earlier.

'Shall we go to Fortnum and Mason's for ice-cream?' I suggested.

'No, thank you, Mummy. I think I'd like to go home now, please,' Maude said in a small voice.

I thought she would love the necklace. It seems that I can never please her.

RICHARD COLEMAN

I noticed them immediately. Kitty was in the hallway, preening herself in the mirror before we left for Mother's party. Jenny stood holding her wrap while Maude watched from the steps. Kitty's dress was cut low, and as I glanced at her décolletage I recognised the emeralds. I had seen my mother wear them many times when she and my father went to parties and functions, and once to meet the Queen. They looked hideous now, made up in a new necklace with other stones.

I said nothing – Kitty's blackmail has effectively cut out my tongue. Instead I grew furious with myself for being so powerless with my wife. Surely this was not how a husband should be, so helpless and without authority. Kitty knew exactly what she was doing.

Later, when I saw the look on my mother's face as she gazed at Kitty's necklace, I could have throttled my wife's lovely white throat.

EDITH COLEMAN

I think she enjoys tormenting me.

It has been bad enough this past year the few times when, for form's sake, I have had to visit my son at their house. Worse still when she was sent to Holloway and the Coleman name appeared in the papers. I was mortified, but it blew over more quickly than I had expected. My friends — my good friends — did not mention it, sparing me further embarrassment. I was just glad that James is not alive to see his name brought so low.

But the worst has been the emeralds. James's mother gave them to me the night before our wedding, with the understanding that I would cherish and preserve them, to pass on to my own son's wife. In those days such an understanding was unspoken. It would never have occurred to me to do anything other than wear the emeralds proudly and pass them on willingly when the time came. It could never have occurred to any of us Coleman women to desecrate them as Kitty has done.

She wore them to my annual May party, with a dark green silk dress cut far too low. I knew immediately what they were, even if the necklace itself was not familiar to me.

I would have known my emeralds anywhere. She saw me recognise them as well. Poor Richard standing next to her had no idea. Emeralds are in a woman's realm, not a man's. I shall never tell him.

I did not make a scene — I could not in front of everyone, and I would not do so to please her either. Instead I waited until the last guest had gone. Then I sat in the dark and wept.

June 1908

LAVINIA WATERHOUSE

At first I refused to help Maude. I wanted nothing to do with any suffragettes' banners. But Maude is no seamstress, and when I saw her poor fingers at school one day, all pricked and torn from the needle (someone must teach her how to use a thimble properly!), I took pity on her and began going over in the afternoons to help.

It is a good thing I have! She is so slow, the dear, and her awful mother has left her with the most impossible pile of banners to sew. It was odd at first sitting in that morning room sewing – I was worried that at any minute Maude's mother would come in, and I have not felt comfortable around her ever since I Found Out. As it happened, though, she is rarely at home, and when she is she is talking on the telephone she had installed, and doesn't even notice us. That telephone makes me nervous – I always jump when it rings, and I would hate to answer it. Maude has to all the time when her mother is out, and takes endless messages about meetings and petitions and other nonsense.

Luckily my sewing is very good – I get through three banners to Maude's one, and you can see her stitches. And it is rather fun sitting there together – we talk and sing, and sometimes Maude gives up sewing altogether when her fingers are bleeding too much, and reads a book aloud while I work. Jenny brings us endless cups of tea, and even coffee once or twice when we beg her.

All we have to do is to sew, thank goodness. We receive the cloth and letters already cut, and the slogan written on a piece of paper pinned to the cloth. The letters are usually white, the cloth green or black. I don't think I could make up a slogan if you paid me. Some of them are so complicated I can make neither head nor tail of them. What on earth does TAXATION WITHOUT REPRESENTATION IS TYRANNY mean? Or worse, WOMEN'S 'WILL' BEATS ASQUITH'S 'WON'T'? What does the Prime Minister have to do with it?

The best part has been the mistakes. It first happened when I was sewing on letters for one of the endless banners that read DEEDS NOT WORDS. (I am sick to death of those words!) As I was folding the finished banner I happened to glance at it and discovered I had sewn on WORDS NOT DEEDS. I was all ready to unpick the letters, but I peeked at Maude and saw that she hadn't noticed — she was frowning over her banner, sucking on another pricked finger. So I quietly folded the banner, put it on the pile, and smiled to myself. Apparently there are to be thousands and thousands of banners — women all over the country are sewing them. Every few days Maude's mother rushes in, grabs the pile of finished banners, and rushes out again without so much as a thank you. I doubt anyone will trace the mistake back to me.

After that I began to make more 'mistakes' — a few more WORDS NOT DEEDS, and then I sewed WEEDS NOT RODS, and stuffed the extra D in my pinafore pocket. It was great fun creating errors: WORKING WOMEN DEMAND THE VOTE became VOTING WOMEN DEMAND WORK; HOPE IS STRONG became ROPE IS THONG.

I had done half a dozen or so when Maude caught me out. She was helping me fold one when she suddenly said, 'Stop a moment,' and spread out the banner. It read WHO WOULD FLEE THEMSELVES MUST STRIKE THE BROW.

'Lavinia! That's meant to read "Who would be free themselves must strike the blow"? You know, from Byron!'

'Oh dear,' I said, and giggled.

'Haven't you even been reading what you're sewing? And where are the B and E for "BE"?'

I smiled sheepishly and pulled the letters out from my pocket. 'I thought they were left over, or a mistake,' I said.

'You know very well what it was supposed to say,' Maude muttered. 'What shall we do with it? It's too late to change it, and we can't hide it − Mummy's sure to count them and will want to know why one is missing.'

I struck my own brow. 'Oh dear, I'd best flee.' It was silly but it made Maude laugh. Soon we were laughing so hard we were crying. It was good to see her laugh. She has been so serious these days. In the end we simply folded up the banner and added it to the pile.

I had not thought I would go to the Hyde Park march − the thought of being among thousands of suffragettes made me shiver. But after so many days of sewing and overhearing things about it, I couldn't help but wonder if it wouldn't be rather fun. There are to be women from all over the country, not all of them per se, and there will be bands and speakers, and spectacles all over. And then Maude told me everyone is to wear white and green and purple, and I thought up the perfect outfits for us. We would wear our white dresses, and trim our straw hats with flowers from the Colemans' garden. Maude's mother may be sinful, but she has cultivated the most wonderful flowers.

'Delphiniums, cornflowers, star jasmine and Persian jewels, all wound round with green leaves,' I decided. 'It will look ever so beautiful.'

'But you said you didn't want to go,' Maude said. 'And what will your mother say?'

'Mama shall come with us,' I said. 'And we won't necessarily march, but we can be spectators.'

Maude thinks Mama will never agree, but she always says yes to me.

GERTRUDE WATERHOUSE

I felt very silly doing it, but I couldn't see any other way to stop her. When Livy and Ivy May came home from school my ankle was wrapped in a bandage and propped on a footstool. 'I tripped over the threshold,' I said when Livy exclaimed over it. 'It's only a sprain, thankfully, no broken bones.'

'Oh, Mama, you are so clumsy,' she said.

'Yes, I know.'

'How long did the doctor say you must stay off it?'

'A week at least.'

'But that means you can't take us to the march Sunday!'

'Yes, I know. I'm sorry, dear – I know how much you were looking forward to it.' I myself had been dreading it.

Livy cried out. 'But we must go! We can't miss it, can we, Ivy May?'

Ivy May was inspecting the bandage. I should have wound it more tightly.

'Perhaps Papa can take us,' Livy suggested.

'No,' I said quickly. I would not have Albert involved. 'You will be at church with him in the morning, and he is playing cricket in the afternoon. No, I think it best if you stay home.'

'Well, then, we could go with Maude and her mother.'

'No,' I said again, even more quickly.

'We'll be perfectly safe.'

'No.'

Livy glared at me so hard I almost couldn't bear it. 'Really, Livy, dear,' I said as lightly as I could, 'I don't understand why you want to go so badly anyway. It's not something that is of interest to you; nor should it be. I'm sure whoever you marry will be quite capable of deciding for you whom to vote for.'

'On the contrary,' Livy announced, 'I do support woman's suffrage.'

Ivy May tittered. 'Livy doesn't want to be left out,' she said.

'Shush, Ivy May, I'm sure you want to go to Hyde Park too,' Livy said.

'Do you really support woman's suffrage?' I asked, surprised at my daughter.

'I do! I think the colours are splendid – the scarves and jewellery in violet, green and white. And the women whizzing about in motor-cars, so lively and passionate –' Livy stopped when she saw my face.

'I do not approve of the suffragettes, nor of the march,' I said sternly, hoping that would be the end of the matter.

Of course it was not. Livy cried for two days and would not speak to me, until at last, the night before the march, I gave in. Nothing stops her getting what she wants, not even her silly mother's schemes. I did not want Livy to discover I had tried to deceive her, so in the end I could not even go with them, but had to hand them over to Kitty Coleman.

Ivy May caught me walking on my 'sprained' ankle. Bless her, she said not a word.

MAUDE COLEMAN

We got off the omnibus at Euston Station and began to wade through the crowds of people already gathered on the pavement. Women were pouring out of the station, having ridden down on special trains from the north. Lavinia and I each grabbed one of Ivy May's hands and held tight as we were pushed and shoved among a sea of accents from Birmingham and Manchester and Lancashire.

Mummy moved quickly through the crowds – the crush did not seem to bother her, which surprised me given how much she hates being confined. When we got to the road in front of St Pancras Station, she began scanning the faces of women in white dresses who had gathered in the road with their banners. 'Ah, there they are!' she cried, and pushed through the crowd on the pavement to get onto the road itself.

There I breathed more freely, for there was more room. It was strange to stand in the middle of such a big road and have no coaches or carts or cabs to dodge – just a long line of women in white dresses stretched ahead and behind, with men and women on the pavement watching us.

Mummy led us over to a group of women, many of

whom I recognised from her At Homes. 'Here they are, Eunice,' Mummy said, laying her hand on the arm of a tall woman with a face full of freckles who wore a sash that read BANNER CAPTAIN. 'And there's Caroline!' Mummy cried, waving. 'Caroline!'

Caroline Black hurried over, flushed, her hair coming down from under her hat. Over her shoulder she carried a large bundle tied to a pole. Mummy kissed her. 'Have you got everything?'

'Yes, I think so,' panted Caroline Black, 'though thank heavens I gave the boy the armour yesterday to bring down. I'd never have made it otherwise.'

I did not know what they were talking about, but before I could ask, Mummy turned to me. 'Now, Maude, I'm going to leave you with Eunice, who will look after you.'

'But you're marching too, aren't you?' I asked, trying to keep the panic out of my voice. 'You're marching with us.'

'I will be in the procession, yes, but I've got something to do in another part of it. You'll be fine here — you know most of these women.'

'Where are you going? What are you doing?'

'It's a surprise.'

'But we thought we were going to be with you. We told Mrs Waterhouse you were looking after us.'

Mummy shook her head impatiently. 'What I have to do is far more important than looking after you. And frankly, Eunice is probably better at sorting you out than I would be. She's Banner Captain for this section of the procession and is very capable. You're in good hands with her. I'll meet you at the end of the day, after the Great Shout at five o'clock. Come to Platform 5, where Mrs Pankhurst is speaking. I'll see you there. Now, we really must be off. Have fun, girls! Remember, Maude, Platform 5 after the Great Shout.' She took Caroline Black's arm and rushed away into the crowd. I tried to keep my eyes on them but couldn't – it was like following the progress of a twig through a fast-flowing stream.

Lavinia had turned pale. 'What shall we do without her?' she moaned, which was rather hypocritical given how much she dislikes Mummy.

'Well, girls, we'll have a grand day, eh?' Eunice cried as she helped two women next to us secure their banner that read HOPE IS STRONG. 'I've got to check the other banners along my section. You stay here by this banner until I return.' She strode away before we could say anything.

'Bloody hell,' I said quietly. We had been abandoned.

Lavinia looked at me, shocked as much by my swearing as by our predicament, I expect. 'Perhaps Mama was right,' she said. 'Perhaps I should have stayed home. I'm feeling rather faint.'

'Stop it,' I said sharply. 'We'll manage.' It was going to be a grim afternoon, and worse if she fainted as well. I looked around for something to distract her. 'Look at the band – the Hackney Borough Brass Band,' I read from their banner. 'Aren't their uniforms lovely?' I knew Lavinia preferred men in uniforms. She was already saying she planned to marry a soldier. The musicians were smirking at the surrounding women. A euphonium player winked at me before I could look away.

Lavinia was staring up at the banner we were meant to stay with. 'Rope is thong,' she announced suddenly, and giggled.

'What did you say?'

'Nothing, nothing.'

After a bit we began to feel better. The women around us were all talking and laughing, clearly excited to be there. The overall effect was of a great buzz of female sound, at times high-pitched, loud but not frightening as it might be if it were all men. It was hard not to be infected by the high spirits. And they did not all appear to be suffragettes. Many of them were just like us, there for the afternoon out of curiosity, not necessarily waving a banner and shouting. There were lots of women with their daughters, some of them quite young. There were even three little girls, all dressed in white with green and purple ribbons in their hair, sitting in a pony-cart near us.

Lavinia squeezed my arm and said, 'It is terribly exciting, isn't it? Everyone is here!'

Except Mummy, I thought. I wondered what she and Caroline Black were doing.

Then the band, led by a man with a handlebar moustache, began to play a march from *Aida* and everyone stood up straighter, as if a wire had been pulled taut all up and down the procession. An expectant hum rose from the crowd. Eunice reappeared suddenly and called out, 'Right, then, banners up!' Women around her raised their poles and fitted them into the holders at their sides; then others who saw those banners go up lifted theirs, until as far ahead and behind as I could see there were banners sailing above a sea of heads. For the first time I wished I too was carrying a banner.

The hum died down after a few minutes when we hadn't moved.

'Aren't we ever going to start?' Lavinia cried, hopping from foot to foot. 'Oh, I can't bear it if we don't go soon!'

Then, suddenly, we did. The banners ahead jerked and a space opened up in front of us.

'Onward!' Eunice cried. 'Come, now, girls!'

As we began to walk, the spectators on the pavement cheered and I felt tingles up and down my back. There were six other processions beside ours, coming from points all around London, bringing marchers towards Hyde Park. It was terribly thrilling to feel a part of a larger whole, of thousands and thousands of women all doing the same thing at the same time.

It took some time for the procession to assume a steady pace. We kept stopping and starting, making our way past St Pancras, then Euston Station. On both sides, men watched us pass, some frowning, a few jeering, but most smiling the way my uncle does when he thinks I've said something silly. The women on the sidelines were more supportive, smiling and waving. A few even stepped in to join the marchers.

At first Lavinia was very excited, humming along with the band, laughing as a banner ahead of us caught a breeze and started to flap. But once we began walking more steadily, when we had passed Euston and were heading towards Great Portland Station, she sighed and dragged her feet. 'Is this all we're going to do? Walk?' she complained.

'There will be speeches at Hyde Park. It's not so far. And we'll be going along Oxford Street and you can see the shops.' I said this with authority, but I didn't really know where the route would take us. My London geography was shaky – I had not been into town very often, and then I simply followed Mummy or Daddy. I knew the principal rivers of Africa better than the streets of London.

'There's Simon.' Ivy May pointed.

It was a relief to see a familiar face among the mass of strangers. 'Simon!' Lavinia and I called at the same time.

When he saw us his face lit up and he stepped out of the crowd to fall in beside us.

'What are you doing here, naughty boy?' Lavinia asked, squeezing his arm.

Simon turned red. 'Came to find you.'

'Are you going to march with us?' I asked.

Simon looked around. 'There ain't no men, is there?'

'The bands are all men. Stay with us.'

'Well, maybe for a little bit. But I has to go and get the horse at Hyde Park.'

'What horse?'

Simon looked surprised. 'The horse for the ladies. For your ma. Didn't she tell you?'

'Mummy doesn't have a horse. She hates horses.'

'It's a friend of Mr Jackson what has the horse. They're just borrowing it for the day.'

'Mr Jackson? What does he have to do with it?'

Simon looked like he'd rather not have said anything. 'Your ma asked Mr Jackson if he knew anyone could lend her a horse. A white horse, it had to be. And he has a friend has one, up off Baker Street. So he lent it to her, and asked me to fetch it and bring it back. Paid me and all.'

The band began to play the Pirate King song from *The Pirates of Penzance*. I was trying to take in what Simon was saying, but it was difficult to think in the middle of so many people and so much noise. 'Mummy never goes to the cemetery. How could she see Mr Jackson?'

Simon shrugged. 'He visited her at Holloway. And I heard 'em talking at the cemetery not long ago – about the suffragism and that.'

'She's not riding the horse, is she? Where exactly is she?'

Simon shrugged again. 'See for yourself. They're at the start of the procession.'

'Is it far?'

'I'll show you.' Simon immediately plunged back into the crowd on the pavement, probably relieved to leave the procession of women.

I began to follow but Lavinia grabbed my arm. 'What about me?' she cried.

'Stay here. I'll come back to you.'

'But you can't leave me alone!'

'You're not alone – you're with Ivy May. Stay with the banner,' I added, gesturing at HOPE IS STRONG. 'I'll come back to you. And Eunice is bound to return soon. Tell her I've gone to look at the banners. Don't say I've gone to see Mummy.'

'We're coming with you!' Lavinia cried, but I wrenched my arm away and pushed into the crowd before she could follow. Whatever Mummy was doing, I didn't want Lavinia to see it.

SIMON FIELD

All I can say is, Mrs C. weren't wearing that when I handed over the horse to her earlier. Must've had it on under her dress.

I'm surprised but try not to show it. Can't take my eyes from her legs. I only seen a woman's legs like that once at a panto of Dick Whittington, and even then she wore tights and the tunic came to her knees. Mrs C. ain't dressed as Dick, though, but as Robin Hood. She wears a short green tunic belted in the middle, little green boots, and a green and purple cap with a white feather in it. She's got bare legs, from her ankles up to – well, up high.

She's leading the white horse what Miss Black's riding. You'd think Miss Black'd be dressed as Maid Marian or Friar Tuck or some such, but instead she's got on a full suit of armour and a silver helmet with a white feather in it that bobs up and down in time with the horse, just like the ostrich feathers on the horses in a funeral procession. She holds the reins in one hand and a flag in the other with words on it I can't read.

Maude just stares. Who can blame her – everyone's staring at Kitty Coleman's legs. I has to say – they're fine legs. I'm bright red looking at 'em, and go hard, right among all them people. Has to cross my hands in front of me to hide it.

'Who's Miss Black meant to be?' I ask, to distract myself.

'Joan of Arc.' Maude says it like she's spitting the words.

I never heard of this Joan, but I don't tell Maude. I know she don't want to talk.

We've been standing on the pavement a bit ahead of 'em, so we can watch 'em approach. As they pass by Maude looks like she wants to say something to her ma, but she don't. Mrs C. ain't looking at her – she has a funny smile on her face and seems to be looking way ahead, like she sees something on the horizon she can't wait to get to.

Then they're past. Maude don't say nothing, and neither do I. We just watch the procession go by. Then Maude snorts.

'What?' I say.

'Caroline Black's banner has a mistake on it,' she says, but she won't tell me what it is.

KITTY COLEMAN

For most of the march I felt as if I were walking through a dream.

I was so excited that I hardly heard a thing. The buzz of spectators, the jangling and creaking of the bridle, the clanking of Caroline's armour – they were all there, but distant. The horse's hooves sounded as if they were muffled by blankets, or as if sawdust had been strewn along the route, as it sometimes is for funerals.

Nor could I really see anything. I tried to focus on faces along the route but they were all a blur. I kept thinking I saw people I knew – Richard, John Jackson, Maude, even my dead mother – but they were just resemblances. It was easier to look ahead towards our destination, whatever that would be.

What I did feel sharply was the sun and air on my legs. After a lifetime of heavy dresses, with their swathes of cloth wrapping my legs like bandages, it was an incredible sensation.

Then I heard a bang that was not muffled. I looked into the crowd, suddenly able to see, and there was someone who looked like my late brother on the pavement opposite me. He was staring at Caroline with such a perplexed expression that I couldn't help but step across to see what he was looking at.

There was another bang. Just before the horse reared I saw Caroline's banner – it read WORDS NOT DEEDS.

Blast, I thought, who made such a silly mistake? Then the hoof came down on my chest.

LAVINIA WATERHOUSE

At first I would not speak to Maude when she and Simon came back – not all the way down Portland Place or Upper Regent Street, nor when we were stopped for a time along Oxford Street. I could not forgive her for leaving me like that.

She did not speak either, just marched with a face like thunder, and did not seem to notice that I had sent her to Coventry. There is nothing more annoying than someone not realising you are punishing them. Indeed it rather felt as if it were me being punished – I was immensely curious about Maude's mother and the horse but since I was not speaking to her I could not ask about it. I wished Ivy May would talk to me, to make my silence with Maude all the more pointed. I straightened her hat for her, as it was tilted dangerously far back, but Ivy May simply nodded at me in thanks. She was not in the habit of saying things when one wanted her to.

Then the procession halted again. Simon ran off to collect his horse, and we moved towards the Marble Arch entrance to Hyde Park. We were pressed closer and closer together, as many of the people on the pavement squeezed into the crowd to enter as well. It was like being a grain of sand in an hourglass, waiting our turn to funnel through the tiny hole. It grew so crowded that I grabbed Maude and Ivy May's hands.

Then we were through, and suddenly there was open space, sunny and green and full of fresh air. I gulped at it as if it were water.

A great sea of people had gathered in the distance around various carts where handfuls of suffragettes perched. In their white dresses and all piled up above the crowd they reminded me of puffy clouds on the horizon.

'Move along, move along,' called a woman behind us who wore a sash reading CHIEF MARSHALL. 'There's thousands more behind you, waiting to get in. Move along to the platforms, please, keeping in formation.'

The procession was meant to continue all the way to the platforms, but once inside the park everyone began rushing to and fro, and we lost all order. Men who had been spectators along the route were now mingling with all the ladies who had marched, and as we moved willy-nilly towards the platforms it became more crowded again, with them pushing in on us. Mama would be horrified if she could see us, unchaperoned, caught among all these men. I saw that silly Eunice for a moment, shouting at someone to bring her banner around. She was hopeless at looking after us.

There were banners everywhere. I kept looking for one I had sewn but there were so many that my mistakes were lost among them. I had not imagined that so many people could gather in one place at one time. It was frightening but thrilling as well, like when a tiger at the zoo stares straight at you with its yellow eyes.

'Do you see Platform 5?' Maude asked.

I couldn't see numbers anywhere, but Ivy May pointed to a platform, and we began to make our way over. Maude kept pulling me into walls of people, and I had to grip Ivy May's hand harder, as it was growing sweaty.

'Let's not go any further,' I called to Maude. 'It's so crowded.'

'Just a little bit – I'm looking for Mummy.' Maude kept pulling my hand.

Suddenly there were too many people. The little spaces we had managed to push into became a solid wall of legs and backs. People pressed up behind us, and I could feel strangers pushing at my arms and shoulders.

Then I felt a hand on my bottom, the fingers brushing me gently. I was so surprised that I did nothing for a moment. The hand pulled up my dress and began fumbling with my bloomers, right there in the middle of all those people. I couldn't believe no one noticed.

When I tried to shift away, the hand followed. I looked back – the man standing behind me was about Papa's age, tall, grey-haired, with a thin moustache and spectacles. His eyes were fixed on the platform. I could not believe it was his hand – he looked so respectable. I raised my heel and brought it down hard on the foot behind me. The man winced and the hand disappeared. After a moment he pushed away and was gone, someone else stepping into his place.

I shuddered and whispered to Maude, 'Let's get away from here,' but I was drowned out by a bugle call. The crowd surged forward and Maude was pushed into the back of the woman ahead of her, dropping my hand. Then I was shoved violently to the left. I looked around but couldn't see Maude.

'If I may have your attention, I would like to open this

meeting on this most momentous occasion in Hyde Park,' I heard a voice ring out. A woman had climbed onto a box higher than the rest of the women on the platform. In her mauve dress she looked like lavender sprinkled on a bowl of vanilla ice cream. She stood very straight and still.

'There's Mrs Pankhurst,' women around me murmured.

'I am delighted to see before me a great multitude of people, of supporters – both women *and* men – of the simple right of women to take their places alongside men and cast their ballots. Prime Minister Asquith has said that he needs to be assured that the will of the people is behind the call for votes for women. Well, Mr Asquith, I say to you that if you were standing where I am now and saw the great sea of humanity before you as I do, you would need no more convincing!'

The crowd roared. I put my hands on the shoulders of the woman beside me and jumped up to try and see over the crowd. 'Maude!' I called, but it was so noisy she would never have heard me. The woman scowled and shrugged off my hands.

Mrs Pankhurst was waiting for the sound to die down. 'We have a full afternoon of speakers,' she began as it grew quiet, 'and without further ado –'

'Maude! Maude!' I cried.

Mrs Pankhurst paused, and jerked her head slightly. 'I would like to introduce –'

'Maude!'

'Lavinia!' I heard, and saw a hand fluttering above the crowd far to my right. I waved back and kept waving as I began to push towards the hand.

Mrs Pankhurst had stopped again. 'Shh! Shh!' women on

the platform began to hiss. I continued to push, forcing spaces to open in front of me, ignoring whatever was happening on the platform. Then ahead of me I saw the garland of delphiniums and star jasmine I had woven that morning for Maude's straw hat, and with one last shove I had found her.

We held onto each other tightly. Maude's heart was beating hard, and I was trembling.

'Let's get away from all these people,' Maude whispered. I nodded and, still holding tight to Maude, let her push away from the platform and out of the jam of people listening to Mrs Pankhurst.

At last there was space again. When we reached the trees on the far edge of the crowd I stopped. 'I'm going to be sick,' I said.

Maude led me to a tree, where I could kneel away from everyone. Afterwards we found a shady spot to sit a little away from the base of the tree. We didn't say anything for a few minutes, but watched people stroll or hurry past, detaching themselves from one wheel of spectators around a platform, joining another. We could see four platforms from where we sat. In the distance the women speaking on them were tiny figures whose arms moved about like windmills.

I was very thirsty.

Maude would speak eventually, I knew, and ask the question that must be asked. I dreaded it.

'Lavinia,' she said at last, 'where is Ivy May?'

For the first time all day I began to cry. 'I don't know.'

MAUDE COLEMAN

Mummy was sitting just two trees away. We didn't discover that until after the meeting had ended.

There was no point in searching for anyone while the speeches were being made and the crowd so tightly packed in. Lavinia was in despair, but I knew that Ivy May was a sensible girl – she might say little, but she heard everything, and she would know that we were to meet Mummy at Platform 5 after the Great Shout, whatever that was.

That is what I kept telling myself, and repeating to Lavinia, whenever she would listen. Eventually she laid her head in my lap and fell asleep, which is just like her in a dramatic moment. It is melodrama that she loves – to her true drama is dull. I fidgeted, waiting for the speeches to finish and for Lavinia to wake.

At last a bugle sounded. When it sounded a second time, Lavinia sat up, her face red and crumpled. 'What time is it?' she said, yawning.

'I'm not sure. Close to five o'clock, I expect.'

The distant crowds were waving their arms and cheering. The bugle sounded once more. A chant rose up like an orchestra swelling to a crescendo in a symphony. It sounded as if everyone were saying, 'Folks are swimming'. Only the third time did I realise they were calling, 'Votes for women!' The last one was loud like a thunderclap, and the cheers and laughter that followed like rain released from clouds.

Then, suddenly, the crowd broke up and a surge of people moved towards us. I scanned the passing faces for someone familiar. I did spy Eunice, who rushed past with a stray banner and pole. She did not see us and we did not try to stop her.

'We should go to Platform 5,' I said. 'Someone is bound to be there.'

We linked arms and began to wade through the crowd, but it was very difficult as everyone was moving away from the platform rather than towards it. Everywhere there were exhausted faces — thirsty children, impatient women, concerned men wondering how they would get home through such crowds. Now that people were not marching in organised processions, the streets outside Hyde Park would be in chaos, jammed with people and cabs and overfull omnibuses. It would take hours to get home.

Finally we drew close to what I remembered as Platform 5, but the banner with the Number 5 on it had been taken down. Mrs Pankhurst and the other women had climbed down from the cart, and a man was hitching a horse up to it.

'They're taking away the platform!' I cried. 'How will we ever find Mummy without it?'

'There's Caroline Black,' Lavinia said, pulling at my sleeve. 'What on earth is she wearing?'

Caroline Black was hopping from foot to foot, still in her Joan of Arc armour. The white plume in her helmet bobbed up and down as she moved. She looked very grim, and my stomach turned over to see her alone.

'There you are!' she cried, not smiling sweetly at me as she usually did. 'Where have you been? I've been looking for you for ages!'

'Where's Mummy?' I demanded.

Caroline Black looked as if she might cry. 'Your mother – she's had a little mishap.'

'What happened?'

'It all went so well, that's the shame of it.' Caroline Black shook her head. 'We had a marvellous time, with such support from our comrades and the spectators. And the horse was lovely, so gentle and a dream to ride. If only –'

'What happened? Where is she?' It was all I could do not to shriek the words.

'Someone let off firecrackers in the crowd along Oxford Street. The horse shied, and at that moment Kitty stepped in front of it to look at my banner – I don't know why. The horse reared – I just barely kept my own seat. When it came down it kicked her in the chest.'

'Where is she now?'

'The daft thing insisted on finishing the march, leading the horse and all, as if nothing had happened. She said she was fine, just a bit breathless. And I stupidly allowed her. Then she wouldn't leave during the speeches – she said she had to be here to find you afterwards.'

'Where in God's name is she?' I cried. Lavinia jumped at my tone and people around us stared. But Caroline Black didn't even flinch.

'She's sitting over in the trees.' She pointed back the way we had come.

Lavinia grabbed my arm as I began to walk towards the trees. 'What about Ivy May?' she cried. 'We must find her!'

'Let's get to Mummy and then we'll look for her.' I knew Lavinia was angry at me but I ignored her and kept going.

Mummy was propped up against the trunk of the tree, one leg folded under her, a bare leg stretched out in front.

'Oh my Lord,' Lavinia murmured. I had forgot that she hadn't seen Mummy in her costume.

Mummy smiled as we came up, but her face was tense, as if she were struggling to hide something. Her breathing was laboured. 'Hello, Maude,' she said. 'Did you enjoy the procession?'

'How do you feel, Mummy?'

Mummy patted her chest. 'Hurts.'

'We must get you home, my dear,' Caroline Black said. 'Can you walk?'

'She mustn't walk,' I interrupted, remembering my first aid lessons from school. 'That may make it worse.'

'Going to be a doctor, are you?' Mummy said. 'That's good. I thought you might become an astronomer, but I've been known to be wrong. As long as you become something, I don't mind what it is. Except perhaps a wife. But don't tell Daddy that.' She winced as she took a breath. 'Go to university.'

'Hush, Mummy. Don't talk.'

I looked around. Caroline Black and Lavinia were watching me as if I were in charge.

Then I saw a familiar figure striding towards us.

'Thank heaven you're here, Mr Jackson!' Lavinia cried, grabbing his arm. 'Can you find Ivy May for us?'

'No,' I interrupted. 'You must get Mummy to a cab. She needs a doctor quickly.'

Mr Jackson looked at Mummy. 'What has happened, Kitty?'

'She's been kicked by a horse and can't breathe,' I said.

'Hello, John,' Mummy murmured. 'This is what happens, you see – I dress up as Robin Hood and get kicked by the pantomime horse.'

'Ivy May is lost, Mr Jackson!' Lavinia shouted. 'My little sister has been lost in that horrid crowd!'

Mr Jackson looked from Mummy to Lavinia. I knew he could not make the decision himself – I would have to do it. 'Mr Jackson, go and find a cab,' I ordered. 'You're more likely to get one than me or Lavinia, and you can carry Mummy to it. Caroline, you wait here with Mummy, and Lavinia and I will look for Ivy May.'

'No!' Lavinia cried, but Mr Jackson had already run off.

Mummy nodded. 'That's right, Maude. You're perfectly capable of taking charge.' She remained against the tree, with Caroline Black kneeling awkwardly beside her in her armour.

I took Lavinia's hand. 'We'll find her,' I said. 'I promise.'

LAVINIA WATERHOUSE

We did not find her. We searched everywhere, but we did not find her.

We walked back and forth across the park where the crowds had stood, the grass all trampled as if a herd of cattle had passed through. There were many fewer people now, so it should have been easy to see a little girl on her own. But there were none. Instead there were groups of young men roving about. They made me very nervous, especially when they called out to us. Maude and I linked arms tightly as we walked.

It was so frustrating — we could not find any policemen, nor even any of the suffragettes who had been running about during the procession wearing sashes that read BANNER CAPTAIN or CHIEF MARSHALL. Not one responsible grown-up was about to help.

Then a group of very rough men shouted, 'Ahoy there, girls! Fancy a drink?' and came towards us. Well. Maude and I fairly ran our legs off to get out of the park. The men didn't follow, but I refused to go back in — it was far too dangerous. We stood at the Marble Arch entrance and looked out across the grass, shielding our eyes from the early evening sun.

I was looking not just for Ivy May, but for Simon as well. We had not seen him since he left the procession to go and collect the horse (led by Maude's mother in that costume! I am speechless. It was no wonder that the horse kicked her). He had said he might come back to the park after. I kept thinking as I looked that they would be together — that Simon would appear, leading Ivy May by the hand. They would be eating ice-creams and they would have them for Maude and me as well. Ivy May would give me a cheeky look, with a little smile and glittering eyes, and I would pinch her for frightening me so.

'She's not here,' Maude said. 'We would have seen her by now. Perhaps she's gone home. She may have retraced the route we took, back to Euston and got on an omnibus. She's not stupid, Ivy May.'

I held up the little purse that dangled from my wrist. 'She had no money for the bus,' I whispered. 'I made her give it to me for safekeeping, so she wouldn't lose it.'

'She may have found her way back,' Maude repeated. 'Perhaps we should walk along the procession route and look for her.'

'I'm so very tired. I don't think I could take another step. Let's stay here just a little longer.'

Then we did see him coming towards us. He looked so small in that great grass expanse, with his hands at his sides, kicking at things that had been left behind — bits of paper, flowers, a lady's glove. He seemed unsurprised to see us, and unsurprised when Maude said, 'Ivy May is missing'.

'Ivy May's gone,' I said. 'She's gone.' I began to cry.

'She's missing,' Maude repeated.

Simon gazed as us. I had never seen him look so grave.

'We think she may have gone along the route we marched,' Maude said. 'Come with us to look.'

'What were she wearing?' Simon asked. 'I didn't notice before.'

Maude sighed. 'A white dress. A white dress like everyone else. And a straw hat with flowers around the brim, like ours.'

Simon fell in beside us and we began walking back down Oxford Street. This time we could not walk down the middle of the street, for it was full of horse-drawn cabs and omnibuses and motor-cars. We stayed on the pavement, crowded with people walking back from the demonstration. Simon crossed over to search the other pavement, looking in doorways and down alleys as well as scanning the faces around him.

I could not quite believe we were going to have to walk the whole route again — I was so thirsty and footsore that I did not think I could manage it. But then, as we were going along Upper Regent Street, I saw down a mews a pump for watering horses, and went up and put my whole face under the stream of water that gushed out. I didn't care if the water was bad or my hair got wet — I was so thirsty I had to drink.

The bell in the clock tower of St Pancras Station was striking eight when at last we arrived back at our starting point.

'Mama will be frantic with worry,' I said. As tired as I was, I dreaded arriving home to face Mama and Papa.

'It's still so light out,' Maude said. 'It's the longest day of the year — did you know that? Well, second longest, perhaps, after yesterday.'

'Oh, for pity's sake shush, Maude.' I could not bear to hear her talk like a teacher in a classroom. Besides which, I had a fearsome headache.

'We'd best go home,' Maude said, ignoring me. 'Then we can tell your parents and they can contact the police. And I can find out about Mummy.'

'Your mother,' I began. Suddenly I was so angry I wanted to spit. Maude had sent Mr Jackson off with her mother rather than have him help us. He would have found Ivy May, I was sure of it. 'Your bloody mother got us into this mess.'

'Don't blame her!' Maude cried. 'It was you who wanted so badly to come on the march!'

'Your mother,' I repeated. 'You don't know the half of it about her.'

'Don't, Livy,' Simon warned. 'Don't you dare.'

Maude looked between us. 'I don't want to hear it, whatever it is,' she said to me. 'Don't you ever say a word of it to me.'

'Go home, both of you!' Simon said. I'd never heard him raise his voice before. 'There's an omnibus there.' He even pushed us towards it.

'We can't leave Ivy May,' I declared, stopping in my tracks. 'We can't just jump on a bus and leave her at the mercy of this awful city.'

'I'll go back and look for her,' Simon said.

For that I could have kissed him, but he was already off at a run, back down along the Euston Road.

JENNY WHITBY

Never did I expect to see such a sight.

I didn't know who it could be, ringing the bell on a Sunday evening. I'd just returned from Mum's, didn't even have my cap and apron on yet. I weren't even there normally – I usually came back later, after Jack was asleep, but today he were so tired from running about that after tea he just fell into his bed.

Maybe it were the missus and Miss Maude, had their key pickpocketed in the crowd. Or a neighbour meaning to borrow a stamp or run out of lamp oil. But when I opened the door, it were the man from the cemetery, carrying the missus in his arms. Not only that – she weren't wearing a proper skirt! Her legs were bare as the day she was born. Her eyes were just open, like she'd been woke up from a nap.

Before I could say a word but stare with my eyes popping, Mr Jackson had pushed inside, with that suffragette lady Miss Black fluttering behind him. 'We must get her to her bed,' he said. 'Where is her husband?'

'At the Bull and Last,' I said. 'He always goes there after his cricket.' I led the way upstairs to her room. Miss Black was wearing some sort of metal suit what clanked as she went up the stairs. She looked so strange I began to wonder if I were dreaming it all.

Mr Jackson laid the missus on her bed and said, 'Stay with her — I'll get her husband.'

'And I'll fetch a doctor,' said Miss Black.

'There's one on the Highgate Road, just up from the pub,' I said. 'I can —'

But they were gone before I could offer to go so Miss Black could stay with her friend. It were like she didn't want to stay.

So it were just me and the missus. She lay there staring at me. I couldn't think what to do. I lit a candle and were just about to close the curtains when she whispered, 'Leave them open. And open the window.'

She looked so silly in her green outfit, her legs all naked. Mr Coleman would have a fit if he saw her like that. After I opened the window I sat on the bed and began to take off her little green boots.

'Jenny, I want to ask you something,' she said real quiet.

'Yes, ma'am.'

'Does anyone know about what happened to me?'

'About what happened to you, ma'am?' I repeated. 'You've had a little accident, is all.'

The missus' eyes flared and she shook her head. 'Jenny, there is no time for this silliness. For once let us be clear with each other — does anyone know what happened to me two years ago?'

I knew what she were talking about the first time, even though I acted like I didn't. I set the boots on the floor. 'No one knows but me. And Mrs Baker — she guessed. Oh, and Simon.'

'The cemetery boy? How could he know?'

'It were his mum you went to.'

'And that is all — no one else knows?'

I didn't look in her eyes, but tugged at the green cap in her hair. 'No.' I didn't say anything about Miss Livy's letter. There seemed no point in agitating her in her state. Simon and Mrs Baker and me, we could keep our counsel, but there was no guessing what Miss Livy might say one of these days — or said already, like as not. But the missus needn't know that.

'I don't want the men to find out.'

'No.' I reached round and began to unbutton the back of her tunic.

'Promise me they won't.'

'They won't.'

'Promise me something else.'

'Yes, ma'am.'

'Promise me you won't let my mother-in-law get her claws into Maude.'

I pulled off the tunic and gasped. Her chest was one big black bruise. 'Lord, what happened to you, ma'am?'

'Promise me.'

Now I understood why she was talking like that. 'Oh, ma'am, you're going to be just fine in a day or two. The doctor will be here soon and he'll sort you out. Miss Black's gone to fetch him. And Mr — the gentleman's gone to get your husband.' The missus tried to say something, but I wouldn't let her — I just ran on and on, saying whatever popped into my head. 'He's down the pub just now, but it won't take him a minute to get back. Let's just get this nightgown on before they come, shall we? It's ever so pretty, this one, what with the lace at the cuffs and all. Let's just pop this over your head and pull it down. There. And your hair, that's it. That's better now, ain't it?'

She lay back again, like she were too weak to fight my words. Her breathing were all wet and ragged. I couldn't bear to hear it. 'I'll just run and light the lamps,' I said. 'For the master and doctor. Won't be a second.' I ran out before she could say anything.

Mr Coleman came home as I was lighting the lamps in the front hallway, and then the doctor and Miss Black. They went upstairs, and then it went all quiet up there. I couldn't help it – I had to go and listen outside the door.

The doctor had such a low voice that all I could hear was 'internal bleeding.'

Then Mr Coleman laid into Miss Black. 'Why in hell didn't you find a doctor the moment the horse kicked her?' he shouted. 'You were boasting there would be a huge crowd – surely among 200,000 people there was a doctor!'

'You don't understand,' Caroline Black said. 'It was so crowded it was difficult to move or even speak, much less find a doctor.'

'Why didn't you bring her home at once? If you had shown any sense whatsoever she might be all right now, with nothing more than a few bruises.'

'Don't you think I didn't beg her to? You clearly don't know your wife well if you think she would have done what I asked her to. She wanted to get to Hyde Park and hear the speeches on such an historic occasion, and nothing I nor anyone else – not even you, sir – said could have dissuaded her.'

'Hyperbole!' Mr Coleman shouted. 'Even at a time like

this you suffragettes resort to hyperbole. Damn your historic occasion! Did you even look at her chest after it happened? Did you even see the damage? And who on God's green earth told Kitty to lead a horse? She's a disaster around horses!'

'It was her idea. No one forced her. She never told me she didn't like horses.'

'And where's Maude?' Mr Coleman said. 'What's happened to my daughter?'

'She's – she's on her way home, I'm sure.' Caroline Black was crying now.

I didn't stay to hear more. I went down to the kitchen and put the kettle on. Then I sat at the table and began to cry myself.

IVY MAY WATERHOUSE

Over his shoulder I saw a star fall. It was me.

SIMON FIELD

I never seen a dead body before. That sounds strange coming from a gravedigger. All day long I got dead bodies round me, but they're in boxes, nailed shut tight and covered with dirt. Sometimes I'm standing on a coffin in a grave, and there's only an inch of wood 'tween me and the body. But I ain't seen it. If I spent more time out of the cemetery I'd see dead bodies all the time. Funny, that. Our Ma and sisters has seen hundreds, all them women and babies died in birth, or neighbours, died of hunger or the cold.

It's strange seeing someone I know like that. If I didn't know to be looking for her I wouldn't recognise her. It's not that she's cut or crushed or anything like that. It's just that she ain't there. There are the legs, arms, head, all in the right places, lying down the back of a mews behind a stack of bricks. And the face is clean and smooth even, the mouth shut, her eyes a little open like she's looking through her lashes and don't want you to know she's looking. But when I look at the face I just can't see her. She ain't a person no more, but a thing like a sack of spuds.

'Ivy May,' I call softly, squatting beside her. I say it even though I know she's dead. Maybe I'm hoping she'll come back if I say her name.

But she don't. She don't open her eyes and look at me with that look she has of knowing everything what's happening and never saying. She don't sit up with her legs straight out in front of her the ways she likes to sit. She don't stand solid, looking like you could never knock her down, as hard as you pushed.

The body just lays there. And I have to get it back somehow, from a mews off the Edgware Road to Dartmouth Park.

How am I going to get her all that way without someone seeing me? I wonder. Anyone sees me will think I did it.

Then I look up at the end of the mews and see a man standing there. A tall man. Can't see much of his face 'cept the glint of his specs in the streetlamp and a thin moustache. He's staring at me, and when he sees me looking at him he steps back behind the building.

Could be he thinks I've done it and he's off to tell someone. But I know he's not. It's him what done it. Our Pa says men can't leave their crimes alone — they got to come sniffing round again, like worrying a loose tooth or picking a scab.

I run out the mews to look for him, but he's gone. I know he'll come back again, though, and if I don't take her now he will.

I straighten out her dress a bit, and her hair, and I buckle on one of her shoes what'd come off. When I lift her onto my back I see her straw hat's been under her. It's all broken, and the flowers crushed, and too much trouble to pick it up with Ivy May heavy on my back, so I leave it on the ground.

If anyone asks, I'll say she's my sister and fallen asleep. But I stay away from the pubs and keep to the little streets and then the parks, Regents then Primmers Hill then the bottom of the Heath, and I don't see many folk. And none ask. That time of night the people out are too drunk to notice, or else up to their own mischief and don't want to draw attention to themselves.

All the way home I keep thinking 'bout that hat. I wish I hadn't left it. I don't like leaving any part of her there. So when it's over, when I've got her home, I go back, all the way through the parks and the streets. It takes no time, not without her weight on my back. But when I get to the mews and look behind the bricks the hat is already gone, flowers and all.

MAUDE COLEMAN

I waited on the wrought-iron steps that led from the French doors down into the garden. The air smelled of jasmine and mint and grass sprinkled with dew. I could hear frogs croaking in the pond at the bottom of the garden and, from the window below me, Jenny sobbing in the kitchen.

I have never been good at waiting — it always seems so wasteful, and I feel guilty, as if I should be doing something else. But I could not do anything else now — there was nothing to be done. Grandmother had arrived and was sitting in the morning room, knitting furiously, but I did not want to be busy like that. Instead I looked up at the stars, picking out the constellations — the Great Bear, the Crow, the Wolf.

The church bells close by struck midnight.

Daddy came and stood in the open French doors and lit a cigarette. I did not look at him.

'It's a clear night,' he said.

'Yes.'

'Pity we can't set up the telescope in the garden — we might even see Jupiter's moons. But of course it wouldn't be right, would it?'

I did not answer, though I'd had the same thought myself.

'I'm sorry I shouted at you when you arrived home, Maude. I was upset.'

'That's all right.'

'I was afraid I'd lost you too.'

I shifted on the cold metal. 'Don't say that, Daddy.'

He coughed. 'No, you're right.'

Then we heard the scream, long and high-pitched, from the direction of the Waterhouses' house. I shivered.

'What in God's name was that?' Daddy asked.

I shook my head. I had not told him about Ivy May going missing.

A throat cleared behind us. The doctor had come downstairs to get us. Now that the waiting was over I did not want to move from the steps. I did not want to see my mother. I had been waiting for her all my life, and now I preferred to be waiting for her always, if that was the only alternative.

Daddy flicked his cigarette into the garden and turned to follow the doctor. I could hear it sizzling in the dewy grass. After it stopped I went inside too.

Mummy was lying very still, her face pale, her eyes open and unnaturally bright. I sat down next to her. She fixed her eyes on me. I knew she was waiting for me to speak.

I had no idea what to say or do. Lavinia and I had rehearsed such scenes many times when we were play-acting, but none of that seemed right now that I was actually here with Mummy. It felt silly to say something melodramatic, ridiculous to say something banal.

In the end, though, I did resort to the banal. 'The garden smells nice tonight. The jasmine especially.'

Mummy nodded. 'I've always loved jasmine on a summer's night,' she said. Then she closed her eyes.

Was that all we were going to talk about — jasmine? It seemed so. I squeezed her hand tightly and looked hard at her face, as if that would help me to remember it better. I could not bring myself to say goodbye.

The doctor touched my shoulder. 'It's best if you go now, Miss.'

I let go of Mummy's hand, and went downstairs and back out into the garden, wading through the wet grass down to the back fence. The ladder was still there, although Lavinia and I did not meet each other over the fence so much now. I climbed to the top of the wall. The Waterhouses' ladder was not up. I balanced there for a moment, then jumped, landing in the wet grass and smearing my dress. When I got my breath back I walked up the garden to the French doors that led directly into the Waterhouses' back parlour.

The family was arranged in a semicircular tableau that a painter might have set up. Ivy May lay across the chaise longue, hair spread around her face, eyes closed. Lavinia lay at her sister's feet, her head resting on the edge of the chaise longue. Mrs Waterhouse sat in an armchair near Ivy May's head, holding her hand. Mr Waterhouse leaned against the mantelpiece, a hand covering his eyes. Simon hovered near the door with his head bowed.

I knew just from looking at them, gathered together yet so separate in their grief, that Ivy May was dead.

I felt as if my heart had been hollowed out, and now my stomach was too.

When I came in they all looked at me. Lavinia jumped up and threw herself into my arms, weeping. I gazed over her shoulder at Mrs Waterhouse. It was as if I were seeing myself mirrored in her face. Her eyes were quite dry, and her expression was of someone who has been struck a blow from which she will not recover.

Because of that, I spoke the words directly to her. 'My mother is dead.'

KITTY COLEMAN

All her life Maude was a presence at my side, whether she was actually there or not. I pushed her away, yet she remained.

Now I was holding on to her hand and I did not want to let go. It was she who had to let go of me. When she did at last, I knew I was alone, and that it was time for me to depart.

SIMON FIELD

Next day Mr Jackson went out and shot that white horse through the head.

Later, as our Pa and Joe and me was digging, the police came to take me away for questioning. Our Pa didn't even look surprised. He just shook his head and I knew what he were thinking – I should never have got in with them girls.

The police asked me all kinds of things about what I did that day – not just about looking for Ivy May, or finding her, but about the horse and Kitty Coleman and Mr Jackson. They seemed way off the mark to me, and none too nice about it neither. It were like they wanted to make their lives easy and say I did the crime.

When it sounded like they was ready to accuse me I said, 'Who would be stupid enough to do that to a girl and then bring her home to her parents?'

'You would be surprised what criminals do,' one of the policemen said.

I thought of the tall man with the specs at the end of the mews. But when it came time to describe finding Ivy May I didn't tell 'em about him. Would've been easier on me if I had – given 'em someone else to look for.

But I knew he was long gone — them bumblers would never find him.

I would, though, some day. Find him. For Ivy May.

JOHN JACKSON

I arranged to meet Miss Coleman at her family grave. I'd considered asking her to come to Faraday, where her mother and I used to meet. But it was a silly, sentimental thought, and risky besides – questions might be asked if we were seen alone in the Dissenters, whereas in the meadow we could be thought to be discussing burial arrangements.

She was dressed all in black, with her hair up under a black straw hat. I had never seen her before with her hair up – she looked several years older. She has no idea but she is beginning to resemble Kitty.

'Thank you for coming, Miss Coleman,' I said as we stood side by side next to the grave. 'I'm so sorry for your loss. It has been a great shock to us all. But your mother is with God now.' I blinked rapidly at the ground. I often express my condolences to mourners at the cemetery, but this time I felt the inadequacy of the words.

'My mother did not believe in heaven,' Maude said. 'You know that.'

I wondered what those last three words were meant to signal. How much did she know about my intimacy with her mother? Her expression was so guarded that it was impossible to guess.

'Simon didn't tell me what you wanted to see me about when he delivered the message,' she said. 'I assume it is to do with my mother's burial, which I thought my father went over with you.'

'He was here yesterday, yes. There was something I wished to discuss with him but did not. I thought that perhaps you and I might do so.'

Maude raised her eyebrows but said nothing.

There was no easy way to say it — no stock expressions or careful euphemisms to smooth the shock of the idea. 'Your mother told me she wished to be cremated rather than interred.'

Maude looked up at the Coleman urn, studying it as if she had never seen it before. 'I know that. She was always worried she might be buried alive.'

'Then perhaps you could tell your father what she told you.'

'Why didn't you tell him yesterday?'

I paused. 'She spoke of it only unofficially — she did not put it in writing or tell her husband. It would not be appropriate for me to tell him.'

Maude pursed her lips. 'Daddy already knows she wanted to be cremated. They used to argue about it. He feels we should do what society dictates concerning the disposal of — of bodies.'

'He won't agree to it even if he knows it was his wife's fervent wish?'

'He'll do what looks best.' Maude paused. 'He lost her, and now he has got her back he will be sure to keep her.'

'What people do with their dead is usually a reflection of themselves rather than of their loved one,' I said. 'Do you think all these urns and angels mean anything to the dead? It takes a very unselfish man to do exactly what his wife wants without his own — or society's — desires and tastes entering into it. I had rather hoped your father was that man.'

'But surely if all these monuments mean nothing to the dead, then nothing we do to them does?' Maude replied. 'If they don't care, shouldn't we then do what is important to us? It's we who are left behind, after all. I've often thought this place is really for the living, not the dead. We design the grave to remind us of the dead, and of what we remember of them.'

'Will the urn on your family grave remind you of your mother — of what she was and what she wanted?'

'No, there is nothing of my mother on it,' Maude admitted. 'If my mother were to choose her own grave it would have a statue of Mrs Pankhurst on it and under her name it would read "Votes for Women".'

I shook my head. 'If your mother were to choose her own grave there would be no monument or words at all. It would be a bed of wildflowers.'

Maude frowned. 'But Mummy is dead, isn't she? She really is dead. She's not going to design her grave.'

She was a remarkable young lady — there are few who could say what she said without flinching.

'And because she's dead,' she continued, 'surely she won't care what happens to her body. She won't be buried alive — we know that. It's we who care — my father most of all. He represents all of us, and he must decide what is best.'

I leaned over and brushed away a spider from the Water-house grave. I knew it was not fair of me to make demands on her — after all, she was only thirteen years old and has just lost her mother. But for Kitty's sake I must. 'All I would ask of you, Miss Coleman,' I said gently, 'is that you remind your father of what you know — of what he must already know — of your mother's wishes. It is of course for him to decide what will then be done.'

Maude nodded and turned to go.

'Maude,' I said.

'Yes?'

'There is something else.'

She closed her eyes briefly, then looked at me.

'Your mother's —' I stopped abruptly. I could not tell her — it would be a breach of my professional duties, and I could lose my position for saying anything. But I wanted somehow to warn her. 'It would be best if you spoke to your father sooner rather than later.'

'All right.'

'It is a matter of urgency. Perhaps more than you know.'

'I'll speak to him today.' Maude turned and hurried down the path that led to the entrance.

I stood there for some time, studying the Coleman grave. It was hard to imagine Kitty being buried there. That absurd urn made me want to snort with laughter.

RICHARD COLEMAN

She came to see me in my study as I was going through papers. I stopped writing. 'What is it, Maude?'

She took a deep breath – she was clearly very nervous. 'Mummy said to me once that she wanted to be cremated and her ashes scattered.'

I looked down at my hands. There was a spot of ink on the cuff of my shirt. 'Your mother said a great many things that have not come to pass. She once said she wanted four children. Do you see any sisters or brothers about? Sometimes what we think and what we do are not meant to be the same.'

'But –'

'That's enough, Maude. There is nothing more to be said on the matter.'

Maude shuddered. I'd spoken more sharply than I'd intended. These days I find it difficult to control my tone.

'I'm sorry, Daddy,' she whispered. 'I was only thinking of Mummy. I didn't mean to upset you.'

'You haven't upset me!' I pressed my pen so hard into

the paper that the nib suddenly cracked. 'Damn!' I threw down the pen.

Maude slipped out without another word.

The sooner this week is over the better.

LAVINIA WATERHOUSE

Purchased from Jay's in Regent Street, 22nd June 1908:

1. 1 black dress in paramatta silk for me — for the funeral
   and for Sundays; my old merino dress is for everyday.
   There was an even lovelier silk dress, with crape all
   round the neck, but it was too dear.
2. 1 black bombazine dress for Mama. It looks so cheap and
   shiny that I tried to convince her to buy paramatta
   instead, but she said we didn't have the money and she
   would rather I had the silk as it matters more to me.
   Sweet of her.
3. 1 black cotton petticoat for me, 2 pairs bloomers threaded
   with black ribbon.
4. 1 black felt hat with veil for me. I insisted on the veil —
   I look so awful when I've been crying and shall need to
   pull down the veil often to hide my red eyes and nose.
   Mama did not buy a hat for herself but said she would
   dye one of her bonnets. She did at least buy a few ostrich
   feathers to trim it with.
5. 2 pairs black cotton gloves for Mama and me. They have
   4 lovely jet buttons up the cuff. Mama had chosen

plain ones without buttons, but did not notice when I switched them. Also, pair of gloves, a hatband, and black cravat for Papa.

6. 7 black-edged handkerchiefs — 2 for Mama, 5 for me. I wanted many more but Mama would not let me. She has not cried at all, but I insisted she should have a few, just in case she does cry.

7. 200 sheets stationery with medium-band black edging.

8. 100 remembrance cards on order that read as follows:

IVY MAY WATERHOUSE
AGE 10

'A lovely flower, soon snatched away,
    To bloom in realms divine;
Thousands will wish, at Judgement Day,
    Their lives were short as mine.'

I chose the epitaph, as Mama was overcome in the shop and had to go outside for some air. The shop assistant said the epitaph was meant for a baby, not someone Ivy May's age, but I think it's lovely, especially the phrase 'To bloom in realms divine', and I insisted it remain.

I could have spent all day in Jay's — it is so comforting to be in a shop devoted entirely to what one is experiencing. But Mama refused to linger and became quite short with me. I don't know what to do about her — she is very pale, poor dear, and hardly says a word except to be contrary. Much of the time she remains in her room, lying in bed as if she is ill. She rarely emerges for visitors, and so it has been up to me to see to the entertaining — pouring out cups of tea, asking Elizabeth to bring in more cake and crumpets. So many cousins arrived today that we ran out and I had to send Elizabeth to the baker's for more. I myself cannot eat a thing, except for the odd slice of currant bread, which the King's physician recommends for keeping the strength up.

I have tried to interest Mama in the letters of condolence we have received, but she does not seem to read them. I have had to answer them myself, as I worry that if I leave them with Mama she will simply forget, and it does not do to delay a reply.

People have said the most surprising things about Ivy May – how angelic she was, how she was the perfect daughter and such a support to Mama, how tragic for us and how much she will be missed. Indeed, I sometimes want to write back and ask if they thought it was *I* who died. But instead I make sure simply to sign my name large and clear, so that there will be no doubt.

Mama said to me at breakfast that she does not want me to go back to school, that I can finish the term by studying at home. (Just as well, as I am in no mood to sit in class. I should probably interrupt everything by weeping at the wrong moments.) And that next term I am to switch schools and attend the Sainte Union on the Highgate Road. My heart did a little leap, as the girls there have such smart uniforms. I was surprised, of course, as the school is Catholic, but perhaps I shouldn't be – Mama asked for the priest from St Joseph's in Highgate to come and see her last night. Papa said not a word. If reverting to Catholicism is a comfort to her, what is one to say?

Papa has been kept very busy with the arrangements, and that is good, I think. I helped him when I could, as Mama is unable. When the undertaker came to see us it was I who chose the dress Ivy May is to wear (white cotton with puffed sleeves that used to be mine) and the flowers (lilies) and what to do with her hair (loose curls and a crown woven of white roses). Papa answered the other questions about the coffin and horses and such. He also met with the cemetery people and the vicar, and with the police.

The latter gave me rather a shock, as Papa brought a policeman home to question me! He was nice enough, but asked me so many questions about that awful afternoon in Hyde Park that I began to be confused about exactly when Ivy May went missing. I tried to be brave but I'm afraid I went through all the handkerchiefs we had just bought. Luckily Mama was upstairs and so did not have to hear the details. Papa had tears in his eyes by the time I finished.

The policeman kept asking me about the men in the crowd. He even asked about Simon, as if Simon were someone to be suspicious of! I put him straight there. And I told him about the men who chased Maude and me at the demonstration, and how frightened we were.

I did not tell him about the man who put his hand on my bottom. I knew that I should have, that it was just the thing he was looking for. But I was embarrassed to have to speak of it. And I could not bear to think that that man got hold of my sister. Telling the policeman about him would be like an admission that he had. I wanted to keep Ivy May safe from him, in my mind if nowhere else.

No one has talked about what actually happened to Ivy May. But I can guess. I am no idiot. I saw the marks on her neck.

Tonight I was standing at my window when I saw Maude

standing at hers. We waved to each other, but it felt very peculiar, and after a moment I stepped back from the window. We are not allowed to visit each other, as one is not meant to pay visits while in mourning. Besides which, I don't think seeing Maude would bring much comfort to me now – all I can think of is her mother abandoning us in that huge crowd, and Ivy May's sweaty hand slipping from mine.

I sat on my bed and looked at Ivy May's little white bed in the corner. We would never lie in our beds again at night and whisper and tell each other stories – or rather, I told them and she listened. I am all alone now.

It hurt so much to look at that bed that I went down right then and asked Papa to move it.

GERTRUDE WATERHOUSE

I am so heavy with guilt that I cannot get out of bed. The priest has come, and the doctor, and neither can rouse me.

I did not tell them, nor Albert either, that I pretended to have a sprained ankle. Albert, bless him, thought it was real. If I had not pretended, if I had taken the girls to the march – or indeed if I had stood up to Livy and not allowed her to go – Ivy May would be sitting here with me now.

I have killed my daughter with my own stupidity, and if she is not here I do not want to live either.

EDITH COLEMAN

The first thing I did was to give that impertinent maid her notice. I am sorry to admit that anything in a house of mourning could give me satisfaction, but that did. Of course she wailed and wrung her hands, but her dramatics had no effect on me – if anything they made me more determined that I had done the right thing, and none too soon.

Jenny had the nerve to mention Maude. 'What will she do?' she kept crying.

'Maude will continue as she has always done. I will look after her – I have come to stay and will remain for as long as I am needed. But that is no concern of yours.'

Jenny looked stricken.

'I let you go two years ago,' I reminded her, 'for reasons I'm sure you remember. My daughter-in-law should never have taken you back. Pack your bag and go. Your final wages will be sent to you.'

'What about my reference?'

I snorted. 'Do you think I would give a reference to a girl like you?'

'But how am I to get another position?'

'You should have thought of that when you lay with that man.'

The girl ran from the room. To my surprise Mrs Baker appeared a few minutes later, asking me to keep Jenny on.

'Why should I keep on a girl of such lax morals?' I replied. 'Believe me, she will be much better off staying home and looking after her child, the poor mite.'

'And what will she feed him – air?'

'I beg your pardon?'

'Never mind about Jenny's son, ma'am,' Mrs Baker said. 'It's for Miss Maude's sake that I'm asking you to keep Jenny. The poor girl's just lost her mother – I hate to see her losing the people round her too. Jenny's been here since Miss Maude was a baby. She's like family to her.'

'That girl is nothing like family to Maude!' I was so furious it was a struggle to keep my voice down. 'How dare you compare her to the Colemans! And Maude doesn't need her – she's got me.' By losing a mother, she has gained a grandmother, I almost said, but thought the better of it.

So Jenny went. Maude said, not a word, though she stood in the hallway and watched her go with a very pale face.

Then, for her sake and Richard's, I made another decision. Already the morning after Kitty's death the flowers had begun arriving – elaborate arrangements of lilies, irises, cornflowers, white roses, all tied up with purple, green and white ribbons. The cards read things like 'To our Fallen Comrade' and 'Hope is Strong – In Heaven as on Earth' and 'She Gave Herself to the Cause'. And that infernal telephone rang so much that I had a man come and disconnect it. Then suffragettes began coming to the door to ask about the funeral, until I had the hired girl who replaced Jenny turn them away. It was clear that Kitty was becoming a martyr to them. I dreaded to think what would happen if the suffragettes turned up en masse to the funeral – they might take it over and turn it into a political rally. I would never forgive myself for allowing James's family name to be dragged through the mud yet again.

I would not let it happen. I spoke to Richard of my plan and he readily agreed. After that it was not so difficult to arrange things to our satisfaction – after all, discretion is paramount in the undertaking trade.

JENNY WHITBY

She come running after me as I walked down the street with my bag. I'd stopped crying by then – I were too scared of what was to become of me even to cry. She didn't say nothing, just threw her arms round me and hugged me tight.

There ain't nothing she can do – a girl of thirteen up against such a grandmother? I feel terrible for breaking my promise to her mum about that witch, but I got no influence with someone like that – the missus should've known that. Nor can I do nothing about keeping her secret from the men. That's in God's hands now – or Miss Livy's, more like.

None of this should be my concern now, though – I got my own troubles, like how to keep me mum and me son and me on no wages and no reference. I've no time for tears. I've the rest of the missus' silverware in my bag, but that won't last forever.

ALBERT WATERHOUSE

I am rather ashamed of my daughter. I know these are difficult days for her, as they are for us all; indeed I've wondered if she would hold up under the strain. But I wish Livy and Maude had not said such awful things to each other in public, and right at Ivy May's grave – my poor Ivy May, whom I could not protect from evil men. I am just glad Trudy was being comforted by a sister and did not hear them – she would have been horrified to hear herself argued over.

It was at first something to do with Maude's dress. I am no judge of these things, but she was wearing a rather fine silk dress that Livy clearly envied. Livy said something about the dress being ostentatious for a girl of thirteen to wear.

Maude then replied, 'Lavinia, you can't spell the word, must less understand what it means. Mourning dresses by definition are not ostentatious.'

I was a bit surprised, as Maude is usually so soft spoken. But then, she has just lost her mother. And Livy was shocked – and livid, I am sorry to say.

'I know enough to know that you should not be wearing

a boater with that dress,' Livy said. 'Nor should you put your hair up under a boater — it just looks silly. And it's coming down at the back. Your hair isn't thick enough to put up the way mine is.'

'Perhaps you forget that I have no mother to ask advice of,' Maude said. 'Nor a sister, nor even a maid, now.'

'I don't have a sister either! Have you forgot that?'

Maude looked mortified at her slip, and if Livy had allowed her to apologise, as she seemed about to do, their argument might have blown over. But of course Livy couldn't resist pressing her point. 'All you think of is yourself. Have you spared a thought for poor Mama, who has lost a daughter? Is there anything worse than losing one's child?'

'Losing one's mother, perhaps,' Maude said in a low voice.

These comparisons were so odious that I finally had to step in — wishing I had done so earlier. (I often wish that, when it is too late.) 'Livy, would you like to walk with your mother down to the carriage?' I asked, at the same time giving what I hoped was a sympathetic look to Maude.

'Papa, how often must I remind you — it's Lavinia.' Livy turned her back on Maude and went over to her mother. I was about to say something — what, I did not know — but before I could, Maude slipped away and ran up the path farther into the cemetery.

Later that night, I could not sleep and came downstairs with my candle to get out *Cassell's* and *The Queen*. I have never looked in women's manuals before — thankfully I have little to do with household sorts of things. But at last I found what I was looking for: both manuals say that a child mourns its parent and a parent its child for the same period of time — one year.

I left both books on the table open to those pages, but when I came down the next morning they had been put away.

MAUDE COLEMAN

I could not stop shaking. I have never been so furious.

What I hated most were the horrid things I said as well. Lavinia brought out the worst in me, and it is much harder to live with that than with her remarks. I have learned to expect her to say silly and stupid things, and I have usually managed not to sink to her level, until now.

I sat for a long time by the sleeping angel. I had not known where I was running to until I ended up there. And that is where he found me. I suppose I knew he would. He sat down at the end of the slab of marble but did not look at me or say anything. That is his way.

I looked up into the bright blue sky. It was an obscenely sunny day for a funeral, as if God were mocking us all.

'I hate Lavinia,' I said, swatting at some vetch that was growing at the base of the angel's plinth.

Simon grunted. 'Sounds like something Livy would say.'

He was right.

'But you ain't Livy,' he added.

I shrugged.

'Listen, Maude,' he said, then stopped.

'What is it?'

Simon tapped his finger on the marble. 'We're digging your ma's grave now.'

'Oh.' I could not think what more to say.

'It's too early to be digging it. For a funeral meant for the day after tomorrow, in sandy soil? We should be digging it tomorrow afternoon. Else it could cave in, sitting there an extra day. Dangerous enough as 'tis. Shoring don't always work in sand. And Ivy May's grave so close. Don't like to dig two graves close together like that at the same time — the dirt don't hang together so well on that side. No choice about it, though, is there?'

'Who told you to dig Mummy's grave now rather than tomorrow?'

'The guvnor. Told us this morning. Our Pa tried to argue with him but he just said to get on with it once Ivy May's funeral's done. Said he'd handle the consequences.'

I waited for Simon to continue. I could see from his face that there was something he would eventually tell me, laying it out step by step in his own time.

'So I had a little look round. Couldn't see nothing from the work map in the lodge. Then I heard that the chapel here's been booked for tomorrow morning. Now I knows the other graves dug for tomorrow's all got coffins coming from outside. Don't say which the chapel is for.'

I shook my head. 'Mummy's service is at St Anne's on Friday afternoon. Daddy told me.'

'Then one of the mutes at Ivy May's funeral just now told me they're doing a funeral at the chapel here tomorrow,' Simon continued as if I had not spoken. 'Has to be your ma. Hers is the only grave ready with nothing to go in.'

I stood up – it hurt to hear him talk about Mummy like that, but I did not want him to see how much his words upset me. 'Thank you for telling me,' I said. 'I'll try to find out from Daddy if something has been changed.'

Simon nodded. 'Just thought you'd want to know,' he said awkwardly.

I wondered if Simon knew that Mr Jackson had asked me about cremation – he seemed to find out about everything else. If he did, though, he didn't say. At Ivy May's grave Mr Jackson had caught my eye, and to his unspoken question I'd simply shaken my head. He must have guessed by then anyway that Daddy had said no – otherwise he would have heard from us.

Instead I asked Simon about something else – something I was sure he knew. 'What happened to Ivy May that day?' I said, looking straight at him. 'No one will tell me.'

Simon shifted on the marble. For a long time he didn't say anything and I wondered if I would have to repeat myself. Then he cleared his throat. 'Someone strangled her.'

His answer was so stark that I could feel my own throat tightening. 'By a man?' I managed to say.

Simon nodded, and I saw from his face that I should not ask more.

We sat for a moment without speaking.

'I'm sorry 'bout your ma,' Simon said suddenly. He leaned across and quickly kissed me on the cheek, then jumped off the grave and was gone.

Back at home I ran into Grandmother in the front hall, inspecting a bouquet of flowers that had arrived – lilies tied with green, white, purple and black ribbons. 'Suffragettes!'

she was muttering. 'Just as well we —' She stopped when she saw me. 'Back already from the meal?'

'I haven't been to the Waterhouses' yet,' I confessed.

'Not been? Get you over there, then. Pay your respects. That poor child's mother is grey with grief. Such a terrible terrible death. I hope they catch the man who —' She stopped herself.

'I will go,' I lied. 'I just — need to have a word with Mrs Baker first.' I ran downstairs so that I would not have to tell her why I was not going to the funeral meal. I just could not bear to see Mrs Waterhouse's face sucked dry of life. I could not imagine what it must feel like to lose a child, and to lose her so awfully and mysteriously. I could only compare it to how I felt losing my mother: an aching emptiness, and a precariousness about life now that one of the things I had taken for granted was gone. Mummy may have been absent or remote these past few years, but she had at least been alive. It was as if Mummy had been shielding me from a fire and then was suddenly taken away so that I could feel the scorching flames on my face.

For Mrs Waterhouse, though, there must be simply a feeling of horror that I could not begin to describe.

Was one worse than the other, as Lavinia seemed to suggest? I did not know. I just knew that I couldn't see Mrs Waterhouse's dead gaze without feeling an abyss open in myself.

Instead of going to the Waterhouses' funeral meal, I went down to ask Mrs Baker about ours. Since she was preparing it, she of all people would know if there had been a change in the arrangements.

She was stirring a pot of aspic on the range. 'Hello, Miss

Maude,' she said. 'You should eat — you haven't touched your food these last few days.'

'I'm not hungry. I — I wanted to ask if everything will be ready for Friday. Grandmother wanted me to find out for her.'

Mrs Baker gave me a funny look. 'Course it will.' She turned back to the pot. 'I just spoke to your grandmother this morning. Nothing's changed in two hours. Beef jelly will set overnight, the ham's to be delivered this afternoon. It should all be ready by the day's end. Mrs Coleman wanted me to get everything ready early so I can help her with other things tomorrow — she's not happy with the temporary help. Not that I do just anything. I won't work on my knees, no matter what.' She glared at the pot. I knew that she missed Jenny, though she would never say.

She clearly thought the funeral would be on Friday. If Daddy had changed the day, no one knew but him and probably Grandmother. I could not face asking either of them, and I knew they would not tell me anyway.

When I came down to breakfast next morning both Daddy and Grandmother were sitting at the table in their best mourning clothes, untouched cups of coffee in front of them. They had peculiar looks on their faces, but they simply said, 'Good morning, Maude,' as I sat down to a bowl of congealed porridge. I tried to eat but could not swallow, so I simply pushed at the porridge with my spoon.

The doorbell rang. Daddy and Grandmother jumped. 'I'll get it,' Grandmother said to the hired char, who was lurking by the sideboard. I frowned at Daddy but he would not look at me — he kept his eyes on the newspaper, though I don't think he was really reading it.

I heard low voices in the front hall and then heavy footsteps on the stairs, as well as creaking. Soon the footsteps sounded overhead, in Mummy's room, and I knew Simon was right.

'Why have you done this, Daddy?'

He still would not look at me. 'Finish your porridge, Maude.'

'I'm not hungry. Why have you changed the day of the funeral?'

'Go and change into your new dress, Maude.' Grandmother spoke from the doorway.

I did not move from my chair. 'I want to know why you've done this. I have a right to know.'

'You have no rights!' my father roared, banging his hand on the table so that coffee slopped from both cups. 'Don't ever let me hear you say that again. You are my daughter and you will do as I say! Now go and change!'

I did not move from my chair.

Daddy glared at me. 'Do I have no authority in my own house? Does no one obey me? Has her influence extended so far that my own daughter won't do as I say?'

I did not move from my chair.

Daddy reached over and knocked my porridge bowl to the floor. It smashed at the feet of the terrified maid.

'Richard,' Grandmother warned. She turned to me, her face more lined than usual, as if she had not slept well. 'Your mother's funeral is to be this morning. We felt it best to have a private service so that it is not taken over by the wrong element. Now, go upstairs and put on your dress. Quickly, now, while I have a word with Mrs Baker. The carriage will be here soon.'

'I didn't want it to be hijacked by the suffragettes,' Daddy said suddenly. 'You saw what happened when she was released from prison – it was turned into a victory celebration. I'm damned if I'm going to let them make a martyr of her. Fallen comrade, they call her. They can go to bloody hell!' He sat back with such a pained look that I could almost forgive him his behaviour.

I knew there was nothing I could do, so I ran upstairs. As I passed Mummy's room – which I had avoided all week, leaving anything that needed doing in there to Grandmother – I could hear tapping. They were nailing the coffin shut.

In my room I dressed quickly. Then it came to me that there *was* one thing I could do. I found paper and pen and scribbled a note, pausing for a moment to recall the address I had seen printed so often on the letters page of the local paper. Then, grabbing my hat and gloves, I raced downstairs again, passing Daddy and Grandmother's surprised faces in the front hall as I continued down to the kitchen.

Mrs Baker was standing by the table, arms crossed, glaring at the spread of food laid out, a large ham glistening with jelly the centrepiece.

'Mrs Baker,' I whispered, 'if ever you loved my mother, please find someone to take this immediately. Please, for her sake. As quick as you can, else it will be too late.'

Mrs Baker glanced at the address, then without a word she strode to the back door and wrenched it open. As I was stepping into the carriage with Daddy and Grandmother I saw her stop a boy in the street and give him the note. Whatever she said to him made him run as if he were chasing his hat in the wind.

It was pouring with rain. The undertaker had spread straw

in front of our house to muffle the horses' hooves, but it was not necessary – the rain drowned out the sound anyway. A few neighbours had seen the funeral carriages and were standing in their doorways, but most were not expecting to do so until the next day.

No one spoke in the carriage. I stared out of the window at the passing houses, and then the long brick and iron fence that separated graves from the road. The glass sides of the carriage carrying the coffin were splashed with rain. All along the route people took off their hats for a moment as we passed.

At the cemetery Mr Jackson stepped up to the carriage with a large umbrella and helped down first Grandmother and then me. He nodded at me briefly, and I managed to nod back. Then he led us through the gate to the chapel entrance, where Auntie Sarah was waiting for us. She was twelve years older than Mummy and lived in Lincolnshire. They had not been close. She pecked me on the cheek and shook Daddy's hand. Then we went into the chapel for the service.

I sat in the front pew between Daddy and Auntie Sarah, with Grandmother next to Daddy. At first it was just the four of us and the vicar of St Anne's, who led the service. But when we began the first hymn, I heard voices behind me joining in to sing 'Nearer my God to Thee', and turned to see Mr Jackson and Simon standing at the back.

Just as we'd finished the second hymn, 'Abide with me' (which, of course, Mummy had detested), the door banged open. Caroline Black stood in the doorway, breathing heavily, her hat askew, her hair tumbling down. Daddy stiffened. 'Damn her,' he muttered. Caroline Black took a seat halfway up the aisle and caught my eye. I nodded at her. When I turned back to face the front I could feel Daddy's fury next to me, and I smiled a little and lifted my chin, as Mummy used to do when she was being defiant.

Damn you, I thought. Damn you yourself.

When it was all done – when the coffin had been taken into the cemetery and laid in the grave with the gigantic urn looming over it; when Simon and his father began to fill it, working steadily in the pouring rain; when I stepped away from my mother to begin the journey home – Caroline Black reached over and took my hand. It was then that I at last began to cry.

DOROTHY BAKER

The waste of all that food was a crime. She didn't even apologise — just said there had been a change in plans and there would be just four for the funeral meal. And there was me preparing for fifty!

I nearly walked out then and there, but for Miss Maude. In a week she's lost her mum and Jenny — and her best friend, from what the Waterhouses' char says. She doesn't need me leaving too.

SIMON FIELD

What happens today I'll never tell Maude. Probably won't tell no one.

After Kitty Coleman's funeral our Pa and Joe and me start filling the grave. The soil's sandy, makes it hard to shovel much in at once, even in the rain. It's always harder digging in the meadow, in the sand. Clay needs more cutting with the spade, but it sticks together so you can handle it easier than sand.

We been real careful with this grave, it being so close to Ivy May's. It's twelve feet deep, so Maude and her Pa and Gran can fit in when their time comes. We done extra shoring and made sure the wood were tight as we could get it against sand. Sand can be a killer if it ain't handled right.

We're shovelling in the sand a while, and the grave's half full. It's chucking down rain and we're soaked. Then our Pa's cap falls in.

'I'll get it,' I says to our Pa.

'Nah, son, I'll get it,' he says, and jumps right in like he's a boy again. Lands straight on his cap and starts to laugh. 'Bull's eye,' he says. 'You owe me a pint.'

'Where are you going to get a pint?' I laugh. 'You'll have to walk a long way for it.'

Only pub round here that'll serve gravediggers is the Duke of St Albans the bottom of Swain's Lane, and they won't let our Pa in any more 'cause he got so drunk he tried to kiss the landlady, then wrecked a chair.

Just then there's a crack and the shoring on the side by Ivy May's grave pops out. It does that when the ground round it's shifting. Before our Pa can do anything but duck the flying wood, that side of the grave collapses.

It must happen fast, but it don't seem like it. Seem like I got lots of time to watch our Pa look up like he's just heard thunder overhead and is waiting for the next flash of lightning. 'Oh,' I think I hear him say.

Then the dirt is raining down on him, piling round him up to his waist. There seems to be a little pause then but it can't be long 'cause Joe and I ain't moved at all yet, ain't said a word, ain't even breathed.

Our Pa catches my eye for a second and seems to smile at me. Then a pile of dirt comes down and knocks him over.

'Man in!' I shout as loud as I can through the rain. 'Man in!' It's words no one likes to hear in this place.

The dirt is still moving like it's alive but I can't see our Pa now. Just like that he's not there. Joe and I scramble round the grave, trying to keep from setting off more dirt. The hole's three-quarters full now. We need a big timber or ladder to lay 'cross the hole, to give us something stable to work from, but there ain't one around. We had a ladder but someone's borrowed it.

There ain't no time to wait when a man's buried like

that. He'll die in a few minutes if he ain't got no air. I jump into the hole though I'm not supposed to, landing in the mud on all fours like a cat. I look and look and then I see the thing our Pa taught me. I see his finger sticking out the dirt, just the tip of it, wiggling. He remembered to put his hand up. I start clawing round the finger with my hands. Don't dare use a shovel. I dig so hard the sand gets jammed under my nails and it hurts bad.

'Hang on, our Pa,' I say as I'm digging. 'We're getting you out. I see your fingers. We're getting you out.'

Don't know as he can hear me, but if he can it might make him feel better.

I'm digging and digging, trying to find his face, hoping he put the other hand up to it. There ain't no time, not even to look up. If I did look up, though, I know I'd see Joe standing on the edge of the grave, looking down at me, hands at his sides. He's a big man, and can dig for hours without stopping, but he's no thinker. He don't do the delicate work. He's better off up there.

'Joe, start counting,' I say as I keep clawing at the sand. 'Start from ten and keep counting.' I reckon I've dug ten seconds.

'Ten,' Joe says. ''Leven. Twelve.'

If he gets to two hundred and I ain't found our Pa's face it'll be too late.

'Thirty-two.'

'Sixty-five.'

'One-twenty-one.'

I feel something overhead and look up. There's a ladder 'cross the grave now. If more dirt comes down I can reach up and grab hold of the rungs so it don't get me. Then someone jumps into the grave beside me. It's Mr Jackson. He reaches out with his arms wide and hugs the pile of dirt I been digging. I didn't think he were that strong but he shifts the pile back so I got more room. He do just what I need him to do without me having to say it.

'One-seventy-eight.'

My fingers touch something. It's our Pa's other hand. I dig round the hand and find his head, then dig round that and lift his hand so his mouth and nose are clear. His eyes are closed and he's white. I put my ear up to his nose but don't feel a breath tickle it.

Then Mr Jackson pushes me aside and puts his mouth over our Pa's like he's kissing him. He breathes into his mouth a few times, then I see our Pa's chest go up and down.

I look up. Round the grave, all silent and still, there's a circle of men standing − other diggers, gardeners, masons, even dung boys. Word got out fast and everybody came running. They've all took their caps off, even in the pouring rain, and are watching and waiting.

Joe's still counting. 'Two-twenty-six, two-twenty-seven, two-twenty-eight.'

'You can stop counting, Joe,' I says, wiping my face. 'Our Pa's breathing.'

Joe stops. The men all move, shifting feet, coughing, talking low − everything they held back while they was waiting. Some of 'em don't like our Pa for his love of the bottle, but no one wants to see a man caught down a grave like that.

'Hand us a spade, Joe,' Mr Jackson says. 'We've got a lot of work to do yet.'

I never been down a grave with Mr Jackson. He ain't so handy with a spade as me or other diggers but he insists on staying there with me till we get our Pa out. And he don't tell the other men to get back to work. He knows they want to see this through.

I like working side by side with him.

It takes a long time to uncover our Pa. We have to dig careful so we don't hurt him. For a time he has his eyes closed like he's asleep, but then he opens 'em. I start talking to him as I'm working so he won't get scared.

'We're just digging you out, our Pa,' I say. 'The shoring come down with you in the grave. But you covered your face like you taught me, and you're all right. We'll be moving you out in a minute.'

He don't say nothing, just keeps looking up at the sky, with the rain coming down so fast and going all over his face. He don't seem to notice it. I start to have a bad feeling which I don't say nothing 'bout 'cause I don't want to scare nobody.

'Look,' I says, trying to get him to say something. 'Look, it's Mr Jackson digging. Bet you never thought you'd see the guvnor digging for you, eh?'

Our Pa still don't say nothing. The colour's coming back to his face but something's still missing from his eyes.

'Expect I owe you that pint, our Pa,' I say, desperate now. 'Expect there's plenty of men'll be buying you a pint today. I bet they'll be letting you back in the Duke of St Albans. The landlady might even let you kiss her.'

'Let him be, lad,' Mr Jackson says real soft. 'He's just been through an ordeal. It may take him some time to recover.'

We work without talking then. When at last our Pa's

uncovered, Mr Jackson checks for broken bones. Then he takes our Pa in his arms and hands him up to Joe. Joe puts him in a cart they use to haul stones, and two men pull him down the hill towards the gate. Mr Jackson and I climb out the grave, both of us muddy all over, and Mr Jackson starts to follow the cart. I stand there not sure what to do — the grave's not filled and it's our job to do it. But then two other diggers step up and take up the spades. They don't say nothing — they and Joe just start filling the rest of the grave.

I follow Mr Jackson and the cart down the path. When I catch up to him I want to say something to thank him, something that connects us so I'm not just another digger. I was close to him in Kitty Coleman's grave and I want to remind him of that. So I say the thing I know 'bout him and her, so he'll remember the connection and know how grateful I am to him for saving our Pa.

'I'm sorry 'bout the baby, sir,' I say. 'I bet she were, too. She weren't never the same after that, were she?'

He turns and looks at me sharp like. 'What baby?' he says.

Then I realise he didn't know. But it's too late to take the words back. So I tell him.

May 1910

LAVINIA WATERHOUSE

The first thing I thought when I heard the bells tolling was that they might disturb Mama in her delicate condition. But then, Mama has never been so fond of this King as she was of his mother. His death is, of course, very sad, and I do feel for poor Queen Alexandra, but it is not like when Queen Victoria died.

I threw open the window to lean out. It should have been raining, or foggy, or misty, but of course it wasn't — it was a beautiful May morning, sunny and soft. The weather never does what it ought.

Bells seemed to be ringing everywhere. Their noise was so mournful that I crossed myself. Then I froze. Across the way Maude had opened her window too and was leaning out in her white nightgown. She was staring straight at me, and she seemed to be smiling. I almost stepped away from the window, but it would have seemed very rude since she had already seen me. Instead I stayed where I was, and I was rather proud of myself — I nodded at her. She nodded back.

We have not spoken in almost two years — not since Ivy May's funeral. It has been surprisingly easy to avoid her. We no longer go to the same school, and if I have passed her in the street I've simply turned my head and pretended not to see her. Sometimes at the cemetery when I've gone to visit Ivy May I've seen Maude at her mother's grave, and then I've crept away and gone for a walk till she's done.

Only once did we come face to face in the street. It was over a year ago now. I was with Mama and she with her grandmother and so it was impossible to avoid her. Maude's grandmother went on and on giving her condolences to Mama while Maude and I stood there gazing at our shoes, not a word passing between us. It was all terribly awkward. I did manage to glance up at her from time to time, and saw that she was wearing her hair up for everyday now, and had begun wearing a corset! I was so shocked I wanted to say something, but of course I couldn't. Afterwards I made Mama take me straight out to buy a corset.

I have never said much to Mama about falling out with Maude. She knows we fought, but not why – she would be mortified if she knew it was in part over her. I know she thinks Maude and I are being silly. Perhaps we are. I wouldn't admit it to Maude but I do miss her. I have not met anyone at the Sainte Union who comes close to being the kind of friend Maude was. In fact the girls there have been rather awful to me, I think because to be honest I am so much prettier than they. It can be a burden having a face like mine – though on balance I prefer to keep it.

I expect my nod at Maude means I have forgiven her.

I went down to breakfast, still in my dressing gown, with a suitably sad face for the King. Mama, however, seemed not to notice the bells at all. She is so big now that she cannot sit easily at the table, and so she was eating a plate of marmalade toast on the chaise longue while Papa read the paper to her. Even as he read out the news Mama was smiling to herself, with a hand resting on her stomach.

'Such sad news,' I said, depositing a kiss on each of their heads.

'Oh, hello, dear,' Mama said. 'Would you like to feel the baby kicking?'

Really, it was enough to make me flee the room. It is one thing for Mama to be pleased about the baby, especially at her age, and it is good that she has some colour in her cheeks. But she seems to have altogether forgot Ivy May.

Papa smiled at me, though, as if he understood, and for his sake I stayed and managed a bowl of porridge, though I did not feel much like eating.

When I went back upstairs to change, I stood in front of my wardrobe and debated for a long while about what to wear. I knew I should wear black for the King, but just looking at that old merino rag hanging there made me feel faint. Perhaps if I'd still had the lovely silk from Jay's I would have worn that, but I burned it a year after Ivy May's death, as one is not meant to keep mourning clothes – they might tempt Fate to make one need to use them again.

Besides, I wanted to wear my blue dress, which I love. It has a special significance – I have been wearing it as often as possible, especially leading up to Mama's imminent confinement. I want a baby brother. I know it's silly, but I thought wearing the blue would help. I don't want another sister – it would hurt too much, and remind me of how I failed Ivy May so miserably. I let go of her hand.

So I put on my blue dress. At least it is dark blue – dark enough that from a distance it could be taken for black.

What is sad about today is not simply that the King is

dead, but that his mother is truly gone now. If it were she who died I would not have thought twice about wearing black. I have begun to feel recently that I am the only one who still looks back to her as an example to us all. Even Mama is looking forward. I am getting tired of swimming against the tide.

MAUDE COLEMAN

I lay in bed for a long time and tried to guess which bells belonged to which church: St Mary's Brookfield up one hill, St Michael's and St Joseph's up the hill in Highgate, our church, St Anne's, at the bottom. Each rang just one low bell, and although each was at a slightly different pitch and tolled ever so slightly more or less slowly, still they all sounded the same. I had not heard such a noise since Queen Victoria's death nine years ago.

I stuck my head out of the window and saw Lavinia crossing herself in her window. Usually when I caught a glimpse of her somewhere – in her garden or on the street – a jolt ran through me as if someone had shoved me from behind. But now it was so strange to see her make such a foreign gesture that I forgot to be upset at seeing her. She must have learned to cross herself at the Sainte Union. I thought of her years ago being frightened of going into the Dissenters' section of the cemetery where all the Catholics are buried, and smiled. It was funny how things change.

She saw me then, and, hesitating for a moment, she nodded to acknowledge my smile. I had not meant it as a smile at her, really, but once she nodded I felt I ought to nod too.

We turned away from our windows then, and I went to get dressed, hesitating over the dresses in my wardrobe. The black silk hung there still, but it would need altering to fit me now — I had filled out since last wearing it, and I was wearing a corset besides. I had worn black for almost a year following Mummy's death, and for the first time I had understood why we are meant to wear black. It is not just that the colour reflects a mourner's sombre mood, but also that one doesn't want to have to choose what to wear. For the longest time I would wake in the morning and be relieved that I did not have to decide among my dresses — the decision had been made for me. I had no desire to wear colour, or to be concerned about my appearance. It was only when I did want to wear colour again that I knew I was beginning to recover.

I wondered sometimes how Lavinia fared with such a long period of mourning for Ivy May — six months for a sister, though I expect she kept up with her mother and wore black for a year. I wondered now what she would wear for the King.

I looked at my dresses again. Then I saw Mummy's dove-grey dress among them and thought that perhaps I could manage that. It still surprises me that her dresses now fit me. Grandmother does not approve of me wearing them, but the stroke has left her unable to speak easily, and I have managed to ignore her dark looks.

I suppose she is thinking in part of Daddy, and I do try not to wear Mummy's dresses in front of him. I could see him now, smoking a cigarette out in the garden — something Mummy forbade him to do, as he always flicks the butts into the grass. I went downstairs in the grey dress and slipped out before he saw me.

On Swain's Lane the paperboys were crying out about the King's death, and some shops were already hung with black and purple banners. No one was painting their ironwork black, though, as they had done after the Queen's death. Some people were dressed in black, but others weren't. They stopped to speak to one another, not in the hushed tones of mourners, but jovially as they spoke of the King. I remembered that when the Queen died everything ground to a halt — no one went to work, schools were closed, shops shut. We ran short of bread and coal. Now, though, I sensed this would not happen — the baker would deliver his bread, the milkman his milk, the coal man his coal. It was a Saturday, and if I went over to the Heath children would still be flying kites.

I had been planning to return a book to the library, but when I got there it was shut, with a small notice announcing the King's death pasted to the door. Some still honoured the tradition. I glanced across the road at the cemetery gate, remembering the white banner from the library falling onto the funeral procession, and Mr Jackson, and Caroline Black. It seemed a long time ago, and yet I also felt as if I'd lost Mummy only yesterday.

I didn't want to go home, so instead I crossed the road, entered the gate, and began walking up the path towards the main part of the cemetery. Halfway up Simon's father was sitting on a flat tombstone and leaning against a Celtic cross. He had a hand on each knee and was gazing into the distance the way old men do by the seaside. His eyes flashed with the blue of the sky so that it was hard to tell what he was looking at. I wasn't sure that he saw me, but I stopped anyway. 'Hello.'

His eyes moved about but did not seem to fix upon me. 'Hello,' he said.

'It is a shame about the King, isn't it?' I said, feeling I ought to make conversation.

'Shame 'bout the King,' Simon's father repeated.

I had not seen him in a long while. Whenever I looked for Simon at work, his father did not seem to be digging with him, but was off getting a ladder or a wheelbarrow or a bit of rope. Once I had seen him propped up against a grave, asleep, but had thought he was sleeping off a night of drink.

'Do you know where Simon is?' I asked.

'Where Simon is.'

I put my hand on his shoulder and looked deep into his eyes. Although they were turned in my direction, they did not show any recognition. It was as if he were blind, though he could see. Something was wrong with him – he clearly would not push a spade into clay again. I wondered what had happened to him.

I squeezed his shoulder. 'Never mind. It's been lovely to see you.'

'Lovely to see you.'

Tears pricked my eyes and nose as I continued along the path.

I tried to stay away from our grave, and wandered for a time around the cemetery, looking at the crosses, columns, urns and angels, silent and shining in the sun. But somehow in the end I still found my way there.

She was already waiting for me. When I saw her I thought at first that she was wearing a black dress, but when I got closer I realised it was blue – which was what Mummy had worn so scandalously for Queen Victoria. I smiled at that, but when Lavinia asked why I was smiling, I knew better than to say.

SIMON FIELD

They're sitting each on her own grave, like they used to. I ain't seen them together in a long time, though neither would ever tell me what the matter was with the other whenever I saw one alone. Too much happened in too little time for them girls.

They don't see me – I hide well.

They ain't quite themselves now – they don't have their arms linked, and they don't laugh the way they used to. They're sitting far apart and making polite talk. I hear Maude ask, 'How is your mother?'

Livy gets a funny look on her face. 'Mama is going to have a baby any day now.'

Maude looks so surprised I almost laugh and give myself away. 'That's wonderful! But I thought – I thought she was too old to have children. And – after Ivy May . . .'

'It seems not.'

'Are you pleased?'

'Or course,' Livy says. 'Life does go on, after all.'

'Yes.'

They both look at their graves, at Ivy May's and Kitty Coleman's names.

'And your grandmother — how is she?' Livy asks.

'She is still living with us. She had a stroke a few months ago and can't speak.'

'Oh dear.'

'It's just as well, really. It's much easier to be with her now.'

The two of 'em giggle as if Maude's said something naughty. I come out from behind a grave and scrape my feet in the pebbles on the path so they'll hear me. They both jump. 'Hello,' Maude says, and Livy says, 'Where have you been, naughty boy?' and that's like old times. I squat by our Granpa's grave across from them, pick up two pebbles from the path, and rub 'em 'tween my fingers.

'How did you know we were here?' Maude asks.

I shrug. 'I knew you'd both come. King's dead, ain't he?'

'Long live the King,' they say together, then smile at each other.

'Isn't it a pity?' Livy says. 'If Mama has a boy she shall have to name him George. I don't like that name as much as Edward. Teddy, I would have called him. Georgie isn't quite so nice.'

Maude laughs. 'I've missed your silly remarks.'

'Hush,' Livy says.

'Simon, I saw your father just now,' Maude says suddenly.

I let the pebbles drop back onto the path.

'What happened to him?' she asks real quiet.

'Accident.'

Maude don't say nothing.

'He were buried. We got him out, but . . .' I shrug again.

'I'm sorry,' Maude whispers.

'And I,' Livy adds.

'I got something to ask you,' I says to Livy.

She stares at me. Bet she's thinking 'bout that kiss down the grave, years ago. But that's not what I'm going to ask her.

'You know I marked all the graves here. Got all of 'em in the meadow, far's I know. 'Cept yours.' I jerk my head at the Waterhouse angel. 'You told me not to, all them years back, after the Queen died. So I didn't. But I want to now. For Ivy May. To remember she's there.'

'What, to be reminded she's just bones?' Livy says. 'That's horrid!'

'No, no, it ain't that. It's to remind you she's still there. Some of her rots, sure, but her bones'll be there for hundreds of years. Longer'n these stones, even, I'll bet. Longer'n my mark. That's what matters, not the grave and what you put on it.'

Maude looks at me funny, and I can see that all these years she ain't understood my skull 'n' crossbones either, for all her being smarter than Livy.

Livy don't say nothing for a minute. Then she says, 'All right.'

I get up and go behind the plinth with my pocket knife.

While I'm back there, scratching the mark, they start talking again.

'I don't care if Simon marks the angel,' Livy says. 'I've never felt the same about it since it fell. I'm always expecting it to fall again. And I can still see the break in the nose and neck.'

'I have never liked our grave,' Maude says. 'I look at it and none of it makes me think of Mummy, even though her name's on it. Did you know she wanted to be cremated?'

'What, and placed in the columbarium?' Livy sounds horrified.

'No, she wanted her ashes scattered where flowers grow. That's what she said. But Daddy wouldn't do it.'

'I should think not.'

'It's always felt wrong, burying her here, but there's nothing to be done. As you said, life goes on.'

I finish the mark and fold up my knife. I'm glad to have done it, like I finally scratched an itch on my back. I've owed Ivy May a long time. When I come out I nod at them. 'I has to get back to work. Joe'll be wondering where I am.' I'm quiet a minute. 'You'll be coming back to see me, both of you?'

'Of course,' they say.

Don't know why I asked that, 'cause I know the answer, and it ain't the one they gave. They're growing up and they don't play in the cemetery any more. Maude's got her hair up and looks more like her mother every day, and Livy's — well, Livy. She'll be married at eighteen, to a soldier, I expect.

I hold out my hand to Maude. She looks surprised but she takes it.

'Goodbye,' I say. She knows why I'm doing it, 'cause she knows the real answer too. Suddenly she steps up to me and kisses my dirty cheek. Livy jumps up and kisses the other one. They laugh, then they link arms and start down the path together towards the entrance.

I got an idea back there behind Ivy May's grave. Listening to Maude made me think about her ma's grave, and how our Pa got buried in it. I always thought maybe it were a sign she didn't want to be buried there. Sometimes I think Mr Jackson thought the same thing. The look on his face when her coffin were lowered into the grave was like a knife turning in his gut.

I go down to see Mr Jackson. He's in the lodge meeting with a family 'bout a burial, so I wait in the courtyard. A line of men are pushing wheelbarrows 'cross to the dumping ground. This place don't stop even for a king.

When Mr Jackson's showed his visitors out, I clear my throat. 'Can I have a quick word, guvnor?' I say.

'What is it, Simon?'

'Something I need to say inside. Away from everybody.' I nod at the wheelbarrows.

He looks at me surprised, but he lets me into the lodge and shuts the door. He sits behind his desk and starts straightening the ledger he's been writing in, recording the next burial — date and time and place and depth and monument.

He's been good to me, Mr Jackson. He don't never complain 'bout our Pa not digging. He even pays him same as ever, and gives me and Joe extra time to finish. Some of the other diggers ain't happy 'bout it, but Mr Jackson shuts 'em up. They looks at our Pa sometimes and I can see 'em shiver. 'Grace of God,' they whisper. 'There but for.' They don't talk to us much, me and Joe. Like we're cursed. Well, they'll have to live with me. I ain't going nowhere, as far as I can see. 'Cept if there's a war what Mr Jackson sometimes says there might be. They'll need diggers then.

'What did you want, Simon?' Mr Jackson says. He's nervous of what I might say, wondering if I got any more surprises to tell him. I still feel bad, giving that one up 'bout Kitty's baby.

It ain't easy to say it. 'I been up at the Coleman grave,' I says at last. 'Maude and Livy were there.'

Mr Jackson stops moving the ledger and lays his hands on the desk.

'Maude were saying how her mother wanted to be burn – cremated. And how she looks at the grave now and there ain't nothing there of her mother 'cept her name.'

'Is that what she said?'

'Yep. And I were thinking –'

'You were thinking too much.'

I almost don't go on 'cause he sounds so miserable. But something about Kitty Coleman keeps linking him and me.

'I think we should do something 'bout it,' I say.

Mr Jackson looks at the door like he's scared someone might come in. He gets up and locks the door. 'What do you mean?' he says.

So I tell him my idea.

He don't say nothing for a time. Just looks at his hands laying on the desk. Then he balls his hands into fists.

'It is the bones that pose the problem,' he says. 'We have to get the fire hot enough for long enough. Special coal, perhaps.' He stops.

I don't say nothing.

'It may take some time to organise.'

I nod. We got time. I know just when to do it – when everybody's looking somewhere else.

GERTRUDE WATERHOUSE

When she came in I didn't say a word to Livy about the blue dress. I hadn't noticed her wearing it this morning. Though it did surprise me, I managed to hide it behind burbling about the baby. I hope at least that she wears black on the day of the King's funeral. They say it is to be set for a fortnight's time.

But then, perhaps it is just as well that Livy is wearing blue. I don't think just now that I could face the drama she brings to mourning. Dear Ivy May would have been appalled at how her sister has carried on over her, when she never did when Ivy May was alive.

I do miss her. That feeling never leaves, I have discovered, nor my guilt – though I have managed at last to forgive myself.

Perhaps I am being unfair on Livy. She has grown up quite a bit over this past year. And she said that she has made it up with Maude. I am glad. They need each other, those girls, whatever has happened in the past.

'Do you know, Mama,' Livy was saying just now, 'the Colemans have had electricity installed? Maude said it's wonderful. Really I think we should have it too.'

But I was not listening. I had felt something inside me that was no kick. It was beginning.

ALBERT WATERHOUSE

I confess I'd had a fair few. What with toasting Trudy's health and the old King's passing and the new King's health, the pints did add up. And I was in there since mid-afternoon when Trudy started. By the time Richard came in I was more or less propping up the Bull and Last's bar.

He didn't seem to notice. Bought me a pint when he heard Trudy was abed, talked about the cricket and which games would be cancelled for the King.

Then he asked me something peculiar. Fact is, I still wonder whether or not he did say it or it was the pints talking in my ear. 'Maude wants to go to university,' he said.

'Come again?'

'She came to me today and said she wants to go to a boarding school that will prepare her for the exams to get into Cambridge. What do you think I should do?'

I almost laughed — Richard always has trouble with his womenfolk. But then, anything can happen with those Coleman women. I thought of Kitty Coleman holding my arm that time I took her home, and her ankles flashing slim and lovely under her skirt on her bicycle, and I couldn't laugh.

I wanted to cry. I studied the foam on my beer. 'Let her,' I said.

Just then our char ran in and told me I have a son. 'Thank God!' I shouted, and bought the whole pub a round.

RICHARD COLEMAN

Maude sat with me in the garden tonight while I smoked a cigarette. Then Mrs Baker called for her and she went inside, leaving me alone. I looked at the smoke curling through my fingers and thought: I will miss her when she goes.

DOROTHY BAKER

I shouldn't have waited so long to bring Miss Maude into it. But I wasn't to know, was I? I try to mind my business. And I couldn't say anything while her grandmother was running the house. That stroke has been the biggest blessing in disguise. I could see Miss Maude blossom once her grandmother's mouth was stopped.

I didn't say anything straight away after the stroke – it would've looked bad to go against a woman after something like that. But the other day a letter I'd meant for Jenny was returned, reading 'gone away'. Of course the letter had been slit and the coins stolen. I'd been sending her the odd shilling when I could spare it, trying to help her out. I knew they were close to the edge, her and her mother and Jack. Now it seemed they couldn't manage the rent.

Later when I was going over the week's menus with Miss Maude, I decided I had to say something. Perhaps I should have said it more casual, but that's not my way. We finished, and I shut the book and said, 'Something's wrong with Jenny.'

Miss Maude sat up straight. 'What's the matter?' We don't speak of Jenny, so it was a surprise to her.

'I've had a letter returned – she and her mum have moved.'

'That doesn't mean something's wrong. Perhaps they've moved someplace – nicer.'

'She would've told me. And she doesn't have the money for nicer.' I'd never told Miss Maude how bad it was. 'Fact is, Jenny's had a hard time of it ever since your grandmother let her go without a reference.'

'Without a reference?' Miss Maude repeated like she didn't understand.

'Without a reference she can't get another job as a maid. She's been working in a pub, and her mum takes in washing. They've hardly a shilling between them.'

Miss Maude was beginning to look horrified. She is still innocent of many of the ways of the world. I didn't dare tell her what working in a pub can lead to.

Then she surprised me. 'How can she raise a son on that?'

I hadn't been sure till then that she knew Jack was Jenny's son. But she said it calmly, as if she wasn't judging her.

I shrugged.

'We must find her,' Miss Maude said. 'That is the least we can do.'

'How? It's a big city – she could be anywhere. The neighbours would've given the postman a forwarding address if they knew it.'

'Simon will find her,' Miss Maude declared. 'He knows her. He'll find her.'

I was going to say something, but she was so trusting in the boy that I didn't have the heart to dash her hopes.

'Suppose we do find her,' I said. 'What do we do then? We can't have her back here, what with the new maid making a good job of it. It wouldn't be fair to her.'

'I shall write the new maid a reference myself.'

It's surprising how quick a girl can grow up when she's a mind to.

SIMON FIELD

When Maude tells me to find Jenny, I don't ask why. Some-times I don't need to know why. It ain't so hard to do — turns out she's been to see our Ma, who tells me where she is. When I go there her and her mum and Jack are in a tiny room with not a crumb of food 'tween 'em — Jenny spent all her money on what our Ma could do for her.

I take 'em to a caff and feed 'em — Maude's given me money for it. The boy and his Gran eat everything in sight, but Jenny just picks at her food. She's grey in the face.

'I don't feel well,' she says.

'That'll pass,' I say, which is what our Ma always says after a woman's been to her. A few years back Jenny wanted nothing to do with what our Ma does for women, but things is different for her now. She knows what it's like to have a child don't get enough to eat. That'll change anyone's mind about bringing another mouth into the world you can't feed.

I don't say nothing, though. Jenny don't need me to remind her how things change. I keep my mouth shut, and get her to have a little soup.

Guess I've caught her just in time.

LAVINIA WATERHOUSE

Well. I don't know. Truly I don't know what to think. Maude has often said I must try to be more open-minded, and I suppose this is one of those moments when I should try. But it is very difficult. Now I have two more secrets to keep from her.

I have just come back from the cemetery, of course. Our lives seem to revolve around it. I had gone there on my own to visit our grave. I wanted to, just before the King's funeral. Mama, of course, couldn't come because she is still in bed, with little Georgie at her side. When I left they were both asleep, which is good as I didn't want to leave her alone otherwise. Elizabeth is there, though I don't trust her with Georgie — I'm sure she would drop him on his head. Papa is at work, though he said it has been very dull and quiet there this week, everyone with long faces and doing very little — waiting for the King to be laid to rest.

I could have asked Maude to go with me, but we spent all of yesterday together, queuing up Whitehall to see the King lying in state, and I was rather happy to be in my own company.

I went to our grave and placed a new posy for Ivy May,

and weeded a bit — around the Colemans' as well as ours, for it needed attention. The Colemans can be rather lax on that front. And then I just sat. It was a lovely, sunny, quiet afternoon. I could just feel the grass and flowers and trees around me growing. I thought about the new King — King George V. I even said it aloud a few times. It is easier to accept him now that I have a brother named for him.

Then I had the idea to tour the angels. It had been so long since I had seen them all. I began with ours, of course, and walked around counting. There are far more than thirty-one now, but I looked only for those old ones from my childhood. It was like greeting old friends. I reached thirty but for the life of me I couldn't find the thirty-first angel. I was deep in the cemetery, up by the northwest corner, still searching, when I heard the bell ring for closing. Then I remembered that I had forgot the sleeping angel, and hurried down the Egyptian Avenue to it. Only when I'd seen it, lying on its side asleep, wings neatly tucked, did I feel I could go.

I rushed down the path towards the entrance. It was really very late — no one was about, and I worried that the gates might already be locked. None the less, I ran into the meadow just for a moment to say goodbye to Ivy May.

And there I found Simon and Joe and Mr Jackson, beginning to pry up the granite slab on the Coleman grave! I was so shocked I just stood there, my mouth hanging open. For an awful moment I thought I had lost Maude too. Then Simon saw me and dropped his spade, and Joe and Mr Jackson stopped as well. They all looked so guilty that I knew something was wrong.

'What in heaven's name are you doing?' I cried.

Simon glanced at Mr Jackson, then said, 'Livy, come sit a minute.' He waved at the foot of my angel. I sat under it rather gingerly — I have never quite trusted it since it fell.

Simon explained everything. At first I could say nothing. But when I had got my breath back I said, 'It is my Christian duty to remind you that what you are doing is both illegal and immoral.'

'We know,' that naughty boy replied — he said it almost gleefully!

'It is what she wanted,' Mr Jackson said very quietly.

I gazed at him. I could have his job, and Simon's. If I told the police about this, I could ruin his life, and Simon's, and upset Maude and her father dreadfully. I could.

But that would not bring back Ivy May.

They were looking at me fearfully, as if they knew what I was considering.

'Are you going to tell Maude?' I asked.

'When the time is right,' Mr Jackson said.

I let them wait a little longer. It was very quiet in the cemetery, as if all the graves were waiting for me to reply.

'I shan't tell anyone,' I said at last.

'You sure, Livy?' Simon said.

'Don't you think I can keep a secret? I haven't told Maude about what happened to her mother, you know — about the baby. I did keep that secret.'

Mr Jackson started and turned red. I looked at him and, after years of leaving the puzzle unfinished in my mind, I at last allowed him to take his place next to Kitty in the story. To my great surprise I felt sorry for him.

Another secret. But I wouldn't tell. I left them to their gruesome task and ran home, trying not to think about it.

It was not so hard – once I'd got in and was holding my baby brother in my arms, I discovered it was quite easy to forget everything but his sweet face.

MAUDE COLEMAN

It was long past midnight when Daddy and I came to the top of Parliament Hill. We had gone to the Hampstead Scientific Society's new observatory by Whitestone Pond to look at Halley's Comet, and were walking across the Heath on our way home.

It has been a disappointing viewing – the waxing moon was shining so brightly that the comet was rather indistinct, though its long curved tail was still spectacular. But Daddy loves the observatory – he campaigned so hard to have it built – and I did not want to spoil his evening there by complaining about the moon. I was one of the few ladies present, and kept very quiet.

Now, though, with the moon lower in the sky, the comet was more visible, and I felt more relaxed than I had been in the dome with its narrow slit of sky, crowded with men drinking brandy and smoking cigars. Lots of people were still out on the hill, looking at the comet. Someone was even playing 'A Little of What You Fancy' on an accordion, though no one danced – the King was being buried in a few hours' time, after all. It was strange that the comet should be in the sky the night before his funeral. It was the kind of thing Lavinia would make a great deal of, but I knew it was simply a coincidence, and coincidences can often be explained.

'Come, Maude, let's go home,' Daddy said, flicking a cigarette butt into the grass.

Something flared in the corner of my eye. I looked across at the next hill towards Highgate and saw a huge bonfire burning, lighting up the trees around it. Among the dancing branches I thought I saw the cemetery's cedar of Lebanon.

That fire was certainly no coincidence – someone had probably lit it for the King. I smiled. I love fire. I felt almost as if it had been lit for me as well.

Daddy disappeared down the hill into the darkness ahead of me, but I remained a little longer, my eyes flicking back and forth between the comet and the flames.

SIMON FIELD

It takes a long time. We're at it all night. He were right 'bout the bones.

Afterwards as the sun's coming up we get some buckets and half fill 'em with sand. We mix the ashes into it and we sprinkle it all over the meadow. Mr Jackson has plans to let wildflowers grow there, like she wanted. That'll make a change from all them flowerbeds and raked paths.

I still got a little left in a bucket and I goes to our Granpa's rosebush and dump the rest there. That way I'll be sure of where some of her is, if ever Maude wants to know. 'Sides, bonemeal's good for roses.

ACKNOWLEDGEMENTS

The Acknowledgements is the only section of a novel that reveals an author's 'normal' voice. As a result I always read them looking for clues that will shed light on writers and their working methods and lives, as well as their connections with the real world. I suspect some of them are in code. Alas, however, there are no hidden meanings in this one — just an everyday voice that wants to express gratitude for help in several forms.

Sometimes I wonder if Acknowledgements are even necessary, or if they break the illusion that books emerge fully formed from a writer's mind. But books don't come out of nowhere. Other books and other people contribute to them in all sorts of ways. I used many books in the making of this one. The most helpful were *The Victorian Celebration of Death* by James Steven Curl (Stroud: Sutton Publishing, 2000), *Death in the Victorian Family* by Pat Jalland (Oxford: Oxford University Press, 1996), *Death, Heaven and the Victorians* by John Morley (London: Studio Vista, 1971), and, my favourite, *On the Laying Out, Planting, and Managing of Cemeteries, and on the Improvement of Churchyards* by J. C. Loudon (1843; facsimile published Redhill, Surrey: Ivelet Books, 1981).

It is a novelist's privilege to make up what she likes, even when real people and places enter the story. The cemetery in this book is made up of a lot of fact and a fair bit of fiction – concrete details and flights of fancy interwoven, with no need to untangle them. While a real cemetery exists where this book takes place, I have not tried to recreate it completely accurately; rather it is a state of mind, peopled with fictional characters, with no resemblances intended.

Similarly, I have toyed with a few details in the suffragettes' history in order to bring them into the story. I have taken the liberty of putting words into Emmeline Pankhurst's mouth that she did not actually say, but I trust I have kept to the spirit of her numerous speeches. Moreover, Joan of Arc and Robin Hood did march in a procession, dressed as I have described, but it was not the Hyde Park demonstration. Gail Cameron at the Suffragette Fellowship Collection of the Museum of London was very helpful in providing me with useful resources.

Finally, thanks go to my quartet of minders – Carole Baron, Jonny Geller, Deborah Schneider, and Susan Watt – who remained steady when I wobbled.

The Virgin Blue

TRACY CHEVALIER

The compelling story of two women, born four centuries apart, and the ancestral legacy that binds them.

Ella Turner does her best to fit into the small, close-knit community of Lisle-sur-Tarn. She even changes her name back to Tournier, and knocks the rust off her high school French. In vain. Isolated and lonely, she is drawn to investigate her Tournier ancestry, which leads to her encounter with the town's wolfish librarian.

Isabelle du Moulin, known as Le Rousse due to her fiery red hair, is tormented and shunned in the village – suspected of witchcraft and reviled for her association with the Virgin Mary. Falling pregnant, she is forced to marry into the ruling family: the Tourniers. Tormentor becomes husband, and a shocking fate awaits her.

Plagued by the colour blue, Ella is haunted by parallels with the past, and by her recurring dream. Then one morning she wakes up to discover that her hair is turning inexplicably red . . .

'Tracy Chevalier's first novel is a triumph. Excellent.'
Time Out

'An intriguing and poignant read.'
Sunday Express

'Such an achievement for a serious writer that you feel it deserves an award.'
Independent

ISBN 0 00 710827 3

The Lady and the Unicorn

TRACY CHEVALIER

It was the commission of a lifetime.

Jean Le Viste, a fifteenth-century nobleman close to the King, hires
an artist to design six tapestries celebrating his rising status at Court.
Nicolas des Innocents overcomes his surprise at being offered this
commission when he catches sight of his patron's daughter, Claude.
His pursuit of her pulls him into the web of fragile relationships
between husband and wife, parents and children, lovers and servants.

It was a revolutionary design.

In Brussels, renowned weaver Georges de la Chapelle takes
on the biggest challenge of his career. Never before has he attempted
a work that puts so much at stake. Sucked into a world of temptation
and seduction, he and his family are consumed by the project and by
their dealings with the rogue painter from Paris.

The results changed all their lives.

'A beautifully written tale, I could not put it down . . . This is not just
a novel about the creation of a work of art, but a tale of ambition,
lust, betrayal and heartbreak . . . a compelling and enormously
enjoyable work.'
Evening Standard

'*The Lady and the Unicorn* will perhaps eclipse *Pearl Earring*.'
Guardian

ISBN 0 00 714091 6